WOMEN LIKE US

BOOKS BY ERICA ABEEL

Women Like Us

The Last Romance

I'll Call You Tomorrow
and Other Lies Between Men and Women

Only When I Laugh

WOMEN LIKE US

Erica Abeel

TICKNOR & FIELDS

New York

1994

TO MAUD AND NEILSON

For information about permission to reproduce selections
from this book, write to Permissions, Ticknor & Fields,
215 Park Avenue South, New York, New York 10003.

Library of Congress Cataloging-in-Publication Data

Abeel, Erica.
Women like us / Erica Abeel.
p.   cm.
ISBN 0-395-62150-X
I. Title.
PS3551.B333W66   1994
813'.54—dc20   93-30721
CIP

Printed in the United States of America

BP   10   9   8   7   6   5   4   3   2   1

Book design by Anne Chalmers

The author is grateful for permission to quote from the following
songs:
"The Great Pretender," by Buck Ram. Copyright © 1955 by Pan-
ther Music Corp. Copyright renewed. International copyright se-
cured. All rights reserved. Used by permission.
"Smoke Gets In Your Eyes," written by Otto Harbach and Jerome
Kern. Copyright © 1933 by Polygram International Publishing, Inc.
Copyright renewed. Used by permission. All rights reserved.

PART ONE

Chapter 1

DAISY FRANK had been at college barely a week when she found all her classmates preparing to desert for the weekend.

That Friday in the fall of '54, Daisy, a public school girl with patrician nerves, stood alone on the stage of empty Reisinger Theater. She stood downstage right, arm stretched high on the diagonal, palm upturned, a single spot picking up her rapt face and a curve of thigh in pink wool tights. Once again she marked her solo, the only sound in Reisinger her feet drumming the floor and voice murmuring the counts. Then she danced it full out, pacing herself, using the adagio to hoard power for the final burst: diagonal run, grand jetés melting into a pivot — right *here* she'd zing it over the footlights. She was an old hand at playing an audience.

Satisfied, she slung on a raincoat and threaded her way through a labyrinth of blue cinder-block halls. Outside Reisinger the fall dusk was crystalline and chill, with a scent of woodsmoke. Daisy sped under a long arbor toward Westlands, a gray stone Tudor mansion and hub of the college, then cut to the right toward Titsworth — incredibly, the name of her dorm. With a warm rush, she pictured the after-dinner scene: in the ground floor common room a bull session, collegial and stimulating; girls in plushy bathrobes and pink curlers discussing Camus's man in revolt, or Wittgenstein, or the Dartmouth Winter Carnival.

At her hall, Daisy found instead a fever of packing: girls cramming black patent-leather hatboxes with Fair Isle Shetlands, Capezios, crinolines, Mum; peeling out of paint-stained Oxford shirts and sour leotards; tossing stinky sneakers in a corner; pulling on oatmeal cashmeres; stepping into pleated wool tartans fastened with a giant safety pin. Touch Blue Grass to the pulse points, and voilà! Shrugging on their camel's hair coats, they flowed around Daisy, who stood in the hall in her raincoat like a displaced pillar. She heard their luggage slapping down the stairs as they raced to catch the cabs idling in front of Westlands.

Daisy prayed it was just Titsworth. She loped through the falling light along Kimball Avenue toward Kober House, off-campus haven to the hard-core rebels, and bounded up a curve of marble staircase. The only girl left was Diana Dew, a Charleston deb, prom queen pretty, with a kittenish nubbin nose and matching attention span. With one hand Diana flipped chicken-wire rollers from her head to the bed; the other hand fumbled at an udderlike garter.

"Why, hon, you not goin' to the game?" Diana squinted at Daisy, unable to place her — the college admitted girls of all backgrounds. "Princeton, Yale," she clarified.

"Oh, I have rehearsals all weekend," Daisy lied, pointing her sneakered foot. "And I *loathe* football."

A cab honked twice from the courtyard below. Diana pulled a white angora sweater over twin circle-stitched cones. "Come to think of it, I hate it myself. Freezin' my rear end off in those stadiums." She paused, arrested by this insight. Shrugged. "Gotta humor Frank Hilliard though. Guess it's trainin' for life." She winked and zipped her plaid hatbox shut. "Bah, hon."

Daisy stationed herself by a round leaded window, shivering in the dorm now deserted but for a ghost of White Shoulders cologne. Down below a few stragglers piled into a cab for the Bronxville station, squealing with merriment. Daisy heard her stepparents: We sent her to that fancy college to play Cinderella? Even though she was sending herself, with a full scholarship. Sarah Lawrence awarded them for dance instead of football.

That evening Daisy got a choice table at Bates. The dining hall was a grand high-ceilinged room with French doors opening on rock gardens. A few other public school pariahs were sowed throughout, eyes on a book as they wolfed their chicken à la king. In a corner sat a sullen girl in befogged harlequin glasses; strictly Lizzie Borden material, but Father was in oil. Daisy had never felt so lonely. Of course, she'd been lonely all her life. At least the times had caught up; it was now fashionable to be an Outsider.

Next weekend, same ritual.

Daisy's education had begun. She learned that come Friday everyone but the grinds deserted the campus to pursue their true course of study. In Manhattan, the boarding school girls took trains to Harvard, Yale, or Princeton, where they were met by preppies in white bucks and a last name for a first name, preppies they'd known all along from the circuit of privilege: Northeast Harbor, Maine; the Debutante Christmas Cotillion; mixers with Hotchkiss, Saint Paul's, Andover — to Daisy, talismanic names evoking rosy-cheeked jocks with the souls of poets standing in early morning chapel with hard-ons.

Daisy learned that even the Jewish girls joined the exodus. They took the IRT up to Morningside Heights for dates with pasty Columbia pre-meds who commuted to college from the Bronx and never bragged about passing out behind a rosebush. Those from private schools like Brearley and Dalton had entrée to the Ivy campuses. But they would never dine at an eating club of the caliber of Cottage or Tiger Inn; they would break bread at Prospect Club, Princeton's salute to the shtetl.

Since her male classmates from Jamaica High were either at Parris Island boot camp, Manoloking Automotive Trades, or reform school, Daisy stayed put.

To save face, she took to grabbing a burger Friday nights at the Caf with the other theater and dance people, who were just making a pass at college. She wrapped herself in dreams of greatness. She had her career to nurture. Hadn't Martha Graham singled her out? Anointed her?

Daisy would date the true start of college three years later, spring of '57, that Friday she first went to Harvard, the weekend that brought Gerrit and Ben and all the rest; the weekend that brought her Delphine Mortimer, resplendent in the spring of '57.

Alone in Reisinger, she was rehearsing "Wings," a solo created on her movement style by Janice Haydee of the Graham company — a signal honor. The piece was to premiere at the following Friday's "New Dance" concert at the Y, an event covered by the press; the Graham people would be on hand, scouting for new talent for the company. She'd been preparing for this concert all her life.

As she hurtled through a thorny passage, applause burst from the dark belly of the theater. Daisy froze. Shaded her eyes and peered into the blackness.

"Bravo-o, you're *good*."

Phantom footfalls descended the aisle. Daisy recognized the slow pelvic roll and long neck of Sally November. Sally stopped at the apron of the proscenium stage; her lips were jam red in her white face.

"C'mon, let's bug outta here. We're going to Harvard for the weekend."

Still unnerved, Daisy did a double pirouette — *tzoom* — landed in a perfect fourth, then turned her back and sauntered upstage. A pity the offer hadn't come from someone else. Because then, she thought, amazing herself — why, then she'd be tempted. Sally November was famous around campus for growing pot in a planter and wearing her diaphragm on blind dates. Daisy concurred with Delphine Mortimer, whom she'd overheard one evening in Bates loudly proclaiming in her society honk that Sally was Snow White as nymphomaniac.

"C'mon Daisy, whaddya say?"

"Thanks, but I've got a dress rehearsal." Mystified by Sally's persistence. "For the Y concert," she added unnecessarily; posters all over college proclaimed the event. Daisy trotted around the stage in a figure eight. The weekend loomed like a Sahara; she couldn't even light into a Sara Lee cheesecake with the other wallflowers for fear of ballooning before Friday night. And what an achingly beautiful spring. Buried in Reisinger, she could sense the air outside, warm and wild, inciting folly. Overnight the campus had turned into a budding grove. Along Westlands tulips thrust up reddish green ovals with a silken sheen. The apple trees behind Kober were studded with white buttons. The magnolias, sheathed in downy pods, looked ready to pop.

Hands on her hips, Sally contemplated Daisy, a campus star and one of its more conspicuous virgins. "Don't you ever get outta here? Don't you want to live?"

"Oh, I once got bird-dogged at Princeton." Her entire sentimental history to date. She'd abandoned her dreary date for Amory Blaine, who'd left her stranded in a boardinghouse on Witherspoon Street.

"Tsk-tsk, rotten form. I hope Amory was worth it. Listen, Rudi is playing in a concert at the Fogg tonight, and I'm sure we can get you a ticket."

Daisy's mind raced: Call the choreographer and plead a torn metatarsal. She can hear Janice. "Just tape it, we all dance over pain. I made this dance for you, it's your big moment."

"Be a pal," Sally wheedled. "Look, the truth is Mia just copped out on me. I can't drive all the way to Boston alone. I promise, you won't regret it."

A rush of excitement. Oh, she couldn't. Could she? "Waaall, I suppose I can rehearse next week. We do have four days —"

"Wait a sec," said Sally, sensing her advantage. "Hold it, don't say another word." She stepped onto the apron of the stage, her face disappearing in darkness, and moved close to Daisy. Her breath smelled of cherry Charms. "Daiz, do you realize what's walking around in Cambridge? The fucking *Aga* Khan."

Outside Reisinger, Daisy blinked in the violent natural light; she was Persephone sprung from the underworld! She hurried toward Westlands under the long arbor feathered with gray-green tendrils of wisteria. She hoped to catch Franca Broadwater, preparing this very moment to leave for her family's twenty-room "cottage" in Lenox.

One of the local aesthetes, wearing all black and dirty sneakers, floated by, inches above sea level, nose in a script. Then, with a little thrill, Daisy saw Delphine Mortimer. Delphine strode smartly toward her, chin jutting, her boyfriend trotting at her heels. She wore a pink peony in her reddish brown mane, and some sort of gold filigree necklace, and a long white skirt, like an Edwardian lady dressed for tennis.

"You *crowd* me, Dudley, you don't allow me to *breathe*," Delphine threw behind her as she passed Daisy.

Incredible! Anyone else would kill to be crowded by Dudley Hunnewell, Yale sculler, golden boy. For two years Daisy had longed to be part of Delphine's inner circle, but only admired her from afar: her theatrics, her style of a mad czarina. It was rumored she'd had an affair with the marquis de Portago, who'd died at Le Mans. She kept a wolfhound in her room, or a man, depending on her mood, along with a harpsichord, which she often played naked.

At the entrance to Westlands, Daisy nearly collided with two generic debs who were giggling about falsifying an address at the sign-out desk manned by Miss Blodgett. The debs' blond pageboys lifted in the breeze all of a piece, like the smooth helmets of Wrigley's gum ads.

Westlands's Great Hall mimicked an English country house: stone pillars and oak paneling, the Gothic gloom shot with light from stained glass windows with *faux* coats of arms. Daisy improvised an address for poor Miss Blodgett, who had chin whiskers and a baritone, no doubt from sexual deprivation. Then she skedaddled up a rear spiral staircase. A narrow cedar-scented hall led to a warren of attic rooms once reserved for servants.

Franca stood packing a Lufthansa flight bag. The afternoon sun streaming through the casement windows spun her crown of braids into a nimbus of light. She had blue eyes that sloped downward at the corners, and the rarefied sweetness of an Arthur Rackham princess. Franca reeked of class. She was Daisy's only friend.

"Well, I'm about to blow it for the Graham audition and ruin my goddamn life." Daisy flung herself onto a rocker and rocked furiously.

"Why do I hear Holden Caulfield when you talk?" Franca laughed. Then, considering Daisy's announcement, "Well, I hope you're planning something *amusing*. Lord knows you deserve a little fun after all that self-flagellation in your dance studio."

Of course Franca couldn't have understood. Even at Sarah Lawrence, a caldron of creativity, Art was just an exalted form of occupational therapy; you didn't sacrifice romance on its account.

"As a matter of fact, I'm going to Harvard. I'm so tired of watching the Great Party from the sidelines. I want to start my life."

"Then start! This very minute. This weekend you'll . . . ." She paused and threw Daisy an odd appraising look. "Well, think of it as your coming-out party. Now. What can you wear?"

Franca inspected her closet, absurdly — Franca was a size 6 to her own 10. The skin on Daisy's arms prickled agreeably; she loved being the object of female fussing. She'd connected with Franca the past fall at the lottery for Joseph Campbell's sellout mythology course. Daisy picked a bad number and must have oozed disappointment. Franca offered her own number, mumbling she was overscheduled. A fabrication, Daisy later discovered, to her shame. Franca was an altruist, the genuine article; she had a constitutional need to see other people happy. This had won her comparisons around campus to a Russian holy fool and Dostoyevsky's idiot.

Franca lit a Player's and exhaled, the smoke floating lazily on a shaft of sunlight from the casement windows. Tucking a hand into her armpit in a way she had, she again contemplated Daisy as if through a new lens. "You look lovely."

"You kidding? I need a goddamn shower." Daisy rose and moved in front of the bureau mirror. She wore a long-sleeve black leotard and embroidered Mexican skirt knotted at the waist, from the Panamanian Shop, a costume that signified, in the shorthand of the day, Arty Girl Who Puts Out — a riposte to the Smithies' uniform of Oxford shirt, argyle knee socks, and those detestable Bermudas. Copper hair snatched back in a bun — a piquant contrast, the spinsterish style framing radiant youth. Eyes the identical color, disconcertingly, as her hair. A bee-stung mouth she considered deformed — and "minimized" with exercises from *Seventeen*. A coltish, leggy body, owned in that way dancers possess their bodies. Daisy had been studying her "line" in mirrors since age four; narcissism went with the trade. Behind her in the mirror she noticed that Franca was still appraising her.

"You *must* look up Peter," Franca ordered in her mock bossy manner. She scribbled a number and thrust the paper at Daisy. Stationery from the Pink Sands in Bermuda.

Peter Tabori, Franca's boyfriend, was a hotshot director at Harvard, famed for his withering putdowns. Daisy had more than once been their object.

"Uh, thanks, but I probably won't have time to look him up. I'm going with Sally November and we'll be with Rudi and his musician friends from Adams House. Different crowd from Peter's." Harvard's token public school minority. The ones they let in as a nod to democracy, Daisy didn't add, out of deference to Franca's benign view of the universe.

"But Peter would be offended if you didn't look him up."

"More likely relieved."

"Nonsense, you've got so much in common. You're both in the theater." She wadded up a cashmere and stuffed it into the bag. Then she looked at Daisy again, something shadowing her eyes, like a cloud darkening water. "And you're lovely, Daisy. You just don't know it yet."

They roared up the Merritt Parkway in Sally's blue Beetle, long missing its muffler. Daisy took great draughts of air, drunk on freedom. She was racing to catch up to herself; at nineteen she was practically a nun.

Sally gabbled on about her sexual exploits, remarkably varied considering the rampant niceness of the age. There'd even been rough stuff with a semifamous photographer. Sunday nights in Titsworth, Sally showed anyone hanging around the hall the pink welts beneath her shoulder blades. By New Haven, Sally was just getting to her current beau, Rudi Urdang, a flutist at Harvard.

"Actually I don't need a man to get turned on," Sally confided. "I'm kind of, you know, self-activating?"

Daisy knew; self-activating was *all* she knew. She inhaled the milky scent of her own forearm, propped on the window, and struggled to produce a highlight from her own sentimental history. She got only D. H. Lawrence and *The Amboy Dukes*. And the fiasco in Princeton. After the football game, she'd drunk too much Dewar's and ended up in the back seat of someone's car with Amory Blaine. While they were kissing, Amory casually unveiled his cock. No-no-no — for such a moment she wanted swelling violins, a shower of meteors! And it wore an odd little hat.

As Sally slowed for the weekend traffic, the late sun blinding them, Daisy was swamped by panic. She was deserting her Grand Plan, her solace and bulwark, her shelter from ordinary dangers since age four. If she wasn't a dancer, who was she? She'd always been Vickie from *The Red Shoes*. *Why do you want to dance?* Vickie: *Why do you want to live?* Martha Graham had watched her in class with gimlet eye. "You are very exciting, my dear. You have the unlearnable quality, presence." Her classmates at Jamaica High mooned around in transparent nylon blouses, dreaming of Tab Hunter. She was hot for Nijinsky. They yearned to make varsity cheerleading. She would dance Joan of Arc in *Seraphic Dialogue*.

She loved to dance for her father, evenings in their living room in Queens. He had charged her, she believed, to become an artist. "Learn to love solitude; on the stage you are alone." She sometimes suspected she'd only imagined him saying those words, sort of to give herself an ally. Her father was long since dead in a plane crash over Mexico City, yet it was still for Arthur Frank that she danced.

"What I really like is whipping Rudi's cock with my wet hair," Sally was saying.

"Uh, could you pull over? I need some air."

"With this traffic? There're cops all over. And we're almost there" — a sidelong glance at Daisy. "Uh-oh, maybe I better."

Daisy stood on the grassy bank, lit a Marlboro, and focused on the Charles, its separate strands of motion. Wasn't she ready to leave? She didn't want the "life." A few ecstatic moments on stage bought poverty, loneliness, and, after thirty-five, exile to the boonies to teach. The dread Main Street of Sinclair Lewis. The life was so mean and thin, closed down so early. She wanted richness, excess. Tender evenings in the Swedish countryside. She wanted a Grand Passion. Love would set her whole world right . . .

"Would you come back here, we're about to get arrested!" Sally signaled frantically from the car window.

Daisy had turned so pale her freckles stood out. "Oh, for heaven's sake," Sally chortled, "they're just guys." She nosed the car into the traffic flowing sluggishly up Memorial Drive.

Molten light dappled the water of the Charles. A single figure in a scull pulled against the oars, shooting into the dazzle. Couples strolled along the riverside path, arms about each other's waists, or lay enlaced in the young grass.

"Ta-da! We're almost there," said Sally as the domes of Harvard came into view. There were actual *domes,* a cluster of mini-Vaticans, temples of love. Eliot House or Dunster House — Daisy barely listened as Sally named buildings — was topped by a gleaming blue dome. Celestial blue, the color of paradise. Beneath it Roman urns with flame tongues of stone. Above it, a gold spire stabbed the sky. And streets cobbled in brick! Cobbled, narrow, slanting streets, like lithographs Daisy had seen of Cambridge, England. Imagine, they'd reproduced it here for the delectation of American girls. Daisy felt delirious. For a moment she wanted just to prolong this vision of bliss — Cambridge, Harvard, and its domes, bricks, and spires — and then, sated, turn around and go home.

.   .   .

They'd arrived too late for dinner with Rudi; by now he'd be at rehearsal. Sally suggested ducking into the Hayes-Bickford on Mass. Ave., across from Harvard Yard. The H-B, explained Sally reverently over coffee, was the greasy spoon favored by Harvard misfits. These alienated souls had wangled letters from psychiatrists declaring them too fragile to withstand the hurly-burly of the houses; to survive, they needed to live off campus. Many of Harvard's brightest and craziest had filtered into the shabby genteel rooming houses of Cambridge.

Sally then led Daisy down a narrow brick-paved walk to Mount Auburn Street, where they passed Elsie's restaurant, Harvard's low-life hangout. Here, explained Sally, students ambivalent about their studies or gripped by an existentialist *crise* frittered away the afternoon, and their lives, playing pinball.

Preppies sauntered by in worn tweed and heather Shetlands, lordly and clear-eyed as mythic heroes, green book bags slung over their shoulders. Their eyes snagged on two exotic birds, no 'Cliffies: Sally with her pixie bangs, neckerchief, and circle skirt, a tarty Audrey Hepburn; Daisy, a flame float of hair, ocher smock, lavender stockings — What have we here?

The concert was at Harvard's Fogg Museum, in the Loggia, a reproduction of a seventeenth-century Italian courtyard. In the corners, four ficus trees rose from fat tubs; a high, columned balustrade circled the courtyard, which was canopied by a skylight. Folding chairs, arranged on a diagonal to face the players' space in the far right corner, had been set out for the concert. Daisy and Sally sat up front in the second-row seats Rudi had reserved. Who needed music? Watching the audience was spectacle enough. Never had Daisy seen so many elbow patches and patrician profiles.

The Harvard Chamber Orchestra filed in. Applause, ceremonial bows. Rudi beamed a smile at Sally. He had shaggy blond hair and wore a mangy corduroy jacket. Rudi's shabbiness was the real thing: his father was a Commie folksinger who'd refused to name names and now worked in a hardware store in Brooklyn.

The 'Cliffie musicians opening their scores or tuning fiddles all looked identical: stringy hair, no makeup, bony wrists. What confidence, to look so ugly.

The orchestra struck up the opening of Mozart's *Sinfonia Concer-*

tante. Barely a dozen bars in, they hit a few clinkers. Daisy, morbidly attuned to music, winced. In the next moment she heard a choir of angels. Before her, cradling a French horn, sat a vision. He had cut-glass green eyes, unseeing, absorbed in the dream of the music. An abrupt nose, high color almost feminine, a mouth made for love. A Roman cap of curls feathered his forehead and spiked his collar. His noble head reduced his crew-cut neighbors to so many Jugheads.

Daisy felt calmly elated, like a wanderer returned home. Here they were, her fantasies since girlhood, in the flesh.

"Check out the French horn," murmured Sally.

From behind came a *sshhh!* Daisy inventoried the vision's every detail: the regulation chinos, pulling tight across skier's thighs; Birkin's thighs, if he had skied. The faded blue work shirt and Irish wool tie. The greenish tweed jacket, perfectly worn-looking, with see-through elbows. In the close air of the Loggia Daisy shivered.

A pause before the second movement. A tuning up and plink-plunking and rustling of pages. The horn player upended his horn and, in time-honored fashion, tipped out spit. The gesture enchanted Daisy. And the way his tweedy arm cradled the horn's brass whorls. Then his eyes slowly roamed the audience — seeking someone? Daisy stiffened — the eyes caught on her, and stayed. A slow investigation, ice green and bemused. The tap-tap of the baton broke the moment. The sweet languor of the second movement filled the hall, stretched to the white marble balustrade. She'd lost him to Mozart. There came a long lull for the horn. His eyes never left the score. He turned a page, so conscientious. Tipped his horn. Turned another page. The faintest yawn dilated his nostril. Mozart had forgotten him, and green-eyes had forgotten her. He looked out toward the audience. She would *will* him to her.

And he came. This time his eyes deliberately sought her. He nearly missed his cue.

"Mass. Ave. toward Central Square, go right on Putnam, then your first right onto Green," repeated Rudi. For the third time.

Daisy didn't care if she never found the goddamn rooming house. She was occupied by two critical questions: Who was the horn player and would he join the crush in the Fogg's lobby? She scanned the crowd for her vision. A sea of clean-cut males in J. Press tweed, one more tempting than the next, but Daisy was the faithful sort.

"Better write it down for her, she's discovered your French horn," said Sally.

Suddenly Daisy saw him, beyond Rudi's right shoulder, leaning against a marble pillar. The curve of his body, elbow against the pillar, was perfectly nonchalant. He was talking to a debutante so slouched she formed an *S*.

"You mean Gere?" Rudi looked disappointed in Daisy. "Or rahther, Gerrit, hard *G*. Gerrit DeWind the third. Or is it the fourth? That stiff? Oh Daisy no, don't do it."

Gerrit, hard *G*. The name fit her mouth to perfection.

"Porcellian Club, the *Advocate*. Prepped — you should pardon the term — at Saint Paul's, or one of the Saint Midas schools. Teddibly, teddibly." He waved an imaginary cigarette holder.

Of course, with his background Rudi would have to despise a Gerrit. Gerrit, in turn, would consider Rudi a *weenie*. And what would he want with a girl from Jamaica, Queens? This idea made him the more desirable. She lusted for his world. There would be a greensward somewhere in New England stretching to the sea, in the center a goldfish pond, the stone mossy and crumbling with age, Gerrit striding across the lawn in a V-neck tennis sweater and white ducks. Her world had leftist folk dance camps in the Catskills. Vacant lots where the local hoods baked "mickeys" in charred pits; where Myrna Fallis, who'd developed early, dropped her drawers for a paying public.

"*Soo* pretentious," Rudi was saying, warming to his portrait. "I once skied with Gerrit. Bromley, someplace. It's barely eleven, conditions are great, and suddenly Gere announces he's packing it in for the day. 'I can't see the point of skiing,' he says. I say, 'What do you mean, man, *point?*' And Gere says — you know, moody as hell — he says, 'Well, first you go up, and then you come down. Then you go up again, and then you come down again. So what's the goddamn point?' "

"Sounds rather existential," said Daisy.

Just then the man of the hour glanced their way. His eyes found Daisy: *I haven't forgotten.* Fire flashed up from her chest to her neck. Gerrit turned to greet a boy with white-blond hair. He'd had an opening and passed. And if he had come over? He would've seen her alarming red neck, about as alluring as psoriasis. And how could Sarah Lawrence artiness compete with triple-threat Radcliffe: genius-level

IQ, old money, and caste. Daisy glanced around in dismay. These 'Cliffies skied and sailed and played tennis with inherited grace. They would have dainty discreet menstruations. She couldn't even eat peas properly. Her stepparents had been too busy taking the goddamn Fifth to coach her in pea consumption.

A red and black lumber jacket wove toward them through the crush. Peter Tabori. Her self-esteem in shards at her feet, Daisy stammered introductions.

Peter, in turn, pushed someone forward, a skinny kid: "Ben Marshak, a friend from my Cronin's poker game. Up to visit his family in Brookline."

The friend stared at her. No, *gawked*. He'd just sighted the promised land. Nerdy black-framed glasses, flattop crewcut, costume by Rogers Peet. He looked wet and new, like something just hatched.

"Wow, some concert" (pronounced *cahn*-cert, with the townie inflection). The kid gestured at the Loggia with splayed stiff fingers. "I love classical music. That Beethoven was the greatest."

The silence ate a hole in the surrounding noise.

"Man, that was Mozart," said Rudi good-naturedly.

Daisy was looking at the kid as though he were dead meat.

This seemed to redouble his interest. "I just landed this great summer job as a waiter. In the mountains," he confided, flashing a crooked smile.

That would explain the zoot suit. She prayed Gerrit wasn't watching.

"Some resaught. They got a casino, a pool to here." Splayed fingers gave the measure. "And, on the buffet table, a champagne fountain with colored lights."

Sally stretched her long neck. "Goodness, how *surreal*."

Mystified, Daisy glanced at Peter, usually a font of intolerance.

He threw his arm around his friend's zooty shoulders. "Marshak is a man to watch. He's in law school at night, he's in the Reserves, *and* he holds down a full-time job. This guy's a winner."

Sally appraised Ben like an object suddenly risen in value. Rudi smiled queasily. And Ben beamed *her* a smile: baby-I'm-yours. Help. Daisy turned away and stared up at the balustrade, where a couple in shadow stood poised and expectant, like enraptured lovers in a pastoral painting.

Over the entrance a clock read nine-fifty-five. The crowd had begun to thin. She had to get to Gerrit before the night swallowed him.

She must send him a note. She would send it before the clock struck ten. But saying what, exactly? And how would she deliver it? What madness, she didn't even have paper. She rummaged in her memory for a line of poetry suitable for the occasion. But suitable, how? Good God, what should it convey?

Ben was now regaling their group with theories on the civil liberties of the insane, chopping away at the air.

It should convey something along the lines of "Gather ye rosebuds while ye may," but less blunt.

Daisy escaped to the far side of a desk. She retrieved Franca's Pink Sands stationery from her bag and scribbled, as best she remembered, some lines from "To His Coy Mistress" by Andrew Marvell: "Now Let us roll all our Strength, and all / Our sweetness, up into one Ball: / And tear our Pleasures with rough strife."

"Daisy's been touched by the muse," joked Rudi.

The girl never made the first move, of course, the Holy Writ of their age. All the more reason to act! Now, how to deliver her note? She looked up at the clock: the minute hand moved, with a shudder, to the twelve. Ten o'clock. Daisy marched over to Sally, pressed the folded paper into her hand, and whispered in her ear.

When she dared look in Gerrit's direction, he'd gotten all chatty with Sally, the treacherous girl. Had she completed a separate mission? Amazed at her own composure, Daisy questioned Ben about his mountain "resaught."

Sally had returned. Sally was pressing something into her hand, cleverly diverting the group with a funny anecdote. Daisy unfolded the pink paper and looked below her right hip. "Glory be to God for dappled things . . . Whatever is fickle, freckled —." Gerard Manley Hopkins, her favorite poet! Then, underlined: "Who the hell are you? Where can I find you?"

Daisy beamed a thousand-watt smile in Gerrit's direction.

Ben moved toward her and blocked him from view. "Kiddo, you've got this knockout smile."

He was ruining the moment! She scribbled her name and college phone number on Franca's stationery. Could she dispatch Sally again? Too obvious. Ben? God, what was she thinking.

Shifting past Ben, she discreetly raised her paper auction style. A woman floated into Gerrit's orbit. Honey-colored and expensive and not quite young. The woman stood thin and palely smiling and rarefied, as Gerrit helped her into a trench coat.

Daisy's arm descended in slow motion. Gerrit telegraphed her a helpless little shrug. He slid his hand beneath the woman's elbow and steered her out the door.

Sunday morning Daisy walked to the graveyard beyond the Harvard Coop to read tombstones. She'd put on her Toulouse-Lautrec outfit: lavender blouse, rust burlap skirt, and a black velvet ribbon around her neck; she might have stepped from the poster of le Moulin Rouge adorning half the rooms at Harvard. Spring had taken cover; the air was raw, the banks of gray clouds pierced by a beam of wan sunlight — perfect for melancholy meditations on love.

Her infatuation with Gerrit was swollen by a long passion for WASPs. She loved their physical proportions, the longish space between nose and upper lip, the longish torso and shortish legs. The English schoolboy haircuts. The grace and lack of straining, their golden carelessness. Every morning when she woke she had to invent a life. WASPs woke up to automatic membership in a world that had been there always.

Daisy studied a tombstone inscription for a Barnard Wyeth. At least, she consoled herself, she hadn't been *nice*. She'd long been at war with the whole culture. She hated the notion of "saving" yourself for your wedding night. That smarmy "Tell Me Doctor" column in the *Ladies' Home Journal*. Doris Day with her goody two-shoes Ipana smile. Women's perms, the rows of tight curls immovable, defeated. Those modesty bands on bathing suits, like a webbed crotch. Iron maiden girdles with four rubber udders — *monogrammed*, for God's sake. Suburban developments of tract houses with picture windows, each framing a mom in apron strings. Split-level heaven, pastel colors, I-like-Ike.

From Jamaica, Queens, Daisy had sighted the Sarah Lawrence standard of rebellion snapping in the breeze. The place was notorious up and down the eastern seaboard for gorgeous avant-garde girls who flouted Convention and went *all the way;* Ivy Leaguers came snuffling round them like hogs after truffles. Even Franca, with her Brahmin background, politely ignored the reigning properties. She and Peter Tabori shacked up weekends in his stepmother's townhouse in Murray Hill, with its Hollywood bed and bathtub. Delphine Mortimer and her band of hell raisers didn't even bother with discretion. Daisy had often overheard them in Bates. They always sat in a cloud of smoke at the same corner table next to the French windows, legs crossed at the knee like men, hooting with laughter. Over endless cups of coffee — to crank them up after a strenuous (and sleepless) weekend — they compared notes on dates, Tantric sex, whatever that was, or Keressa, some dynamite Oriental technique where you don't move.

The clock on the church belfry tolled once. Four long hours before Daisy was due to collect Sally from Rudi's room in Adams House, where they'd hung out a Do Not Disturb sign. Anything in Cambridge not nailed down must be doing it. Suddenly Daisy realized that she could call Peter Tabori — Franca had been so insistent. In her bag she still had the crumpled piece of stationery from the Pink Sands.

Peter lived on the second floor of a mustard-colored frame house with a sagging porch. Two scrawny kittens frolicked on the brown lawn and a few crocuses poked up like sparse patches of hair. Peter's movie mogul father lived in the Beverly Hills equivalent of Franca's mansion in Lenox; like the heiresses at Sarah Lawrence, he courted squalor.

Daisy followed Peter's corduroys upstairs. The hang of his pants suggested a number of sensual pursuits; she averted her eyes. Peter seated her on a Goodwill special leaking stuffing from its underside. Then he kicked off his Bass Weejuns and sprawled across from her in a shiny black chair with a Harvard crest on its back. On the poster behind his head Rhett Butler prepared to ravish Scarlett O'Hara.

Now what? Suddenly Daisy couldn't remember why she had come. She was flustered by Peter's maleness, scarcely knew where to rest her eyes. Franca had always stood between her and this oppressively physical Peter; the tight body, gray eyes with dark brows, thin sardonic mouth. The small, even teeth of a killer fish. Back in New York, he'd been a great yakker, old Peter, mixing up batches of banana daiquiris, extemporizing on his prowess as a man of theater, his plans to inherit the mantle of Elia Kazan, while Franca functioned as waitress and cheering section. Actually he was kind of a self-centered shit, not to put too fine a point on it. What redeemed him was having chosen Franca.

This afternoon he was not rude, but not exactly oiling the conversational flow. Daisy did her damnedest to "draw him out," as savvy girls ought; questioned him closely on the Second City–type revue he was staging in the basement of the Brattle Theatre; asked enough questions to write a goddamn thesis. He returned thorough answers, like an earnest schoolboy, but each time he let the talk languish, let it curl up and die.

Silence.

"You made a deep impression on my friend Ben," Peter said thickly.

"Rough jewel, your friend Ben," Daisy murmured, mystified by his tone.

"The man couldn't stop talking about your smile."

Daisy shrugged, reflexively tried to suck under her pulpy upper lip.

"He has good taste" — Peter's breath caught — "my friend Ben."

She focused on Scarlett O'Hara's cleavage. Peter became fixated on Daisy's leg, crossed at the knee and marking some beat.

Daisy yielded to his silence, troubled, but not enough.

It dawned on her that she had come because Peter planned to seduce her.

Mercifully, he stood and pulled out his guitar from behind a desk. He sat on the floor, his back against a daybed with regulation Indian madras bedspread, and picked out "Greensleeves." When he lost the words, he hummed with his eyes closed. This gave Daisy a chance to regroup. Franca's man — good God, what kind of friend was she. Unrequited lust for Gerrit geysered onto whoever was at hand.

Abruptly Peter stopped playing. He upended the guitar on the floor with a twang. "Like a drink? Sorry, should've asked sooner, but there's no ice. Afraid all I have is Dewar's."

Daisy hadn't drunk since getting bird-dogged at Princeton. She remembered the Scotch and the good feeling of the Scotch, not the badness it unleashed, and she wanted to feel that way again.

Peter handed her a jelly jar filled with amber and cocked his head at her. "You don't look comfortable. I mean, perched up there. Come sit on the floor." He squatted down and patted the space beside him.

Here Daisy lost track. Later she was driving Sally's blue Volkswagen back down U.S. 1, Sally nodding off beside her, she was swigging black coffee so hot it raised blisters on her lips; and every time she got to the floor part, she lost it.

She remembered the burn of the Scotch, and that her dress was amber, and that inside she was amber, same as the liquid in her glass.

And every so often the sky would open up and drench the room in amber. At some point, too — Daisy could not have said when — she'd lost the sense of sequence, which was maybe what getting loaded was about, all the edges rounded, no corners, no elbows, everything fluid and seamless. "I will kiss you here," Peter said. "And here. And here."

Before that, he moved close to her on the floor, a hand's width away. "You're so lovely."

Franca's phrase. Daisy's hands jumped on the wheel; the car swerved.

He brought his face close to hers, like an inquisitive but well-behaved child.

"We can't, you're spoken for," Daisy said. And, trying levity, "I've got the wrong lines. Those should be *your* lines."

"It's all right" was all Peter said. He drew two fingers along her lavender leg, from knee to ankle. Then he undid the strap of her ballerina, took off the shoe, and kneaded her instep. She noticed that desire was a close cousin of nausea. Everything slowed. She had a sense of perfectly filling time.

After a while, Daisy said feebly, like a person very ill, "I love Franca."

"So do I."

As if that were all they needed to know.

Chapter 2

IN FIFTIES U.S.A., jug-eared boys borrowed Dad's car and tootled off with their dates to sock hops and weenie roasts. June of graduation from college, you married the last person you went steady with. Advance to middle age without passing youth. Husbands positioned themselves to mount the organizational ladder. Brides quit their make-work jobs the second the rabbit croaked from the pregnancy test, their sigh of relief audible throughout the land, and prepared to be taken care of forever. In suburbia's tract-house heaven, families embraced Togetherness — though where was Daddy? Busy climbing the corporate ladder — and all was for the best in the best of all possible worlds.

But there was a flip side to the Doris Day era: pockets of naysayers, Wild Ones romancing self-destruction, rebels without a cause. At Sarah Lawrence the reigning idols were Holden Caulfield, hater of "phonies" who sold out — wasn't it better to end up, like Holden, in the bughouse? Dostoyevsky's epileptics and visionaries with itchy trigger fingers. The boozers and fuckups of the Lost Generation. Young Werther pickling in his Sorrows. And, at a further remove, beamed in from pop culture, James Dean and Montgomery Clift, purveyors of glamorous doom.

The Ivy campuses had their dissenters, too. It was cool to put down studying — cracking the books was for nerds and fruits — even flunk out, and watch the old man hit the rafters. It was cool to spend the four years shit-faced and pass out behind the azaleas. One Yalie threw up in a corner of his room, then tossed some Brooks shirts over the mess. The lexicon of boozing would fill a small book. Reckless speed was cool, driving drunk cooler; the Ivy League's finest raced their MGs and Austin Healys up and down the steeplechase of Merritt Parkway — weren't they all in training for Le Mans? One way to defeat the phonies was to blast out early. Getting dead was the one thing you could do and really mean it.

That April of '57, though, Daisy and Sally wanted only to get warm. They stood shivering on Kimball Avenue, noses pressed to the wrought iron college gate. Stamped like fillies, hugging their own bodies against the early spring freeze, bladders near bursting. On a rise beyond the gate loomed the unattainable dorms, black hulks with sparsely lit windows, frigates in the night.

They'd overshot the curfew by a good forty-five minutes. Old Amos, gatekeeper and lech, would admit you after witching hour in exchange for a feel. But he was nowhere in sight. Daisy parted lilac bushes, trying to locate the breach in the fence that served as emergency entrance. Sally squatted behind another bush and peed. Someone must have repaired the fence. A breeze knifed through Daisy's thin cardigan. They'd have to hit the Greasy Spoon, the all-night dive down by the railroad tracks.

A gunning motor — *vroom-vroom*. A screech of brakes. Some horse's ass playing Indy 500. A natty little MG with top down took the hairpin curve of Kimball Avenue on two wheels and bore down on them. Another screech of brakes.

"Good evening — or is it good morning?" A slow nasal honk laden with breeding. "What *are* you people up to? Has our Amos packed it in for the night?"

At the wheel Daisy recognized Delphine Mortimer. The street lamp, or the moon, picked out her rippling mane and a long white satin muffler circling her neck.

"Careful with that scarf. You might find yourself imitating Isadora," called Daisy, pleased with her reference to Isadora Duncan's garroting by her own scarf.

"I'd rather go *à la gloire* than any other way." It'd turned so cold, Delphine's breath made little puffs in the air.

"The guardians of virtue have mended the fence," said Sally, prancing in place.

"*Quel* drag," said Delphine. "Why don't you come over to Kober with me. You can flop in the living room. We'll find you a sleeping bag or you can borrow my new Arabian horse blanket."

Daisy and Sally looked at each other stupidly; of course, the off-campus houses had no curfew.

"Well, come along, it's not exactly balmy out here. I've got some champagne and paté and cornichons. I'm having a celebration."

"We'll follow you in my Beetle," Sally said.

Ignoring Sally, Daisy climbed in next to Delphine. "What are you celebrating?" She wanted to hear Delphine's voice, a unique vintage of Locust Valley lockjaw, extreme to the point of parody.

"Oh, let's see. *The New York Times* just asked me to do an article on us — 'The Silent Generation.' And I've landed a summer job on the *Village Voice*, but I don't know, it's not really any one thing." She took the curve without braking, clipping the curb and dragging a garbage pail. "This afternoon I was reading *Three Sisters*, and I got to the part where someone asks poor Masha why she's all in black. And Masha answers, 'I'm in mourning for my life.' And I thought, Well, I'm celebrating *my* life."

No wonder everyone was mad for Delphine! Daisy bounced along in her low-slung seat, leaning into the curves, and admired the workings of fate. Because Sally's appetites had made them late, she, Daisy, was sitting here next to Delphine, a girl she'd idolized since sighting her in the fall of '54, their freshman year, striding up the path to McCracken Library in her long green velvet coat, hair streaming; playing Scarlatti on her harpsichord, naked — a girl convinced that in her absence the world went out.

Delphine's driving must have been known to the Westchester police. She took the turns with a screech, downshifted with an impressive *vroom-vroom,* braked unpredictably — to punctuate a thought — and sometimes turned full around toward Daisy, the better to make a point, terrorizing the odd driver on the road at that hour. They jolted to a stop in a cobbled circular driveway to a smell of burning rubber.

Though it was past one A.M., Kober House, a Tudor gray stone manor with peaked dormers and leaded windows, blazed with lights.

Inside was not much warmer than outside, like a true English manor house. Toting their patent-leather hatboxes, Daisy and Sally traipsed after their hostess up a curved marble staircase. It was lined with portraits of pigeon-breasted dowagers, a futile reminder of the college's origin as a finishing school for well-born girls.

Delphine's room flickered with red light. Daisy felt she'd entered an enchanted grotto. Several girls lounged about in bathrobes, wreathed in cigarette smoke; Vivaldi fiddled from a record player on the floor. Daisy took in a girl named Ginny Goldberg, in a pink quilted robe, seated on the bed under the eaves — Jesus, wearing *bunny slippers*. There was Mia Sils-Levy, an actress, in her usual black on black, hunched on a stool like a raven; Grace Omura in a yellow kimono, cross-legged on the bench in front of the harpsichord.

"Finally!" cried Ginny. "Let the party begin." She swooped down on Delphine's Harrods shopping bag. Sally flopped in the space vacated by Ginny and curled up in fetal position. Daisy sat timidly on the floor against the bed. Everyone else swung into action. With practiced hand, Delphine uncorked the champagne, jumping backward to escape the fizz. She filled a ruby and crystal goblet that flamed red in the light, and passed it round. With swift precise movements, Grace laid out the paté and cornichons on a paper plate. Mia ran to her room for a knife. She returned with a silver letter opener and a plastic toothbrush glass.

In her wake strode Froyda Maidman. Even at this hour she wore her uniform, inspired by Vita Sackville-West: cream silk blouse — it was said Froyda bought them by the dozen — antelope vest, fawn suede boots. She was famous for her epic poem on Amazons, as well as losing her father's Cadillacs around Bronxville. This spring half a dozen girls were sick with love for her; one had left a pearl-handled dagger wrapped in a handkerchief at her door. She sat on the floor next to Daisy, smelling of suede and — was it jasmine?

Ginny raised her goblet. "To Delphine's portrait of the class of fifty-eight! But let's hope we don't recognize ourselves *too* well." She surveyed the group in mock alarm.

Delphine threw back her head and laughed. Perfect white teeth, almost *too* even. Statuesque, she was often called — fancy for over-weight — but Daisy was bedazzled. Delphine had wild eyes with something animal and keen in their shine, a powerful throat, a racy black mole just above her lip, which Daisy planned to reproduce above her own. She wore a strange brocade blouse shot through with metallic glints and a long billowing skirt, like some Pre-Raphaelite Grace.

A mirror set in an antique bureau in the corner caught her from behind, so Daisy could see her twice.

Suddenly Delphine brought her finger to her mouth and froze, eyes closed. "Vivaldi's a genius, just listen to that modulation, sliding from key to key. It's just like coming."

Dreamy nods of agreement; Delphine always found the perfect image.

Sally lifted a groggy face from the bed. "Sometimes when I *pee* it feels like coming," she offered, and sank back into sleep.

Ginny opened her eyes wide and asked no one in particular, "How do you know when you've had an orgasm?"

Stunned silence.

"O Eustace Chesser, where are you now that we need you?" groaned Delphine, head thrown back. "Dearie, I'll lend you my copy of *Love Without Fear*. If you have to ask, you haven't had one," she added unhelpfully. The subject was now closed.

While everyone busied themselves spreading paté and passing the goblet, Daisy's eyes roamed the room. The russet light came from a lamp with a dark red, perforated shade and an outside spot shining through a small red mullioned window. On the bureau she noticed a silver-framed blowup of Delphine and a group of golden girls and boys on a sailboat. Daisy zoomed in on a Gerrit lookalike at the helm; he wore a rakish smile and a cigarette dangling off his lip. Of course. Delphine and Gerrit were of the same clay.

Delphine dwarfed her courtiers, Daisy decided (as always, hyper-critical, though hardest on herself, a habit contracted from years studying her "line" in dance studio mirrors). Ginny was a large pale blur of a person waiting to happen. Her broad moon face hinted at Mongol raids on the old shtetl. She had downy, baby-fine skin — which seemed somehow squandered on her — and hid her body beneath men's Oxford shirts. Delphine must need Ginny as ballast to keep from flying into the stratosphere.

From her command post, Delphine tapped the letter opener against Mia's plastic glass. "A toast to us, to our brilliant futures! Women like us — we're going to play it different." She upended her glass, then passed it, as Ginny wrestled with another bottle of champagne.

"I can picture exactly where I'll be in ten years," said Delphine, eyes half closed. Dramatic pause. "By thirty I'll be editor in chief of a publishing house."

A collective intake of breath.

"I can picture my office already. A big corner office it'll be, overlooking Madison Avenue on one side, Saint Patrick's Cathedral on the other. I'll paint it Chinese red and have masses of ferns and begonias."

"I'm going to become a disciple of Frank Lloyd Wright in Taliesin," said Froyda Maidman. Booted legs crossed at the knee, she puffed away on a cigarillo, thrillingly androgynous. Daisy wondered what women did together. Probably something silken and delicious they'd burn you in Salem for and that she owed it to herself to try.

"I'm going to live in the Village and stage an avant-garde opera," piped Grace Omura in her singsong. Surprised looks. Little Grace wrote haiku, perched in the crotch of the apple tree behind Westlands. Tough to picture her ordering around an army of spear carriers.

Daisy now wanted nothing so much as Delphine's admiration. She marshaled her nerve (only on stage did she lose her shyness). "I'm going to be an expatriate and live in Paris and all. In an atelier." She cursed the quaver in her voice.

Silence, as curious eyes converged on Daisy. A campus star, yet a loner. Unplaceable, as though she'd been born from someone's head.

"Marvelous!" said Delphine, peering down at her. "You'll be part of the last post-Hemingway wave."

"And what will you *do* in your atelier?" asked Froyda in a smoky voice.

"I'll write of course." She'd just thought of it. Why not, it was perfect. She'd be a writer! She's always kept diaries and journals.

"But you must dance, too," said Delphine.

"Oh, I don't know. To dance you have to give up life, capital *L*." The vertigo again; saying it out loud made her defection real. How could they all be so certain of what they were about?

"You have star quality, a gift that shouldn't be squandered," Delphine scolded. "You mustn't *ever* not dance." Her violet eyes bored into Daisy, who could feel her own neck burning.

"I'm going to get a master's in early childhood education," announced Ginny, to Daisy's relief.

Awkward hush; no one appeared impressed. Daisy couldn't feel sorry for her. Ginny would get a teaching license, as "something to fall back on" and then "marry up."

"Someday I'm going to play Nina in *The Seagull*," breathed Mia.

"You do have an affinity for suicidal heroines," said Froyda. Chin in palm, Mia gazed into space without answering, a habit that had marked her as profound.

Froyda went on, "Of course, Camus believed — and I quote — 'There is but one truly serious philosophical problem, and that is suicide.' "

Everyone pondered this, possibly thinking of Swarthmore, which had a monopoly on suicides. Delphine glanced feverishly around.

"I'd say it's far more serious to be out of champagne!"

Grace Omura took a corkscrew to a bottle of Chianti. "I'm going to marry a rock 'n' roll star," she volunteered.

Stunned silence. Then everyone gabbled at once.

Well, of course there would be a husband somewhere down the line. But a long way down, quite a long way. He would likely do something practical, like earn a living. Maybe he'd be a Renaissance businessman, but of course no one would be so crass as to marry for money.

"An architect is ideal," said Delphine. "Someone who'll spur *my* creativity."

"The thing is not to be like other women," said Mia. "Like our mothers, shadowy and self-effacing. What've they actually accomplished?"

"They know how to set up for a mah-jongg game," offered Ginny.

"And choose a furrier," said Froyda. Whinnying laugh.

Daisy couldn't remember her mother, and her stepmother was like a chilly older sister. "In the evening we'll hold *salons*," she said to distract herself. "Like women in eighteenth-century Paris, or Alma Mahler. Surround ourselves with fascinating people from every field."

They'd read their work aloud to one another, or play chamber music, chimed in Delphine. The conversation would scintillate. As wives, they would provide intellectual stimulation, something a husband might well lose touch with in the hurly-burly of nine to five.

They segued into what they would not do, not ever, on pain of death.

"The worst," said Delphine, "is to marry before graduation and become a cow. Or get knee-jerk married in June. Like at Smith."

To a stiff who would have "shown respect" by not "going all the way." Or a dentist or insurance salesman — groans — a guy who'd attend a stag dinner before the wedding and guffaw over dirty jokes — puleeze — and on the wedding night put shoe trees in his shoes before claiming his bride, said Delphine. Shrieks of laughter. Or to one of those animals from Dartmouth, a bullshit artist with a "line" a mile long, the kind who said to his cronies in private — Delphine had actually *heard* this — Boy, has she got a pair on her — or had he said "jugs"?

She couldn't picture herself pushing a stroller laden with shopping bags and babies, said Ginny. *Babies?* They looked at her in horror. Her hallmate Muffie had left college to get married last year, Ginny said, because she was "preggers" — "Muffie used that word, so help me God."

The worst, said Froyda, would be to settle in the suburbs. Think of it: rows of identical houses with picture windows in a development like Levittown. Wall-to-wall pile carpeting, identical Norman Rockwell prints, *Life* magazine on the coffee table. Formica counters. Golf clubs. Car pools. Barbecue pits. The American Dream! So plastic and uptight and antisexual. Did everyone in those developments turn out the lights and assume missionary position at the exact same moment?

Sally sat up with a start and rubbed her eyes.

A heart-shaped face with starry eyes blossomed in the doorway: Diana Dew, wrapped in powder blue fleece. The queen of Sigma Chi wandered onto the wrong set.

"Come toast the future with us." Delphine, the munificent hostess, waved her in. Her room apparently magnetized the late-hour, roving population of Kober. Daisy wondered uneasily whether Franca was at large in the house.

Delphine filled a plastic glass with Chianti. She passed it to Diana, who wrinkled her pert nose at Froyda's cigarillo. A large blue-white rock glinted on her fourth finger.

"Y'all have to celebrate with *me*," said Diana. "Girls" — a huge intake of breath — "Frank and I are gittin' *married*! This June. Y'all are invited, of course."

A thunderous silence.

"Congratulations," said Ginny several beats late. "Let's all drink to the soon-to-be Mrs. Frank Hilliard." She shot Delphine a stage frown — *Be civil!* — and upended her goblet.

Silence.

"So you'll be commuting to college all the way from Charleston?" twittered Grace.

"Why no, hon, I won't commute at all. I mean, we don't know yet where Frank's goin' to be workin'. He's received offers from *three* law firms. So" — she toyed with the belt of her robe — "I won't be comin' back to college."

"But see here, surely you plan to finish college," said Delphine, hugging her own chest, as if trying to rein herself in.

"Well, I'll — I'll take some courses at the community college. But Frank wants to start a family right away."

"What about you? What do *you* want?" asked Daisy.

Diana looked puzzled by the question. "Why, hon, what *Frank* wants." She added, "We're real like-minded."

Cigarettes were lit. Vivaldi's *Winter* pounded the dead air.

Diana flicked lint off her bathrobe. She set her glass of Chianti on the harpsichord. Faced them down, eyes glittering. "Y'all think you're so damn superiuh. Anyone who gets married is sellin' out or some-thin'. But I think y'all envy me."

"Oh, good God," murmured Delphine, the heel of her hand to her forehead.

"Yes, you're jealous! I have a man who truly wants me, warts 'n' all, a man who wants to spend the rest of his life with me. That's real square, right? And what've *you*-all got? Besides your su-periority? Lust in the dust."

The only sound now was Vivaldi's strings. Daisy had to concede that Diana had a point about the men. Weekends with high-strung poets in filthy lofts didn't exactly lead to matrimony — but so much the better!

"Y'all are real smart, compared to you I'm a dumb hick," said Diana without sarcasm. "But y'know something?" She looked surprised by what she was about to say. "Lord knows how y'all will end up. And I'm going to have a wonderful life."

Chapter 3

SOMETIME before dawn Daisy lugged her hatbox and Delphine's sleeping bag down the long curve of white marble, past the pigeon-breasted dowagers. She headed for a dimly lit living room to the right of the stairs. There in a sleeping bag on a couch lay Franca.

She wanted to dive back into the night. She wasn't ready for this; mañana would be too soon, but the sleeper had opened an eye. Franca offered a rumpled smile and struggled to sit. Her fair hair fell over a man's blue pajama top. "Greetings. Come into my parlor."

They laughed, and for a second Daisy felt false relief, as if her treachery had not happened. She bummed one of Franca's Player's, lit it with shaking hand, and collapsed onto a sofa catty-cornered to Franca's. Then Franca nattered on about the sailor in her lap on the Greyhound bus home while Daisy hated herself. She was punchy from no sleep. *Les plaisirs d'amour ne durent qu'un instant* went the French song. Yeah, but one instant of love's pleasures, and au revoir friendship. Just the sort of issue she would have liked to explore with Franca.

"Well? How'd it go in Cambridge?" said Franca with a yawn.

Daisy looked down at the strap of her ballerina, felt Peter's thumb kneading her instep. A pang of desire. What did Franca know? *This is just for us,* Peter had said. "At the concert I met someone, sort of," Daisy said.

In the same moment Franca asked, "Why only sort of?" Daisy asked, "Have you spoken to Peter?"

Silence. "Not since Friday." Franca ground out her barely smoked cigarette and lit another. The match went out. She went on shaking it.

Daisy thought, She knows. Better just do this swiftly and then disappear back into the night, into the orchard behind Kober House, where she could sleep under an apple tree and catch pneumonia, the least she could do to atone. She went to Franca's couch and squatted beside her. "I did something terrible, and if you hate me I'll understand. I saw Peter. I mean, I did look him up, after all. Almost as a favor, you were so insistent. And then we were just, you know, very attracted." She flushed. "We were guzzling Scotch, and things kind of went out of control. I never intended what happened. Though not all that much happened."

Say something for God's sake. But Franca just stared into space, unreadable thoughts pooling in her eyes.

"No, *I'm* the bad guy," Franca said abruptly. She tucked her fist beneath her armpit and looked at Daisy. "We kind of planned it. Oh damn!"

"*Planned* it?" Creakily Daisy rose, stupid, not yet caught up to her anger. She shook her head no, even as it made sense. Of course. Peter had seemed too unrepentant, even for him. The whole thing had smelled fishy.

She walked to a bookcase in the corner and pulled out a book. She'd been about to tell Franca they hadn't actually *gone all the way*. It no longer seemed pertinent.

"Please come back here and let me try to explain."

"Oh you're really something, you know? A real phony. *You* of all people — how could *you* set me up?"

The worst was, she'd imagined Peter found her irresistible.

"Let me *try* to explain. What happened was, last weekend Peter and I, well, we got engaged. He wants it kept secret because he thinks engagements are corny and bourgeois, and —"

"So that's why he never mentioned it."

Ignoring the sarcasm: "Surely you've noticed Peter has always been attracted to you —"

"Oh, right, I'm, uh — how'd you put it? — so lovely."

"And he had this demented idea that if he made love to you, and our relationship could survive that — well, that would somehow be a test we would pass as a couple. And then we could move forward and get married." A moment. "Do you know, I actually *believed* that? When all he really wanted was a last fling. With my blessing."

"And you gave it." It struck Daisy that Franca hadn't mentioned her willingness to be seduced; a little righteousness sputtered out, like air from a balloon. She looked at the book in her hand: *Ideal Marriage* by Van de Velde.

"The horrible thing is I always go along with him. It's always me, catering, placating, that keeps us in forward motion. As long as I'm *with* Peter, physically, it's like I'm under a spell, I'm hardly aware of humoring him. I sometimes think he could ask me to slit someone's throat or sell atomic secrets, and I'd do it." She sighed. "Peter provides all the energy, all the excitement. He rescues me from being the boring person I essentially am. Without Peter I'd hardly exist." A silence. "How could you understand? You *are* someone."

Was. The vertigo again. Daisy noticed the book in her hand. She put it back on the shelf. With her back to Franca: "Goddamn, you were the only person I trusted," she said, voice cracking. She went and flung her sleeping bag on the couch and yanked at the caught zipper.

Franca sat cross-legged on her couch, watching. "You still have me, if you want me."

Daisy yanked savagely. She couldn't trust herself to speak. Outside in the Kober orchard she heard the faint twittering of birds announcing dawn.

Franca came over. "Here, allow me." She worked the zipper free. "Daisy," she said carefully, "Peter thought of you as the ultimate test."

The words settled into her like unguent.

"You'll probably think this *perverted*," Franca continued, "but if Peter had to do this with someone — well, I'm sort of glad it was you."

The idea made them both smile.

Still, Daisy didn't like it. As if she'd incurred a debt she'd have to repay when least expecting it.

Several hours later Daisy was in the Caf, gulping down a cup of coffee — sleep then was only the least interesting way to spend the night. She had just time to make Zimmer's class, The Romantic Quest. She sped under the arbor and cut right around Westlands. Over the weekend the campus had bloomed, like flowers opening slo-mo in Walt Disney; there were mauves and froufou pinks, the frothing red tongues of tulips, fuchsia banks of azaleas.

The classroom was secreted in the dank basement of Titsworth. (There were no purely academic buildings at Sarah Lawrence.) Its windows were level with a path that snaked along the back of the college parallel to Kimball Avenue. Daisy slipped into a seat at the oak seminar table near the door, hoping for low visibility. Her well-honed insights on *Madame Bovary* had evaporated. She was still high from the red room and Delphine. And scheming how to reunite with Gerrit, convinced now that they had a future; Peter's view of her as "the ultimate test" had perked up her self-image. In one weekend, it seemed, her life had begun in earnest.

Zimmer launched into a lecture on Flaubertian-style realism in the famous carriage scene, when Roderick seduces Emma. Hmm, maybe she could learn from Roderick? A scent of lilac wafted through the open casement windows, mingling with Froyda's jasmine. Was there anything this morning that wasn't sex? Sally November sat hunched over her journal with a colored pencil, drawing one of her famous orgasms, a tightly patterned mantra of magenta, yellow, and green. A hieroglyph, Daisy imagined, for some cosmic commotion, an aurora borealis of the senses. Across the table, Froyda Maidman was falling in love slow motion with Mia. Diana Dew knitted an endless muffler, smiling dreamily. Only Ginny Goldberg took notes.

Zimmer was a pretty hot item himself, if you preferred European suave to clean-cut Ivy. He'd published only a slim monograph on Gertrude Stein; this merely endeared him to his students, eager to shore up a wounded genius manqué. A shock of black hair fell diagonally over his brow. He flipped it back with a toss of the head — his trademark, along with the pipe and the itchy tweed jacket that more than one debutante in revolt imagined grazing her cheek.

With a start Daisy noticed that Zimmer had abandoned Emma Bovary for "Franny" — how had she missed the transition? The new story by J. D. Salinger had just appeared in *The New Yorker;* everyone, Daisy included, had stormed the newsstands to buy a copy. Franny visits her boyfriend, Lane, at a big football weekend at Yale. Over lunch, Franny enthuses about various Eastern theories of mysticism, and ends up fainting.

"What do you suppose was wrong with Franny?" Zimmer asked.

Froyda's hand shot up. "On the face of it she was having a nervous breakdown, or maybe just a massive case of heartburn or something, but it was really a religious *crise,* a dismissal of the whole goddamn *ego* thing, you know, egotism — of the 'I' that Lane represents, of Western I-centered civilization really; she doesn't *want* to goddamn compete and play the game, like everyone expects you to, she wants to, like, rachet herself up to a higher level, through the medium of prayer, though Lane tries to reduce it to mere neurosis, when in effect she's attempting to change her whole way of *thinking*."

Zimmer nodded at Froyda above his pipe smoke. "Your point is well taken," he said.

What point? "I think Salinger is a clubby snob in this story," Daisy heard herself say. "If you're not part of his elite band of Zen mystics, you're either a phony or a boor."

Mouths opened; she'd scribbled *fuck* on an icon.

"I mean, in the final analysis, Franny aspires to become an absolute nobody, I think is what she says. What's so great about wandering around the desert, praying nonstop and saying *om*? It's a nihilistic cop-out."

Zimmer smiled and pulled on his pipe. He always enjoyed Daisy's fierceness, her refusal of cant.

"Clearly, you have no religious vocation," said Froyda to Daisy.

Just then Daisy noticed a pair of skinny shanks at the window just level with the path, directly behind Zimmer. Above the legs hung a flower print dress — ugly, red poppies or something. The legs remained at the window, their owner in no hurry to move on — someone from building and grounds?

"But to get back to Franny's malaise, don't you think there might be a simpler, more prosaic explanation?" asked Zimmer. "After all, when she disappears into the ladies' room, why does Lane become irritated by the sight of her raccoon coat over the chair — or more accurately, the wrinkled silk lining? What is Salinger suggesting?"

Silk-lined fur — oh God, Zimmer was brilliant! Salinger was a genius. A little tremor ran around the room. Diana's knitting needles stopped clicking. No one breathed.

Daisy noticed the legs had disappeared from the window.

Zimmer relit his pipe and drew on it. "So perhaps there's a simpler explanation for what ails Franny. Lane reflects that it's been too long between drinks, as he crudely puts it. The last time more than a month ago. I leave you to draw your own conclusions."

Daisy placed her tomato-soup red tray on the slopping pile, and pondered how she could remeet Delphine. She drifted with the eddy of girls heading for the mail room, the true nerve center of the college. Here destinies were forged or exploded. Equally important were the hall phones and message pads, a yellow pencil tied to their coils by a dirty string. Only Lizzie Borden and the other certifiables found Marx or Mendel's peas more consuming, more crucial to their well-being than the messages from Ivy-town scrawled on those pads.

Suddenly Daisy spotted Delphine. Gesturing frantically from the shadowed stairwell that led to faculty offices on the second story of Bates. Delphine signaled at Daisy not to blow her cover. She was wild-eyed, hair tumbling from its pins. From behind, Daisy heard someone whistling Vivaldi. The moment Sally passed, Daisy headed for the stairwell.

"I cannot abide that girl," Delphine murmured. "If she gets the same B.A. as me, I don't want it. *Tu dois me rendre un service,*" she said, switching into the language of diplomatic missions. "I've left something upstairs in one of the offices. Be a dear and get it for me."

"Of course," murmured Daisy, flattered and intrigued.

Delphine blew a strand of hair out of her eyes and lit a Camel. Her nails were bitten, shockingly, below her fingertips, the third finger was stained yellow with nicotine. She smelled of B.O. cut with cologne.

"It's in Zimmer's office. The bathroom adjoining it, to be exact." She exhaled over Daisy's shoulder. "It's, uh, something I left there, in the bathroom. Last night before I picked you up. I was in such a dither over celebrating. Seems like ages ago, doesn't it?"

Daisy nodded matter-of-factly, wrestling to conceal her amazement: Delphine and Zimmer? Certainly there were no tutorials Sunday night, at least not the usual sort. And where did her regular, old Dudley Hunnewell, figure in?

"I can't go myself because I just spotted his wife skulking around up there, and she's already suspicious as hell. If she sees me anywhere near his office . . ."

How did you do it with two men? From the standpoint of hygiene.

Did you douche or something in between? And with a man Zimmer's age. He had to be thirty-five.

"Bring me a blue plastic, uh, case that looks like a miniature flying saucer. I think it's right on the sink. Better hurry. Zimmer leaves the door unlocked. I owe you one."

"What if he's there?"

"He's gone to a faculty meeting."

"Blue flying saucer," repeated Daisy solemnly.

She bounded up the stairs and walked down a dim, wood-paneled hall. She wondered about poor Dudley Hunnewell, so overbred he could only marry a cousin, which Daisy believed Delphine to be.

At Zimmer's door, Daisy glanced both ways. She silently turned the knob, and walked through the book-lined study to the bathroom. No trace of a flying saucer. She opened the medicine cabinet: nothing but a bottle of Chanel after-shave cologne. She recognized the original of the scent she'd just smelled on Delphine. She scanned the floor, thought she heard footsteps. She speedily checked the study, even behind the throw pillows on the sofa. She felt remiss for not accomplishing her mission. As she slipped out the door, she collided with Hannah Zimmer.

"You are perhaps looking for something in the professor's office?" said Mrs. Zimmer in her German accent.

"I came up to check Professor Zimmer's office hours," Daisy managed. Her leotard had turned moist with sweat. She closed the office door with exaggerated care. There on the door were posted the office hours.

Mrs. Zimmer's liver-colored eyes betrayed no expression. She was square-framed with hair like yellow raffia, Hansel's aging Gretel. She unsnapped her pocketbook and drew out a blue plastic disk. "You are perhaps looking for this?"

Daisy stared at the object as if it were radioactive.

"You will do me a favor by taking this," said Mrs. Zimmer firmly. She grasped Daisy's right hand, placed the disk in it, and closed Daisy's fingers around it.

"Mrs. Zimmer, this is a mistake —" Out of loyalty to Delphine, she stopped.

Mrs. Zimmer studied her. "You must think me very stupid. You're a child. Annika, our daughter, would have been your age." Her nostrils looked pinched, her skin waxen. What had happened to Annika? Daisy wondered. She wanted to ask, but didn't dare. She felt encumbered by her own animal vitality.

"There have been many girls, very many. You are all so beautiful. Your figures, your skin, your long shiny hair. I sometimes wonder, do you know the power you have?"

Daisy flinched, though Hannah made no motion, her pink-knuckled hands hanging by the sides of her flower print dress.

"No, you don't know, you understand nothing. You become invisible," she said, half to herself. "You wonder, do you exist? When he does see you, his eyes look trapped. You have become his prison. You become all the time suspicious, of every girl. I see a girl looking at me a moment too long, and I think, Is she the one?"

"Oh, Mrs. Zimmer," Daisy blurted, "it's bound to blow over."

Something relaxed around Mrs. Zimmer's eyes. "Well, precisely. So you do understand something. But you are so sloppy, you must take better care. Now listen to me. Be a good girl, and do not tell the professor of our little meeting."

"No, of course not."

"*I* certainly will not tell him. You see, I don't want him to know what I know. Because then there would be a scene, and he would feel . . . *schuldbewusst —*"

"Guilty?"

"Yes, just so. And he would say, 'You deserve better, this is so unfair to you.' And then he would have his reason for leaving. At my age, I do not want to rock the boat."

Mrs. Zimmer turned and walked stiffly down the hall. Daisy watched her square shoulders in the flower print dress till she vanished around the corner. She heard her footsteps, growing fainter, in the stairwell.

Daisy stood in the same spot a moment longer, clutching her booty, troubled by an afterimage of red poppies. Then she remembered the dress she had spied outside Zimmer's class.

Chapter 4

MISSION FLYING SAUCER clinched their friendship. Daisy never told Delphine about the encounter with Hannah Zimmer, though. Taking the rap for Delphine appealed to Daisy's exalted notions of friendship — she was Oliver shielding Roland from the Saracens! And she was spooked by Hannah's misery; it was like some ugly graffiti scrawled across the window of the future.

That week in mid-April their foursome became official. It fell naturally into place. Delphine and Ginny had been a duo since sophomore year; Daisy brought in Franca.

Delphine's crowd, they were called around campus. They were envied; they had their sights fixed on a future over the heads, so to speak, of everyone else. Resented: their clique closed others out. Feared: Delphine was like Genghis Khan — the mere sound of her slow honk sent the Miss Porter's girls scurrying.

"Let's all unhook our bras and talk about Wittgenstein," Delphine would start, sliding into her seat at "their" table in Bates. Hooting with laughter, she slashed at "TFBs" — trust fund babies, and never mind that she was one herself — "saving" it for the wedding night, Tupperware parties, Mamie Eisenhower's bangs, her mother, Merry "the lush." Nor did she exempt herself from the rampage. "I haven't

38

got much," she announced loudly, blowing a wisp of hair off her cheek, "but what I've got *sags*."

Delphine accepted Franca grudgingly. "I'm a lapsed debutante," she told Daisy one night over coffee in the Caf. "I can't abide all that Social Register crap. But Franca, you know, in her core she belongs to that world. She's an eccentric socialite." She cited Franca's love of needlepoint. Her plans to *quit college* and marry, though for some reason she kept the engagement secret.

Delphine also joked behind Ginny's back that Ginny was sexually retarded, perhaps missing a crucial anatomical part. "I mean, she's actually unacquainted with lust. Maybe someday she'll be kissed awake by a great cocksman."

Bitchy, hypercritical, disloyal — Daisy saw these traits in Delphine, but they slid off her. Delphine could have been Tokyo Rose. Daisy was infatuated. She had found the friend of her heart.

They needed one another to complete themselves. You became how the others saw you.

Delphine was the flamboyant one, their inspirational leader and beacon, *called* by a brilliant destiny. Ginny, a psych major and plodder, was the pragmatic one — Daisy thought of her as ballast that kept the three of them from capsizing; her traffic with mundane things, like her seasonal old clothes sales, was reassuring as Ovaltine. Franca was the angelic one, interpreting each to the other, healing rifts, a Pollyanna censoring the evidence of reality.

Daisy was the artistic one, the group's child, the one they worried and clucked over, which Daisy soaked up, ever in search of a missing mother; the intellectual, since she had read *Ulysses* and most of *Being and Nothingness,* and could work the word *reification* into a sentence without a beat missed.

After rehearsal or a session in McCracken Library, Daisy headed for Delphine's red room in the perfumed night. She collapsed backward onto the bed, leg crossed at the knee. "I can't *live* without some consuming project," she groaned, dragging on her new Dunhill cigarette holder.

"I see you doing something significant," said Delphine, pacing. "You'll harness all that discipline from your dancing."

"Maybe I'll study literature in Heidelberg, and stroll along the Neckar, and discuss Schopenhauer with a blond German too young to have been a Nazi." By midnight it was settled: she would be a scholar and wear clunky brown oxfords and rimless glasses and deliver papers on the bildungsroman at international conferences.

"Whatever we do, we'll never live like a cow!" cried Delphine. "So long as I escape the family taint," she joked, mysteriously alluding, as she sometimes did, to some dark family history. She fell on her harpsichord, and ripped through a Scarlatti sonata.

With the deepening night, Daisy felt the boundaries blurring. Delphine became her double: the best she could be. Perhaps the worst, too.

"We come from different planets," Daisy wrote in the journal she kept — since she was now a writer. "When I think 'Christmas' I remember my stepfather's harangues on religion-the-opiate. Or the hand-me-down present from my stepmother, the blue flask of Evening in Paris cologne she'd received from her fifth graders. For Delphine 'Christmas' means sepia-colored rooms burnished by firelight; tree-trimming parties, midnight mass with Handel's *Messiah,* skiing in Saint Anton.

"When I think 'school' I get P.S. 127: the words *kike* and *fuck* scrawled in the stairwell; the vomitous lunchroom smell of navy bean soup and margarine sandwiches and orange peels during the war; the greasers baiting us Jews in the halls for getting skipped to Rapid Advance. For Delphine 'school' is La Roseraie in Switzerland and Rosemary Hall; mixers with Hotchkiss or Choate; singing 'Jerusalem' and 'A Mighty Fortress Is Our God,' horny as all get-out in freezing early morning chapel; field hockey in the long golden New England afternoons."

Daisy was especially entranced by an image of Delphine in her green velvet coat, haunting the sandstone cliffs outside Rosecliff, her family's "historic pile" in Newport, Rhode Island. Yet she never envied Delphine. Delphine was her window onto a magical world, like the scenes inside Easter eggs, snow eternally floating over a perfect winterscape. What Delphine possessed couldn't be acquired: inborn confidence and nerve. She was a queen, laying about her and smashing rules, inventing her own, answerable to no one.

·   ·   ·

One evening they took their trays onto the lawn behind Westlands to eat supper *sur l'herbe,* as Delphine called it.

"Men get on my nerves, with their incessant demands," said Delphine. "*Quel* drag. I need to clear my head. I'm calling a man strike."

Delphine actually meant it, Daisy marveled. The other girls who gathered in the red room, conjuring brilliant careers, weren't they phonies? Just sneakier versions of Diana Dew? Because the careers were window dressing, part of the enterprise of attracting a husband. By adding to their dowry artistic inclinations, they were simply positioning themselves to attract a better-grade husband.

The saccharine voice of a countertenor singing Purcell floated down from an open window, its yellow curtain fluttering in the breeze. From Sally's bathroom in Titsworth, Rudi Urdang could be heard singing in the shower. Froyda Maidman rolled up the path arm in arm with Mia Sils-Levy, a couple out for an evening stroll.

"My, my, don't they make a handsome pair," said Delphine.

"They're shacking up together," said Sally, who'd joined them. In a loud whisper: "I've heard Froyda is anatomically weird. They say she's got a miniature set of male organs way up inside."

Delphine fell back on the grass, exposing a gray bra strap, and whooped with laughter. "Sometimes I think we should go for broke and make this the best goddamn dyke college in the country."

Daisy reveled in these evenings, savoring every detail. The jonquils nodding their orange ruffs in the breeze. Grace Omura, perched in the apple tree, silhouetted against Westlands, composing haiku. The syrupy countertenor singing "Come, come, ye sons of art," pouring from an open window. She had always pitted herself against everything that surrounded her, taking refuge in novels and her Grand Plan. For the first time she relaxed into a circle of belonging. She wanted to freeze time. She wanted never to leave Arcadia.

Delphine proposed they form an "SOS" Club. "When any of us is in deep shit, wherever we are, the club will come to the rescue. Just like in fairy tales."

For all her bravado, it was Delphine, as it happened, who needed the SOS Club most. It was formed just in time, too. Because then came the awful business with Dudley Hunnewell.

.   .   .

Delphine discovered she was pregnant. "I have very suggestible ovaries," she told her group in Bates, shaking her hair free. "All I do is
look at an erection and I get knocked up."

The Miss Porter's girls at the next table collected their things and left
in a jiffy.

Delphine's cavalier tone was a pose. After lunch, she roamed the
little orchard behind Kober House, frantic. How could she have done
this *again*? Twice she'd journeyed to Pennsylvania, to the sainted Dr.
Spencer; and the last time to Havana (bringing back coffee and Macunado cigars). She had vowed to herself, Never again. Yet in the heat
of the moment, the "precautions" always seemed such an affront.
She'd also taken enough abnormal psych with Clara Winternitz to
suspect that maybe, just maybe, she was punishing herself, anteing up
for past sins.

That evening in the red room, pale and too queasy to smoke, Delphine grasped Daisy's arm: "God help me, I don't know whose it is."

Daisy flashed to Kurt Zimmer in that class two Mondays back. No
wonder he'd abandoned Madame Bovary for Salinger's pregnant
Franny!

Delphine decided not to tell Dudley. Wouldn't he feel it increased his
claim on her in some way? And she'd been trying for months to let him
down easy. She just hadn't found the language yet.

Love, though, made Dudley hyperobservant. That weekend in New
Haven he sensed Delphine was different in some way, *tasted* different;
tasted somehow . . . pregnant. Gazing at her across the table in the
beery basement of the Rathskeller, Dudley asked her to marry him.

"Dudley, I —"

"*Our* child," he went on in wonderment. "We could go to a justice
of the peace in New Haven. We could go right now, this very moment,
as soon as I pay the check! But knowing your mother, maybe we'd
better produce a big June wedding."

Delphine blew out in exasperation. "Dudley, there's something you
ought to know." As delicately as she could, she confessed to confusion
about the baby's father.

Dudley's left eyebrow shot up; his expression was otherwise unchanged. He lit a Camel; holding it between thumb and third finger,
he smoked it down.

Delphine now regretted her confession; she hated cutting off options.

Finally Dudley eyed her, flushed with daring. "It's no one's business but our own," he said.

Delphine caught her breath, stared at him in disbelief. She hadn't suspected the depth of his loyalty. She now felt trapped! "Dudley, really, is this some antiquated notion of honor?"

"He is *ours,*" said Dudley with a lift of his chin. "Regardless."

To lobby for marriage and the family, Dudley abandoned Skull and Bones, classes, and everything he owed his future, and haunted the Sarah Lawrence campus. He could be seen in his Burberry, his yellow head against the black bark of the Westlands apple tree, gazing into the middle distance, a button-down Young Werther. He made such a pest of himself, Delphine ordered him to stop coming round. He kept coming. She refused to see him.

"He's just being pig-headed," she told Daisy in the red room. "After all, when has Dudley not gotten what he wants? The bottom line is I could never marry the dear fellow. He's so predictable and cautious and dreary. His biggest accomplishment was getting tapped for Skull and Bones. Marrying Dudley would be like getting to the ending without a beginning and middle."

One Sunday afternoon Dudley ambushed her in the kitchen of Kober House. "I won't stand for this," he announced, an ugly glint in his eye.

"Are you threatening me? Are you mad?" Delphine escaped up a back stairs to her room and locked the door.

A furious pounding. "It's me, Kurt."

Jesus, she'd forgotten all about Zimmer. Where the hell was Dudley?

Zimmer had come to arrange about money.

"I find your attitude ignoble," said Delphine. "Your only concern is your reputation."

She was not off the mark. Zimmer had tired of Delphine. He was comfortable with Hannah and her policy of appeasement, the harmony of their little design for living. And Delphine was so confrontational, always in need of drama. It was all rather exhausting. Lately her astonish-me antics made him want to take a nap. As for her indifference to birth control . . .

While Zimmer tried to organize an abortion, they heard hollering from the courtyard below. Dudley stood beneath Delphine's window, calling up obscene threats. Delphine went to the window and peered down at him, fascinated that a person of good breeding could descend to this. For his part, Zimmer had had enough Grand Guignol; he wanted the quiet and order of his study. He slipped out Kober's back exit.

Delphine cowered on her bed and covered her ears. Through her hands she heard shrieks. She ran to the window.

Dudley was on fire. Turned in profile he had a long flaming tail from head to foot, like a brontosaurus.

She ripped her Arabian horse blanket from the wall, leaned way out the window, and flung the blanket down on Dudley. Then she hurtled down the hall and phoned the police, barely making herself understood.

"They swaddled him in the horse blanket and carried him off on a stretcher. Daisy, he actually torched himself. His face — he'll be hideously disfigured. It's all my fault —"

"But it's *not*."

"Yes, it's happened again, don't you see, just like the other time."

Daisy sat beside her on the bed. "What other time?"

"Everything I touch turns to horror." In bits and pieces the story came out. There was a first lover, when Delphine was sixteen. Raoul Peña, son of a tackle shop owner in Newport. Merry found out and forbade her to see him.

"One night Merry was crocked and shooting moles in the lawn with a rifle from a second-story window. She saw Raoul leaving the house, running across the lawn in the moonlight. Mother fired at him, several shots — I heard the shots from downstairs in the library. The booze wrecked her aim. She only crippled him." Bitter laugh. "The Mortimers bought off the cops, got names erased from the records and all the rest. We paid off the Peñas. Raoul's mother — I remember her in their shop when I was a child — she went bonkers after that. Walked up and down Thames Street swearing she'd kill me, kill us all. They packed her off to Westwood Lodge instead of Bridgewater State, thanks to our money. She's probably there to this day." Delphine gnawed a nicotine-stained cuticle. "Something else I never told you:

when I was eleven, Father" — she shuddered — "got electrocuted. In
the new shower in the Rosecliff gatehouse. Faulty wiring, they said. I
recently found out he was shit-faced when it happened. I mean, look
at us, the whole lot of us. We're cursed. To think we were given so
much . . ." She sagged against Daisy. "All I want is to be safe."

Trying to comfort Delphine, Daisy silently agreed that the Mortimers were indeed a magnet for calamity. Close up the glamorous
doom that emanated from Delphine seemed less glamorous. Daisy
wondered that the poor fetus didn't spontaneously give up the ghost.

Later, Ginny, back from a weekend in Cleveland with her family,
stopped by with a vial of Miltown. She talked to Delphine for hours
in a hypnotic monotone, repeating over and over that Delphine could
not, must not, blame herself for Dudley's insanity. Finally, sporadi-
cally shaken by a leftover sob and zonked on tranks, Delphine fell
asleep. Ginny alone, Daisy realized, could reason with Delphine.

Next day at lunch, Delphine slid into her customary chair at their
windowside table and announced a fresh crisis. Dudley had escaped
with only second-degree burns on his face and back. But Bronxville
General, lacking a mental ward, had shipped him to Bellevue.

"They've thrown him into the snake pit!" She had recently seen the
movie through a scrim of smoke at the Thalia, a foul-smelling rerun
house on the Upper West Side. "I mean, he's high-strung, the dear
fellow — depleted gene pool and all — but he's hardly *insane*."

By dinner Delphine was having second thoughts about the abortion.
"Maybe I'll *have* the baby. I'll go away to Switzerland for a few
months, to the mountains, the Upper Engadine. Then I'll put my son
up for adoption. No — once I see his dear little face I could never let
him go. But I could arrange to have him raised by some village people —"

"This is not an opera, this is your life," protested Ginny.

"I don't mean to nag, but how many weeks is it now?" said Daisy.

The real reason Delphine was stalling was that Dudley had finally
made an impact.

"I mean, it's so romantic what Dudley did. I think I've fallen back
in love with him. Think of it, he was actually willing to die for me. Like
that boy in *The Dead*."

For days she vacillated back and forth. Finally her friends prevailed.

Delphine flew to Havana — dangerously late — and brought back Kahlua, a box of Macunado cigars, and a uterine infection.

The following week, over shepherd's pie, still pale and hollow-eyed, Delphine demoted Zimmer to "an intellectual comrade."

Daisy liked that; Hannah's gamble had paid off. So life offered second chapters. Postscripts.

Dudley's family retrieved him from Bellevue and shipped him to the Hartford Institute for Living. Delphine fumed: "Forget the fancy title, he's a prisoner there. Girls, do we know any lawyers?"

They looked blank.

"Wait a mo, what about that friend of Peter's, from his poker game," said Franca. "Peter's in awe of him."

"Ben Marshak, he calls an average of four times a week," said Daisy. "On a slow night in my hall, he provides the evening's entertainment."

"Call Ben," said Delphine.

"Oh brother." Daisy rolled her eyes. "Well, okay. Only for you. I'll ask him to find us a lawyer who specializes in — what? Crimes of passion directed against oneself?"

Inspired by Daisy's call, Ben was so persuasive he could have gotten Jack the Ripper a year on probation.

Then, suddenly, it was Daisy's turn.

Chapter 5

THEY WALKED in the orchard behind Kober House; the apple trees thrust jets of white blossoms skyward; fragrance rained down on them. She'd imagined him so hard, the Gerrit walking beside her felt unreal.

She had just danced "Wings" in a concert at Reisinger, delivered a performance she judged honorable, if not brilliant. She stood in the dressing room in her aqua silk kimono, a glob of Albolene on her index finger, poised to erase the Moira Shearer eyes complete with red dots in the inner corners. Then she saw him. In the mirror, behind her, at the dressing room door. Her hand froze in midair, her heart fluttering wildly, and their eyes in the mirror locked. He was more slightly built than her fantasy. But the green gaze, ironic and bemused, the cap of curls, Amory Blaine with a hint of Roman charioteer — all that was as she remembered.

She was prepared to drive off with him, anywhere, no questions asked. But apparently you had to talk first.

He had come down from Harvard with his stepbrother, Lucien, Gerrit explained. Lucien wanted to see a girl named Mia Something, an actress, who was giving him a hard time. He himself was going on to New York to see his stepmother off on the *Ile de France*. Binky, as he called her, ran an art gallery on Fifty-seventh Street, and was going to Belgium to look at Magrittes.

"Then Lucien mentioned the dance concert. I said to myself, The girl I saw in the Fogg *looked* like a dancer. And she was wearing lavender stockings. And quotes Andrew Marvell. Then I thought, Wouldn't such a girl go to Sarah Lawrence? Imagine, I almost started applauding when I saw you up there on the stage tonight! I didn't even know your name till I saw it in the program."

Daisy scarcely grasped his words; she was busy finding her way around this voice: nasal and overbred and thrilling.

He added, "You ran off so fast the other night in the Fogg."

She had a different memory of "the other night in the Fogg" — yet she was going to quibble? When life laid your heart's desire at your feet?

Their shoes crunched on the spongy grass. His gait enchanted her — a rolling sailor's gait, or maybe a skier's — and his green wool turtleneck, and the threadbare elbow of his tweed jacket. *Crunch, crunch.* Why were their footsteps so loud? She felt vaguely responsible. No words came. The words compacted in her heart these many years — they wouldn't come out. Tristan and Isolde drank the love potion and never had to make small talk. How did anyone get love off the ground?

"Uh, where are you from?" Daisy asked.

"Here and there — everywhere." *Crunch-crunch.* "Father worked in the American consulate in Rome," Gerrit went on in his nasal drawl. "The truth is, I sometimes feel more Italian than American."

Her Italians were the Donofrios in Jamaica; at night you could hear them hollering through the common wall of their semiattached house. Once some knife play brought the cops. Cutting a look at Gerrit's perfect profile, she saw he'd turned somber — her fault?

"Listen," he said with sudden urgency, "I've got to tell someone about this madness. I scarcely know you, but I sense I can trust you." A moment. "I'm quitting Harvard." Sidelong glance to gauge her reaction.

Daisy nodded sympathetically. A man never quit college — only the serious mental cases. How wonderfully *perverse* to leave the hub of the universe! Though self-destructing lost something without the right audience.

"You can't imagine how stultifying Harvard is. The snobbery, the clubs. So phony and empty, though I have to admit I'm part of it. Or *was*. I'm about to get booted from Porcellian for pinching their booze and a couple of books." *Crunch-crunch*. "My clubmates are effete, God knows, but at least they're gentlemen, if you get my drift."

Daisy nodded, mystified.

"Now the place is overrun with weenies. Cracking the books to pull down A's. Christ amighty, on a Saturday night, all the lights are blazing in Widener Library!"

Daisy couldn't muster much dismay; wasn't she of the same tribe?

"Let them have the goddamn place," said Gerrit. "I need the real world. How else will I write the great American novel?" he added with a tortured laugh. "A writer owes it to himself to experience everything. *Everything*." He paused and drew a paperback from his jacket pocket: *Lafcadio's Adventures*. "Like Gide's Lafcadio here, pushing someone off the train just" — he snapped his fingers — "for the hell of it. *L'acte gratuit*." In the dappled light his face suddenly looked devoured by rot. He replaced the book in his pocket and strolled on. "Of course, Father will blow a gasket. He regards writing as a woman's hobby."

Daisy quickened her step, elated. Gerrit had tapped her as his ally. They had a project: saving Gerrit for Art.

"*Do it. Take* a year off to write. You owe your talent more than you owe your father."

Gerrit stopped and gazed at her face offered up in the moonlight, the tip of his tongue grazing the corner of his lip. "Thank you for that." They'd reached the end of the orchard, a little bower. A few blossoms floated down. *Now*. He would pull her to him. She became acutely aware of their four hands hanging chimpishly at their sides. Something wrong here. In the dorm everyone bitched about guys trying to score.

Gerrit started to retrace. "Tell me who you are. I can't for the life of me place you," he said, unburdened and happy.

She could sound exotic too. "My father was Arthur Frank, former head of the Jackson School, a Marxist institute shut down by McCarthy." Instantly ashamed at using her family's travails as seduction.

"*Heavens!* You're not serious." He turned toward her, eyes sparkling. "Binky would have a fit. She practically underwrites *The National Review*. She's a bit of a snob, the old dear." His eyes turned reflective. "Hmm, Arthur Frank, you don't say."

Daisy prepared to expand the theme of who she was, but Gerrit seemed satisfied. He stopped and murmured close to her ear, "I've never known a real Red. *Are* you?"

The double-entendre cut off her breath. She would streak straight to heaven, like a reverse comet. "I'm apolitical," she managed. "You know, the Silent Generation and all?"

Up in her room in Titsworth he grabbed her. All she could think was, Thank God, thank God, thank God. She felt him through his chinos, gigantic, delicate, *sprung*. She couldn't breathe him in enough. They fell onto her narrow bed with its faded madras cover, and he knelt beside her and buried his face in her neck, murmuring, "I think I'm a little in love with you."

A fever of anticipation. She was in a force field, moving toward Gerrit with the inevitability of natural law.

So why was she on the six-twenty to New York, for a date with Ben Marshak? Because she always kept her word was why. From her father she'd inherited good character and no money — and suspected you were better off with bad character and money. She was determined to go through with this evening, though she was wheezing and sneezing from the spring's pollinations — and, said Delphine, prolonged virginity.

Chief among Ben Marshak's many sins was the appeal he'd have for her stepparents. Ira and Dora Frank wouldn't view Ben in the manner of normal Americans, the ones who ate Velveeta cheese and celebrated July Fourth and hoped their daughter would marry a capitalist. They'd smell a fellow "lefty" — Daisy vaguely remembered Ben's spiel on civil liberties at the Fogg; they'd *kvell* over his Good Politics. At last a nice "progressive" to take her off their hands!

She couldn't oblige them. She knew enough about good politics to keep her distance. She'd gone and hidden in the pantry, sitting on the worn spot in the linoleum, knees drawn to her chin. Even with her eyes and ears shut she could hear Ira's monotone behind the closed bedroom door. Useless to ask Dora — she just sat at the kitchen table, head in hands, weeping. Terror seized Daisy; her stepparents never displayed emotion. Then she saw the newspaper. *The New York Times,* flung catty-cornered on the yellow-and-green-flowered oilcloth of the kitchen table. On the bottom of the front page, the photos, a row of them, like the inky shots of criminals in the post office. In the middle, the round spectacles dominating his face: Ira Frank. Uncle Ira, her father's brother. 8 TEACHERS OUSTED, SUSPECTED AS REDS, the headline said in fat ugly black. *Specific Charge Is Refusal to Tell If They Are Communists.* Suspended without pay . . . Charged with insubordination and conduct unbecoming teachers . . . Ira Frank accused of being a party member . . . Frank termed the action a "heresy hunt" . . . designed to strike terror into the teaching staff for daring to fight for a salary increase . . .

"CommieJew," the O'Donahue kids said distinctly as Daisy walked past their yard with her red tin lunchbox on the way home from school. The Donofrios looked at the Franks with flinty eyes, then looked away. They were subversives, with horns and cloven hooves, conspiring to sell the Land of the Free to the Russian devils.

Ira took the train to Washington to testify before the Committee. Some of their friends named names. Ira — there had never been any question — took the Fifth.

Daisy stayed home from school. She stopped dancing. The Franks joined the stream of defrocked Reds migrating to California. Ira reinvented himself as a lay analyst and put up a shingle. He turned reclusive and crotchety and took up knitting; Dora retreated into rheumatoid arthritis.

In 1953, the year before Daisy left for college, the Rosenbergs were executed. Daisy read in the paper that Ethel sang "Good Night Irene" in Sing Sing. She read that it took an extra jolt to kill Ethel.

Even now, in 1957, with McCarthy and HUAC discredited, if someone mentioned H-bombs or atom spies or the Cold War, Daisy stared into the middle ground. She liked Ike. She liked Ike just fine.

Underneath she kept the faith; the world's savagery did not invalidate her father's ideals; a diet of lefty idealism imbibed since childhood stays in the cells, like Catholicism. And she worshiped Arthur Frank, like a Russian peasant an icon. Wherever she landed, Daisy kept on her bureau a faded photo in a silver frame of a man with smoky wide-set eyes and thick sandy hair.

Her traitorous heart, though, coveted the enemy. Her father's "ruling class." She coveted the exotic alien, his cultivation, assumption of belonging, and silky textures. He would not smell like Ira's cohorts in short-sleeve shirts, of acrid immigrant striving, and socialist meetings in bare halls, and punch ball, and cabbagy tenements. He would smell of blond sweat, old houses, country lanes after rain. Insouciance. He would be safe. At the farthest possible remove from the Franks' doomed circle.

Il Gran Ticino, on Sullivan Street just up from the San Remo, was the quintessential bohemian, Villanger restaurant of the fifties. Red checked tablecloths, candles stuck in Chianti bottles encrusted with multicolored wax, sawdust on the floor, bocce out back — perfection! Young men on the make — both senses — took their dates there for dinner, before or after a foreign movie. What better way to impress a girl with one's sensitivity and urbanity.

Life had not coddled Ben. Father dead of an embolism, mother supporting them as a waitress at the Circle Lounge in Brookline. He worked days as a bookkeeper while putting himself through Brooklyn Law at night.

No self-pity here, thought Daisy. Great guy — for someone else. As he laid out his grueling schedule, she took him in: the decent navy summer suit — since the Fogg he'd discovered Brooks Brothers; a clownish bow tie, like a kid playing dress up. His eyes hungry behind the smudged lenses. The crooked smile that tugged at her.

"Tell me, Ben, when do you sleep?"

He looked caught out; workaholism wasn't yet in fashion. "I don't much. But after the Bar I'm planning to take a three-week intensive course on how to relax."

Cancel the smirk, he's serious.

"Then I'm going to work for Legal Aid. Right now I'm volunteering for a group trying to get reparations for victims of McCarthyism."

Daisy heard Ira applauding from Culver City.

"I may also go into politics, make a run for Congress," Ben went on, misreading Daisy's alert expression. "There's nothing I can't do, I'm unstoppable. Just you watch." A right-hand chop. His every gesture jeopardized the glassware. "You don't know the man I am."

Suddenly her eye snagged on his right pinky, oddly crooked and swollen. "Your finger — what happened to it?"

Ben looked puzzled, then covered the offending finger with his hand. "Oh, that. I guess I hurt it playing handball."

"You *guess*? It looks broken."

"Yeah, maybe."

"But we should take you to Saint Vincent's — immediately."

"Look, it's nothing, really. Let's talk about you and me."

"But if it's broken, doesn't it *hurt*?"

Sheepish: "I haven't really noticed. I have the constituency of an ox."

Er, constitution? Even an ox would notice pain. She was horrified and impressed, both. He *was* unstoppable; she saw him blasting up the highway of life, impervious to every obstacle. The triumph of energy.

"I think you are going to have a very exciting time," said Daisy, and fell on her shrimp marinara.

Ben watched her eat. "You have a knockout smile," he said.

She was too busy scarfing the tails of the shrimp, and the shells, to return the compliment.

"Tell me what you're thinking," said Ben.

"Oh, let's see. I was thinking about the Brahms *Liebeslieder Walzer*." She hummed a couple of bars.

Leaning across the table, he seized her hand. "You're so refined. You're everything I've ever wanted."

Daisy gently reclaimed her hand and looked up at the painting above their table. "Would you please tell me what this gondolier is doing on a lake? He belongs on a canal, not a goddamn lake."

Ben wouldn't play ball.

She brushed bread crumbs into a little pile. Then she braved his eyes. That was love. Coming from the wrong quarters, yet she tangoed with it for a second before returning to the dumb gondolier. Suddenly she felt nauseated. Gerrit's eyes were always mocking.

"I wanted you from the moment I saw you," Ben said.

"For God's sake, it's not *me* you want, it's an image. Refinement. Dance. Sarah Lawrence." She snuffed an urge to mimic his accent. "You don't know the first thing about me."

Ben considered for a moment. "It doesn't matter," he said.

Christ.

"When can I see you? Next Saturday?"

"Rehearsals."

"Thursday then? We'll go dancing in this great place I know in Jersey, Bill Miller's Riviera." Gesture toward Hoboken. She rescued his wine glass. Shook her head no.

Ben assumed a bullish expression. "Sunday, how's Sunday?"

"Ben, I can't —"

"Okay, then let's get married."

He was kidding.

Her smile froze. He wasn't kidding. It would be incest, she thought suddenly.

"Listen," said Ben, a burr in his voice. "I'm gonna marry you. And you're gonna marry me. You'll see."

She reached into her bag for a train schedule. Lightly: "Is that a prophecy or a threat?" Her heart ached. He was just a kid, alone and unsponsored, ready to cast his lot with her, no looking back, like her forebears or someone in Odessa. Yet all she'd done was act like a bitch? There was something seriously wrong with love.

And with this schedule, too — maybe because she was reading it upside down.

Nodding off on the train back, she guessed she had just passed up a chance to avoid one shitload of trouble. But there were plenty worse things than trouble.

Three portentous knocks on her door.

"Hello, Daisy."

Finally.

"Come up to Cambridge, Daisy."

Finally.

"Come this weekend. I promise I won't lay a hand on you."

Of course he wouldn't.

Of course he would.

It never failed: hop a Greyhound bus, and you got a garlic-hal sailor in your lap, and a headrest anointed with Wildroot Cream Oil. Daisy scrunched way over toward the window of the two-oh-five for Boston. In her black patent-leather hatbox she'd packed Mum to ensure "daintiness" — at all costs be dainty — Evyan's White Shoulders, and a long white cotton gown from the Panamanian Shop, like Jean Peters wore in *Viva Zapata!*, virginal yet suggestive. The Greyhound stalled in the rush-hour traffic piled up outside Hartford. Out the window lay a forbidding maze of gasworks pipes. Her sailor snorted and jerked awake and breathed in her direction. Pressing her nose to the window, she burrowed deeper into anticipation.

Daisy had always suspected in herself a serious vocation for the sensual; she would be *wild*. Of course she had already experienced love, with Robert E. Lee Prewitt in Hawaii, and in that Italian hospital with Captain Henry, and with Jake Barnes in Paris and Spain (*she* would have cured him). She'd embraced the knees of countless Russian counts. Her main conduit to bliss was D. H. Lawrence, his women like delicate flames, their upturned faces shining flowers, while cosmic currents streamed from Birkin's loins. Though where exactly *were* loins?

Nor could she square love's choreography in novels with the tidbits gleaned from Sally. How she could come when Rudi sucked her nipples. How the best position was "doggies." Or "scissors," the one she was going to patent. And Delphine carried on about "rhythm": andante, allegro, pizzicato. A lover she called the Miles Davis of the sheets. Rhythm was the God-granted gift of great cocksmen, not unlike the genius of Mozart. How to square that with "Take me" and "kisses of fire"?

Cronin's smelled of corned beef and beery piss. It had bruising wooden booths, tables gored with graffiti, and the blue lighting of a morgue. The sons of the ruling class gathered here to get down with the townies and chugalug low-life brews while quoting T. S. Eliot and parading existential angst.

Seated in the hub of the universe opposite Gerrit DeWind, Daisy could scarcely believe her luck. With his wide-spaced jade eyes and high color he might have stepped from a Dutch old master.

Gerrit toyed with his swizzle stick and poisoned the air with Gauloises. He drummed his fingers on the table, surveying some hangman's landscape. Daisy's euphoria faded. Where was the prince who'd knelt by her bed? How could he fall out of love in a week? She hadn't even had time to disappoint him.

Fearful of invading his misery, Daisy sipped her Dewar's and pretended to listen to Johnny Ray on the jukebox. *Oooh, I'm the great pretender / pretending that I'm doing well . . .*

A dusky Armenian-looking girl sidled down the aisle. Her blue-veined bosom was displayed in a peasant blouse straight from *The Outlaw*. As she passed, she and Gerrit traded loaded looks.

Too real is the feeling of make believe / too real when I feel what my heart can't conceal . . . Oooh, yes . . .

A blond boy appeared at their booth. Wind-burned cheeks, like a Norse girl. Gerrit introduced Lucien Chatfield. Lucien sent Daisy a slow smile, as if they shared a secret. As he left, he gave Gerrit's shoulder a squeeze.

"My stepbrother," said Gerrit absently.

The shoulder squeeze lingered unpleasantly.

Gerrit cast a disgusted look around. "Well, I've broken the news to Father. He had the predictable shitfit."

Daisy upended her glass. "Congratulations. On to the great American novel!" Maybe it wasn't a bad idea for Gerrit to leave the hub of the universe.

She listened distractedly as he laid out his plans: job at Time Inc. — Binky knew Luce — sublet in the Village. Where was "I'm a little in love with you"? She had to get him back to plan A. Oh, to have Delphine's thinking on this. She would undoubtedly counsel bold action, like reaching under the table and grabbing him.

Gerrit was now shaking his head no. "It's bad timing, our meeting now. I just seem to be causing people pain."

Daisy's throat constricted. He was signing off before . . .

Gerrit seemed to notice her for the first time. "You see?"

"No, no, you make me happy. I've been happy ever since we met."

He reached for his Gauloises. "I couldn't bear to harm you."

"But why would you?"

He looked surprised by the question. "You're so delicate and open and exposed. Somehow I want to protect you. The good part, anything about me that's worthwhile wants to protect you — from myself."

"I don't want to be protected from you."

His eyes turned mulish and hooded. "Don't you see? I'm tied up. Tied up in knots." He ran his hands through his hair. "But dammit" — he reached for her hands — "I feel this powerful connection with you. I do, I do."

All lovers, she thought confusedly, had to pass through a ring of fire or two. She would, if need be, love *for* him.

The white frame rooming house past Longfellow Park, off Brattle Street, was perfect. She was none too sober after two Dewar's and no chow — Who could eat on such a night? There was even a crazed landlady in a ratty cardigan, straight out of Dostoyevsky, who led them, muttering, up stairs disinfected with pine. The smell made her sneeze. And the landlady's sweater stretched over a hump. No kisses of fire for *her*. Daisy wished she weren't blitzed; she would have liked to be tremendously lucid.

A high lumpy bed covered in white chenille ate up the room. Their room, thought Daisy confusedly, feverish. From the wall leered a white plaster death mask. Two fake kerosene lamps stood sentry on the night tables. A breeze fingered the white lace curtain in the bay window. Drunken voices floated up from the street, the sound of glass shattering on pavement, a trill of laughter.

She was poised to cross the Great Divide. They stood at the foot of the bed for long moments, since there was no place to go but the bed.

Taking her cue from the Russians, Daisy threw her arms around Gerrit and slid down his chest to embrace his knees, but in the same moment he stepped backward, and she fell forward as if she were tackling him. "No-no-no," he murmured, trying to raise her. "No-no, we mustn't."

Below, bewilderment. Why mustn't we? She tasted blood; she must have bitten her own tongue in the heat of passion and the goddamn dust down here was making her sneeze.

He got her to the bed. She fell back on the pillow and pulled him over her, but another sneeze welled up; she turned her face just in time, then another sneeze; she couldn't stop.

Gerrit sat back on the edge of the bed. "D'you have a cold?" he asked testily.

"No, it's just allergies. I'm allergic to house dust, molds, and dander."

"Dander? What's dander?"

"You know, the stuff that comes off dogs, cats, pet pumas." Why were they talking about dander? She willed a sneeze into oblivion. *Damn* Dr. Weinberg, all those shots to no avail.

Gerrit drew away and folded his hands primly in his lap. "Well, I'd best be going."

Everything in the room locked in place and engraved itself on her memory.

She watched him take a white handkerchief from one of those inside jacket pockets men have. "Here. Something's happened to your lip." He touched the handkerchief to her mouth.

They both stared at the spot of blood.

Within the week Daisy received a thin blue letter postmarked Cambridge. It contained only a cryptic utterance, written in a crabbed hand: "You would have hated me." Signed with a large ornate *G*.

Chapter 6

TERM'S END was upon them. For once people remained on campus for the weekend. From every dorm window sounded the scattershot of typing. High on Dexedrine and assorted uppers, the girls were rolling all their insights into one ball, preparing to inflict on their dons the turgid papers the college labeled "contracts."

With summer looming, the class of '58 hurled itself into job hunting. They red-penciled want ads in the Sunday *Times* and *Village Voice.* They blackened forms and warmed metal chairs in seedy employment agencies that promised "glamour jobs" for "gal Fridays" — perhaps this summer they would not, like last, end up waitressing at Stouffer's or selling chocolates in Schrafft's.

Franca was spending the summer on Cape Cod, where Peter had just landed a plum as assistant director at the Dennis Playhouse. They were planning an autumn wedding. Delphine had nailed down a coveted spot as researcher at the *Village Voice;* she'd work on her "Class of '58" article for the *Times* magazine evenings and weekends. Daisy took a summer stock job in the Westbury Music Circus on Long Island. She was one of six chosen from two hundred hopefuls who showed up for the audition. After her White Night, as she'd named the

Gerrit fiasco, she'd instinctively turned to dancing, as to a first lover who had loved her well.

As for Ginny Goldberg, the SOS Club never paid much attention to her plans. She was the tortoise (and, they whispered, the grind). She was annoyingly punctual, a reproach to the girls who straggled in late to chill morning classrooms, haggard and still wearing pajamas under their trench coats. She took meticulous notes in an even, right-slanting hand. Submitted her neatly typed contracts *a week before the deadline,* her effort never loosing the torrents of praise awarded Delphine's. Surrounded by high-flying artists, Ginny slogged along, steady and reliable, traits that would serve her well in early childhood educa-tion — and won her zero points around SLC.

Beneath the orderliness she was a mess. No accident, that fat. Ginny Goldberg was Hello, I'm-fucking-myself-over-fat. You couldn't be a member of Beechmont Country Club, Shaker Heights's best club for non–Our Crowd Jews, without learning that the blubber was a capital offense — against yourself, your mother, and Israel. Since she had pleasant features and that luscious glowy skin, naturally she'd had to hear all her life, "Honey, if you lost twenty pounds, you'd be a knock-out."

She'd always lived in her body as with an antagonistic stranger. At fourteen, following minor surgery for a gyn problem, she became persuaded she was disfigured "down there." In high school the pop-ular girls were all jocks. The worst humiliation came when they chose up teams. She would stand forlornly on the hockey field in her gray cotton gym suit, eyes focused on someone's dimpled knees, always the last girl chosen. She suspected she might spend her life trying to over-turn the verdict of those team captains. She would *show* them — show them what, though, for God's sake? She'd selected SLC over Bryn Mawr because she wouldn't have to expose her thunder thighs in Bermudas. Of course, she would never admit any of this to Delphine and the others.

The spring of '57, though, a new Ginny began to emerge, surprising everyone, most of all herself. She dropped ten pounds, a sign in wo-men's lives that love interest has entered the plot.

"His name is Tom Puccio," Ginny, all aflutter, told her crowd, over dinner *sur l'herbe.* The entire campus was in flower, a gouache of hibiscus pinks and misty blues and amethyst freckled with ocher; with the Tudor gray stone and shingled gables, it could have been spring in the Cotswolds. "This is a look-no-further," Ginny added gravely.

Tom Puccio was an intern at New York Hospital. Ginny had met him at the Academy of Medicine library while researching a paper on the latency period and sexual awareness.

"He's *northern* Italian — clean-cut, not greasy. He's got an exhausting, inhuman schedule. But one thing he won't give up is opera. Tom knows Verdi so well, when we went to *La Bohème* last Saturday, he slept through all the recitatives, or whatever those things are, and woke up just in time for the arias." She laughed giddily.

They stared at her — so unlike Ginny!

"Uh, I don't mean to quibble, but *La Bohème* is Puccini, not Verdi," said Daisy.

"Never mind, she'll bone up on opera," said Franca. "But Ginny, you *hate* classical music."

Ginny peered at her from behind her harlequin glasses. "Oh, I do? Just watch me."

"I'll give you a crash course in music," offered Daisy. Panicked at being left behind with her postnasal drip and virginity, the last unloved person on earth.

The final day on campus they gathered in Franca's aerie to await Ginny's return from her interview for a social work job, or something of that nature — it was hard to focus on Ginny's plans.

Delphine horsed around with her tennis racket and lectured Daisy on love. "Treat 'em like shit, and they come yappin' round. It's hideously boring of men to be so predictable. My rule is, Only worry when they start asking if you've just eaten scallions."

At that moment Ginny loomed in the doorway — Ta-da! She eyed them triumphantly. She was dressed in full job-hunt regalia: navy sack dress with white Peter Pan collar, white gloves, her Ronay black patent bag with a shine to damage the retina, matching black patent pumps.

"Soooo?" said Franca.

"Yikes, I'm so excited I can hardly *stand* it!" squeaked Ginny, waddling in.

"I take it the interview went well," Delphine drawled in her best lockjaw.

"Actually, by the time I arrived, they'd *filled* the job, though they said they'd keep my résumé on file. But I got a different job. You're not going to believe this —"

"Why don't you sit down, unhook your bra, and tell us all about it," interrupted Delphine.

"I'm a college guest editor at *Mademoiselle*."

Silence.

"What a brilliant coup!" cried Franca.

Delphine frowned at her racket strings. "Wasn't that the job Sylvia Plath had before she cracked up?"

"My word, what a horrible thought," said Franca.

"Does your family have an in at Condé Nast?" pursued Delphine.

Ginny snorted. "Lot of good it would have done me. Their only ambition for me is to marry Bernie Bergstein and join the Beechmont Country Club. In the interim — that's how they view life-before-marriage, an interim — I should get certified as a schoolteacher. You know, 'something-to-fall-back-on'?"

"How'd you pull it off? Start at the beginning," ordered Franca, pushing forward a rocker with a paisley throw.

"I'm too excited to sit." Ginny sprawled in the rocker anyway and kicked off her heels, crossing ankles not much slimmer than her calves. "Let's see . . . First I go to Career Blazers, and they tell me I'm not qualified for one of those deadly clerical jobs. I can type, but seems you need steno. Same story at three other agencies. It was so dreary, the thought that I didn't qualify for dreck, instead of getting discouraged — I know this sounds crazy — I got *energized*. I said to myself, Ginny Goldberg, where would you like to be ideally?"

"You said that out loud right there in the agency?" asked Delphine.

"Honestly, Delphine, what is *wrong* with you?" Franca asked.

"I figured, what did I have to lose?" Ginny rattled on. "So I looked up *Mademoiselle* in a corner phone booth and went to 350 Madison Avenue. This dragon with red talons and a mustache said they had nothing for a girl with my qualifications. Then she said they did have this opening as a guest editor, because the girl they'd been counting on suddenly eloped to Peru or something. But they'd held a national competition to fill those jobs — which naturally eliminated me. Then I said to myself, Why not Ginny Goldberg? I had this crazy belief I could do the work as well as anyone. I started thinking of

Marlon Brando in *On the Waterfront* saying, 'I coulda been a con-tenduh,' how terribly easy it is to *miss* doing what you want to do, and then spend the rest of your life regretting it. By then I think I was high as a kite on caffeine, I'd had only black coffee all day. So I said to myself, Ginny Goldberg, you're not walking out of here till you nail down that job.''

Silence. Delphine tapped her racket strings.

"So I just embroidered on the truth, you might say. I told red talons I'd done tons of editing and rewriting for an author. Even though all I'd ever done was file and answer the phone for this friend of my mother's, who was writing something called 'The No Nonsense Nails Book.' And before I knew it, they sent me to a huge corner office to see this *terrifying* creature, a tough old buzzard, who looked like she'd have me for lunch. Actually, she's a legendary editor, Gertrude Al-cott." A shrug: "They were desperate. And I was there."

"Bullshit," said Daisy. "Why play You mean, you want li'l ole me? I bet you were damn impressive."

"I'm gonna fall on my face," said Ginny miserably.

Daisy summoned a burst of niceness. "Naah, you're gonna take Manhattan. Congratulations!" she said, hoisting an invisible glass.

Daisy knew from the juices churning inside her what was bugging Delphine. *They* were the contenduhs, not Ginny Goldberg. Certainly not Ginny Goldberg.

When Franca Broadwater woke the next morning before dawn to find Peter's place in the bed empty, she suspected she might have woken to trouble.

His blue pajama bottom lay bunched on the floor. It brought back a delicious memory of the night: Peter stood at the side of the bed and slid his hands beneath her and scooped her onto him so she could lock her legs around his waist, the rest of her still on the bed, and they'd made love that way, slowly, so slowly, for the longest time. He'd known exactly what he was about. She stretched luxuriously. She loved Peter's commandingness.

Franca inspected herself in the bureau mirror and combed her fingers through her yellow hair. She had small, chubby breasts, a rounded pink and white body that seemed to exist in the mirror before her because Peter adored it. *"You're a Renoir bather."* A twinge of worry brought her fully awake: Why was he up so early? She didn't want any quarrels before he left for the Dennis Playhouse.

Peter lay beneath a coverlet of bubbles in his mother's peach tub, staring straight ahead. Oh dear, just as she'd feared: he was in the "trough." Life with Peter was a bit like sailing in gale winds: towering highs followed by dizzying free falls. "Smoke Gets in Your Eyes" started up on the radio on the marble sink. *They asked me how I knew / my true love was true* . . .

"What is it, sweetheart, you couldn't sleep?"

"Franca, try to understand."

She went alert as a deer caught by headlights.

"Darling, I'm just so terribly conflicted about this whole marriage trip. I wanted to talk about it now — before you and your mother start organizing the wedding of the century. My head says to go ahead, we're perfect for each other. But my gut tells me I just can't — I *can't* get married right now."

Rage knifed through her. She pulled a towel around her.

Something here inside / cannot be denied, sang the radio.

"Getting married now after two years of the purest happiness feels too much like an ending. Sort of an anticlimax. I'm about to graduate college, for Chrissake. The world should be opening out for me — for us, for both of us." He looked at her, suddenly hopeful. "Maybe you feel the same way?"

The only sound was bubbles fizzing. She was trying to envision the world without Peter, saw her life scrolling up like a piece of foolscap. She realized she was not entirely surprised. How could she have counted on a man whose condition for marriage was to make love to her best friend?

Peter sank into the foam to his chin. "But I don't want to lose you. Franca, try not to be angry — don't do the obvious thing and turn this into an adversarial situation. We're both in this together. Here's what I'm thinking: for the moment, couldn't we just go on having fun together, and then just . . . see what happens?"

Franca had always been a good early morning person. Thoughts and decisions came fresh and clear and fast. Mother had been right about "playing the game"; and she deluding herself to think you could break the rules.

Her second thought: there would be no recriminations.

She told Peter no. We get married in September, or you will never see me again.

She gave him one week to make up his mind.

Then she noticed his erection, a periscope nosing its way up through the suds. His head was at war with his gut, and his cock had yet another agenda. An image came to her, of hanging over Peter like a she-wolf. Something yielded behind her knees. It was five-thirty A.M., and the birds were starting to cheep in Murray Hill's stunted maples. Too early for the first bus to Lenox. She dropped her towel and climbed into the tub, and they entered their strange new limbo with a rousing fuck.

Afterward, since there was nothing more to say, Franca dressed, packed her flight bag, and took a taxi to Port Authority. She sat on a bench for an hour or two, among the unwed mothers and bums, shivering, her hair damp on her shoulders, waiting for the eight-fifty Bonanza bus to Lenox.

From the Cape, Peter pounded the Maginot Line with phone calls, letters, telegrams. Not even in the beginning had he been this attentive. "I'm pining for you. I can't bear for us to be on bad terms. Can I fly up and take you to Tanglewood? Will you at least have dinner with me, dammit?"

He wept into the phone. She had never heard Peter cry.

He stormed and whined. "Can't you be more understanding? This is difficult for me too."

Franca held firm. She sat on the flowered chintz–covered sofa in the library, entirely numb but for this pain that throbbed, like stigmata — it was the damnedest thing — in the palms of her hands. Deprived of Peter, his plans and excitement and energy, she felt herself deflating like an inner tube. Her first love, he was inseparable in her mind from love. Down the road she'd marry someone cobwebby and kind, as a sort of social gesture, and slog along in honorable fashion. But she knew with perfect clairvoyance that the passion she felt for Peter would not come her way again. She would have died for him. Like Alcestis in her childhood book of Greek myths, offering to die in place of Admetus — "Oh, I am so glad that he will live!"

It was strange, this sudden lust for sleep. She'd always been a rotten sleeper.

It occurred to her that she was pregnant.

She would not use it. Everyone did, of course; you could practically hear the shotgun weddings exploding throughout the land. But Peter would never forgive her. She would not forgive herself.

She sat unmoving among the cabbage roses on the sofa, needlepoint on her lap, turning her few ideas over and over like pebbles, too lethargic even to call Delphine for Dr. Spencer's number in Pennsylvania. Then she downed two Miltowns, pulled an afghan throw over her head, and hoped not to wake anytime soon. The lilac was magnificent that June. Its perfume filled the room.

Mrs. Broadwater had seen this coming; courtship had been invented, after all, to protect women from such disasters. She'd never liked that snippety little Hungarian from Hollywood, even if he *had* gone to Harvard. He was a quick study; anyone could see he was poor husband material. But she had some sense of his hold on Franca. She asked the housekeeper to bring them tea in the library.

"If you really want this man —" (She deleted "dreadful.")

"I've never wanted anything but Peter."

"Then why not try a bit of time-honored witchcraft?"

"Witchcraft?" Franca offered a wan smile, buoyed by the solidarity. Her mother was a dear friend, so different from Delphine's horrid Merry; and poor Daisy never really had a mother. It was so easy to forget one's own good fortune.

"Well, nowadays we call it reverse psychology."

A moment. "No." Franca shook her head vehemently. "No tricks. I will do nothing shabby or manipulative."

"I'm going to Italy for the summer," Franca heard herself chirp over the phone. "With Cousin Edith. And then I'll spend the year in Florence."

"Italy? Florence? Why Florence?"

"To study art history."

"Why Edith? You've always hated Cousin Edith. Oh, I get it. I get it. You're *punishing* me."

"Peter, you know me better than that." Then, in an earnest tone, perfected after much coaching, Franca told him that she, too, was now having second thoughts.

Silence rushed into her ear; she counted to five. "You're the most wonderful man I could imagine and I adore you. But I don't know if you're built for the long haul. You crave excitement and tumult all the time, and why not? You've a right to that, if it's what you want. But marriage is sort of boring and tranquil. And I truly believe in that 'till death do us part' stuff. I guess I'm an old cornball, just like you've always said. And — this is painful for me to say . . ." A sigh; she counted again to five. "Peter, I'm no longer sure *I* want to marry *you*."

After they hung up, she sat unmoving on the couch. Funny, she almost believed it.

The weather for the seven-day crossing was idyllic: calm sunny days, vaulted starry nights. The *Queen Elizabeth* might have been boiling along on air. In all their travels, the passengers agreed, they'd never experienced a pleasanter crossing.

Franca Broadwater alone was seasick. Even though she'd spent summers cruising in New England's rougher waters. From dawn to dusk she lay wrapped in a blanket on a canvas chair on the second deck, her skin grayish, the whites of her eyes like burnt hard-boiled egg. The nausea was as unremitting as the horizon; she was too ill even to throw up. Cousin Edith spooned Bovril into her three times a day to prevent dehydration. In the portion of her brain still functioning, Franca recited over and over the phone number Delphine had given her of the private clinic in London. Before sailing she'd asked the family lawyer to advance her extra money for a "surprise" she was planning for Mother. If she could just get to the clinic and get through the abortion, some form of life might be possible on the other end.

The third day of the crossing Franca started to bleed. The blood, bright red, not the usual color, traveled from her body in clots the size of silver dollars, pygmy fists, small crabapples. It soaked through the tripled Kotex she wore like diapers, to her shame staining the khaki canvas deck chair. Toward evening — she'd lost all sense of time — cramps hammered her lower back, and she felt something bell up inside; she knew she had to get to the head. Seated trembling on the can, she felt something huge and livery slither out, then came a rush of blood. She peered between her legs into the rank toilet, and fainted.

June tenth, the morning before they were to dock in Cherbourg, Cousin Edith brought a telegram to Franca's bedside in sick bay. White-lipped, Franca waved it away and declared herself too weak to be bothered. Edith opened it and read aloud: COME BACK AND MARRY ME. STOP. UNDYING LOVE PETER.

Slowly Franca sat upright in the bed, Lady Lazarus.

Franca checked into Delphine's clinic after all; she needed a curettage. Though still anemic from blood loss, she shopped with Cousin Edith for her trousseau in Harrods, and she bought Peter a green-and-white-striped shirt on Jermyn Street — perfect for openings at the Brattle Theatre! Then she and Edith made a quick tour of the Cotswolds, just to make it worth Edith's while.

She had won, reflected Franca on the plane home, lulled by the hum of the engines. Though she would have preferred not to *have* to win. Of course, she would never tell Peter about the miscarriage. Why sour things; she wanted to start right this time. And Peter couldn't deal with blood and mess and illness; he would be disgusted, appalled by such misery. He was more fragile than she'd realized. The dear fellow hadn't been able to manage without her. Funny, she'd always thought *she* was the weak one.

Chapter 7

TO CELEBRATE the end of the "hiatus" with Franca, as he named it, Peter Tabori threw a summer solstice party at his mother's "little place" in Katonah. Through a chain of marriages to Texas oil, Peter's mother had leveraged herself to great wealth and acquired little places on two continents. The spread in Katonah included tennis courts, a pond stocked with black bass, a bathhouse with sauna, and a collection of vintage cars housed in their own garage.

Delphine amassed a host of reasons for not going. She enjoyed the Amazonian feeling of spending Saturday night writing, holed up in the little Village apartment she shared with Gina and Daisy. She never worried about meeting men. How did you *not* meet them? Once she'd had to deposit a stool sample for a parasite infection after a trip to the Yucatán. The doctor phoned with a report on her amoebas — and an invitation to dinner! Plus they all wanted to get married. Men divided women into two distinct breeds — the ones you slept with and the ones you married — but her they regarded as both. She'd climb into bed with a guy on the first date if she felt so moved, or had downed enough gin, and by daybreak he imagined himself engaged. Men liked the idea of taming her. The way she saw it, they'd keep her baking corn bread in the wagon camp while they, hogging all the fun, went thundering off in search of buffalo.

A secret worry teased her: Was she becoming prematurely jaded? When it came to men, what could astonish her?

Eventually, the heat and bongo drums of the summer Village drove her out of the apartment and up the Henry Hudson to Katonah. Halfway to Westchester she pulled over to a grassy shoulder of the Taconic Parkway and wrestled down the top of the red MG Dudley had bequeathed her as an elegant gesture or an oversight. The weather had migrated from hot to torrid; distant thunder crackled, ominous and exciting. Delphine turned off the parkway onto the green back roads of posh upper Westchester. Every so often the car hit a zone of cooler air, like a thermal memory. She wound past ersatz Tudor houses hugged by banks of fuchsia azaleas and tonsured lawns, their glassed-in verandas flaming orange with a last blast of sun. Each spread touted the income and importance of its owner. The American Dream, thought Delphine. Was there anything more sterile? You would want for nothing, but you would *want* nothing — she recoiled, like a horse ducking a bridle. She intended to "earn her death" first, in the phrase of some expatriate novelist.

She turned up a poplar-lined drive aspiring to Versailles. At its far end squatted a giant architectural statement in fieldstone and white stucco. In the entry hall lay a zebra hide, its black mane erect. Delphine shuddered. Armed with a flute of champagne, she wandered through rooms that announced a serious confusion over theme. In one room the owner had gone Santa Fe: whitewashed walls, bulging hearths sporting tin crosses, a massive refectory table from the Inquisition. The adjacent sitting room was wallpapered in red velvet and furnished in rattan, part gaslight brothel, part safari. Peter's preppy classmates, more accustomed to venerable Victorian, clustered together for protection.

A male appraised her in that tiresome way and broke loose from his group. Lucien someone — Chatfield? White-blond hair and tortoiseshell glasses: a Dudley clone. She'd met him the past summer, cruising in the Gulf of Maine. He droned on in a British monotone, complete with stutter, about a recent race. "We were m-m-moving right along . . . good stiff b-b-breeze . . ." Delphine let a yawn escape through her nostrils. He needed a good shot of testosterone.

Champagne hitting her wrong. She accepted a refill — *It's what gets you through.* There was Daisy, standing under an assemblage of antlers and cow skulls mounted on the wall. She looked quite beautiful in a black Empire dress with a tiny flower print, copper hair straggling out of a bun, and seemed oblivious to the carnage hanging over her. Delphine recognized that she ought to have honored her original impulse to stay home. While her nostrils dilated with another aborted yawn, her tearing eyes panned across the room — and snagged on a face.

She'd been doused with ice water. She shook her head, blinked several times, rudely gave Lucien her shoulder.

The man had pale blue almond-shaped eyes, wild *Tartar* eyes, a sultry mouth. Waffled, battened-down hair.

Leaving Lucien midsentence, she drifted over.

The man was telling army stories, hilariously, to judge by his listeners. "So we're standing in the chow line and this cat muscles in and the guy in front of us says, 'Where you think you goin', muthuh-fuckuh?' And the first guy says, 'You callin me muthuhfuckuh, muth-uhfuckuh?' And the cat says, 'Listen muthuhfuckuh . . .'"

The accent was perfect. He wore a cornflower blue shirt and bleached Mexican pants closed with a drawstring, a bandito among the button-downs.

He'd segued into the role of museum guide. Pretending to conduct a tour of the premises, unconcerned his host might be within earshot. "A schizophrenic's wet dream," Delphine made out. "And over there we have the Lucrezia Borgia room, reserved for clients with a penchant for flogging." He gestured in the direction of a study with dark paneling and billowing wine velvet drapes. "And the Gunga Din room, for big-game games. And beyond that an antebellum boudoir from *Gone With the Wind,* for anyone wishing to play Rhett and Scarlett."

A smile played over Delphine's lips. She felt suddenly easy through all her body. "Okay, who is he?" she asked Lucien, who'd trailed after her.

"Jake, uh, Mikowski, Mikulski, something. Friend of Rudi Ur-dang's. Studying architecture at Columbia. Very talented, won the P-P-Prix de Rome. Anything else you care to know?" Lucien added, looking wounded.

"Well, is he pinned?" she asked rudely.

"He *was* — at any rate, madly in love with a girl I know from Deer Isle. Mimi Van Doorn. Jake was always hanging around her family's camp. I think they actually eloped, not six months ago. Old man Van

Doorn nipped *that* in the bud, and maybe something else as well. Guess he figured Jake wasn't in it for love alone. After all, a poor architect could do worse than marry a Van Doorn . . . And Jake's pretty pushy."

"You know your trouble?" asked Delphine with a lift of her chin. "You've never *had* to push. Maybe that's what you need, to *push*." She placed her hand on Lucien's sternum and gave him a little shove. Then she edged deeper into Jake's group.

The look she lobbed him went off like a hand grenade. Jake trailed off midsentence and rocked slightly on his heels, swallowing hard. They drank each other in.

Then Delphine did a military about-face and walked fast, as if hurrying to catch a train, attracting curious looks; walked as far away as she could get, to the Victorian parlor, to a velvet-cushioned window seat cut into a bay. There she stared out into a border of white phlox, seeing nothing.

"May I join you? Or would you rather be alone?"

Delphine's eyes traveled slowly up the Mexican pants and blue shirt to meet Jake Mikulski's. He sat beside her, hand on the window seat, carefully distant from her skirt. With a feeling of helplessness, she noted his shapely fingers, the fine brown hair on his wrists.

"That was a pretty tacky thing you did back there, making fun of your host," she said faintly.

"You were laughing, I noticed."

"Regrettably, yes."

"I was hoping I'd find you."

"I was praying you wouldn't."

He nodded. "I think I understand. Perhaps I should go."

"Perhaps you should."

He stayed put. They both looked at his hand on the window seat for a while.

"I'm not ready for this," said Delphine, who was trembling.

"I know. Me neither."

"What's with those two? They look ready to kill each other," someone said, nodding in the direction of Jake and Delphine.

When the person next looked, they had disappeared.

.   .   .

In another corner of the house Peter Tabori was teaching Daisy Frank to smoke dope. From a tiny roach she sucked smoke deep into her lungs and held her breath, then suddenly sputtered and choked, her eyes tearing.

When her vision cleared, first thing, she saw a Roman profile and cap of curls. Just several heads away.

Tiny cold needles pricked all through her. She quickly turned and focused on a cow skull. An afterimage persisted: the blond Slouch attached to Gerrit.

Daisy walked purposefully toward the kitchen.

"Hey, where you going? The lesson's not over," called Peter.

She turned and blew Peter a kiss.

Gerrit, who stood along the same fault line, blew her a kiss back.

Fuck you, she murmured with a smile.

Grabbing a bottle of Veuve Clicquot off the kitchen counter, she left by the servants' exit. She followed a down-curving path marked with oiled bags containing candles. Maybe the path led to the parkway, where she could hitch a ride back to New York. It abutted on a little adobe house. She opened the door: a blast of cedar-scented heat — the sauna? A fine place to cook herself into oblivion, and why not? Since the Cambridge fiasco, Daisy was persuaded that, at twenty, her amorous career was over. After lengthy analysis, she'd blamed its demise on the dander discussion — they'd descended to such a subject! To Gerrit it probably evoked some racial defect. Clearly she was repulsive, with her pulpy upper lip. She would have liked to hose down her psyche and emerge a blithe spirit. A golden Slouch, like the one draped over Gerrit.

How had she gotten *here*? She was sitting on the coolish sand, watching the pond. Where had she put her bag? Had she left it up at the house? Hold it — she couldn't reconstruct the past minute. She didn't mind. Not a bit. Ho-ho, it was all pretty funny, her lost bag, and Gerrit with the golden Slouch, ho-ho-ho. Hey, yeah, *stoned* . . .

She sat in an endless present, absorbing the pond's secret life. From its far side sounded a chorus of croaks, bullfrogs telling their love. Bubbles and widening circles probably signaled the passing of fish, beautiful fat black bass, taut and chill, driving through the depths, pure sex. She devoted an hour or so to following the bass in her mind.

A mist had settled over the pond, like in those Swedish flicks where the lovers frolic naked among the bullrushes. From high above in the house, laughter tinkled, faint and disembodied: the sounds you'd hear after you died. Her naked white knees looked like faces. Funny, she couldn't remember taking off her clothes. This puzzle detained her for some time. Then she waded into the water, dove, and struck out for the middle of the pond in a smooth, powerful crawl; she'd always been a good swimmer. She was purely motion and breath, violating the pond's silence, cutting a scar into its surface. Suddenly she felt woozy, there in the black heart of the pond. The champagne mixed with dope. She tried to stand, but her feet stabbed a void; there must have been a steep shelf. She pictured the Marianas Trench. Who would hear her call? Arms windmilling, she struck out for shore. After a long time, she felt for the bottom. Nothing. Had the shore receded? She shot into a side stroke, heart hammering in her ears, a prow cutting inward toward the light, till her outstretched fingers struck bottom.

She stood and laughed aloud, letting a handful of cedary silt dribble through her fingers. Because of the floodlights, she half expected applause.

"What's the joke?"

She submerged with a splash. That voice she knew.

"Why didn't you answer my letters?"

A figure detached itself from shadow and walked to the water's edge. She recognized the cowlick sticking up in the floodlight. Squatting, Gerrit DeWind splashed water in her direction.

"Why didn't you answer my letters?" he repeated.

"They didn't invite an answer."

He continued splashing.

"And I hated you," she added. Noting her past tense.

He stopped splashing. "Are you trying to drive me mad?"

Huh? She squinted at his features in the darkness; she'd never heard the language of male chutzpah in full flower.

"All right, come on out now, you're going to catch cold," he scolded.

"Then go away."

"Wait, don't move." He sprang up, ran to the pool house, and emerged holding out a white terry robe. He walked to the water's edge and stretched it toward her, bending awkwardly from the waist. "Here, put it on."

She didn't budge.

"Rise from the briny deep like Botticelli's Venus. God, that's who you look like, the girl on the scallop shell. C'mon, I'll close my eyes. Trust me."

After near drowning, what could she fear? She rose and stage-walked to the outstretched robe. Only then did she see that his eyes were indeed squinched shut, like a kid's.

"Here I am."

His eyes opened. "Yes indeed! You certainly are!" He drank her in, her glistening perfection of youth. She offered him a good stiff draft, then turned and slipped into the robe.

He set to work drying, using the robe as a towel. Rubbed her arms, shoulders, the ends of her hair, her back, rubbed and rubbed. She went floppy under his hands, like a child getting dried after its bath. Then the work stopped. She felt him behind her. In one motion his hands crushed her breasts and she spun around and they crashed together, striking teeth.

"No!" She jerked backward, brought her hand to her mouth.

"Okay. Okay."

He knelt, lifted the hem of the robe, and planted a kiss on the inside of her right knee. "Let me just adore your knees for a while. Your glorious dancer's knees." He kissed the other knee, the bastard.

"Dancer's knees are a mess," said Daisy, buying time.

"Not these," he muttered, kiss-kissing away, little childish yet insistent kisses.

"Even worse are the feet," she said weakly.

"Oh?" He smiled up at her, his teeth white in the shadow. She felt the rough of his beard against her calf, and his breath. Then he crouched way down and set to work planting slow, insistent kisses on her arch, an erogenous zone never mentioned in *Love Without Fear*.

She sank slowly like a doomed ship as he rose to meet her. Kneeling, they feasted on each other. He tasted of animal health, clover, champagne.

"C'mon," he murmured, his mouth still on hers, gesturing toward the pool house. "No, I've got a better idea. Let's go."

"Yes, where?"

"Maybe you should get dressed first."

He helped her pull the black organdy dress over her head.

"My bag." She looked wildly about.

"In the pool house." He ran for it.

She stuffed her bra into her bag. They were both moving fast and jerky, as in silent films.

She had supposed they were headed for some back wing of the house, but he steered her toward the driveway. She recognized Delphine's MG. Gerrit's car, a black Triumph racing job, was parked carelessly on the bias. She got in. He tossed her a checked lumber jacket from the back seat. Turned the key in the ignition.

"By the way, where we going?"

"My stepmother's place. On Tenth Street. She's in Italy."

"One thing I'd like to know," said Daisy as they pulled onto the Taconic Parkway.

"No, don't. Don't hold me to account. Please."

"I insist."

He slumped down behind the steering wheel.

"I'd like to know whether I'm eloping with Gerrit DeWind the third or fourth."

A relieved chuckle. "Oh, you are tough. Okay, the fourth. The original practically got here before the Indians. Father hired someone to trace the whole genealogical tree. But who gives a rat's ass?"

After that, neither spoke. They possessed a history and could live off the interest.

It was not until the toll that Daisy remembered Gerrit's discarded date. At the second toll she remembered her self-respect, and by the third that was lost in the wind, too.

Brenda Chatfield's place could have been a gentleman's club imported from London. Claret red walls, celadon velvet couches flanking a fireplace with marble mantel cluttered with silver-framed photos. In bookshelves either side of the mantel Daisy saw the titles *Country Houses Designed by Delano and Aldrich* and *Frescoes from Venetian Villas*. On a table she noticed an odd-looking lot of horns.

Gerrit absently stroked a tortoiseshell one. "Binky's collection of Scottish horn snuff boxes," he said. "It was just photographed for *House and Garden*."

His stuffy expression only excited Daisy the more.

The living room also contained a great many photos of a woman trying to pass for Grace Kelly. They infested the gleaming Steinway grand piano dominating one corner. There was Grace in yachting cap on a lawn sloping to the sea; there was Grace gracing Machu Picchu.

Daisy inspected a photo of Grace with — why, Gerrit, in a white suit, standing on a balcony overlooking a Venetian canal. Next to them stood a portly gent with thinning hair combed sideways to hide the baldness.

"Who's the guy?"

"Father." Gerrit added, "They're estranged."

For a second he lapsed into that absent mode she remembered from Cronin's. Then he bowed. "Allow me to show Madame zee bedroom."

"Thanks, no." Officially, she was still semipissed.

"Okay, you can sleep on the sofa bed in here," said Gerrit affably. He sauntered toward the bathroom, whistling.

While she was still wrestling with disappointment, he slid in beside her.

"Only if you promise not to lay a hand on me," she murmured into the pillow.

At that moment she again remembered his date at the party, but the wonder of skin on skin made short work of such thoughts. Heat licked through her belly and groin. She wouldn't let it happen, though. Toward dawn — he must have been touching her a particular way — an electric firestorm flashed through her, she cried out like a lost sailor sighting land. Then she wept great wracking sobs, like a child, and he held her.

Never a sleeper, Daisy watched the pale light stripe the blinds on the windows facing Tenth Street. A collage of Sunday morning sounds floated up: a church bell striking; a car door slamming, then a motor turning over; a dog with a tinny bark. The sounds of happiness. Gerrit slept turned away from her, his arm trapped under the weight of his body, his hair mussed in a touching, defenseless way. She went to the little galley kitchen in search of juice or a Coke, anything to quench a ravening thirst. Then she squeamishly brushed her teeth with Binky's guest toothbrush. The moment she slid back under the sheet, Gerrit moved toward her, and then, still half sleeping, over her.

And so, on a Sunday morning on Tenth Street in Greenwich Village, they finished the phrase begun that Friday night at Harvard in the Fogg.

As she walked home through the summer Village streets, she thought, echoing Julien Sorel, Is that all?

Chapter 8

H E W R O T E her letters, several a day, on the blue stationery, though she lived only seven blocks west of Binky's, on Bethune Street. "You are a wildflower, like heather," he wrote. "I kiss your neck with a thousand little kisses."

She quit the Westbury Music Fair after the second rehearsal of *Brigadoon,* and took a job as a typist at an ad agency.

"*Advertising!* That's murder of the soul," squawked Delphine.

"May it rest in peace," Daisy shot back.

Westbury would have interfered with Gerrit's death-watch hours — ten P.M. to four A.M. at Time Inc. This she didn't reveal to Delphine, partly because she couldn't justify it to herself. But then, she didn't even try.

From long habit she continued to take class at Graham, often just marking combinations, hiding in the back row. Her body mutinied; it wanted no quarrel with gravity; it wanted to sink into a swamp of pleasure.

She had come into her true vocation: love. What a peculiar phrase, "sex life" — Was there another life?

"It's never been like this with anyone," Gerrit told her, looking at her with genuine surprise. "You're incredible. So responsive."

She discovered she preferred love andante, when Gerrit wasn't sprinting for the finish line, when they lingered, more vegetable than human, on the lip of Vesuvius. One night he festooned her with yellow freesias, arranging them around her hair, upper and nether, exclaiming over colors like a mad painter: "Your hair is pink, copper, gold — even *green*." He sat back on his heels. "My God! I just realized who you look like. Simonetta Vespucci, Botticelli's mistress and model. I'll have to show you the original at Chantilly."

I'll show you. More than art and flowers, Daisy retained tenses, allusions to a future. Like most fifties girls, her thinking automatically slid into that groove. Summer before senior year, after all, was the next-to-final lap in the race to mate. And without the future, she and Gerrit amounted to meaningless sex. That was not acceptable even to Delphine.

She gamboled around Binky's apartment in Gerrit's blue work shirt. Assaulted him with schlurpy kisses. After her shower Gerrit dried her hair with Binky's plush gold towels, and they reminisced about "their" pond in Katonah. He rubbed rose-scented oil into her dancer's tortured feet. Amazingly, he was domestic, and loved to rustle up spaghetti carbonara in Binky's kitchen, with its gleaming copper pans hanging on the brick wall.

After dinner — which she left uneaten; love left no space for food — he pulled her onto his lap on the velvet couch facing the fireplace. The pale green echoed his eyes. Did she imagine it, or was the whole apartment keyed to his beauty? Daisy nuzzled his stubble cheek and silky hair, rooted around for his smells, the babyish Johnson's shampoo scent around his scalp.

From Friday night to Sunday they rarely left the sofa bed. The "command post," Gerrit dubbed it. They napped rather than slept, then started all over. In those days it wouldn't stay *down*. They needed the booze: Dewar's for Daisy, Jack Daniel's for Gerrit, chased with Binky's Meursault. The booze dissolved inhibitions — Gerrit seemed embarrassed by too much pelvic action — put sex in soft focus, its scents of low tide and, oh God, *noises*. The booze muted the shock of sex out of wedlock; for all their flouting of convention, they were secretly amazed at themselves.

They read Gerard Manley Hopkins — "their" poet — aloud, declaiming and gesturing and pacing like ham actors. " 'Glory be to God for dappled things,' " Gerrit boomed.

" 'For skies as couple-colored as a brindled cow,' " Daisy took up.

" 'For rose-moles all in stipple upon trout that swim' — Like you, you're all in stipple." He pushed her down on the couch and nosed up her T-shirt. "Hmm, what have we here . . ."

She read each new installment of his novel-in-progress and praised it lavishly. (So it sounded like Holden Caulfield Takes His Nervous Breakdown to Harvard; so all fledgling novelists were derivative.) By night she lay on her side, chin cupped in her hand, and watched over his sleeping profile. She smiled in the blackness like a maniac. At dawn she slipped into sleep, and woke to find him floating over her, tugging at her hair; she could just about come through her scalp. He told her, "You're the only good thing — well, almost — in my life."

Happiness was a high-wire act needing constant vigilance; no wonder courtesan was a full-time job. Gerrit grew moody when simultaneous orgasm eluded them, according to *Love Without Fear* a sacred duty. Daisy sometimes felt he'd entered them in the Great Fuck Sweepstakes, and they were competing with their own previous record. If they didn't top it, she — or the mysterious entity "the relationship" — was to blame. Ecstasy was pretty demanding. And image maintenance. It was tough playing La Bella Simonetta round the clock, making certain always to offer her best profile. At times she just wanted to yawn like a hippo and shuffle around in grotty ballet slippers, unimproved by Midnight Azure mascara and Revlon's Cherries in the Snow. She worried that the at-ease, off-camera Daisy would send him packing. He was awful finicky. Jesus, did anyone ever get carte blanche just to *be*?

She administered a mental slap. Hey, dope, this is happiness. You are *happy*. She didn't know much about this happiness stuff. She'd never been in this neighborhood.

And then she stopped being happy.

She received the news like a neurologically damaged person who touches a hot stove and gets the message late.

Monday night, the Time Inc. "weekend," and Gerrit was canceling. After she hung up she remembered — stupidly, it took a while to wrap her mind around the thought — that he had canceled the last two Mondays as well.

Tuesday night. *But it's ten o'clock, I've been waiting in this joint for an hour.* She's at the White Horse, hollering into the phone mouth-piece over the racket.

"Don't *yell.* Look, I told you, I got tied up with Binky's lawyer. She's getting royally screwed by an art dealer and she's hopeless about money."

"Why are you always so concerned about Binky?"

"Oh Daisy, that's unworthy of you. I hate it when your voice gets that edge. You know what? I think you're determined to wreck this evening. Well, congratulations. You've succeeded."

The dial tone stung her ear. She stared at the receiver. Wait, wait, *wait* a minute . . . How had they gotten *here?*

Everything now offended. Her new yellow toreador pants. Her "Queens accent." Her allergies — "No dander in this apartment!"

"Incidentally, there's something I've been wanting to ask you. Why are you working at that dumb ad agency? When you could've done summer stock?"

Why, to be with you. She'd only done what all girls did, and were careful to camouflage lest they appear too eager: arranged herself around his life.

She caught him studying her. Across the table at Chumley's. From Binky's couch. One night, glancing up from his manuscript, she saw his eyes on her, weighing. Tinged with panic. Like a kid with a mouthful he's not sure he can swallow.

"I'm all fucked up," Gerrit announced. "The timing's all wrong. I warned you, I *did,* that night in Cronin's. You deserve better."

He looked so tormented, she was tempted to commiserate. She marked her place in his manuscript. "But . . . what's wrong with the timing?"

"Let's just say I'm in over my head." Nasty smile. "Maybe I didn't know I would like you so much." He lit a Marlboro, eyed her with *dis*like. "Now don't start imagining some" — he waved his ciga-rette — "some white picket fence deal in Darien."

She went and shut herself in Binky's pink bathroom and sat listening to the pipes in the brownstone knock and groan. Hearing the venom in his voice. She could muster no activity outside of loving Gerrit. She was like an ocean liner unable to change course.

·   ·   ·

Nights on Bethune Street she swung in a bucket chair suspended from the living room ceiling, at her feet a stiff vodka gimlet. What had she done wrong? (She didn't for a moment believe his cryptic nonsense about "timing.") She sifted July for a turning point, the earliest symptom of Gerrit's defection. Reviewed each of their meetings for crimes and misdemeanors, some damning word or act or smell that had escaped her, a smile flashed with spinach in her teeth. She'd been so busy being happy she hadn't noticed when the lease ran out.

She went on sleepathons. Craved unconsciousness almost as much as she craved Gerrit's hands on her body, his tender invasions. She was exhausted, falling out of Gerrit's love, as if she were actively collaborating in it. The crazy part was she was the same person Gerrit had once thought he somewhat loved. Into the bargain, a great lay. Could that be the problem? No one ever rhapsodized about Isolde or Juliet being great lays. No fiancée was ever a great lay.

At odd moments she grasped at hope: he needed her critical eye, her editorial judgment. He needed her to help make him an artist.

One evening on Binky's couch, she read a passage about the hero's burgeoning attraction to his aunt Olga, an exotic Russian older woman. He falls in love with her on a boat crossing the English Channel.

Daisy went on red alert. Till now the novel had mirrored Gerrit's life; she recognized most of the players, including the Slouch, Father, and settings from his anecdotes about his past. So who was Aunt Olga? Or was he now working purely from imagination?

Hoping to draw him out: "You know, the scene on the boat — the one with Aunt Olga? It's the best thing you've written so far. It has an immediacy, the ring of truth."

His eyes shone with joy. "You think so? Yes. You may be right. I'm so glad you like it."

Daisy confided her troubles to Delphine, who said, "Fee, fi, fo, fum, I smell another woman."

Who? Daisy zoomed in on the sooty-eyed brunette from Cronin's. Beth Kavafian, an actress, Gerrit's flame from sophomore year. He claimed, suspiciously, she thought, to despise her. Or was it the Slouch from Katonah, the skeletal descendant of Corning Glass, abandoned but not forgotten?

When Gerrit went down to the corner deli for Marlboros and groceries, she scoured Binky's place for clues. Discovered only a crumpled envelope from Lucien postmarked Mykonos. At that moment the phone rang; when Daisy answered, the caller hung up. Every day Gerrit's life grew more cluttered — with Binky, Lucien, the spirit of loves past; the phantom phoners; letters to Harvard deans and his house master; summit lunches with Father at the Brook Club.

One night they went to dinner at Il Gran Ticino with Lucien and one of his generic debs. As Daisy was waiting to get into the ladies' room, her eyes panned across the sawdust floors and diners. Lucien stood behind Gerrit's chair. He gave Gerrit's shoulder a squeeze, then bent and whispered in his ear. Daisy recognized the shoulder squeeze from the night at Cronin's — only five months ago? Gerrit turned his head upward, baring a sculpted white throat, and they both laughed, a complicitous private laugh. Lucien was so pink and effete.

"Do you think — Is it possible Lucien's in love with you?" Daisy blurted that night on the sofa bed.

Gerrit groaned and pulled the pillow over his head. "Why do you always start in late at night, when I have to work tomorrow? He's my stepbrother, you silly person. That's the sickest thing I've ever heard."

One Saturday night the phone woke them. Daisy checked the little squat-legged alarm clock on the end table: two-ten. She tiptoed to the bedroom; the door was shut, but she understood he was talking to Binky. She semiheard his end of an argument. The phrase "know where my duty lies" . . . then "we'll make the time." But mainly her ear picked up tone. So Gerrit spoke to Stepmom in his private voice? The nasal tenor he drew across *her* nerves like a bow? Daisy studied the silver-framed photos on the wall outside the bedroom. She was the color of topaz, this Binky, with her heavy dark blond hair coiled at the neck. Her wounded gaze and loose mouth, erotically relaxed — most unstepmotherlike. Familiar somehow.

Could it be? The woman in the raincoat that night at the Fogg?

At Foote, Cone, and Belding they played the jingle "You'll wonder where the yellow went." They played it in rhythm 'n' blues, rock, and country western. Daisy stared at the page in her typewriter, but she was watching a tableau vivant starring Gerrit DeWind, watching it through a gauzy scrim. She could dimly make out players and fleeting gestures, hear odd scraps of dialogue. But what was the plot?

"You're not going to believe this!" Delphine honked from the black bucket swing. "Daisy's jealous of the ugly stepmother."

"But isn't she *forty*?" Ginny bellowed back. She was in the bathroom, giving her hair a hot-oil treatment.

"At least. And with jelly arms and wattle chin," said Delphine.

"About as wattled as Grace Kelly," went Daisy, belly down on the sagging sofa bed.

Ginny waddled into the living room, head turbanned in towels. "Oh, they airbrush wattles," she said with her new expertise.

"And then there's his step*brother,* Lucien Chatfield," said Daisy. "Binky's son. Always hanging around."

Delphine jabbed a finger at Daisy and gave a great whoop of laughter. "D'you realize? I mean, just think: you have the guy balling his stepmother *and* his stepbrother!" Suddenly she looked respectful. "Sooo decadent."

"My *droves* of women?" said Gerrit, his green eyes amused. "Tsk-tsk, let's not exaggerate, you are melodramatic. It's rather an endearing trait. Maybe *you* should write a novel." He slumped way down on the velvet couch, hands dangling over his crotch, his impossibly wide-set eyes fixed on some private vision. "Actually, there's been only one woman that mattered," he offered.

Only one was worse. Daisy shrank so far into herself she grew concave. Her chest was broken out in pink dots. A *poi*-son could develop prickly heat instead of a cold.

"Who?"

He waved her question away. Flicked his half-smoked Marlboro into the fireplace. Dreamily: "Someone in Europe. Autumn of fifty-six."

In a hypnotic monotone: "Where in Europe?"

"Venice, in September — after the tourists go home. There was a festival of baroque music. We stayed holed up in the Cipriani for one whole week."

The Cipriani! Daisy rolled the name on her tongue. A far cry from Ira and Dora's Arrowhead Lodge.

"Every night we'd take the vaporetto to a different palazzo to hear the Solisti di Zagreb. Always worrying about being seen."

"Why'd you worry?"

He jerked from his trance. "Aha! Thought you'd get me, Miss Marple, but I'm too clever. C'mere." He lunged the length of the couch at her, planted soft little kisses on her lips, then thrust his tongue into her mouth. His hands slid under her new Romanian blouse; he had her.

"And now to write about it," he said afterward, pulling on his chinos.

Why did sex grow better? Sex had a parallel life, unconnected with loving kindness. She was running on empty, a monster of desire. They would have burned her in Salem. Visions of sucking and licking filled her. She arrived at his apartment after twenty-four hours of mental foreplay.

"God, I got hard just thinking of you walking down Bleecker Street," he breathed.

They both came fast, too fast, a way of clearing the palate, before settling down to something that possibly resembled murder more than love. One night he checked them into the seedy Earle Hotel on Washington Square. The clerk leered at them, displaying a section of missing teeth. Despite temperatures in the high eighties, Gerrit had asked her to wear black stockings and a white eyelet garter belt with blue ribbons. She kept them on. While foraging in her pocketbook, her fingers struck a tube of Coppertone suntan oil, a memento of a trip to Jones Beach. She kneaded oil into Gerrit's shoulders, then he flipped over and she worked on his chest, ribs, then migrated south to where nice girls never ventured. Her lips existed for this alone. With a groan Gerrit pushed her off him and in one motion fell over and into her and came, and soon grew hard again, and they picked up where they'd left off.

Every time now had a tragic frenzy; every time now they topped their own record — now that he was no longer keeping score. She thought of that Swedish movie she'd seen in her adolescence in Culver City, *One Summer of Happiness,* promising so much. But they'd gotten it wrong, the Swedes, they'd misled her. It was more like three lousy weeks.

Chapter 9

THAT SUMMER of '57, Ginny — plodding and pedestrian, Delphine's confidante and court therapist — suddenly became the heroine of her own story. She was in love, and not just with Tom Puccio, the young intern she considered a "look-no-further." A good fifteen years before the drumbeat of feminism conscripted women into an army of careerists, Ginny fell in love with a job.

And some job. To win the coveted slot of college guest editor at *Mademoiselle,* this intellectual fashion magazine, thousands of girls had submitted essays, poems, stories. Only twenty had been chosen. She had slipped into the elite club by a freak of timing: just before her interview, a shotgun marriage claimed one of the winners, or so ran the rumor around *Mademoiselle.* New York City, usually clamped shut like a clam, magically opened to the guest editors.

They were plied with free ballet tickets, invitations to screenings, openings, promotions of Tupperware or fur pieces. They got free makeovers and hair stylings and personalized makeup kits. They ate four-course lunches on expense accounts with famous authors. Once Ginny got food poisoning from a gamy coquilles Saint Jacques at a restaurant promotion and threw up all night, and Daisy almost had to take her to Saint Vincent's emergency room, but the party at the Waldorf had been worth every dry heave! Somewhere in there they also helped put out a magazine. Of course, she was way out of her league, privately felt herself an imposter. She wasn't even assigned to a specific editor, like the legitimate contest winners. She was a floater, working for the fashion or copy editor, and occasionally the articles editor, Gertrude Alcott, the dragon who had so terrified her at the interview.

She loved everything about the office at 350 Madison Avenue: the towering marble lobby, glacial as a meat locker; the artificial office climate, unrelated to anything in nature; her little cubicle with its corkboard and pushpins, the plushy tip-back swivel chair; the camaraderie around the water cooler. Even if the camaraderie was a bit forced, and she could never truly relax around the other guest editors. They were all out to one-up each other (wasn't it bad enough to compete all the time for men?).

One afternoon, when she was "floating" around the art department, she noticed a fugitive from an old master bent over a drawing board. He glanced up at her. He had round, blissed-out eyes with curly lashes, burnished gold ringlets, the mouth of a cherub.

"My God," she blurted, "you look like an angel. An archangel," she amended, suddenly hearing her father's dreadful word *faygeleh*.

He smiled. Checked his watch. "Well, it figures, since I'm about to go to heaven for lunch. Hamburger Heaven. Oooh, terrible joke. Would you join me anyway? I'm Renato Russell."

More lunches followed. They laughed and gossiped about everyone in the office like two biddies, even confiding about the men in their lives. Renato's was an alcoholic window display artist; Ginny tried not to think what they did in the sack.

The job's expandable hours were perfectly tailored to Tom's grueling intern's schedule, his absentee style of romance. And bringing home work kept her mind off the husband-hunting nurses surrounding the medics. Late into the night, hunched in the black bucket swing, she proofread galleys for fashion spreads using real coeds as models: "This season's Important Sweater wraps up Harriet Rosenfeld, Barnard '59, in a froth of looped mohair rubbed down from a face-framing cowl collar." At her feet lay a manual of editing signs she'd taken out of the library. Sometimes she herself got to write fashion copy, avoiding clichés like land mines — her triumph to date had been converting "forest green" to "bois green." Delphine often slept uptown at Jake's, Daisy at Gerrit's stepmother's place on Tenth Street. Her only company was Erroll Garner's piano chunka-chunking on the record player. Or a neighborhood diva practicing arpeggios — of all the rotten luck; wasn't it bad enough at the opera? The diva set the cats howling on the patio fence until a wino stuck his head out the window and bellowed at the whole lot, "Shaddap!"

One Monday Miss Alcott called Ginny into her office. Surveyed her sourly through rhinestone harlequin glasses and thrust a sheaf of papers at her. "I thought you might like to spruce up 'Breakup' for us," she said with her odd sneer, which Ginny would later recognize as an adjustment of dentures. "It's written in psychologese and needs to be translated into standard English."

Ginny all but skipped down the hall to her cubicle, manuscript clutched to her breast. Its working title was "What to Do When He Dumps You," one of ten topics the women's magazines will recycle until the millennium.

That weekend the temperature reached ninety-eight in the shade, with ninety-eight percent humidity. Delphine and Jake had gone to New Haven to look at the new Louis Kahn art museum; Daisy and Gerrit were in Connecticut somewhere with Lucien; Tom was doing a cardiac rotation at the hospital. Ginny laid in a supply of what her father called delicatessen, pulled the living room table to the window in pursuit of air, and positioned their two fans at her feet. She made a pot of iced coffee. To drown out the local Maria Callas, she put in earplugs.

Reading through the manuscript, she worked up a fresh coat of sweat. Cosmetic touchups wouldn't do it — this dog needed a complete overhaul. She was visited by a terrifying thought: now she'd be *found out*. She'd lied in the interview. What had she ever written but those deadly contracts in college? Was the dragon setting her up to get fired? In a panic, she phoned Delphine at Jake's, then remembered they were out of town.

She went to the kitchen and polished off the whitefish, German potato salad, and a pint of Schrafft's Dutch chocolate ice cream. She eyed a jar of Skippy's peanut butter, queasily decided against it. There was nothing for it but to write. She inserted a daunting white page into her student Royal typewriter and took it from the top.

Late Monday afternoon, Ginny's office phone rang: Miss Alcott wanted her to stop by her office. Walking down the hall, Ginny prepared to be discovered; she composed gracious demurrals — Oh it was nothing, really, so glad to pinch-hit in a crisis. She was especially pleased with her lead, a lead to waken one of Tom's cadavers.

Miss Alcott's pinpoint eyes fixed her through thick glasses. "I'm afraid this won't do. It's riddled with clichés" — she held a page away from her as if it'd wrapped chum — "and it reads like a scholarly treatise. Where are *you* in all this? We need *your* voice, grabbing the reader by the lapel." She riffled through Ginny's perfectly typed pages. "And somewhere in the second paragraph, we need to know why we're being asked to read this. As it stands, we haven't a clue. And may I suggest you start with a lead — You do know what a lead is?"

Ginny carried her manuscript into a stall in the ladies' room, leaned against the door, and wept.

On her way back to her cubicle, she collided, head down, with Renato. One look at her swollen eyes and he said, "How about going out for a heavenly cup of coffee?"

Huddled at the counter: "Okay, what did he do?"

"Who?"

"Dr. Tom. What else could get you in such a state?"

She explained.

"So you'll rewrite it. Everything is fixable. The dragon wants your voice? Let's give 'er voice."

"I wouldn't know my voice if I tripped over it."

"Hmm, why don't you talk the piece through to me out loud, and I'll write down the things that sound most like you, the crème of Ginny Goldberg, the absolute *pearls*."

She couldn't believe his kindness. Tom fixed all the broken hinges on Bethune Street, but he really only talked about himself. Why couldn't all men be sweeter, like women. Like Renato. The confusion of it all made her teary again.

"C'mon, no more of that," said Renato, offering his pocket hand-kerchief. "Now get cracking."

Fifteen minutes later, he handed her the "pearls," scrawled over four napkins.

"But what about a lead?" she said in a plaintive voice.

"After work you'll hit the Periodicals Room of the Forty-second Street library and read a hundred or so leads, and see how the big kids do it. You've got to think like a pro and act like a pro, even if you don't know what the hell you're doing. That's eighty percent of it. Just remember, it's all done with mirrors." He patted her arm. "Hey, I'll bet you next time around the dragon's gonna love it. If I win my bet, you buy me a mai tai punch at Trader Vic's."

"Renato, how come you're such an absolute prince?"

He sighed. "Guess I need distraction. My companion just found a new — richer — caretaker. The worst is, no one needs me anymore. I seem to need to be needed. So" — he flashed his angel smile — "the good Lord sent you."

Ginny's rewrite was never officially accepted. At some point she simply learned that the story slugged DUMPED had found its way to the copy-editing department — and she bought Renato a mai tai punch at Trader Vic's. The following week, Miss Alcott's assistant appeared at Ginny's cubicle with a new writing assignment: a paragraph on the hopes and aspirations of *Mademoiselle* guest editors, to accompany a full-page photo spread. The moment the assistant left, Ginny panicked. Then she heard Renato: *Just remember, it's all done with mirrors.*

Toward the end of July, Delphine packed up and moved into Jake's pad on Morningside Heights. Daisy and Ginny ended up sharing the apartment. And Sally November, Daisy's old partner on the road to Harvard, occasionally subbed for Delphine.

Daisy felt cheated; she'd contracted to live with a soulmate, and she'd gotten Delphine's proxy. She and Ginny cohabitated like two nonwarring yet alien species. Daisy thought Ginny a goody two-shoes, *square*. Ginny never even laughed full out as the rest of them did, practically peeing in their pants. She'd come to Sarah Lawrence, she once confided, because no one wore Bermudas, and she wouldn't have to expose her thunder thighs. After one bohemian summer, Ginny would submerge herself in Dr. Tom Puccio, Daisy decided, and live happily ever after in a split-level ranch house where she would time foreplay.

Ginny, for her part, thought Daisy self-destructive. "Where's it going with Gerrit?" she asked one evening.

"Whaddaya mean, we're not on a train to Kalamazoo." Though if they *weren't* on the train, she and Gerrit were the unthinkable: meaningless sex.

"Where's it 'going' with Doctor Tom?"

Ginny opened her eyes wide and batted her lashes. "Oh, Tom wants a wife."

One evening Tom stopped by Bethune Street for drinks before an evening of music appreciation at the City Opera. He arrived early, creating pandemonium: Ginny's hair was still in rollers. Sally greeted him at the door, her breasts ajiggle beneath her black lace camisole. Leaving Tom wall-eyed in the hall, she sashayed back to the kitchen to tend to her brownies.

It was the first Ginny's friends had viewed the mythic medic. He had slightly bulging eyes, a flattop, and knife-sharp pleats in the chinos he surely called trousers. He might have been boiled in a sterilizer, he was so clean cut.

Straightaway, Tom took his Swiss army knife to the wobbly legs of the Danish Modern table. Next came a monologue on myocardial infarctions. Ginny passed around a plate of potato chips and onion-and-sour-cream dip, and rattled on nervously about the rigors of working for Miss Alcott. Her sleeveless white piqué dress offset her lovely skin, nacreous, almost lavender in the twilight. Ginny was blooming, Daisy noted with surprise. (Somehow their group always discounted Ginny.)

"Bet you dollars to doughnuts your Miss Alcott's an old maid," Tom said, his mouth curving into a mirthless smile. "That's how those career gals end up."

In the kitchen, Sally was seized with a coughing fit.

"Oh, Miss Alcott seems quite content in her way," said Ginny in the demure style she adopted around Tom.

"Naah, that's no kinda life," Tom said, waggling his head. "What kind of life could she have?" He stood and walked to Ginny's chair and positioned himself behind it, hands on her shoulders. They looked posed for a formal wedding photograph. Envy stabbed Daisy. The siren call of security. Ginny needed only hatch babies and open cans of cling peaches, she'd be safe for the rest of her life.

"I wouldn't *allow* my wife to work," Tom said from behind Ginny.

"Uh, isn't that *her* decision?" asked Daisy. She caught Ginny's hand signal: lay off.

Tom pursed his lips. "What is the point of having a family, I want

to know, if my wife ends up abandoning her children to a colored lady
from Harlem?"

Sally came jiggling out of the kitchen bearing a platter.

"Hash brownies, anyone?"

That summer, Tom rechristened Ginny "Gina." Ginny was ecstatic. In
one blow she'd been liberated from a detested name, and Italianized,
made kosher for the Puccios.

Daisy continued to call her Ginny. It was bad enough to fake a
passion for Puccini, but surrender your name?

Each time Daisy saw her, though, Ginny looked less like Ginny and
more like Gina. She shed five, fifteen pounds, subsisting on grapefruit,
parchment-thin wafers, and cans of coffee Metrecal. A waist appeared,
circled with wide elastic cinch belts. Her broad face developed cheekbones to rival Dietrich's. She tossed the glasses for contacts, painted on
black-rimmed doe eyes and a chalk mouth. Dirndl skirts and plaid
Ship 'n' Shore blouses yielded to crisp, boxy little suits from Peck and
Peck or De Pinna, pulled together with summer white beads, earrings,
and pumps. "Renato says the key," Ginny chirped at Daisy, "is knowing how to accessorize."

Like a gap-toothed hillbilly, Daisy watched the metamorphosis from
the living room swing. She thought of Frankenstein. Ginny was a mad
scientist reinventing herself as a cover girl with an Ipana smile. Daisy
wondered if *she* weren't metamorphosing in reverse, passing from
butterfly to something larval. At Foote, Cone, and Belding, she toiled
with the other typist-clericals in the typing pool, a center corral of
females ringed by men in private offices. Her coworkers had long red
talons that tapped about on objects, like dextrous mandibles, even
dialing the phone. From exchanges in the ladies' room, Daisy gathered
that the women regarded the office as a kind of padded holding pen,
which they would soon quit if they played their cards right. They
didn't wonder where the yellow went. They wondered whether Stu or
Vince or Ron would call, so they could say sayonara to the typing pool
and Kotex dispenser and time cards and move to a garden apartment
in Astoria and begin real life.

When Daisy tried to envision her own prospects for real life, she
heard Gerrit's crack about no picket fence in Darien. She suspected
she'd bought a one-way ticket to Heartbreak Hotel. She took to log-

ging the course of the affair in her black-and-white-marbleized notebook — Heartbreak Hotel, it's well known, is the premier writing
school for women. Her scribbles oozed self-pity, but stubbornness
kept her scribbling; this way, somehow, lay salvation.

One sweltering evening, when everyone in the city was felled by temperatures that at night bottomed at eighty-five, into the apartment
swept a live fashion plate. Ginny had just gotten photographed by
Mademoiselle for a makeover. She strutted around the living room
while Daisy, wearing only Gerrit's undershirt, gawked from the swing.
They'd given Gina — the only possible name now — a glossy helmet
with flip-up ends, a saucy white bow clamped on one side; white
button earrings the size of silver dollars; a navy Chanel suit with white
braided edges; navy and white spectator sling-back pumps; and a
working set of pearly talons.

"You can't waste all this on us chickens," Daisy said.

"As luck would have it, I'm seeing Tom tonight."

"I hope they're not doing Wagner. Five hours with the Valkyries,
and Tom won't get a chance to appreciate the new you."

Coy smile. "He's cooking dinner. At his place. This may be *the*
night." She laughed, eyes flashing with something akin to terror.

It happened because suddenly she started to feel good through all her
body in a way she never had before.

After they finished washing the dishes, she went to the bathroom,
which was off Tom's bedroom. When she came out, he took her in his
arms and kissed her. Usually she hoped a roomie would arrive to break
up the clinch, but the roomies were all out. Then something amazing
happened: suddenly she stopped waiting for a roomie to come, because she *liked* it; their tongues did lovely velvety things, and she
wanted never to stop. His hands slid down to her hips — too big, but
he made her feel feminine, gathered in.

"Let's just lie down for a minute so I can hold you, just for a
minute," he murmured over her feeble protests, "just to hold you."
Truth was she really wanted to. She trusted Tom, so cautious; usually
he was the one to apply the brakes. They stretched out on the Indian
spread, and they hugged each other — not dangerously; Tom seemed
almost asleep; he was always exhausted from the hospital and drop-

ping off at odd moments. Then his hands started to roam her body, like a sleepy child's. A hand squeezed her breast; she stiffened; the hand left off, and Tom again seemed to doze, then the hand returned to her breast, and she got used to that idea, loved this sensation in her nipple, mysteriously connected to her crotch, growing hot and wet.

One caress segued dreamily into the next and suddenly, she could hardly believe it, he'd pushed aside her bra and was suckling her. She covered her breast with her hand: he'd see her stretch marks! Removing her hand, Tom said, "You're beautiful." He kissed the palm of her hand, then nosed her breasts like a hungry baby. His hand slipped down into her pants — *down there*. She stiffened. *No, we can't.* Praying he wouldn't stop, but he did! She moved his hand back, and he sucked at her nipple while his fingers probed and played. Oh my God, Ginny groaned.

Suddenly he was atop her, spreading her legs open with his. He'd broken the spell. She wanted the other way, the dreaminess, but he was groaning and pumping against her — "I want you so badly."

"Oh Tom, we'll get married, won't we?"

"I love you," he growled, a hand fumbling with his pants. He pulled aside her underpants and rammed into her and pumped once, twice, three times, then rapidly pulled out, and a wetness spurted onto her thigh. He fell to one side.

"Of course we'll get married," he murmured, and began to snore. She wanted to cry. It'd been so quick: had he not found her sexy? It hadn't hurt; she hadn't felt anything; suddenly she'd gone numb. And now this soreness. She slipped off the bed and went to the bathroom. She stared at her image in the mirror; her mascara had left dark smudges beneath her eyes; the white bow was still in place.

Another detail tormented Ginny. Why hadn't he kissed her *during*? She was dying to ask Daisy or Delphine, but they would just cackle and mock; she thought of calling Franca on the Cape, but it was past midnight. Maybe she was just naive. Maybe, like whistling and humming, you couldn't kiss and have sexual intercourse at the same time.

Next morning Daisy was fumphering around the kitchen in her pre-coffee torpor when she heard the assorted bolts and cylinders turn over in the triple-locked door. Ginny appeared at the kitchen. Her make-over looked practically intact. Daisy wondered if Ginny weren't, too.

"Soooo?"

Ginny broke into a smile and clasped her hands in front of her. "We're pre-engaged!" she squeaked. "We'll make it official after Tom finishes his residency."

"Congratulations!" Daisy laid down a fresh coat of sweat. Every time she looked, a new bride walking into the sunset. At least Delphine would never capitulate. Of course with Ginny, you could've seen it coming. Daisy did not press for further details about the sleepover. With nice girls like Ginny there wouldn't be any.

The following Sunday when Daisy returned from Gerrit's, she found the door locked only once. Yet the apartment was empty, Thelonius Monk racing dizzily on the record player. She checked all the rooms, even the back patio, calling Gina's name. Scenting catastrophe. In the living room, the swing — was she imagining it? — moved slightly, as if just abandoned. A tall frosted glass lay overturned beneath it, spreading a cranberry puddle. A section of the Sunday *Times* lay like a crumpled tent beside the puddle. Wait, hadn't Gina said something about tea with Miss Alcott? But it was only one, too early for tea. Going on instinct, Daisy streaked down Bethune Street toward the little triangular park on Abingdon Square.

Ginny sat on the first bench. Two black guys were squatting at her feet, peddling a plaster bust of Jesus. She stared straight ahead at the nursing home across the square. Her bow perched at an odd angle.

"Boy, am I glad to see *you*." Daisy collapsed on the bench next to Ginny. Ginny kept staring at the nursing home, as if awaiting a signal. The guys wrapped their Jesus in newspaper and carted him to the next bench.

"Phew! Hot enough for you?" Daisy asked. They often joked about this favorite question of New York doormen. Daisy fanned her thighs with her skirt.

Ginny stayed stony.

"Cigarette?"

Ginny shook her head no. Daisy lit up, sat smoking for a while.

"Well. Now that I know where you are, guess I'll go home." She didn't move.

"He's engaged," Ginny said suddenly.

"What? *Who* is?"

Ginny's lip trembled. "*He* is, I read it in the *Times*."

"You must have read wrong. He's engaged to *you*."

Daisy ground out her half-smoked cigarette on the pavement. "Ginny, are you *sure*?"

Ginny squinched her eyes shut.

"Jesus, it's like one of those creepy movies where the guy's been leading a double life. Listen, you're lucky."

"Real lucky."

"I mean, you could've married a closet ax murder. Shit, he's probably been promised since birth to someone back in Sicily."

"Family's from the North."

"Well he can't get away with this, you've got some rights. Call him immediately and demand an explanation." As the words left her mouth, Daisy knew that he *could* get away with it. Ginny would never get an explanation. What was Tom going to say? I wanted to get laid, and the nurses are off-limits. Or maybe the explanation didn't exist. Not even for Tom.

"Listen, a Catholic — it would've killed your mother. You'd be raising a dozen bambinos, your insides would've dropped out. You would've lost bladder control. Started peeing in your pants —"

"They have something for that now," said Ginny, as if she'd considered this eventuality. "It's called the Kegel exercise. You stick a pencil in and grip. Tom once told me about it."

An Indian wearing a turban sat down across from them. He sent little smooching sounds their way and bent to peer up their skirts. It started to rain. The Indian left. Ginny refused to budge, so Daisy sat on beside her in the rain. She thought of Miss Havisham in *Great Expectations,* permanently sidelined, but decided Ginny didn't have the makings of a serious nut. Daisy punched her lightly on the arm. "C'mon, you've got that fabulous job. You've got Miss Alcott."

Ginny turned and for the first time looked at Daisy. The rain had plastered her bangs to her forehead. "That job means nothing. It's what I did because Tom was always busy. It's what I did to impress him. Make him believe I was important and glamorous. It was all for Tom."

Daisy sensed that wasn't so, but now wasn't the moment to contradict her.

The sky opened up. She persuaded Ginny to come home. The rain had only steamed the heat, yet Ginny couldn't stop shivering. Daisy rummaged in her drawer and found her a Lanz granny gown, which she'd bought from Ginny at one of her rummage sales. She made Ginny drink a shot glass of cognac. Then Ginny went into her bedroom. She sat on the end of the bed, very still, hands folded on her knees, brow furrowed, concentrating hard on something. An hour later, when Daisy peeked in the door, she was still sitting in the same position, her face a field of emotion, as if she were watching a movie.

Daisy was touched by her silent stoicism. It reminded her for some reason of a fox biting off its own foot to escape the teeth of the trap.

All afternoon Daisy half expected the phone to ring, with the news there'd been some weird mix-up, or it was all a sick joke, Tom had never even met Miss Funicello or whoever — a Nancy Malfitano, Daisy read in the crumpled Engagements section lying next to the swing, a cement heiress. The only call was from Miss Alcott, concerned over Gina's no-show.

Daisy's sleep was marbled with old nightmares, pictures from an ancient scrapbook. A voice from the console radio in the living room says Flight 171 exploded in midair . . . A small girl stands at the door of a row house in Queens, howling into the night . . . Daisy woke to the feeble cheeping of New York's morning sparrows. And the swoosh of water — *running* water.

She hurled herself out of bed toward the bathroom. The door was closed. She flung it open. Darkness. There in the murk in the nearly overflowing tub lay Gina, her face a chalk white death mask. At Daisy's shriek, Gina's eyes opened. The death mask broke into a hideous red-lipped grin.

"An herbal mask." Gina pointed at her face. "Rejuvenates the skin by sloughing off dead cells. It's part of the makeover."

Daisy fumbled at the faucets. "Why's it so goddamn dark in here?" She flipped on the light.

"Oooh, don't. The instructions call for a serene atmosphere."

Chapter 10

THE WEEK BEFORE Labor Day, Delphine called an SOS lunch to buoy Gina — somehow the name had taken.

"I don't think she needs buoying," said Daisy. "She's so cheerful it's gonna crack every plate in the cupboard."

"Let's all have lunch anyway. Schrafft's this Tuesday?" Mysteriously, urgently: "I need you. I need to see you."

Delphine's muumuu, Garbo shades, and thong sandals produced an instant scandal at Schrafft's. She was followed by Sally November, who had invited herself along, in a transparent lace camisole and black toreadors. The natives blinked at them from under heavy-duty millinery. Hats like hot water bottles or oversize doilies. One little straw number featured a Robin Hood feather angled downward — "Like a listing cock," Delphine said audibly.

The hostess swiftly hid them at a back table behind a pillar.

Gina swept in twenty minutes late. Silent ovation from the millinery set. She wore a navy chemise coatdress with huge red chiffon bow; pearl earrings and matching pearl bracelet peeping over little white gloves to the wrist bone; a navy velvet hairband perched on her new short gamin hairdo, each spiky bang glued in place.

"Sorry, I was stuck doing an interview with this divine new playwright, one of England's Angry Young Men." The table turned rancid with envy. To Delphine: "Thanks for arranging this, but I'm great. Couldn't be better."

An awkward silence fell over them. If anyone, it was Delphine in need of rescue. She looked ashy white behind her enormous shades, held together at the earpiece with a safety pin.

They ordered chef's salads and iced tea, except Delphine, who ordered a double bloody Mary and Maryland crab cakes. A *Village Voice* militant had convinced her the female obsession with weight was a diversion created by the military industrial complex. She filled the dead air with stories about the duties of a *Voice* researcher.

"One way to get a writing assignment is to make it with the executive editor on his office casting couch. If I weren't spoken for —"

"How's the piece for the *Times* going?" Gina asked. "By the way, is it sunny in here, or am I missing something? Or did you walk into a doorknob?"

Delphine hesitated a beat. "Nothing like shades to hide the dark circles. Circles look better on Anna Magnani than us pasty WASPs."

Delphine's too-loud voice attracted furtive looks. At the next table a mother in a Carmen Miranda hat and her sweet-faced daughter shuddered visibly.

"Oops, Mom's probably passing on her recipe for tuna wiggle casserole. Tell me, doctor, can this marriage be saved by a chlorophyll douche?" A sigh. "Seriously, I've been up all night for a week typing and editing Jake's article. A profile of Antonio Gaudi for the *Voice.* We've been trying to get Jake an architecture column at the paper. It was Jake's idea, to run a regular weekly column, kind of a personal essay on architecture. Is that not brilliant?"

"For the *Voice,* maybe," drawled Gina. "Provided he says 'fuck' a lot. But how's your *Times* piece on the Silent Generation? I keep worrying we're all in it. I insist on twenty-four hours' notice so I can skip town before it appears."

Delphine poked at a crab cake with her fork. "Actually, the piece has grown too big, it's getting away from me. The subject's too broad. I mean, to sum up our whole generation — I can't get my arms around it."

"But they're counting on you!" cried Gina. "If you blow it, they'll never give you another assignment."

Daisy looked at her in disbelief. When had Delphine ever admitted defeat? Clearly, happiness in love dissolved ambition. You could be cute and dizzy and helpless. *He* would achieve for both of you, so why knock yourself out? Why kill yourself? To prove what?

"Not to worry, dahlink," said Delphine. "They've extended the deadline." She looked past them at a lone luncher falling into her manhattan. "Oh shit. I wasn't planning to tell you this today." To Gina: "I don't want to sound like I'm gloating. When you must be feeling so wretched. Oh shit." She broke into a broad smile, all lips and gorgeous teeth. "I just *have* to tell you."

They waited in silence.

"Are you ready for this?" She looked from one to the other. "Jake and I got married."

Gina jerked forward as if shot in the back; Daisy recoiled.

Sally leapt up with a little yip and ran around the table to kiss Delphine. "I have just the dress to wear to the reception," she cried, striking a mannequin pose. "It's drippy and black, sort of Charles Addamsy. I found it at Goodwill."

She was losing Delphine, thought Daisy. Women formed temporary alliances, pending *his* arrival. She wanted to hang on forever to everyone she'd loved, and here they were all deserting her. "Congratulations," she said in the voice of a gravedigger.

Delphine's smile had faded. Her arms locked on her chest. "Okay, okay, I know what you're thinking. But I'm not about to quit college and become a *cow*. Nothing's really changed. Jake and I are a team. We're both going to work, side by side, each in our field."

"And you'll edit his stuff," Sally pointed out.

"Well, yes. Of course. Jake has an IQ off the charts, but he can't spell worth a damn. Or type, for that matter. Or structure an article. His ideas are too profound for the shallowness of journalism."

A silence. "I realize consistency is shallow too, but when I think of all the times you've carried on about June brides," said Gina in her brittle new voice.

Daisy foraged in her chef's salad for a strip of turkey. "I dunno, I feel . . . sort of betrayed. Like you're Galileo or somebody, saying, 'Okay, guys, have it your way, the earth's the center of the universe.' And now we're stranded out here, with our spears and banners flapping in the breeze and — I mean, you've only known Jake six weeks."

"Look, I know the timing stinks. I should've met Jake ten years later — I shudder to think I might never have. But life isn't tidy like that. You have to seize happiness when it's thrown your way. We discovered we loved playing house. I mean, the coziness of cutting our grapefruit together in the morning. It seemed like a terrible regression to start 'dating' again when the fall term started up. In fact, Jake wouldn't hear of it. So one morning we went and got the Wassermans, and a week later we just hopped a subway to City Hall and did it. Grabbed the nearest person as a witness, a pregnant Puerto Rican woman ready to pop. There was a timer ticking during the whole ceremony, we were shaking with laughter the whole way through."

Constipated smiles.

Delphine lit an L and M. "I've never met a man like Jake. The others are so stuffy. Cookie-cutter men. Saint Paul's, Yale, Wall Street, all marching in lock step. You can see the end before you've even begun. They're so bored — so bor*ing* — already. Petrified of what other people think, scared of their own shadow. I mean, the only exciting thing Dudley Hunnewell's ever done is set himself on fire." A snort of exasperation. "Jake doesn't give a damn what other people think. I mean, here he is an architect, a crap shoot of a profession. Only a few titans make it, the rest starve. And he's willing to gamble, even though he's poor as a churchmouse. I'd gamble on Jake's talent too. As much as I'd gamble on my own. Jake — Jake is all I could want in a man."

Gina inspected her glass for stains. "What will your mother say?" asked Daisy.

"Luckily Mother's gone to the Galápagos. To mollify her, we'll produce a proper church wedding next June. Announcements, photo by Bachrach, the works. If I can swing it, we'll never tell her we're already married. Oh face it, no matter what I do, Mother will have a shitfit. She's always been jealous of me and my accomplishments — never used her own brain except to plan buffet menus. And jealous of my sex life; Daddy died so young. First thing she'll ask, 'Is he in the Social Register?' God, Jake Mikulski? A second-generation Pole from Greenpoint, Brooklyn? Well, Mother will just have to adjust."

Gina reached into her bag and consulted her compact.

Delphine's head swiveled from her to Daisy, skipping Sally, who sat in between.

"Dammit, you people are really something. I don't give a good goddamn about Mother. Can't you see I want" — her voice broke — "I'm asking for your blessing." She locked her arms across her chest. "Goddamn it to hell, could you just *pretend* to be happy for me?"

Coming before Labor Day, summer's grand finale, Gerrit's silence felt particularly ominous. Time became distended; each day dawned indifferent and rosy, massed with the others, gathering cumulative force and insult, pressing in with bands of steel on Daisy's skull. She felt as though she were waiting on her own execution. By day eight, as she was planning Gerrit's — she had him face down at Time Inc. in a pool of his own blood — the phone rang.

He missed her, came the nasal honk. He'd been subbing for four other slaveys who were away on vacation, he'd been inundated with work, etc. "Listen, I know this is short notice, but could you come to Binky's place for the weekend? I'm dying for you two to meet. Please say you'll come."

Daisy spluttered that she had to check her calendar.

"You've got to come; I can't face Binky's hordes of relatives without you. We'll go sailing, I'll show you around Mattapoisett in the Land Rover. Oh, and Daisy?"

"Yes?"

"I won't let you alone all night."

After they hung up, she leapt from the swing and let out a great whoop of joy. Everyone knew what it meant when they introduced you to family. It meant you were on the Magic Mystery Express bound for somewhere.

On the train to New Bedford he amused her with anecdotes about Mattapoisett. A village of Victorian frame houses on Buzzards Bay, across from Cape Cod, its dearest hope was to remain sealed off from the rest of the world. "No new families have arrived for generations. Without an infusion of new blood, we'll soon have an upper-crust version of the Hatfields and McCoys. Like our friends across the aisle." He gestured with his head at a slack-mouthed couple.

She loved Gerrit's mockery of his own clan; it thickened *their* complicity.

"I sometimes think if a Negro or Jew crossed the town line, a siren would go off. Don't worry, with your Irish coloring, you'll pass."

Daisy's smile faded. "Uh-unhh, now remember" — waggling his finger — "no melodrama."

He kissed her. It was like nectar, her thighs loosened, she went weak all over, right there on the train. Even though Hatfield and McCoy, across the aisle, had turned full around to watch. Gerrit pulled a yellow sou'wester over them and got the fly of his chinos unzipped and his hand snaked into her underpants. "Ever ready," he murmured in her ear. In her hand his hardness felt mineral. She came painfully, through the ends of her nerves, then felt him beating into her palm. The clackety-clack of the train. He reached into the L. L. Bean bag for a towel. The sink in the train toilet emitted only a hiss of pipes.

"I'm *sooo* pleased Gerrit finally brought you round." Brenda Chatfield kissed Daisy on both cheeks — *sooo* European — and grasped her hands, one of them scented with essence of Gerrit. "I've been [pronounced bean] so eager to meet you."

She'd gotten Binky wrong, thought Daisy, eyeing her surreptitiously from her wicker rocker on the veranda, where the clan had gathered for cocktails. The royal mother was no Grace Kelly. She was Lauren Bacall. A tawny edition, with heavy sunstreaked hair coiled at the nape, and the sleek lines of a racing craft. And that strangely vulnerable loose mouth.

The gin sluiced through Daisy. Here she was, in the cool white epicenter of America. A sagging porch that overlooked a lawn sweeping to the sea. A stone goldfish pond, Old Glory snapping in the breeze. The late sun spangled the water in the harbor, where sailboats rode at anchor. Daisy glanced at the peeling paint on the ceiling, shifted her weight on the lumpy pancake cushioning her wicker rocker — Why did they make a fetish of seediness? Gerrit sat across from her, leg crossed at the knee, *charming* everyone with tales of Time Inc. follies. He looked, for once, untortured. In his natural habitat. He seemed to have forgotten her presence. Now, now, no melodrama.

The talk had switched to sailing. Daisy tuned in and out of chatter about "running before the wind" and "reaching" and "stiff breezes" — she had never guessed the conversational potential of wind. Then her ear picked up the word *Venice*. Someone had just asked Binky about her trip to Italy.

"The place was swarming with peu-fectly ghastly tourists, so loud, the sort that give America a bad name," she said in her booze-and-tobacco-cured voice. She added, "The Cipriani was simply *inundated.*"

Gerrit shot Binky a startled look. Intercepted by Daisy; her euphoria dropped to half mast.

Gerrit winked at Daisy. Abruptly stood and reached for her glass. "May I get you some more of that?"

The last sun struck dazzling sparks off the water. From afar hooters lowed, warning ships off shoals.

Binky turned toward Daisy. "Tell me, deah, where are your people from?"

It was all going so well! She and Binky watched each other like rivalrous fowl in a barnyard, yet Binky was cordial enough, in her languid way. She even complimented Daisy on her peu-fectly charming dress, an orange and pink disaster made of Orlon that kept pilling.

Friday night they made love in Gerrit's little room under the eaves. The pine walls smelled of sea rot; the house had entrapped the sea in its very frame. They smothered their cries in the pillows, then their laughter. Stretched beneath him, her body cupping his in a perfect fit, Daisy knew — absurd thought — she'd beaten out Binky.

Such merriment! It was hard to keep pace. She was always lagging behind tempo; compared to the Chatfields, she was a lumbering yeti. Mentally, too; no one here was analyzing Wittgenstein; in this crowd introspection was bad form. The goal was to *play* till you dropped, perish of "good fun." They screeched into the driveway in Austin Healys and MGs, kicking up a spray of gravel. Fresh from doubles at the club, they were barely sweating. In no time, ice clinked in glasses and the clan assembled on the front lawn for varsity croquet, Daisy cheering Gerrit on from the sidelines. The thunk of wood on wood. "Christ hey," said Drudy. "Good fun!" said Binky. "Neat-o!" cried Meg. All the females had muskratty features and smiled with more gum than teeth. All the males had white-blond hair on their heads and glinting off their terrier legs. A dozen people had two names to go round: variants on Margaret or Andrew.

Such merriment! The party shifted to the *Ainslee,* a fifty-foot ketch. They pitched and rolled over Buzzards Bay, lubed with bloody Marys and something called bullshots. Daisy clutched any solid object within reach, a sporting smile sprayed on with fixative, marveling that the smartly heeling boat didn't flip them into the brine.

Saturday night — was it only *Saturday*? — they were due at Townsend Crawford's. "Townie is my godfather," Gerrit told Daisy as they bounced over in the Land Rover. "He's a crusty old banker from Philadelphia, the city's leading patron of culture. Without Townie, well, the museum, the symphony, simply wouldn't exist. He's a bit of a boozer, but quite delightful. I know you'll enjoy him."

No sign or mailbox betrayed the existence of Crawford's colonial revival clapboard, vast as an institution. It occupied a neck on Buzzards Bay that offered a view of Naushon Island, words everyone pronounced with reverence because it was owned by the Forbeses.

The more Townie drank, Daisy noticed, the lighter he grew. Weaving among his guests, he was now practically airborne, like a small dirigible. She was pretty airborne herself, though to stay up here she might soon need a "transfusion" — Mattapoisett did stretch the vocabulary. The "sauce" was important. Without it she might feel like a Hottentot at Buckingham Palace. She found it hard to contribute when Drudy and Madge — or Andy and Meg? — reminisced about the Snowflake Cotillion. Or a bash at Dark Harbor's Tarratine Yacht Club. Now they were discussing plans to sail down Eggemoggin Reach on the yacht of a man so far right he'd become a mascot of the left.

The phrase "Kill a Commie for Christ" scrolled through Daisy's brain.

Guests surged toward the clam shucker, opening up a vista, and Daisy spotted Gerrit and Binky. They violated the dress code. Gerrit was costumed in a white tennis sweater and white ducks, a visitation from *Brideshead Revisited*. Binky inhabited floaty yellow chiffon, hair tucked up forties style around the nape. She in no way resembled the dowdy wives in their flowered cotton frocks and oatmeal cardigans with grosgrain ribbon down the center. The handsome couple! Their elbows and hips formed congruent angles, as though they were ballroom dancers taking a break. Binky's face was lifted toward Gerrit; he smiled down at her.

The thought massed dark and murderous behind Daisy's eyes, blinding her: Those two were sleeping together. It was perfectly plain in their geometry; how could you miss it? That was it — the picture! The picture behind the scrim! Didn't everyone see it? She looked wildly about.

She moved away from the offending sight and leaned back against someone's chair. Solid, at least. Out on the horizon Naushon Island started to spin.

"Wouldn't trust Drucker, he'd take the gold right out of your teeth," came a familiar voice behind her.

Daisy swiveled her head and saw the sun-blistered top of Crawford's bald dome, his green pants, his cranberry claw grasping a tall glass. He sat in a circle of green pants and red pants. One face was lobster pink. It began singing what sounded like a school song; other drunken voices chimed in.

"Heard the one about the Jewish and the Irish sewer cleaners?" said Crawford.

Daisy was brimming over with her recent illumination, but she kept an ear cocked.

"The Irishman's gotta pass a shovelful of shit up to the Jew, who's working on top. Every night when he comes home, his wife says, 'Paddy, you smell like shit. It's in yerr face, yerr hair — I'd rather wash a rat than touch ya.'"

Applause and guffaws; they loved the Irish brogue, Crawford did the harridan wife to perfection. The lobster was laughing too hard, his laugh went into *Haaaagh . . . aaaagh,* then furious deep coughing.

"So the Irishman greases a palm or two, and *he* gets to be the man on top, while the Jew is down in the sewer."

From a distance Gerrit waved gaily and snaked toward her.

"'Annie,' he tells his wife, 'I've got a great piece of news for ya. Yerr goin' to be so glad. I won't be smellin' so vile anymore. Now Moe is down in the sewer —"

Moe, they loved it. The lobster was weeping — *Haaaagh . . .* He'd taken off his glasses to wipe his eyes.

"'— And now *Moe* passes up the shit to *me.*'"

Gerrit glided over, smiling, his eyes bottle green in the late light, the sea air crimping his hair.

"'*Glad*?' Annie says to him. 'And why should I be *glad*? Now — on top of everything else — now you've got to take shit from a *Jew*?'"

Barks, howls. *Haaaagh . . . aaaagh.* The lobster crumpled forward over his knees.

Gerrit took her arm, but she pulled away and walked carefully, setting one foot before the other over the grass, onto a narrow strip of sand, over blackish seaweed, out onto a pier, and then kept walking with careful measured steps to the end of the pier. The low sun scribbled a bronze pathway over the water. The pier heaved and creaked with each sea swell; far out the groaners lowed. Daisy had turned remarkably sober.

Gerrit had followed her out. "C'mon, Townie's blitzed out of his mind, he's just a sloppy drunk."

"*Sloppy?*"

"Now c'mon, you promised. No melodrama. Townie's my godfather. He's an old, old family friend. Look, I'm sorry, okay? What do you want? I mean, where've you been? People say these things. I'm not my godfather's keeper."

Daisy focused unseeing on the bronze waves. She'd slammed nose first into a giant underwater bunker. This was real, nothing here but this.

"Please, I'd like to go home."

Gerrit shrugged. The expiring sun had bruised the sky purple and green. Just beyond the light lurked a terrible amount of darkness.

"Back to New York," she added unnecessarily.

Gerrit skipped an oyster shell into the chop. Bad throw, it dribbled away. He skipped another shell: it curved out over the water in four clean jumps, maybe five.

"Suit yourself," he said.

The next day at noon they drove in silence to the station in Binky's Land Rover. The station was deserted; no one left Mattapoisett at noon in the middle of Labor Day weekend. She watched Gerrit switch off the ignition. The only sound was the electric thrum of insects, rhythmically waxing and waning. A tender scent of honeysuckle hung in the air. She stared at his hand, lying palm down on his thigh. It seemed the most distant point in the universe.

He got out of the car and lifted her bag from the back seat. He moved with swift efficient motions, like the Chatfields playing croquet. He carried her bag to the platform and stood next to her on the platform. The noon sun blasted down on them. Daisy realized he was waiting with her for the train.

She focused across the track at an ad for *Bridge on the River Kwai.* Since everything was smashed, she said, "You're making it with Binky, aren't you?"

"I hate that voice of yours." Gerrit bent awkwardly at the waist and peered down the tracks.

"The Cipriani, Venice," said Daisy to his yellow-shirted back. "She was 'the only one that mattered.' And I'm the, uh, camouflage."

"Very good, Miss Marple." He turned and regarded her curiously, shading his eyes from the sun. "You know, you're *sick*," he said with a kind of awe. "That is a really sick mind to think of such a thing."

A muffled roar. She saw the train's light, redundant in the sunlight; it grew larger, an oncoming Cyclops.

"I don't want to see you anymore," Gerrit said into the rising roar.

He remained standing next to her on the platform until the train chuffed and clanked into the station.

Chapter 11

THE COMMENCEMENT SPEAKER for the class of '58 was Frank Lloyd Wright, complete with black prairie hat. To receive their diplomas, the graduating class filed slowly toward Westlands under the long trellis. It was now a tunnel of wisteria, slightly monstrous, a topiary boudoir. The lavender-blue blossoms and cloying scent suggested lost afternoons with Blanche DuBois, subverted the onward-and-upward spirit of the occasion. Long after they had forgotten Wright's exhortations to "break the mold" — and his excursions, midceremony, to the john — the class of '58 would remember the treasonous sicky-sweet scent of wisteria.

Delphine Mortimer delivered the commencement address. Standing on the flagstone terrace in front of Westlands, she looked out over a sea of fresh, clear-eyed faces owning the future. Among them were Diana Dew Hilliard and Franca Broadwater Tabori, both pregnant; they'd come up to see old friends and go to the parties.

"We have been *understood* as no generation before us," Delphine intoned. Birds twittered; nervous glances were exchanged: unclear whether "understood" was pejorative or positive. But the ambiguity had a satisfying ring of profundity.

Twenty of the eighty-member class of '58 seated before her were married. Half the remaining group had already mailed engraved invitations to a June wedding; the other half would probably have jumped at any proposal. Delphine herself planned to marry — technically, *re-marry* — Jacob Mikulski the following Sunday in Newport, Rhode Island.

The Kober House hell raiser had hardly, as promised, become a "cow." Though delivered several months late, her article, "Voices from the Silent Generation," finally appeared in *The New York Times Sunday Magazine*. In her senior year Delphine became a local celebrity and precocious spokesman for her generation, such is the awesome power of the *Times*. She was courted and feted, invited to contribute to panels on "Whither Courtship?" at the YMHA. *Glamour* magazine photographed her in a Dior trapeze dress, hovering over Jake at his drafting table; they prefigured the power couple. She was offered a job as a fact checker at *The New Yorker*. She kept them at arm's distance, finding journalism a bit superficial; she thought she might prefer to work in book publishing, and write her own stuff evenings and weekends.

Delphine was to be married in Newport, in the little stone chapel on the grounds of Rosecliff, where Merry Mortimer had been married. The reception would be held in the "great cottage."

"It's a *faux* Norman pile that's been in the family since the arrival of the Pilgrims," Delphine told her crowd. "Now occupied by my four spinster aunties, one loonier than the next."

For four years she'd had a painting of a mansion hanging in her dorm room, painted by Aunt Hildreth, and she'd never once mentioned it was Rosecliff. It perched precariously on limestone cliffs battered by the Atlantic. In stormy weather the waves sent up plumes of sea spray that watered the violet gentians sprouting between cracks in the slate courtyard. A fitting setting for Delphine's nuptials, her crowd agreed: hyperbolic, gothic, old-money cavalier — so like Delphine herself!

On the eve of the wedding, a nor'easter howled around the limestone cliffs, rattled Rosecliff's windows, poured through its sievelike French doors. Delphine sat on her father's blue velvet chair in the oak-paneled library, partied out after a two-day round. She'd seen enough Baccarat crystal and monogrammed silver to last a lifetime. Merry's friends had feted them at the Ida Lewis Yacht Club, and Jake had made a huge hit, but then Merry had spoiled it and started ranting about "pansies" and what they did in the sack, and Delphine had drunk way too much, even for her. Jake, she'd noticed, had kept pace. She leaned her head back and closed her eyes, envisioning the future unfurling before them like a carpet of flowers.

Her stomach flip-flopped and she tasted that taste — metallic, unmistakable — of hormones on the march. Dare she give Jake the news? Her ovaries had outwitted her diaphragm, and she was several weeks late. She had put off telling him because she didn't want to puncture his euphoria; he had a way of blaming her for news not to his liking. The timing couldn't be worse, really. How could they have a baby now, when she was about to start her new job as editorial assistant at Hollinsworth Publishing? And they were counting on their combined salaries to cover the rent for their new Village apartment, a parlor-level floor-through with exposed brick walls.

Jake poured them both a brandy against Rosecliff's permanent deep freeze. Outside, mockingbirds squeezed out ropes of song, the only indication it was June.

Suddenly Delphine remembered their vow to be "emotionally naked" with each other. Taking a deep breath, she told Jake she was pregnant. "But don't worry, darling. I'm not going to go all sentimental on you. Actually it might be amusing to honeymoon in Havana —"

"But darling, *I'm* sentimental. How absolutely marvelous. Forget Havana." He pulled her to her feet and waltzed her clumsily around, calling her *petite maman*. Then his arms fell to his sides and he turned very still, eyes fixed on the middle distance.

"That'll show them."

Delphine's stomach flip-flopped; her mouth went slack. "Show them? Show *whom*?" She collapsed heavily on the couch and covered her face with her hands. "Them" was undoubtedly Mimi Van Doorn, his first love. The Mimi affair had poisoned more than one evening. Old Van Doorn had snuffed the engagement in some despicable manner, and possibly also arranged an abortion. In his sleep Jake still ground his teeth in rage.

"I don't believe it, not that old nonsense again, not tonight," Delphine groaned. "Okay, why don't you tell me once and for all what happened, what did Van Doorn *do*? Oh God, why think of that on *our* night." He was jinxing their future.

Jake stood contemplating some happy vision, a smile curving his sultry mouth.

"I can't believe — have you fucking lost your mind?" She hurled her snifter of cognac across the room, striking a watercolor by Aunt Hildreth.

The crash of glass roused Jake from his trance.

"So you're marrying me because Mimi Van Doorn, the original pea brain, wouldn't have you. Oh, wait — I get it! — in your twisted mind, knocking me up is your revenge on the whole fucking family!" Jake blinked at her, surprised to be in the path of a hurricane. "I do believe you're still in love with that dumb cunt." Delphine rose unsteadily and approached him. "Don't think I haven't seen your stash of photos in your sock drawer. D'you jerk off over them? I'm nothing but a symbol to you," she cried out, half to herself.

"Why are you starting a fight? *Tonight?* Why must you always ruin everything?"

Delphine was a rotten drunk; once she landed in a groove, she bombed down it, pulling everything down around her. The way she kept repeating "dumb cunt" jump-tripped Jake's rage; Jake on the sauce could produce a fancy temper all his own. He seized her wrist and twisted. He wanted just to silence her voice. He twisted and twisted, bending her sideways to the floor, and she screamed, "I'm pregnant, you bastard." He let go her wrist, suddenly frightened for both of them, and Delphine fell heavily on her side, taking a standing lamp with her. It shattered on the floor and the room went dark. Jake flung open the French doors and walked out onto the terrace, where the ocean's roar canceled human voices.

God had delivered ideal weather for the wedding: young June sun in a purple-blue sky, rinsed air fragrant with roses and orange blossoms — a shamelessly gorgeous day from *Bride's* magazine, an all-American sweetheart of a day.

Well before two, guests began assembling in a grassy courtyard in front of Rosecliff's little chapel. Daisy took in the weathered stone walls encrusted with lichen, the pink roses clambering up its sides, the little graveyard out back, its stone crosses askew — and saw the intertwined ghosts of Cathy and Heathcliff.

The cryptlike chill from the chapel fingered her even out here in the sun. She shivered in her lavender cotton dress with plunging neck — a bit Jane Russell for a wedding, she knew, but it was that or last year's pilling Orlon number. She had a touch of stage fright. Their group's first wedding had been Franca's extravaganza the last fall at The Country Club in Brookline. Something here, though, felt volatile, dangerously combustible. The mix of guests maybe.

The Mortimer side had "motored" from Boston, or Bedminster, the fox hunt and gin zone of New Jersey. The wives wore navy head-hugging hats with veils over tight mousy curls. Their husbands were apoplexy pink and walked as if their balls were on fire. They glanced around uncertainly, thinking Merry would have done better to pack Delphine off to Radcliffe, or even Sweet Briar, instead of that appalling Sarah Lawrence, which promoted free love and Godless communism. But at least the dear girl would be safely married; and of course she was *one of us*.

Delphine's four aunts hovered in a cluster next to the roses. They were horse-faced and hairy and mad as hatters. One giggled like a shy debutante, with a handkerchief held to her mouth. Aunt Hildreth, tormented by hormones, had a baritone and a mustache; she cradled Henry, her dirty white Yorkshire terrier and constant companion. Delphine's friends sometimes wondered if she worried about heredity.

Meredith Mortimer stalked about on stiff legs, navigating with the exaggerated care of the practiced lush. She was tall and regal as a clipper ship, with round eyes and a homicidal smile. The old girl was putting as good a face on it as she could. "So nice to see you," she croaked at Delphine's friends, delivering a blast of bourbon. "Please call me Merry."

The groom's side was represented only by a few Columbia College types hiding behind black-rimmed glasses and bushy beards. Mr. and Mrs. Mikulski, of Greenpoint, Brooklyn, had the tact to be dead.

The Sarah Lawrence contingent, in earth colors and dyed cotton stockings, drew alarmed glances. Sally November wore a huge Floradora girl hat laden with posies, a parody of proper millinery, and as for her décolletage . . . Gina Gold, as she now called herself, wore a hat like an upturned straw bowl and powder blue Chanel suit — a copy she'd bought at Loehmann's. She snaked among the guests, scribbling quotes on an impressive reporter's pad. She was writing up the Mortimer-Mikulski nuptials for *Town and Country*. She actually had in tow a photographer sent by the magazine. (So tasteless to court publicity, murmured a Mortimer from the Back Bay.)

Peter Tabori hovered, solicitous, over Franca, who was hugely pregnant. Following her blackmail trip to England, as she privately called it, he'd proven a model husband: attentive, adoring, a little dazed, like a man who has survived a near-fatal accident. "Don't you want to sit down for a bit?" Peter inquired anxiously. Franca laughed. "I doubt whether the mere act of standing brings on labor." "But isn't it chilly out here for you — you know, you two?" he joked. To stop his fussing, she sent him to the car to fetch her Scottish wool shawl.

Delphine had invited her old beaux from Groton and Andover, explaining, "I feel closest to people I've fucked." Several old beaux had tooled in from Cambridge or New Haven in black hearses, the vehicle of choice that year on Ivy campuses. They eyed the fluttering SLC contingent like foxes surveying a henhouse. Daisy pictured them twenty years down the line, these golden eligibles Delphine had fought off since adolescence. They would arrive at their Princeton "homecoming" and tailgate parties wearing straw boaters, grizzled and porky and pickled in booze, but otherwise unchanged. Old boys. Oh God, there was Kurt Zimmer with the missus, who pretended not to recognize her. Daisy prayed not to see Dudley Hunnewell; he might still be nuts enough to play human pyre for the occasion.

Suddenly her eye was drawn to a handsome usher sniffing the roses. (Ushers were Delphine's only concession to Merry; "I refuse to be *given away* by a male authority figure, and I want to walk alone to the altar.") Daisy watched the usher inhale from a tiny flat roach, snuff it against a mashed packet, carefully replace it, and bend to smell the roses. He had delicate features and a naturally bobbed nose that looked almost mismatched with his chunky frame. Beneath the cutaway peeped dirty white topsiders. Uh-oh, a rebel preppy, her nemesis. Topsiders caught her watching. His black Irish eyes beamed mischief; his lips, still holding the joint, curved in a wry smile. Why did she recognize that smile?

"Let's hope the groom isn't marrying for money," came a voice at her ear.

As Kurt Zimmer kissed her, Daisy smelled the Chanel after-shave she had once smelled on Delphine. The dark shock of hair still hung across his brow, but Zimmer had gone fat and pouchy, like a capon.

"And if the groom *is*?" said Daisy with sudden concern.

"Be a damn shame, since Merry's been going into principal for years. And no luck selling Rosecliff. Historic landmarks are unheatable, and every winter the ocean eats a chunk of beachfront. It's your classic white elephant."

Delphine always bitched about Merry's tightness, but was the family actually bankrupt? The weird part was that Delphine wouldn't have concealed it from guile; she'd probably never thought about it.

"At least Jake's getting pedigrees, with all the perks: the River Club, the Brook, the Ida Lewis Yacht Club . . . And the happy couple won't want for invitations. Blood's thicker than money. Even when the dough runs out, tribal loyalty prevails."

Why this sourness? Could Zimmer be having regrets?

He lit his pipe and surveyed her. "Don't *you* look ravishing — lavender is your color. You're all so lovely. La Delphine, a Grace by Rossetti. Franca a little Rhine maiden. And now Ginny. When did she become a sloe-eyed beauty? When I was in love with Delphine —" He caught himself, then tapped Daisy's arm with his index finger. "*You* knew. Anyway it's all past history — *Où sont les neiges d'antan?* — and I've grown lazy and fat." He patted his paunch. "Ah yes, I think I was in love with all of you, collectively, a frieze of maidens. In love with your prodigal youth, your moment of perfect beauty."

During this speech, Daisy scratched Topsiders from her dance card. He looked poised to dive into Sally November's cleavage.

Zimmer followed Daisy's eyes. "Oops, there you go. You all have appalling taste in men. It's your fatal flaw, the one that'll do you in. You all — your whole group, curiously — go for cruel, flashy men. All style, no content. Let's see how long Jake sticks around once Delphine runs through her trust fund. As for the young man ogling Miss November — Fletcher someone — Delphine used to call him the Hun of Hanover. He was famous at Dartmouth for hurling a piano out the second-floor window of his frat house. I'm warning you against yourself because you're a person of consequence. You've got a mind like a glass bell. But for God's sake, find yourself a good man and get married. I'm talking now as your friend, Daisy."

"Joseph Campbell always tells his class, 'Follow your bliss.' "

"He must have meant wedded bliss." Zimmer rubbed his hands together. "Nippy out here in the sea air, sun's deceptive. I hope they serve venison at the reception. Knowing Merry, we'll get cucumber sandwiches."

"But why should we even think about marriage right now?" Daisy

persisted, unnerved. "We've got big plans." She ticked them off: Gina
an editorial assistant at *Town and Country;* Mia Sils-Levy starring in
an off-Broadway production of *Antigone;* Grace Omura working as a
lighting designer with the Living Theater. Delphine was skipping the
honeymoon to start at Hollinsworth Publishing. She omitted Sally
November, who was peddling a novel she'd written on toilet paper
over spring break in Fort Lauderdale.

"And what about you, Daisy, what happened to your dancing?"

"Oh, I'm going to live in a garret in Paris and write the great American novel," she threw out. Suddenly she wanted to drop the subject;
her sense of purpose was too fragile to expose to Zimmer's blitzkrieg.

"Lemme tell you something." He took her arm, and they strolled
along the edge of the courtyard. "Manhattan is filled with hordes of
young women just like you. Liberal arts majors working in publishing,
magazines, art galleries, none of it paying a living wage, of course.
They're fine, those little jobs, but just keep your eye on your number
one priority: marrying a good man. Because that's where your future
lies. I would only say this to someone like you, Daisy; you like to deal
in truth. Never Delphine." His bushy brows shot up. "A grand, delicious girl! But when it comes to her self-interest? Not playing with a
full deck. Who but Delphine would invite a psychotic ex-beau to her
wedding?"

"So why not just skip the little jobs and grab the first nice professional?"

"No, no. *Go* to Paris, my dear, and write for a year. It'll make you
more interesting to a man who's had his nose to the grindstone, preparing to be a good provider." He lit his pipe. Waved his hand excitedly through the smoke. "Think of Moira Shearer. She gave it all
up — dance, art, acclaim — to marry some journalist type and live in
the country. You can't imagine a happier woman."

How the hell did Zimmer know whether Moira Shearer was happy?
And how easy at SLC to forget what the rest of young womanhood
wanted: the provider, the suburbs, Sunday barbecues, togetherness.
What if she woke up in Paris one morning and couldn't figure out the
next step?

"Well, I'd better go find my wife," said Zimmer, his face suddenly
sheepish. "She was none too eager to come, I can tell you."

·   ·   ·

"Lordy, d'you *love* this scene?" said Sally, undulating over. She thrust out her tits and stretched her long neck, like a dodo preening. Out the corner of her mouth: "I dunno about you, babe, but I been workin' the weddin'. No more lust in the dust. I mean, Rudi Urdang wants to play the flute in an orchestra in the boonies. What kind of life is that? I'm in search of serious husband material, Yale Law, a man with ambition and a future." She cocked her head at Daisy. "Speaking of lust in the dust" — Daisy struggled to compose an exit line, though rudeness barely registered on Sally; what a blessing to be insensitive — "remember that gorgeous beau of yours, Garrett, Derek, someone?"

Daisy succeeded in keeping her face stony; this was progress. Though she had a way to go, considering the Tinker Bell dancing in her gut.

"Well, Rudi says Garrett never came back to Harvard. What I heard was — *Wheesh,* this is wild. Garrett was having an affair with his stepmother — you know, his father's wife? And then the old man walks in on them at her place on the Cape. And he's pissed as hell, the old man, even though he hasn't lived with his wife in years. And he cuts Garrett off, won't even pay his tuition to Harvard."

Sally's voice was coming from far away and her cherry lips jumped and jived like a cartoon character's.

"And now Garrett's run off to Mykonos with Lucien Chatfield, his stepbrother. Have I got it right? You practically need a diagram to keep it all straight. Rudi says Lucien is queer, and you know Rudi never maligns anyone. Does that mean Garrett is bisexual? Well, *you* oughta know!" Sally licked her right index finger and tidied a spit curl. "I'm off to *chercher le* husband. Why else did our parents sacrifice to send us to Sadie Lou?"

Daisy wouldn't give Sally satisfaction. "You know what I like about you? You've got real class."

Sally stared at her. "Well, who're you?" she said, waggling her head, "Miss Toplofty?" And she pushed off.

All the color was leached from the day. Even though she'd known it, of course. She'd fucking known all along.

She must have been swaying in the breeze, here was Topsiders grasping her elbows, holding her steady. She felt wonderfully cared for in his hands.

"I saw you looking so wobbly suddenly. Are you all right?"

"Oh, just a passing attack of vapors," said Daisy, raising a hand to her brow.

"I've been dying to talk to you ever since I saw you in the church-yard."

His voice a sweet Irish tenor, soothing her. "Gosh, I just remembered where I've seen you. On Delphine's bureau. In college she had a photo of a bunch of people on a boat. A ketch. Or a sloop."

Amused smile: "A yawl. The *Saskia*. Merry Mortimer's boat." He rolled his eyes, as everyone did at the mention of Merry. Daisy noticed that his were bloodshot.

She refrained from admitting she'd had a crush on the helmsman in the photo, hair damp with sea spray, cigarette butt clamped Bogey-style between his lips — and the same devastating smile now before her.

"Where can I find you after today?" he said urgently. "I don't want to lose you."

Great, five minutes in and they dreaded losing you. "Try the café Deux Magots on the Boulevard Saint Germain."

"You have a Fulbright?"

"Oh, nothing so respectable. I'm just going to Paris to" — snapping her fingers — "make the scene."

"Far out. I've never met a girl who wasn't traveling on a dumb teen tour with a thousand chaperones. Betcha the rest of your class is marrying a doctor or a stockbroker. Or going to Katie Gibbs to learn shorthand until they meet a doctor or a stockbroker."

"I'd rather write poetry at the table where Sartre wrote *Being and Nothingness*." Envisioning this bliss, she half shut her eyes. "And then I'll move on to the Select, Hemingway's café, for a Pernod. And I'll look up my friends the Beat poets in their flophouse on the Rue Gît le Coeur. Then on to Oxford, with its pink roses and gray spires. I'll travel at my own rhythm, accountable to no one. I'll hit the Côte d'Azur and sleep in student hostels, and hitch a ride to Munich, and travel along the Neckar River on a motor scooter with a German too young to be a Nazi. I'll travel light and late, like a murderer or double agent. Arrive in French towns in the dead of night, shuttered up and silent in the moonlight. If the Hôtel de Gare is closed, I'll sleep on a bench at the *gare*."

Fletcher glanced around to make certain no one could hear. "Listen, I know this sounds like a line, but wait for me."

Was he stoned? "Uh, where should I wait? The Deux Magots?"

"Don't" — Fletcher's eyes narrowed and his jaw clamped — "Don't dismiss me. Wait for me to graduate. I'm serious." His chin thrust up and his eyes dared her to mock. "I'm a sophomore," he added.

An organ started up, thank God. From deep within the church sounded the ceremonial strains of milestone occasions. Daisy's throat tightened; tears welled in her eyes. Oh, she was a sentimental slob, must come from her forebears in Minsk. Ushers started escorting guests to their pews. One offered his arm to Aunt Hildreth, tactfully ignoring Henry, clutched to her bosom.

"Ma'am?" said Fletcher with a little bow. He gave Daisy his arm and escorted her into the chapel.

It was as bone chilling as promised. The Mortimer side sat ramrod erect, inured to cold by cruising in the Gulf of Maine. Sunlight fired up the stained glass, the blues were the blue of paradise. The radiant colors, white lilies, and polished stone; the organist, seated to the right of the altar, playing Bach and pumping away with his feet; the light beams forming stairways to heaven and dancing with motes; the carved oak of the stalls; the musty, venerable smells, an odor of Episcopalian well-being — Who would not be seduced by such atmospherics?

Suddenly Fletcher materialized at her pew, slipped her a little bouquet of honeysuckle, and not missing a beat, swiveled with a squeak and sauntered duck-footed up the aisle.

She closed her eyes and inhaled the scent of honeysuckle. An electric thrum of insects, a sound she still woke to at four A.M., in a sweat. Brenda Chatfield, the color of topaz, saying in her booze-and-tobacco-cured voice, "So pleased Gerrit has finally brought you round . . . *sooo* pleased . . . sooo very pleased."

After the Mattapoisett caper, she had sheared off her hair and worn all black. She exuded unavailability, laughing and flirting from another dimension, gesturing with her Dunhill cigarette holder; appeared glamorously wounded, pregnant with disillusion, like Sally Bowles or Lady Brett. Beneath the pose she felt poisoned at her core, like factory workers who have handled radium. She cringed before the hand lifted to strike, and always expected the hand to strike. And now

Fletcher the Hun. What could she fear? She was beyond harm. In his careless way, Gerrit had ruined her.

Something, Daisy realized, was amiss. From his niche on the side of the church, the organist had regaled them with Mendelssohn, Bach, Vivaldi. Now he'd come full circle and was back to Purcell's "Trumpet Voluntary." He cast desperate glances at the little wooden door to the vestry.

"What, is this a musicale?" said a voice from deepest Brooklyn behind Daisy.

One of Jake's smart-ass friends. People stirred restively and heads turned toward the entrance to the church, where any moment now, surely, the lovely bride would appear. To judge by lengthening shadows outside, the hour was advancing.

A tall figure in a veiled hat moved stiffly down the aisle, silk rustling, glancing from left to right. The mother of the bride. Sighting Daisy, she bent, bones creaking. "Come with me, deah."

Daisy tried not to recoil from bouquet of bourbon.

All eyes converged on them as Mendelssohn rang them up the aisle and into the perfect June day.

Outside it was twenty degrees warmer. Hand shaking, Merry lit a Pall Mall with a monogrammed silver lighter. "She'll do anything to disgrace me. Talk to her, for mercy's sake."

Merry led Daisy round the side of the church to the door of the vestry. "I'll leave you alone, she won't listen to me. I always knew she would do this to me." Her eyes watered at the enormity of it and she walked unsteadily off.

Delphine stood in the vestry like a painting of a Spanish infanta. She wore a billowing cream satin gown that pulled across the midsection. An antique lace veil fastened to a tiara of seed pearls half covered her upswept auburn hair. Her eyes, the pearls, the satin of her gown, gleamed in the sepia light. She had never been more beautiful.

"I can't go through with this marriage. I'm pregnant."

Daisy reflected a moment. "But isn't that all the more reason to press on?"

The set of Delphine's features announced determination not to cry. Daisy guessed she didn't want to ruin her makeup, a hopeful sign.

"Are you worried the baby will be born too soon, so to speak? C'mon, who cares. Just the dowagers and stuffed shirts."

Delphine snorted. "If it were only that."

A cruel idea struck Daisy. "Jake doesn't want the baby?"

"Oh no, he *wants* the baby. That's just the problem." Her eyes glittered, her lip trembled dangerously. She steadied herself with her arm lock. Daisy sat on a little oak chair by the door and waited while she fought for control.

Delphine recapped the scene from the night before. "I'm not even a woman to him," she said savagely. A tear rolled down her cheek. Daisy handed her a crumpled Kleenex. "So now you understand why I can't go through with this marriage," she said with finality, peering down at her cream satin toes.

"But what do we do with all these people? You can't just hightail it out of here."

"Oh? Why not? Men abandon *women* at the altar, or just before."

"Well, for one thing, we don't have keys to a car." Daisy groped for a better reason. Circumstances rather narrowed the options. "The fact remains, you love that man."

"Oh, Daisy, how can you be so simple." When in trouble, Delphine always attacked; she'd berate the lifesaver hauling her in. "That was before Jake said what he said last night," she added.

"He was just drunk."

"In vino veritas."

Merry's face loomed at the door. "This is a fucking disgrace. If you don't come along this instant . . ."

"Oh dear, Mother's looped," Delphine muttered. "Just one more moment, Mother," she called. Reflectively: "Actually, I do still love Jake, that's the worst of it."

Daisy realized that Delphine wanted to be persuaded. Maybe she wanted the blessing she'd never given, not at Schrafft's that afternoon or ever, from grief at losing Delphine to a husband.

"You know what?" Daisy said. "I think you're a coward. You don't have the guts to really take a stand, put your mouth where your money is."

"I think it goes the other way around."

"No matter. You used to attack June brides, then you went and got married yourself, because that's what you *really* wanted, that's *you*, Delphine. And now you're just too goddamn stubborn to admit it. As for Jake, he adores you, you're perfect together. But you can't expect him not to resent those people, they treated him like shit. You'll heal him. He'll get past his anger, once you have the baby. God, I sound like the *Ladies' Home Journal,* and 'Can This Marriage Be Saved?' "

Merry loomed darkly in the doorway, making Daisy start; with her big shoulders Merry resembled a linebacker in drag. Fletcher appeared behind her, eyes flashing mischief.

"Well?" Merry rasped.

"Oh hi, Fletcher," Delphine drawled in a bored tone. "Fletcher McHenry, Daisy Frank. Fletcher is Mother's godson."

Topsiders gave a military salute. Daisy stifled an urge to laugh.

"Dearie, I know we agreed you'd walk down the aisle alone. But it's just never done. You heard Reverend Wortham. Frankly, I don't blame you for balking. Fletcher here has offered to pinch-hit and give you away. Haven't you, deah?"

Delphine turned her back to them all, like an actress preparing an impersonation. "I'll be along in a moment," came her muffled voice.

When Merry and Fletcher had left, she wheeled around. "Oh fuck. Daisy, what the fuck am I doing?"

This was no time for the long answer. "You're taking the leap. An existential leap." Daisy smiled at her.

Delphine stared at Daisy for a moment, then smiled back. "That's right. I'm taking an existential leap."

They grinned at each other like maniacs. The smile faded from Delphine's face.

"Pray for me," she said.

They walked arm in arm into blinding sunlight. A darning needle darted past, its blue tail iridescent. They walked past the roses and honeysuckle to the entrance of the church. In the parking lot, a car door slammed. Daisy wondered who the latecomer might be. She saw with a shudder that it was Dudley Hunnewell.

From inside the church, the organist struck up, newly emphatic, the opening notes of Purcell's "Trumpet Voluntary." At the entrance Fletcher offered Delphine his arm and flashed Daisy a smile, quite the loveliest thing she'd seen all day.

She whispered in Delphine's ear, "You'll see, everything will be fine, after you have the baby."

"Baby?" said Delphine. *"What* baby?"

PART TWO

Chapter 12

1960

OCTOBER 1960

Class of '58 (Correspondent: Sally November)

Diana *Dew* Hilliard writes, "We just moved to Chevy Chase with Frank Jr., Sarah, and two English sheepdogs. Frank is at the State Department telling Secretary Dulles what to do."

Congratulations to Gina *Gold*, who is writing features for *Mademoiselle*.

Franca *Broadwater* Tabori's second son, Christopher, was born, appropriately, on Labor Day! Husband Peter is busy directing the Brattle Theatre's new production of Samuel Beckett's *Krapp's Last Tape*.

Grace *Omura* Yakamoto performed her "theater pieces" with husband Jun in Tokyo.

Delphine *Mortimer* Mikulski writes, "My husband Jake and I have just moved into a darling little apartment on 54th Street, overlooking the garden of the Museum of Modern Art."

Yours truly has just gotten engaged to Sheldon Wunderlick, a tax lawyer from Philadelphia! After a year as a practicing astrologer, and then a stint as a model (I did the Midol ads, "Bonnie's blue, now Bonnie's gay" — you know the ones!), I've been working as promotion assistant at Aspen Press. Daisy *Frank,* who never sends in her news — hisss, booo — has just gotten a job in Aspen's Publicity Department.

EVEN IN 1960, two years out of college, September for Daisy meant beginnings, as if the world ran on a giant academic calendar. This morning the city had been laundered by the first fall storm; a north breeze rustled the dry leaves of the sycamores, the air was quick with promise. She hurried east along Twelfth Street, wobbly in her new navy pumps, past the fig-colored brownstones with freshly painted doors and knockers of polished brass. Today was day one at her first real job in publishing, the dream glamour job of every female English major. She was on her way at last.

Ajax Books, a paperback reprint house, had been a mere detour. Marooned in a grungy cubicle, she typed contracts for sci-fi adventures, westerns, and murky whodunits by Ngaio Marsh, stuff that got printed on paper resembling regurgitated oatmeal. The big challenge was to guess from the mementos on his tie what her boss had eaten for lunch. She spent her own lunch hour warming metal chairs at Career Blazers. Or checking in with Personnel at Time Inc., famous for its big salaries and cute Yalies in red suspenders. A futile exercise; who were they kidding? To penetrate Time, you needed a daddy who'd circle-jerked with Henry Luce.

Then Delphine, who heard about it from Sally, phoned about the opening at Aspen Press. It was in Publicity, Delphine cautioned Daisy, the crass commercial end, and workers were paid better in Taiwan. But hell, Aspen was *the* place to be, the sassy bad boy of publishing, a thumb in the eye of bourgeois complacency. It specialized in the risqué and the avant-garde — Henry Miller, D. H. Lawrence, Jean Genet — the authors of those green-covered paperbacks hip Americans smuggled through Customs from France. Aspen's publisher, B. J. Everley, spent his days in court battling for unexpurgated versions, conducting a one-man crusade to make America safe for dirty books.

"Aspen is sort of the Sarah Lawrence of publishing," drawled Delphine in a lockjaw untarnished by two years in Manhattan. "Unfortunately there must be fifty Seven Sisters all panting for the job, all absurdly overqualified. Just be sure to use the word *challenging* three times during the interview, and leave the rest to me. A friend of the publicity director owes me one."

She'd be returning to her old dreams of art, but with a salary, thought Daisy, waiting for the light at Fifth. (Down and out in Paris was existential and romantic; in New York you were just a bum.) At Aspen Press she'd edit absurdist playwrights and avant-garde novelists, play midwife to genius, take authors to lunch. And evenings she'd write her Parisian memoir, *Here Lies the Heart,* named for the street of the infamous Beat Hotel.

A secretary with a single gray braid and an eye tic led Daisy through a forest of partitions in primary red, blue, and yellow. (The home of feelthy books as an X-rated kindergarten?) Nan McIver, the publicity director, pinned Daisy with a vacant blue stare, as if they'd never met, and set her to work filing foreign reviews. Then Nan spread the *Times* on her desk and dialed a number. From the bank of beige file cabinets Daisy listened: in her scorn for publicity, she'd neglected to learn what it was.

"Does it have a real dining room, or just a dining alcove? And when you say 'sliver vu,' waall, exactly how much river *do* you see?" Pause. Sarcastically: "Oh, I see. Thank you." Nan dialed another number. "I'm calling about your ad for a two-bedroom in Gramercy Park."

Nan spent the rest of the morning on the blower with the real estate people. By three she still hadn't returned from lunch. In desperation Daisy refiled reviews, so she'd appear indispensable and not get fired on day one.

Several months in, she'd graduated to updating reviewer lists and addressograph plates; answering phone inquiries about pub dates; mimeographing press releases; and sticking into review copies enclosures that no one read. She still couldn't have said what publicity was, and felt as unemployed as at Ajax.

·   ·   ·

At least there was George Byrne. Aspen's editor in chief was handsome in a stormy Byronesque way, and looked at the world through eyes of two different sizes. Byrne was the key, Daisy decided, to her career advancement. She seized any pretext to sashay by his large office fronting on University Place. But how to approach him? Byrne broadcast the message that nothing, not the death of his own mother, could justify breaking his momentum.

To escape the stupefying boredom, Daisy took to hunkering down in the ladies' room with the latest in Aspen's Black Cat art-porn line. Seated on the closed toilet seat, she lolled about in Parisian hotels with French demimondaines, butt in the breeze, awaiting the arrival of a dandy in yellow gloves with the hot eyes of George Byrne. She felt quarantined in a front for the real Aspen. Where were glamour and creativity? Beckett, Genet, her great project? She sensed you could catch a ride out there to serious excitement, but couldn't figure out how to get on board. Once again she was standing on the sidelines, watching all the stepsisters go to the ball. Even Gina was going to the ball — *especially* Gina, with her byline and fan mail.

She wasn't the only underoccupied female at Aspen. Sally November's main contribution was her nine o'clock arrival — everyone else dribbled in toward ten. Sighing with ease, Sally unwrapped her biale and black coffee, slipped into beat-up Pappagallos, and dialed her first number of the morning with voluptuous slowness. From the cubicle across the way Daisy heard her nasal drone: "So, Aunt Bea, how's the arthritis? . . . Mia, is this a look-no-further?" Then Sally filled the hours till noon pecking out, open-mouthed and all but drooling, the same page of jacket copy. Lunch hour she hunted for silver at Fortunoff, weighing the merits of Rose Ballet sterling over Rondelay. Overall she spent her days in a warm, well-lit place that gave her pocket money and allowed her to say at cocktail parties, "I'm in publishing."

So who in publishing, besides George Byrne, worked?

Nan McIver had a crisp tailored manner and pointless blue stare — impressive, considering the prevailing female dumdum style — but she was eighty percent image. Occasionally a flurry of activity around her desk signaled that she was engineering a stir over a book. Like the morning Byrne handed her the manuscript of a biography of Marcel Duchamp.

"Get me Bloomingdale's!" she called over her shoulder at Daisy. "Whaddya say to a window using Duchamp's painting *Nude Descending a Staircase,* along with a few nude mannequins," Nan quacked out the side of her mouth, her business voice. After a dozen negatives, Nan slammed down the receiver, muttering "Criminy." (Nan never swore, and seemed perpetually shocked by Aspen's titles.)

She finally sold the idea to Bamberger's in Newark. Newark's window-shoppers were baffled and incensed; within the week Bamberger's was forced to dismantle the display.

Daisy cringed in anticipation of Nan's disgrace. How could she show her face at the office? At ten-twenty Nan strode in, swinging her briefcase and whistling the *Egmont Overture.* The bad news was that *Nude* was going home to the Philadelphia Museum. The *good* news was that Greg was coming to look at the apartment in Turtle Bay!

Hunched in a stall with her hookers, Daisy was hit by an epiphany: all these career girls popping out of subways at nine-o-five A.M. and scurrying to offices, clutching their brown bag of Danish and regular-coffee-to-go, were just having a brief fling with work while hangin' around waiting to get married. Even a tricked-up model like Nan, with a title and a peon like herself. For Nan the job was a paid hobby. Her real work was routing Greg from his bachelor digs and resettling him in a normal pad so he'd finally pop the question. Why not write an article that would capture this career girl limbo?

In a fever of excitement Daisy tapped it out over a week of lunch hours.

Even the clever, ambitious girls, the ones with a glitzy job — who are "lucky," as they might put it — are ready to trade in the job for a proposal from a man with the right life plan; or even a proposal from the insurance salesman back home, if you've suddenly grown panicky and tired. Working is a time out; a postponement of responsibility and two-by-two and diapers in the living room. And if you're bored senseless, it's only *for now.* Married, a girl can expect to get taken care of for the rest of her life — which has a way of blunting ambition.

Yet a certain jitteriness prevails. By their early twenties, most girls are safely squared away with an upstanding junior executive, and a pastel split-level house with an American eagle on the door. Stretch career girl limbo too long, and you can fall out of the game. You can become *pfft,* just like that; everyone's mother has tales of such a tragedy — a woman without a country . . .

The article was perfect, Daisy decided, for *Coronet.* She saw her byline in boldface print. Other magazines would commission pieces, as Gina called them. She'd be a social critic and opinion maker, enter the ranks of New York's visible people. Her great project would be journalism.

"Couldn't you give us happier news?" *Coronet* wrote back. "Thank you for thinking of us, and best of luck placing it elsewhere." Ditto from ten other magazines. Each rejection a blow to the body. Doubled over, she reeled about her tiny apartment.

Franca, she needed Franca; you could always count on Franca, joked Gina, for instant ego repair. Her three-story yellow colonial on Brattle Street had become a haven for the old crowd, a reincarnation of Delphine's red room. Delphine had rechristened Franca "the normal one." With the two babies, brilliant husband, dogs, cats, garden club, and Country Squire station wagon, Franca Tabori was an endorsement in living color for Togetherness.

"Am I crazy, or is that child a little *old* for that?" Delphine murmured in Daisy's ear.

Franca sprawled on her side on the living room Persian rug, nursing Christopher, who indeed wore a look of quite unbabyish bliss. She babbled nonstop, unable to finish her sentences, as if she were high, almost, like when they took Dexies to write contracts: Peter said this, Peter did that . . . Chrissie's diaper rash . . . The pediatrician said . . . Her ash blond hair fell over her face and the corners of her lips turned up in a goony grin. "Mmmm, nursing's such a turn-on. Not a bad substitute, especially with Peter so busy. Or tired — Oh God, where's Andy?"

The visitors sprinted in different directions. Daisy found Andy under the kitchen sink, wrestling with a can of Drāno. She scooped him up. "Gotcha." He stared at her with Peter's cool gray eyes, then yowled with rage. She smelled a load. The whole kitchen smelled of upchuck and load. "Let's see, how do we change you," she muttered, holding him at arm's length.

Over Andy's protests she and Gina managed a diaper change. "Good God, where do we throw this? The toilet's already full of diapers," said Daisy. Gina discovered a stain on her new hot pink suit and went in search of club soda.

"I smell doo-doo, even through this bronchitis," said Delphine, holding her nose and coughing. "I mean, Chrissie has teeth and practically talks in sentences, but I think Franca's planning to nurse him till adolescence. So he can stay dependent on her forever, and she can imagine herself in the hot center of life."

"Don't be a bitch," said Daisy, pursuing Andy; with four adults on duty, the place felt wildly out of control.

The doorbell. Nanook bayed like a wolf, baring yellow fangs; cats leapt from high perches, crisscrossed in the foyer, and darted for cover.

"If it's the chimney sweep, let him in!" hollered Franca from the living room.

"Don't you want to cover up first?" called Daisy.

"What for? I need to give him instructions."

The chimney sweep, pale, grimy, an emissary from Dickens, goggled at Franca's bosoms. The friends exchanged looks; in college Franca had always been painfully modest.

Sniffing the air, Daisy asked, "Do you have something in the oven?"

"The blueberry muffins!" Franca scrabbled to her feet and ran for the kitchen, the baby shrieking at losing the nipple, head bobbing. She yanked open the oven door. A tray of little charred soldiers. "Cookie!" said Chris, pitching forward. Franca reached in without a pot holder. Her scream set Chris wailing again.

"Here, let's get you some butter," said Daisy, turning off the oven. "Funny, I still smell burning."

"Peter's shirts!" Franca burst into the pantry. An iron stood smoking a brown hole in a pink shirt. She set down Chrissie, who went crawling off at a great pace, white bottom bobbing. "Watch him! Somebody!" Gina left in pursuit. Franca seized a mixing bowl and poured in flour. "We'll just have to start over!" She broke one egg, two, a shell skittering to the floor. "Now a little milk, a little sugar, more flour." She made quick, spastic motions, spraying flour all around, Chaplin on the assembly line.

Daisy put her arm around Franca. "Sit down, for heaven's sake. We don't need muffins. We came here to be with you." She added, with a smile, "I need you to tell me how brilliant and talented I am, even though I've been rejected by every magazine in New York."

Aghast: "But I promised you home cookin' —" The phone. Franca dove for the receiver. "*Another* one? But Daisy's here, and everyone . . . I thought you had the run-through last night . . . I'm *not* nagging."

A *whomp!* from the living room. Silence — then an animal howl. "Andy!" Franca let the phone drop and sprinted. The phone swung by its cord from the counter. Sighing, Daisy picked it up. "Hullo, Peter?"

Franca came rushing back, Andy bouncing in the crook of her elbow. "Just a wee bumpety-do," she crooned. She'd forgotten all about Peter's phone call. "The Band-Aids, where're the bloody Band-Aids?" She turned her head this way and that, like something motorized. Andy struggled to the floor and picked up *Pat the Bunny*. Chrissie reached for her from Gina's arms.

Franca looked at them dully, as if her thoughts were blurring. "Sorry — I'm so sorry."

For a second Daisy saw her in Westlands, sun through the casement window backlighting her crown of braids, radiant as a June morning.

"I say, let's order in pizza," said Gina in her new Tallulah voice.

Delphine sat at the kitchen table, coughing like a fiend, and pushed back the old breakfast dishes. "I mean, don't take this wrong, but couldn't you use some help here? You can certainly afford it. What happened to that Danish au pair?"

A long moment. Franca sighed. "Daddy couldn't stand having a stranger around the house, could he," she said to Chrissie, who was struggling to get down.

A little mermaid with white-blond hair and stand-up tits, as Daisy remembered. Oh no. No, Peter hadn't. Oh, Franca.

"We're fine without Elke, we're doing fine without her." Franca's smile came and went, like a bulb with bad wiring. She wiped the back of her hand across her forehead, streaking it white. "I better be fine. With Peter's mood swings, I never know who's going to walk in the front door, especially before a show opens. It's me the steady soul around here."

Delphine was seized by a coughing fit.

"I want so badly to please Peter. But I don't know how anymore. He says he wants babies, a big family. Then he turns on me. 'How did you get so boring?' he says. Oh, I know he's dealing with a lot of artistic egos. So my job is to keep us in forward motion. But lately, no matter what I do, I can't" — she looked confused — "I just can't seem to please Peter anymore."

Delphine hawked like a stevedore. "Dearest, have you ever thought Peter doesn't *want* to be pleased?"

Daisy checked her image in the ladies' room mirror: copper hair pinned up in a French roll; round steel-rimmed glasses as befit a serious intellectual; kelly green Empire dress from Paraphernalia, the kicky new boutique on Madison Avenue. Underneath, her new floating action bra, spanking clean, in case she fainted and they phoned the paramedics from Saint Vincent's.

Rehearsing the language a final time, Daisy marched into Byrne's office like Grant leading the charge at Vicksburg.

Byrne's eyes remained on his manuscript.

She addressed the part in his hair. "Hi, my name is Daisy Frank and I was wondering if I could help out with some editing."

Marking his place with an index finger, Byrne let his eyes migrate upward till the larger one saw her. "You wonder if you could help out with some editing," he repeated dreamily. His teeth smiled, but not the eyes. Denise, in her cubicle across the hall, had stopped typing.

"May I ask who the hell you are?"

"Uh, I work here. In Publicity. I've been thinking Aspen ought to utilize the local talent more," she rushed on, like Road Runner pedaling over a void. "I love literature and I lived in Paris for a year —"

"You don't say."

"And I thought I could edit one of our, uh, your French authors —"

"Yes, yes, do get to the point."

Point? That *was* the point. She'd gotten to the point. Now what. She couldn't slink back to Siberia empty-handed. "Actually, I was wondering if I could take a look at the new Samuel Beckett and, well, see if the translation needs smoothing out."

A poisoned smile. "Samuel Beckett, as all the world knows, translates his own work into English from the French. I doubt very much it needs *smoothing out*."

Heat blasted up her neck. "Of course, how silly of me." She refused to cry, she would not cry. Girls were notorious for blubbering in offices. She pictured the leak in her ceiling; that worked for holding off an orgasm.

"Tell me, do you have work to do?"

"Yes but —"

"No, I know. Don't say it. You want something more creative, right? Creative!" He looked around. "They all want creative! All of them! Tell you what, Miss, uh — You see that slush pile over there? It's in there, waiting for you, the great American novel, just waiting for *you,* your creativity. And when you find it, you'll be so kind as to write us a reader's report. Okay? Okay, good." He returned to the place his finger still marked on the page, not without noticing Daisy's glorious legs.

"*Oy oy!* Don't take it personally." Denise had followed her into the ladies'. Daisy looked at her, wild-eyed, hands against the cold porcelain of the sink.

Denise lit a Lucky Strike. "Last week Byrne's wife ran off with her shrink," she went on in her smoker's baritone. "The poor guy's berserko. One minute he's dictating letters to the AMA, the next he's bawling like a baby. You had the worst possible timing. Actually, Georgie's not a bad guy. Just a trifle high strung."

She had to do *something* to head off creeping brain death. Perhaps the moment had come to move *Here Lies the Heart* off the back burner. If not now, when? It'd perched there so long, her Parisian memoir, it'd fallen behind the stove. She hurried down Eightieth Street toward her fourth-floor walk-up in Dr. Penson's brownstone, propelled by a rush of inspiration. The November sky had turned leaden. Don't let it rain. It was hard to concentrate when it rained, because water dripped through her porous ceiling with the steady beat of a metronome.

She would write about her career as a Beat generation groupie, the night she and Gregory Corso got themselves locked in the Panthéon to commune with the ghost of Victor Hugo. And subsisting on potato-noodle soup and Moroccan hash. And the morning she climbed the pissy stairs of the Beat Hotel to Allen Ginsberg's room, and woke him and announced she would do anything for him, *anything* — and Ginsberg said, "Anything?" and asked her to wash his socks. She would leave out her talent for taking up with bad men and getting stranded, without a sou, in exotic ports. She would leave out that she sailed home on the *QE II* because she'd run out of money, and imagination, and nerve. She would leave out that the grand expatriate adventure had somehow eluded her.

From the vestibule of her brownstone, two women butted past, heads down, muttering in Spanish. They'd probably come from a session with Dr. Penson, the Puerto Rican landlord. Daisy suspected Dr. Penson performed abortions in his basement apartment. He was always stomping up the stairs to her pad, brandishing a snake, fuming that he'd found orange hair clogging the drains. Daisy shuddered whenever she saw the snake; she couldn't help associating it with Penson's basement practice.

Sudden hunger drove her to the fridge in her tiny wedge-shaped kitchen. Just a moldy grapefruit half. Standing by the two gas burners, she devoured a bag of Fritos. She mopped the floor. She picked dead leaves off the avocado plant on the windowsill, fashioning a stalk topped with a leafy thatch, her very own topiary art — to what lengths would she go not to write!

The phone. A party tonight on Carmine Street, Dave Amram would be there, maybe even Jack Kerouac. And how could *Heart* compete with Kerouac, even if he was a wino and Mama's boy? Or the odds of meeting a Renaissance businessman? How could *Heart* compete?

Next night a party somewhere else: a BYOB up a rank stairwell in the Village, a Bach solo cello on the record player, hosted by rube intellectual and assman-about-town * * *. After midnight they migrated north to the West End Bar near Columbia. At the parties she met lawyers, creative directors, architects, sound engineers, off-Broadway actors, stringers from Brazilian newspapers, all with big prospects and bigger erections. She met men in espresso coffee houses in the Village — the Peacock or the Figaro — or the San Remo bar on Macdougal Street; at the Museum of Modern Art (a prime pickup place — hard to go wrong with a man who loved Monet); at the headquarters of John V. Lindsay, the young patrician congressman from the East Side's Silk Stocking district; at A-frame ski chalets near Hunter Mountain or Bromley; at "grouper" houses at Fire Island, where the herd gathered for a "sixish" on someone's sagging deck, the clinical light of dusk etching eyes and mouths and chins not yet ragged.

There were always good reasons for sex (in those days not yet

debased currency): the thrill of the forbidden; a failure of imagination — how many hours could you discuss alienation in Antonioni? —
the specter of Sunday morning alone. Leo P., a disciple of Wilhelm
Reich, taught her to bellow during orgasm and gag herself in the
morning to break down muscle "armoring." Adam H., an actor who
played a junkie in Jack Gelber's hit play, *The Connection,* taught her
Keressa. Louis G., a blubbery director, liked to make love on gamy
sheets to a record of whale calls, and gave a little swimmer's kick when
he came. Men were so grateful — imagine, getting laid without an
engagement ring! And she was talented at sex, like someone with an
ear for language. ("I love the way you come," said Louis into her ear
as the whales boomed.) And didn't she like them all, the fat jolly ones,
the jumpy little Woody Allens, their cocks and their asses, their sexual
styles, like some signature of the soul?

She had less talent for love. Somewhere in the heart's region she was
out of order, disconnected — I'm sorry, this is not a working number.
She knew she was kind of young to have gotten ruined so early in the
game, but there it was. Fiction delivered neat endings. The heroine
shot herself offstage or swallowed arsenic or got in the way of a train.
In real-life New York you played hard and stayed out late and learned
to move fast. Speed was of the essence. So you'd be the one to jump
ship first.

When occasionally the supply of dates dried up, there was always Ben
Marshak. After three years at Legal Aid, he was planning a run for City
Council. The frenzy of his schedule plus willful blindness kept him
mostly ignorant of Daisy's amours. New Year's Eve of '61, Ben rescued her from an evening alone on Eightieth Street with her strep
throat. He swaddled her in wool scarves and bore her off in a taxi to
an elegant dinner party on Central Park West. The host was a big-time
lawyer who subsidized Legal Aid, massaging his conscience by en-
abling the folks his clients regularly screwed to have their day in court.
His duplex overlooking Wollman skating rink was done up to look
like an English gentlemen's club, with green-matted hunting prints,
Chesterfield chairs, and a wall of bound leather "books by the yard,"
Dante's *Inferno* nudging *Peyton Place.* Ben proudly introduced Daisy
around. Funny, he didn't *see* her swollen eyes and red schnozz and
greasy hair.

Daisy sensed they were being scrutinized. On the opposite couch sat

Marjorie Morningstar, shoehorned into a white sheath. The host's daughter. Suddenly Daisy pictured Ben through Marjorie's eyes: the tortoiseshells and trendily shaggy hair; skinny boy-lawyer breaking into politics, with ELIGIBLE stamped across his chest. Still dangerous around glassware, but the chest-thumping now translated as confidence, success did that for men.

Marjorie's thoughts crackled at Daisy like static: Whatever does he see in you?

"Why don't you go make nice to the boss's daughter?" Daisy murmured. "Daddy could sure give your campaign a boost."

Ben only turned up the smile. "Don't be a smart-ass."

"But I *am* a smart-ass. That's the trouble. You need someone motherly and gentle and kind, a woman who truly appreciates you, the way you deserve." Safe to say this, she thought fuzzily. If she lost her footing on the high wire, Ben would catch her. Ben was her safety net; he would be there always.

"Thanks for the dime-store analysis, what do I owe you?" He put his arm around her. "The fact is you do appreciate me. You just haven't realized it yet."

Once she'd caught him watching her from across a room, his eyes naked with desire — love? — and she'd been surprised to feel an answering blip. Usually she was counting the ways he fell short of her ideal, or thinking, Incest, might as well do it with Ira, or one of the fellow travelers. What the hell was wrong with her? Maybe she needed to go home and take a hot bath.

Someone was counting down to midnight. Cheers, kisses, the pathetic forced jollity of New Year's Eve. Ben kissed her germy mouth; she turned her face aside to cough.

"To our life together," said Ben.

"Ben," she said with sudden urgency. "Ben dear, you can't let me hold you up like this. You've got to start your life without me."

Ben smiled. "Nonsense. Without my girl, what kind of life would that be?"

Oh brother. It always went like this. Friends snickered and joked. Ben was like the guy in *Of Human Bondage,* only Daisy had more class than Mildred and didn't limp. The story was out that Ben kept a signed marriage contract in his briefcase, hoping to bump into Daisy in the subway or street.

.   .   .

Lunch hour on a rainy Thursday. The slush pile yielded a *Life of Jesus* illustrated with tinted postcards. *A Retelling of the Tarzan and Jane Story* in iambic pentameter. Then she disinterred *Devil's Barge* by Richard Gracchi. A novel. Daisy gave it the first-page test. A narrator who plied the Seine in his barge alluded to an unsolved murder, suggesting his own complicity. His dark voice teased Daisy's curiosity. Tell me more. She carted the manuscript back to her desk. The narrator was involved in contraband transactions, sort of an existentialist petty criminal. He had only one leg. To judge by the women pursuing him, his middle member more than made up for it.

By two P.M. Daisy was still reading, and penciling little notes in the margin. She'd even forgotten her meatball hero, usually the afternoon's peak experience. On the IRT home, she shamelessly beat out an old lady for a seat so she could keep reading. Her jubilation deepened with the night. Around midnight she read the last sentence. She grinned at the banner of rags she'd hung from the ceiling to mute the drip. She'd found an icicle in hell!

She dialed Delphine, then, noticing the hour, hung up.

She hauled her broken Royal portable from the closet and set up at the table. When she next looked up, the sky beyond the Dutch rooftops had turned dove gray.

A week turtled by. No word from Byrne.

"This is worse than after a one-night stand," Daisy groaned on the phone to Delphine.

"Whatever you do, stay away from Byrne. Only thing an editor hates worse than a call from an author is a call from an underling."

Every passing hour chiseled away a chunk of Daisy's self-esteem. She stuck by her judgment like a Christian martyr; dammit, that novel was good. In the way of women, she soothed herself at odd hours with cool creamy desserts.

The third week her intercom buzzed. "Byrne wants to see you," said Denise. In a baritone whisper, "The news is good."

"We'll publish it," Byrne growled at Daisy's midriff. He lit a cigarette and squinted at her with his meaner eye. "Oh, and by the way, *nice* report. You seem to know literature."

She wanted to throw her arms around him. She could hear the homage at the editorial meeting.

"I'll present it at next week's meeting," Byrne was saying. "You see, if the proposal comes from you, it won't sit well with B.J. It needs my, uh, imprimatur. I want to make certain our little book gets off to a good start. We don't want you saying anything silly. Just leave it to me. And don't worry. I'll see you get the credit."

"I appreciate that, Mr. Byrne." She ordered her features to appreciate.

Any minute now, she'd be recognized. Any minute now her career would start in earnest.

The minutes became days, then weeks. She went to bed one night in autumn and woke up to snow. She continued typing perfect stencils, and Nan's perfect pad continued to elude her. Byrne was peculiarly occupied or absent. Why had he not been heard from? Why hadn't B. J. Everley stopped by and invited her to celebrate at "21"? Daisy confided her worries to Sally, but Sally and Shelley Wunderlick had set the date, and the logistics of wedding claimed all her attention.

One lunch hour Daisy flipped through *Publishers Weekly* while munching a chicken salad on rye at her desk. Her eye trolled down the "Talk of the Trade" column, past an item titled "A Dream Come True," and snagged on a name: Richard Gracchi. She gulped and backtracked. " 'It's what I've always dreamed about,' sighs Richard Gracchi happily. He has just signed a contract with Aspen Press for his novel, *Devil's Barge,* an over-the-transom find by Aspen's George Byrne." Heart in throat, Daisy read about expatriate exploits in Paris, Gracchi's long wait for recognition, a new novel in the works, and a "jubilant" George Byrne exulting about "the special pleasure of finding an unagented novel of this caliber."

Daisy stood, *Publishers Weekly* falling to the floor with a slap, her hand at her neck.

Nan glanced her way. "Criminy! Hold it, I'll have to get back to you. Don't show the apartment till I see it first." She sometimes had trouble remembering this girl worked here.

"What, what is it? D'jou swallow a bone?" She pounded Daisy's back.

"The bastard stole my book!" Daisy squeaked, jabbing the air due east, in the direction of Byrne's office.

Nan stopped pounding. "Hush, what are you talking about? C'mon, I think we'd better go to the ladies'."

One of the stalls was occupied; Nan put her finger to her lips. "*Devil's Barge* is mine, my discovery," Daisy hurtled on. "I found it, I wrote the reader's report, and Byrne promised *I'd* get the credit."

"It's not *yours*. You're not even an editor. You simply brought it to Byrne's attention, the way you're supposed to. Look, I know it feels unfair, but these things happen. They're not even all that rare." As she talked, Nan's mind whirred. Barges . . . An author party . . . Eureka! An author party on a barge! On the Hudson! They'd leave from the Circle Line ferry slip off Tenth Avenue. For music they'd have Dixieland, no, something nautical, hornpipes, or that new record of whales mating. As for hors d'oeuvres, why, *fruits de mer,* of course.

"That makes it okay?" Daisy asked.

"Makes what okay? Listen, George hasn't been very productive recently. He's got personal problems, I hear." She offered Daisy a Salem. "Tell me," she said reflectively, "did George say the book needed his — what's the word he uses? — imprimatur?"

"I think that was the word."

Nan nodded her head sagely.

Daisy was puzzled only a second. "You mean George, like, gets up in the morning and makes a *practice* of this?"

A toilet flushed. Denise emerged from a stall.

"Hon," she said to Daisy with a nervous glance at the door, "you never heard this from me. The man signed his name to your report. Sure, he 'rewrote' it. Crossed a few *t*'s, dotted an *i*. But only God could tell the difference."

Daisy clapped her hands like cymbals. "Dammit, I'm going to Everley. No, I'll go right to the editor of *Publishers Weekly*."

Nan aimed her finger like a pistol. "You do that, and you'll never work in publishing again."

Daisy swayed in place. The acid in her gut could dissolve steel. No wonder men got ulcers.

"Why don't you take the rest of the day off?" Nan said in a kinder voice. "Go shopping. See a good movie. There's this new French film at the Paris, *The Lovers*. They show — well — it ain't *Pillow Talk*."

Denise lit a Lucky. "Try not to get so steamed, hon. The book'll probably sink like a stone."

"That's right," said Nan, nodding happily. "Like a *stone*. Not to worry. And try to see it from Georgie's perspective. He has to make his way."

"So do I."

"You know it's not the same for you. This is his life."

"It's mine, my life too."

"It's not, though." Nan drenched her in the blue stare. "Gee willikers, I hope to God it's not!"

Chapter 13

1962

DELPHINE LOVED being married. She loved being married to
Jake in particular, though she suspected that, if not married to him,
she'd be happy even with a lesser man. Coming from distant asteroids,
she and Jake were uncannily similar: they had the same hell-raising
humor, same intolerance for the *Nouvelle Vague* films that phonies
plumbed for hidden meaning, same casualness about balancing check-
books.

She loved their little jewel-box apartment on West Fifty-fourth
Street, overlooking the garden of the Museum of Modern Art. Her
husband-the-architect insisted of course on white walls, and a pair of
expensive leather and stainless steel chairs by Mies van der Rohe, for
which she dipped into principal. Jake detested the Danish Modern in
vogue among young marrieds — "Like motel rooms on the Jersey
Turnpike" — so up they drove to Newport in a U-Haul to raid Rosecliff. Jake then groused about gloomy Victoriana (while liking its odor
of old money). Over Merry's squawks, they lifted from the library the
blue Victorian chair with carved oak crest, its velvet worn silver in the
center. Drew Mortimer's favorite. Flanking their nonworking fire-

place, it cohabited peaceably with Mies. To the left of the mantel they hung a floor-to-ceiling oil painting of Great-aunt Letitia, who'd croaked at the Boston Symphony, her towering height requiring three men to carry her out, like a felled oak. In the dining alcove they hung Jake's blueprints for the Topeka Arts complex, which had won him the Prix de Rome. The hall housed Aunt Hildreth's watercolors of maritime gardens, produced as occupational therapy at Austin Riggs — remarkably similar, Jake enthused, to Monet. They slept in a mahogany sleigh bed. Delphine pictured an ark sailing them high in the sky across a crescent moon.

The dailiness and routines of marriage, the very features considered fatal to passion, made Delphine hum with contentment. Every evening after work she hurried west on Fifty-first Street, then uptown along Fifth Avenue to Fifty-fourth. She wanted to get dinner under control before she heard Jake's key turn in the lock, a lovely sound. It bugged him if she interrupted his train of thought to stir the rice. Sometimes she just heated up coq au vin left over from Saturday night, dousing it with Chianti; she was determined to wear out one of the dozen ovenproof casseroles with mallard motifs they'd received as wedding presents from Merry's friends. Or she set a chuck roast in a nest of tinfoil, punched it full of Accent, smothered it in a can of Campbell's mushroom soup, popped it into the oven, and by eight o'clock, voilà: pot roast. For Sunday lunch she sometimes did leg of lamb with mint jelly, string beans boiled to oblivion, vanilla ice cream with "choc" sauce — a salute to Merry and years of identical bourbon-soaked Sunday lunches at Rosecliff. Monday the lamb encored as shepherd's pie, followed by a Jell-O mold Cling Peaches Jubilee from a recipe she'd clipped from *McCall's*.

To celebrate their three-years-seven-months-four-days anniversary, Delphine whipped up a quickie beef Strogonoff from a *Times* recipe. Jake came home early, high on a triumph at work, and they fell upon each other (she'd noticed a strict correlation between Jake's success and his libido). Too late she remembered the beef; the sour cream had curdled. Famished, they both gobbled two helpings — and took turns all night in the john. Now, to the mystification of friends, the mere word "Strogo" set them laughing.

Weekends were best. She stored memories of them like preserves against hard winters. Saturday night they threw dinner parties. Like young brides everywhere in 1962, Delphine bravely tackled the five-page recipes from Julia Child's bible, *Mastering the Art of French Cooking.* On Friday night she laid the groundwork for a *boeuf Bourgignonne* that called for bouquet garni, mysterious *lardons,* and cheesecloth. (Would the upper layer of Kotex do?) Saturday afternoon Jake poked his head into the kitchen. "Phew, looks like a cyclone hit in here!" Then he dashed off for squash at the Harvard Club on West Forty-fourth Street, Delphine hoping he wouldn't get waylaid by a running backgammon game played for big bucks. Of course his sole contribution to the dinner was bar duty. And the cleanup never satisfied; Jake grumbled about geological layers of grease in the kitchen; Mr. Fastidious needed everything antiseptic — architects were notoriously anal. And sometimes she would have preferred to spend the evening tucked into her father's blue chair with a manuscript. Her boss could barely manage these days without her reader's reports.

But the dinner parties were essential, and she was blessed with boundless energy, stamina born of the sporting life on turf and surf, plus good Yankee genes. Parties exercised Jake's gregariousness and wit, and they buttressed the career of a hot young designer at Johnson and Burgee. She always invited an editor from one of the "shelter" magazines, or a reporter from a newspaper's Style section. Often she included Gina, currently writing stories for *Mademoiselle* on the joys of singledom. Gina was a model "perky girl," complete with a coif that flipped (perkily) up at the ends and velvet headband clamped over bangs. She was always dashing to make a deadline, or decorating her little walkup on East Eighty-seventh Street with perky things, like Rickie Tickie Stickies and macramé flowerpot holders. She'd have perky orgasms, if she had them. Usually she brought to dinner an art director or designer named Sergio or Renato, neither of them Latin.

Jake was above hustling. He belonged to his work, an arts complex for Hampden College, an SLC spinoff in upstate New York, near Albany, that should really put him on the map. Yet did he have to antagonize the money men that everyone else brown-nosed in order to get on? He seemed to go out of his way to provoke them. Though of course he locked horns with them over aesthetic principle.

After the most boffo party, Delphine was happy to see the last guest leave — and so was their neighbor, Mrs. Hawkins, who often complained to the landlord about the noise. "Now you're mine, all mine," Delphine cried, unbuttoning Jake's shirt and snuffling in his chest hair; crazed by his scent, boyish and faint, she wanted more smell, more of *him*. Both sloshed, they slept in a private delirium, tossing, parched. Then, the finest cure for hangover yet devised, Sunday morning love, long and slow, just short of torture, or a fancy high ride, a cakewalk in the sky. Who else made love like Jake?

Her desire for him was open ended. She sometimes wept afterward, unable to reach the end of it. She once came so violently, Mrs. Hawkins pounded against the adjoining wall. To retaliate, Jake played his prized Deutsche Grammophon recording of *Wozzeck* full volume. Nothing had prepared Delphine for the animal abandon of married sex. No need to sneak to the bathroom for a quick toothbrushing in the morning, no need for image maintenance — the audition was over, you were in the show for real. Every fuck was an investment, money in the bank. That much more history bound them.

Their most ingrained ritual, one that suffused all the others, was cocktail hour. Before Jake came home she'd fix a batch of iced martinis in the monogrammed sterling shaker from Abercrombie's they'd received as a wedding present (from her side, like anything connected with booze). She got a head start testing the proportions of gin to vermouth; by his arrival she had a nice buzz. With Jake she put away a couple more. Strung out the high during dinner with rotgut Almaden, capped it with a snort of Jake's Poire. She couldn't say whether they drank too much. Booze was as familiar as the cabbage rose wallpaper in Rosecliff's dining room. As a child, after a party, she went around sipping the sugary dregs of mint juleps, amusing Drew and Merry, by then shit-faced and knocking into furniture. She made her own drinking debut at those tedious debutante balls; *it's what gets you through*. Six P.M. was impassable, the Jungfrau looming in your path; you could just about crawl out of your skin by six without a hit of Tanqueray.

One bitter February night Jake slammed into the apartment and announced that he'd told a senior design partner where to get off. "The guy's constantly at me, hassling me about cost overruns, chiseling away at all the details. The soul of the thing — its *soul* — is in the details." Collapsing in the blue chair, legs akimbo, Jake described the reinforced concrete exterior for Hampden's Fine Arts building. "When the old blowhard gets through, the place'll look like an army bunker."

Delphine refilled her glass at the antique hutch doubling as a bar, walked to the window, and frowned down at MOMA's garden. *Suppose he got fired.* For reasons of temperament. They needed both their salaries; Jake's ten grand — a coup for a young architect — her five. Without Jake's, she'd have to dig deeper into the principal of the trust fund that was finally hers, the interest having paid for college, and she was already depleting it for her weekly sessions with Dr. Beetlebaum. It was Jake who insisted they take this apartment, the stratospheric rent be damned. He'd had it with the rent-controlled roach farms. And they loved the theater, with dinner afterward at Frankie and Johnny's or Orsini's, and sex and rum in San Juan, where they stayed in funky little *pensiones* to save money.

Keep off a touchy subject. And wasn't she crazy to worry? Burgee and Johnson wouldn't fire their hottest young designer, winner of the Prix de Rome. Talent like Jake's wasn't expendable. Freshening her drink, she turned to Jake, who sprawled in the blue chair, drawing maniacally on his Camel.

"I've got a great idea. We need to bug out of here. I know, I know" — she held up the palm of her hand — "you can't take the time. But just for a long weekend. We could go to San Juan over Washington's Birthday. That little *pensione* we went to last time, near the Condado?"

A smile creased his features. "You mean the place with the hookers upstairs? Walking around all night in stiletto heels?"

"And the plastic sheets," she said in her throat. Loving his sultry mouth and Tartar eyes, even his dandruffy lashes; she always saw him for the first time. "The sheets that rustled. Remember, darling?"

They dissolved in laughter, remembering. They'd had a lovely time in that room, even with the plastic sheets that rustled and the stiletto heels. They'd barely made it to the beach. She leaned back against the hutch, weak behind the knees. "If you don't make love to me this instant, I'm not sure I can bear it."

Stumbling toward the bedroom, unbuckling, shedding underwear — no time to strip back the antique lace bedspread, the worse for other impromptu sessions. Suddenly he rolled off her and onto his back and slid upward. She loved that with Jake, being in control, and the overtones of abasement, like hot times in jalopy back seats. When he reached down to touch her, though, she caught his hand and kissed his fingers, one by one. She was miles away. Worries over his job still?

In the living room she poured herself a nightcap. Tasting Jake. Misaligned and gritty from not quite coming. Oh hell, there was always later, or the morning, the whole rest of their lives. She was spooked by happiness was her trouble. As if she didn't deserve it; get too happy and the gods throw you a clip from behind. The affairs before Jake had been nerve ends and histrionics, to fake out the foreboding that stalked her. At twenty-one she'd felt stale, all played out. Jake came along when she'd forgotten what to hope for. She hadn't believed she could love, not like this. Just Don't Blow It! They were golden, she and Jake, the golden couple. Everything was breaking their way.

Working at Hollinsworth Publishing, though, was like wading through molasses. The powers there believed she should praise De Lawd for the privilege of breathing the air in their sacred grove. Meanwhile, she sat in her cramped office, scheming how to make editor in chief by thirty. She would implode with impatience! She could dance circles around her boss, like some female Figaro with ten times the wits of the dim master. Tim Estabrook III, Princeton '56, had weak rabbity eyes and displayed a worrisome lag time between thought and utterance, like someone on the phone from Tokyo. Manuscripts screaming for his attention collected dust on shelves, while she fielded calls from piteous-sounding authors. Oh what she might accomplish in his place!

She'd already tricked him into promoting her from secretary to reader. For two years she'd read manuscripts and written reader's reports on her own time. She could swiftly spot literary merit, or a juicy potboiler for housewives. Tim, she soon realized, didn't know what he thought about a book until she told him. So one afternoon, when he handed her a new manuscript, she fluttered her lashes and confided that much as she wanted to, she couldn't type his correspondence *and* write a reader's report by morning. She didn't add that her working every night bugged Jake; he loved her drive, but not when it cut into their evenings.

Now Tim had gone and fallen in love with her, which made him even dimmer. He stuttered when anxious; in her presence he could barely get out a sentence. You are my destiny, she read in his eyes. God help her. He was a retread of Dudley Hunnewell. But she needed Tim's help, any bit she could get. Women in publishing rose to the top in publicity, promotion, subsidiary rights, but never, except for Blanche Knopf, the boss's wife, editorial. Hollinsworth had one female editor, who handled cookbooks, self-help, and juveniles, and a stooped my-opic copyeditor who looked allergic to daylight. The slot of assistant editor coming open was earmarked for another reader, Graydon Heap, a lightweight with connections up the kazoo. She sometimes felt like a pygmy batting against a giant rampart.

Yet what was her alternative? The Junior League, garden club, car pools. Cowhood. She'd end up turning tricks in the afternoon, like that old classmate from Rosemary Hall she'd just heard about. (Hmm, how about a book on matron hookers?) She'd end up in Austin Riggs, where her family had sent enough fragile souls to underwrite a wing. She must not, like Daisy, give up on herself. Daisy was vegetating at Aspen, de-feated by the times. Lost in husband-hunting and sex, stupidly unaware that the two were mutually exclusive. The thought of Gina, and her expense account, got her even madder. The old sneak, pretending in college to be Miss Drone. Actually, Gina *was* mediocre; she'd simply converted mediocrity into an asset. In her articles she didn't need to *try* to talk down, she was already there. . . . Oh, why am I such a *bitch*?

To learn the craft of editing, Delphine went outside Hollinsworth. She paid a veteran at Scribner's a handsome sum to give her a crash course in how to shape, cut, and "open up" a manuscript. Then she asked Tim Estabrook if he had something in the hopper that needed editing. "I'd do it on my own time, of course," she added with a twinkle.

He stuttered and blinked his rabbit eyes, and fretted several days about neglecting Graydon Heap. Eventually he gave Delphine *The Lady Is a Sleuth,* a mystery novel featuring a spunky female private eye that sort of turned the genre on its head. He gave it to her with a touch of malice. The author, a woman named Lucy Beamish, was a notori-ous pain in the ass. Delete one sentence, query one word, and she shrieked like a stuck pig; you had to wrench her final draft from her; she appeared at the office in carpet slippers, red harlequin glasses, and orange fright wig, clutching a paper bag containing her bologna on white and bottle of Pepsi, presumably to advertise her poverty and extract a larger advance; and her accent made Molly Goldberg sound like Sir Laurence Olivier. But she'd acquired a small loyal readership, and they were forced to tolerate her.

Installed in the blue chair with three number 2 yellow pencils, Delphine absorbed *Sleuth* in one blow as she might drain a tall glass of lemonade. The book was impossibly tangled and windy, subplots spinning off in all directions. But inside it lived an elegant little thriller screaming to get out. Better yet, Beamish had written characters, not the formulaic ciphers typical of the genre. The woman had the potential to write what the industry called a breakthrough book, a mystery with the heft and resonance of serious fiction.

Delphine typed a ten-page memo proposing massive cuts, cliffhanger chapter endings to heighten suspense, and a trimmed roster of characters.

"Good stuff," said Estabrook, taken aback; he himself hadn't known where to begin. He inhaled Delphine's lemony musk and broke out in blotches. "Well, get to work on it. Uh, b-b-by the way, where'd you learn how to do this?"

"You know, by reading novels analytically. Tolstoy, Joyce, Mann. And Agatha Christie, of course."

Lucy Beamish took one look at Delphine's doctoring, put on her carpet slippers and wig, and stormed unannounced into the office. Behind Delphine's closed door her postmenopausal caw was audible for half a block. "A butcher, not an editor . . . No respect for integrity . . . Don't want my name on it . . . Who the hell you think . . ." et cetera, et cetera. Estabrook ducked into a series of all-day meetings.

That afternoon Delphine bought her Scribner's mentor lunch at Chock Full o' Nuts and received lesson number two: "Editing is about tact. You don't tell an author this is a hopeless piece of shit." "But I didn't." "Did you put smiley faces in the margin, and write 'nice'? Another old trick: when you cut, cut about one hundred ten percent of what should go. That way, when the author asks, 'Does this *have* to go?' you say, 'No, let's put it back,' and you restore ten percent. Well, better luck next time. And remember lesson number three: the only good author is a dead author."

Beamish went to the mat with Delphine on every one of her "suggestions."

Eventually the skinnier version of *Sleuth,* plus the ten percent Delphine agreed to restore, became a main selection of the Mystery Book Club and was optioned by Paramount Pictures. Delphine learned through the office pipeline that Beamish thought it miraculous the book was taking off despite ham-handed editing by that "daffy girl who works for Tim Estabrook." Delphine just smiled. She suspected that for her next book Lucy Beamish would demand to work with Delphine Mikulski.

Delphine became something of a presence at Hollinsworth. It was rumored around its stately precincts that in ten years or so — in the unlikely event she stuck with it — she might, just might, make assistant editor. But her style clashed with the Hollinsworth *tone:* her shrieks of laughter, largeness, too audible lockjaw drawling, "Mrs. Mikulski's line" — so *physical.* The position on Delphine was that she was smart all right, but needed a Katie Gibbs for grooming — one week she'd worn the same dirndl skirt pinned closed with a large safety pin, and she had something against deodorant. Tim Estabrook saw only a Pre-Raphaelite painting come to life. He occasionally took Delphine to lunch at the Brasserie, a snazzy new restaurant in the Seagram's building on Park Avenue. He would watch her shape the words *fettuccine Alfredo,* and imagine her fingers digging into his back, and hear her coital cries. All last week Delphine had worn sunglasses in the office. He conjured scenes of unspeakable domestic violence. He had reason to hope.

To become an editor, she needed to acquire books, not just plump the pillows of those brought in by Estabrook. She couldn't very well submit *Pineapple,* a children's book sent her by Grace Omura from red room days. It consisted of blank pages, the odd pineapple perched on a horizon, and inscrutable haiku. One afternoon she received a packet from Aunt Hildreth wrapped in red and green Christmas paper. She prayed no one but the boys in the mailroom had seen it. The packet contained three chapters of a gardening book Hildreth thought ideal for Hollinsworth, complete with her own line drawings. Delphine sighed. She hated to discourage Auntie's occupational therapy — she'd been progressing so nicely.

She flipped through the pages. The drawings looked botanically accurate. They were exquisite, actually, almost the equal of Redouté's, and the writing was zany yet authoritative. Delphine could hear Hildreth rattling on full tilt about walking leaf ferns. She herself cared not a hoot for walking ferns, but wasn't there an audience for this stuff? Why, Aunt Hildreth could do for gardening what Julia Child had done for French cooking! Delphine could even see her discussing fine points of pruning on her own TV show, Henry, her Yorkshire terrier, tucked under one arm. Hildreth had a certain eerie appeal; she resembled a Velázquez duenna with mustache.

Excitedly, Delphine placed Hildreth's pages, accompanied by a memo, on Estabrook's desk. He promptly shot the proposal down, relieved that Delphine's judgment wasn't foolproof. "Come to lunch with me and see what I do with agents," he said as a sop.

In 1962 the Italian Pavilion, secreted in an apartment building on Fifty-fifth Street, was the premier publishing restaurant, along with the glitzier Four Seasons. Delphine barely tasted her vitello tonnato. She was high on the happy hum of editors, agents, and authors getting blitzed on extra-dry double martinis with a twist. She listened avidly while Peter Curry, a young agent from William Morris, expounded on a book proposal titled *Sex Lives of Single Girls*.

"The timing is just right for a book like that," said Delphine excitedly. "Used to be, single girls who admitted to a working acquaintance with sex were labeled, to be blunt, whores." Curry's eyebrow shot up. "But change is in the air. Along with togetherness there's a whole kind of sub rosa, ah, libertinism going on right under our noses."

"Yes, all these girls need is permission to go ahead with what they're already doing, or itching to do," put in Curry.

The book, they decided, would promote the notion that single was no longer pitiable and spinsterish; in fact, it was sexier, more glamorous to be single than married. The tone would be that of a friend taking you aside and divulging her secrets on the art of living, then cheering you on as you practiced them yourself. As Curry and Delphine played off each other's ideas, Curry thought this gorgeous girl and the book were a match made in heaven. Especially compared to that old maid Estabrook.

Estabrook was growing queasier by the minute, and not from his osso bucco. Those two were playing footsie under the table. Could it be? No. Yes! He was certain of it.

·   ·   ·

The week after the Book-of-the-Month Club took *Sleuth* as a featured alternate, Estabrook buzzed Delphine. She appeared in his office before he'd hung up.

"N-nothing d-d-definite yet" — the stutter, she knew, was a good sign — "but we need a new assistant editor, and I'm p-p-pushing for you. You'd work on cookbooks, juveniles, self-help, mysteries."

Delphine geysered appreciation, thinking, *Cookbooks?* Had Maxwell Perkins ever descended to soufflés, or *Andy the Aardvark?* She intended to publish innovative novels, major biographies, seminal nonfiction.

"It's a bit premature, but why don't we celebrate with a d-d-drink after work," said Estabrook.

She braced her hand against the glove compartment to keep her brainpan off the windshield. She could blame only herself; she should never have gone with him to the Brasserie. Sure she'd been aware of his crush, like distant static — she was accustomed to male randiness in her vicinity — but she knew these repressed types, nothing to fear. She hadn't foreseen that after one martini, he'd press his bony shank against her thigh. The car clipped a Checker cab. Now he was going to get them dead! He just missed ramming a bus pulling out. She shrank toward her door, counting the blocks to deliverance.

"Delphine, I don't know how to say this, but for some time I've sensed you're married to a man who doesn't appreciate what an exquisite woman you are." "Good God, where'd you get such an idea?" "He *hits* you," said Estabrook, indignant, hopping a light. A chorus of horns. A cabbie gave them the finger.

How could he —? How did he —? Not even Daisy knew about that. "Mr. Estabrook, I can't imagine why you could think —" "Dearest, call me Tim. Those dark glasses you wore." "Oh *that!*" — laughing wildly — "I have the worst migraines, and I can't tolerate light when I get an attack." A long monologue on warning auras and migraine lore, she stretched it out till Fifty-third Street, happy for the diversion. "But you're kind to be concerned. Oh, turn left here and come back east on Fifty-fourth. I live halfway down the block." She was thrown against him. "Oops! You'd be great at Watkins Glen."

Estabrook braked with a jolt, pitching her against the dashboard. As Delphine turned, trembling, to say good night, he muttered "sweetheart" and grabbed her and brought his mouth hard against hers, forcing his tongue between her lips. She stared ahead unseeing. *He was ruining it for her at work*. There went her promotion! Her nails dug into her palms. It was happening again — Raoul, Dudley, the horror. Everything she touched . . . She twisted her head free. "Mr. Estabrook — Tim — please, I'm a married woman." She groped for the door handle; just about now Jake came home from work.

Tim found her lips again; she clamped them shut; his tongue played over her mouth, his ropy saliva made her gorge rise. "I'll wait for you forever," he muttered.

Jake could walk up the sidewalk any minute. She fumbled for the door handle, found it, pressed down, but Tim's weight against her toppled them sideways, cantilevered over the curb, just as Mrs. Hawkins emerged from the lobby with her three spunky dachsunds.

Overnight, Tim's stutter was cured. The manuscripts Delphine once reported on now went to Graydon Heap. She couldn't swallow for the rage strangling her. She sat doodling at her desk, alarmingly unoccupied. Could she just be Mrs. Jacob Mikulski and entertain his clients and make babies and casseroles? Like everyone else? Maybe her ambition was a form of madness, hubris. It was all too confusing, she felt so alone. The cruelest part was she couldn't confide in Jake. Couldn't reveal the true reason for her fall from grace. She amused herself with homicidal fantasies. Push Estabrook off a cliff. The bluffs at Rosecliff would be perfect. Rosecliff brought to mind Aunt Hildreth. That cockamamy book, Hildreth's gardening follies. The drawings had been quite beautiful. Hell, what else did she have going? And when had she ever trusted the judgment of Tim Estabrook?

Friday evening found her in the silver Volkswagen flattop en route to Marion, Massachusetts, a seaside town bordering the summer retreat of Daisy's old nemesis, Brenda Chatfield. She had a second motive for getting away: exhaustion. For the past week Jake, thwarted by the senior designer, had tied one on every night and picked a fight; by the time they made up it was usually three A.M. She'd been going on caffeine and prayers.

She was startled by the sight of Hildreth's house, a Victorian fantasy with turrets, dormers, widow's walk, and ivy and orange trumpet vines that looked to be eating the place alive. Hildreth lived with her beloved terrier Henry, now stuffed and mounted in a kitchen alcove, some half-dozen cats, and three cousins. One of them never descended from her quarters in the attic.

Over the weekend Delphine and Hildreth sat at the kitchen table among some rather menacing Venus's flytraps, reworking the first fifty pages of *Hildreth's Gardens.* Delphine typed and retyped drafts as she and Hildreth talked them out loud, Delphine trying to ignore Henry's reproachful eyes. Saturday night they broke out the Jack Daniel's and sat in the living room/greenhouse, surrounded by stacks of yellowing newspapers dating back several years and neatly tied with string. The cats danced in their litter, then came traipsing through the Velveeta cheese and liverwurst Hildreth had laid out. From her rocker, Miss Havisham looked on with an antic grin. Delphine prayed the aunt in the attic wouldn't pull a *Jane Eyre* during the night. Some family. Thank heaven she was replenishing the gene pool with Jake, not that she was having any luck getting pregnant.

"Aunt Hilly, let's drink to your future. We're going to package you and make you a star. The Julia Child of gardening! Public television, book and gardening clubs, coast-to-coast promotion. Prepare to become famous!"

Since Estabrook's door was closed to her, Delphine decided to send *Hildreth's Gardens* directly to Hollinsworth's new editorial director, George Byrne. She was not unknown to Byrne; he'd written her a note praising her work on Beamish's *Sleuth;* whenever they passed in the hall, he slowed his pace to smile at her, poised to speak, then hurried on, and she'd occasionally thought that if Jake hadn't blinded her to other men's appeal . . . But pitching Auntie's proposal to Byrne was an all-or-nothing gamble. A lowly reader never went over the head of her boss.

A week lumbered by. Delphine obsessed on the phone to Daisy and added new texture to her smoker's cough. She longed to join the lunchtime lushes at P. J. Clarke's, a white-shoe bar in a narrow free-standing brownstone on Third Avenue. In the back was a restaurant, but most habitués never made it past the liquid refreshment. After the third week, the siren call of Clarke's was beyond resisting. She was going to be fired anyway; they wouldn't continue cutting a check for deadwood. Why not go down in style.

Delphine snaked her way through the gray flannel crowd, male heads swiveling. She ordered a double Dewar's and stood with her elbows propped on the burnished mahogany bar, lost in her reflection in the blackened mirror. On either side, two overripe preppies leaned in with an opening gambit.

"Delphine!" The familiar caw penetrated the noontime gabble. "Delphine dahlink. What are you doing here?" Lucy Beamish butted her way through. She was so short, at first Delphine saw only a traveling hat, like Dali's limp watch, drooped over orange curls. She was lugging a brown Macy's shopping bag. "You're *just* the person I've been looking for."

"It's good to see you, Lucy," said Delphine with tragic dignity. She drained her Dewar's. "Won't you join me here on the road to perdition?"

"What? Lunch I'll have, perdition, no thank you. Why don't we mosey on back and grab a cheeseburger. You have an expense account, no? Oh, what the hell, we'll splurge. Have I got something for you. I can't believe my luck in finding you here. It's providential." Her second finger jabbed downward at her shopping bag. "My new book, dahlink. Untitled. Even *you,* dahlink, are going to like this one." She wheezed asthmatically, Lucy's form of laughter. "This is the one, my big book, the one I've been warming up for. That smarmy George Byrne is itching to get his hands on it. Ever since *Sleuth* took off, now suddenly they want me, *now* they all love me. Before it was, Make way for the bag lady, here comes the yenta. I saw their little smiles. So you know what I said to Byrne?"

Delphine was studying a photo to the left of the mirror of old-timers in bowler hats around a spittoon. Cut down in my prime, she thought. And now my period! It didn't seem fair. She'd failed as both woman and professional, though neither was her fault. Well, she'd get sloshed, just like the old-timers; she felt a solidarity with the world's boozers.

Lucy was tugging on the sleeve of her cardigan. "So you know what I said to the SOB?"

"No, Lucy," she sighed, "what did you say?"

"I said, 'Mr. Byrne, unless I can work with Delphine Mikulski, I will take this book' " — she paused for effect — " *'elsewhere.'* Ach!" She struck her forehead with the heel of her hand. "You should've seen his face."

Slowly Delphine turned and looked down into Lucy's eyes, magnified to large black disks by her bifocals. Her own eyes welled with tears. "You said that, Lucy? You did that for me?"

Puzzled: "What? Hell no, honey, I did it for *me*."

1963

Tonight Delphine couldn't begin to think about cooking dinner. Tonight she and Jake were golden. Tonight they would go to Orsini's and order a magnum of Dom Perignon. She all but polkaed around the living room, listening for Jake's key in the door. She'd phoned his office with the news of her promotion — no great surprise after *Rich and Dead*, as Beamish had called "Untitled," had hit the *Times* best-seller list, though Estabrook could have queered it; God knows he'd tried. Of all the rotten luck, Jake had left for the construction site. Then came the call from Aunt Hilly. With her news that *Hildreth's Gardens* had been taken for serialization by *The Boston Globe*, and PBS was discussing a weekly Saturday morning gardening show.

The slam of the door made her start. Silence. Footfalls. Jake sank into the blue velvet chair without taking off his Burberry.

"Would you care to talk? Maybe take your coat off first?" *Keep it light, Feen* — his bed name for her. She went to the hutch and poured him an iced martini, extra dry the way he liked them. Better save her news for later. Much later.

Jake knocked back his drink and stared past her. "Tell me, since you're an expert on *those people*. To qualify for chairman of the board of trustees, d'you have to have your head up your ass?"

"Could we back up and start from the beginning?" Delphine asked pleasantly. Determined to avoid a fight, which could lead to a week-long sex strike.

"We seem to have hit an impasse."

"Hampden College?"

"No, the fucking Parthenon. *Jesus*, Delphine." Outside a gathering storm grumbled. "It's Houghton, the goddamn chairman of the board. An arch Philistine. Wants the Chem building smack up against the Physics building, when it's plain to any cretin each structure makes a separate statement, and they were never ever meant to squat on top of each other like Siamese twins. So I blew my stack. I told him —"

"Yeah, you told him —"

"It's plain to any cretin each structure makes a separate statement."

"You used the word *cretin*?" she said, striving for a nonchalant tone. From her canvas, Aunt Letitia looked down with disdain. "Is there some way you could make Houghton see that the integrity of the design will be ruined by what he's proposing? After all, the board hasn't pulled all this dough from the alums just to present them with an eyesore."

"Oh sure, it's that simple. And I'm the village idiot who just doesn't get it. Do you honestly think I haven't tried to reason with them? D'you know your most irritating trait?"

No, tell me. Easy, skip the sarcasm. Dr. Beetlebaum had explained that Jake lashed out from unresolved infantile rage; thwarted, he'd attack whatever was at hand. She mustn't "personalize" it.

"It's your condescension. That's your least likeable trait."

She leaned back against the hutch, gripping it. She must short-circuit a scene. Too many scenes lately; Jake might raise questions she never wanted to hear. Suddenly her heart ached for him. He was ashamed. He was losing his footing at work, and his pride made him hate her and need to smash everything, and she didn't know how, without sounding condescending, to tell him, *I can absorb it.*

"You must be sorry you didn't marry Deadly Hunnewell."

"Oh let's not start with that," she said mildly. Dudley, the onetime human pyre, had collected himself and was now Doing Well at Brown Brothers Harriman. She could care less. But for Jake, Dudley embodied a world of insult and injury; he'd gone and married a cousin of Mimi Van Doorn, the woman Jake still loved to hate.

Delphine came and sat on the arm of his chair, and rubbed her cheek, catlike, against his hair. He shrank from her.

"I know you're still hot for ole Deadly. Aren't you. The three-piece suits, the Holland American Club —"

"God, those fascist John Birchers?" Delphine chuckled, semi-pleased; usually it was she jealous of Mimi, with reason.

"Southampton, the Meadow Club, all that dough, just think what you missed —"

"I never think of the silly boy — only when you bring him up." She kissed his ear. "And I can tell you, ole Deadly might still be at the funny farm without Poppy's connections."

"They should've kept him locked up. The nerve he had, doing that number at our wedding. But you people condone it. A *Hunnewell,* after all."

"What's this 'you people'? *You're* my people."

"Uh-huh. Is that why you keep that picture of Deadly in your drawer?"

"That's a picture of *Saskia,* Merry's yawl. Dudley happened to be on board."

"Oh did he. I'm sick of Merry's yawl, and cruising in Eggnog Reach, or whatever the place is you and Hildreth and your brain-damaged relatives gas about when you're loaded." In a sudden motion he stood, dumping her into the chair. His eyes blazed. "You wouldn't have murdered Deadly's child."

She needed a moment to take his meaning. *Oh God.* The "D and C" she'd had after the wedding. She'd thought all that was behind them. "Darling, that's so unfair," she said, tamping down her voice. "You agreed the timing was wrong, you told me you agreed."

His mouth twisted down at the corner. "I don't recall that I had much of a choice."

He headed for the door; she cut him off in the foyer.

"Jake, wait. Is that what this is all about? A baby we both agreed we didn't want? Not right then, because the timing was wrong, totally wrong, and would've wrecked everything?"

"You wouldn't have done it to Deadly's, just had the damn thing scooped out. Some mongrel fetus you just scooped out and tossed in the garbage. Like melon seeds." He looked at her with cold curiosity. "How many, for Lord's sake, how *many?*"

He reached for the door's top lock.

Delphine grasped the lapels of his trench coat. "Don't go, Jake, not tonight. I know you're pissed about Houghton, and you've every right to be, but I'm on your side. I want to help. I have utter confidence in you. I'd — I'd stand by you no matter what. There's nothing you could do to disappoint me, ever."

His lip curled. "Oh, but that's just what you're afraid of. That I will disappoint you. I've disappointed you already —"

"That's *nuts,* Jake. I'm asking you, don't go out tonight. Stay with me. Look" — yanking on his lapels — "I'm begging you, I'm begging you to be with me tonight."

His eyes went opaque. "I need to be alone. Oh don't, don't lay a guilt trip on me." He waved his hand in front of his face. "I gotta get outta this sty. It smells, there's dust all over. Old milk —"

"Old milk? You're talking to me about *old milk*?" She started to cry. He reached for the doorknob.

A howl burst from her, and she hurled herself at him. He caught her by the shoulders. "I hate it when you get like this."

He was out the door, jabbing the button for the elevator. She crumpled to the doorjamb.

"I just got promoted, you dumb fuck!"

Her own sneeze woke her. A rank odor. In the darkness she made out flowers. A hand waving a bouquet of daisies in front of her nose like smelling salts. Jake's face loomed over, foreshortened and loony. "I lost a pile-a clams." Peck's-bad-boy grin. "Backgammon, the Harvard Club." On his breath she smelled stale booze and fear, and she wanted to protect him. Little kisses traveled down her cheek, down her neck. His fingers plucked at the ribbons closing her gown. He nuzzled her chest. "My wife my life." She felt his breath against her breastbone and pulled him to her. "Darling," he said, "so selfish —" She put her hand over his mouth. His muffled voice: *So selfish . . . so sorry.* The clunk of a shoe hitting the floor. *Don't ever let me be such an asshole again.*

Chapter 14

JANUARY. For New York's population of single girls, more socially unmoored than illegal aliens, this was the cruel month. The swells have fled Manhattan's Upper East Side for Barbados, sharply reducing the number of cruisable events; and career girls getting by on sixty dollars a week ply the city's arctic canyons in threadbare coats. One knife-cold evening Gina invited Daisy to the Robert Rauschenberg opening at the Jewish Museum on Fifth Avenue. Renato, Gina's usual escort for glamour events, was down with the flu.

Forty-knot winds rattled the rotting sashes of Daisy's windows. She longed to stay in her lair, hunkered down with the poets, junkies, and paraexistentialists from the Beat Hotel. She'd finally written Chapter 1 of *Here Lies the Heart*. (It was making the rounds of the little literary magazines, and she'd received one rejection that wasn't a form letter.) She wrote to keep her brain alive, and from pique at Gina, now with her own column at *Mademoiselle,* and flashing a press pass, and jetting to L.A. She'd discovered that if you just started typing, you passed through a membrane into your self-made world, where you could live quite happily for hours at a time, like a bear in its cave. *But you're almost twenty-six,* came a niggling voice. That was like the expiration date stamped on pot cheese at Daitch Shopwell — *Heart* could wait. Sighing, she pulled on her Julie Christie mini with hem to *here* and penciled in the new Twinky broken-doll eyes. Get out there, tote that barge.

In the first room of the Jewish Museum, art patrons clustered in front of *White Painting,* a series of panels innocent of any image or even mark. Another gaggle inspected *Black Painting,* torn, crumpled newspapers painted black. On the far wall of the main gallery hung a real quilt and real pillow, schmeared with oil paint. The smartly dressed crowd glanced around uneasily for cues how to react; better appear reverent in the case this *wasn't* the emperor's new clothes. In one corner Rauschenberg himself, wearing summer white and paint-spattered sneakers, held court. "Why are you only interested in ugly things?" Daisy heard a woman ask. "Depends what you mean by 'ugly,' " answered Rauschenberg in a Southern drawl. "Take your mink coat, for instance. Couldn't it be described as the skin of a dead animal?" He was charming and fey, off-limits to women. So New York: at every turn enticements you couldn't have.

Daisy approached an enormous red painting aswarm with mirrors, shreds of underwear, a mashed parasol, postcards, comic strips, re-productions of old masters. The naked light bulb flashing from its center produced dancing red inchworms on her retina. She backed away — into a trio of pinstriped suits. A man with bootblacked hair glanced at her in annoyance, then continued yakking about pork bellies. In a separate klatch the wives agreed they could not survive, not even for a week, without a Hungarian countess on Park Avenue who vacuumed their pores. To think she could be home in Paris with her Beats! She scanned the crowd for Gina. There she was, standing behind a stuffed angora goat wearing an inner tube around its middle. With the discerning frown of a connoisseur, Daisy headed for the goat, when a movement of the crowd threw her sideways against a man.

"Enjoying the show?" he asked.

A kind, avuncular face, bald, a cascade of chins. A Republican banker no doubt. "Not as much as the reactions to it. Everyone's terrified of appearing like a Philistine."

Malcolm Straight, he said, extending his hand. "Oh, they'll catch up with Rauschenberg soon enough. He's already the old master of the new painting. I've been collecting him for some time, especially the silk screens," he added modestly. "I lent the museum *Charlene*." With his head he indicated the eye-damaging canvas.

"D'you have to change her light bulb often?" Daisy asked.

He laughed in a quick complicitous way, as though she'd said something enormously witty; Republican bankers knew how to put a girl at her ease. Straight chatted about his art collection; his preference for the new "pop" artists Andy Warhol and Tom Wesselman; the special intimacy you feel with your dealer. The only dealer she knew was Sally Wunderlick's old hash connection, but she kept that to herself and relaxed around Straight's oddly choked-off voice. His easy chattiness compensated for the oversize head and spreading gut. Semihypnotized, she felt her muscles unclench. So much simpler between men and women with the juice turned off.

She told Straight she worked in publishing. "But I'd rather be where there's more action. At a weekly newsmagazine. Unfortunately I've never gotten past Time Inc.'s typing test."

Straight's gray eyes sparkled behind his specs. "Oh, I sit on a board with the chairman of Time, I'd be happy to call him for you," he said in his unassuming way.

The pork belly maven was heading their way, eyes clamped onto Straight. "Uh-oh, see ya," said Daisy.

"Of course you know who *that* is," said Gina, bustling over. She wore a shocking pink spin-off from Courrèges and white-kid astronaut boots.

"You mean Chubby Checkers? He's the only person here who looked at the art. Maybe I'll call him for a business lunch." She'd just thought of it.

"Now don't tell me you've never heard of Malcolm Straight. *Everybody* knows Malcolm Straight."

"Maybe not west of the Hudson." Gina excelled at making you feel like a hayseed.

"He sort of, you know" — Gina looked vague — "collects companies. They say he's created this brilliant invention called a teaching machine that's supposed to revolutionize Western civilization. He's married to Perdita Jekyll, coanchor of the *CBS Morning Show. Mademoiselle* wants me to do a profile of her." A woman in an inky

beehive and too-dark brows stared at them, despising their youth.
Gina bent toward Daisy's ear. "I hear they've split, but better stay
away. You don't want to be the, uh, interim woman."

"Rather be Typhoid Mary," Daisy assured her. Suddenly she longed
to be curled up on her unfinished sofa with a mug of hot chocolate and
the new novel she'd just started, *The Group*.

At the revolving door she braced for the gales blasting off Fifth. If
only this were fiction, she thought, tonight I would have met my
destiny.

Daisy glared at the slim white envelope from *Prairie Schooner*. Fingered it, suspicious, afraid, not daring to hope. Usually she got a fat
five-by-eight enclosing her spurned chapter. Fat was bad. But thin? She
ripped open the envelope, all but tearing the letter. She reread the two
paragraphs several times, just to be sure. HALLELUJAH! Her cheeks
stretched in a grin. Just then Penson stomped up from the basement,
brandishing his snake. "Look, *orange* hairs —" Daisy beamed at him.
She loved Penson, loved the old grinch. "Never mind. I'll shave my
head. I sold my chapter! I'm breaking into print!" She waved her letter
at him and kissed him on the cheek.

That *Prairie Schooner* was paying one hundred fifty bucks on publication, more than a year away, lowered her to sea level. Writing was
a rich girl's game. Except at Time Inc., home of the living wage. Wait
a sec, that Republican from the Jewish Museum — didn't he know
someone at Time? Sooo serendipitous. Why not call him for lunch?
Connections, everything in Gotham was connections. She liked it; she
was learning to think smart.

It was a trip, driving with Straight. He spun the black Porsche around
every obstacle, moving or stationary, never braking, urbanely chatting, no stitch dropped, *smooth*. A man of surprises, this Straight. The
Republican drove like a cabbie. Daisy reveled in Kraut workmanship,
the buttery leather and expensive clicks, the orange and blue hiero-
glyphs on the baseboard. In the distance loomed a cluster of glittering
monoliths, Manhattan Stonehenge. Time Inc. in there somewhere,
perpetually unreachable, like *The Three Sisters'* Moscow. Unless, of
course, you had entrée.

Straight's agenda was cloudier. He'd canceled their lunch date, but before she could get depressed, he proposed dinner. Well, well. Lunch was platonic, but dinner was open ended into the vast New York night, prelude to anything. The guy was also ancient, fat, and somewhat married. Nonetheless she assembled her war paint and produced her best Keane waif crossed with Twinky tart. A little *coquetterie* kept a girl from dozing into the consommé. Hell, in the old days, Sally November would've worn her diaphragm.

La Caravelle was on Fifty-fifth Street off Fifth Avenue. It was one of those pink and silver preserves with cuisine so haute you could leave your teeth home. As the maître d' led them to their banquette, Daisy caught a blur of svelte women in giant beehives and Jackie-little-black-dresses dining with their fathers. She felt like a dead-end kid out with her rich uncle. In her honor Straight had traded the pinstripes for a bulky leather jacket over a western shirt and flowered tie — slumming, was he? He was cordial and easy the way she remembered. Bashful, more like a Kansas high school boy at prom time than an entrepreneur. A wave of desperation. How would the Time business carry them all the way through to dessert? She sure hoped the food was good. Straight was ordering the Montrachet. Her menu had no prices, so the woman wouldn't know the cost of her favors. She felt worldly and blasé, Sally Bowles in Berlin. She'd wait till the second glass of wine to bring up Time.

"I have a little triumph to celebrate." She told Straight about her letter from *Prairie Schooner*.

He looked impressed. "Bra-vo! That's tremendous!" They clinked glasses. Accustomed to rotgut Almaden, Daisy gulped in amazement the velvety — woody? — Montrachet.

"But what they're paying me," said Daisy, spotting her opening, "is pathetic."

"Those publications are always wildly undercapitalized. God, I admire you for writing a book. The discipline it takes to create your own structure. When I was at Yale I helped edit a kind of alternative literary magazine with something to offend everyone."

"When were you at Yale?" She had him in Kansas City, before the Boer War.

"I was class of fifty-five."

"Really! I thought you were — well, a different generation." She flushed. Oh nice, she'd just blown it — but Straight just looked rosy and content. Success must do wonders for the old self-esteem. Add hair, she reflected, subtract the pounds and a couple of chins, and he could be, well, just shy of thirty. Less of an uncle. Something in the evening shifted. "So, we're pretty much products of the same era," Daisy said.

"Ah, the uptight fifties." He laughed. "What a time. It marked us for life."

"Probably for the worse."

"No, I loved it. All that repression. Necking in the back seat of cars. Button-down everything."

"Merry widows."

"I like Ike."

"Wanda Hendrix."

"Veronica Lake."

"Johnny Ray. 'The Little White Cloud That Cried.'"

"'Red Sails in the Sunset.'"

"Oooh-wah."

"Dooh-wah."

"*Forever Amber* — hot stuff!"

"*Love Without Fear.*"

Laughing, they both upended their glasses. In the same moment they set them down, and their eyes locked, and they kept on looking, and looking, unable to come to the end of what they'd discovered. She was the one to break it. Hold it, *waitaminute*. Not on the agenda. She sipped her wine, marveling, half listening as Straight went on touring the fifties. *Photoplay,* Levitttown, bomb shelters. What's happened? Something momentous. The static is gone. She hadn't noticed all the static. Only Straight coming in now, loud and clear. The gray eyes fringed with jet lashes, feminine and shy, a vertical groove between the snub nose and mouth, horsey teeth, flattened predator's ears. Suddenly everything the world could offer was right at this table.

"You know, we might've known each other in college," she said dreamily.

"Sat at neighboring tables in the Rathskeller in New Haven."

"Passed each other in the lobby of the Taft Hotel."

"Somehow we just missed each other."

They considered this, the tragedy of it. Daisy focused on a vase of gladioli the color of rayon panties, clung to it like a drowning sailor.

"Do you live alone?"

"With my avocado plants. You?"

"I married very young. We're separated."

Oh. Had he answered her question? Did it matter?

They both looked up in surprise. A squadron of waiters leaned over them with chafing dishes and silver and much white linen.

Time Inc., she thought once, giddy, flushed, down the magic rabbit hole.

In front of her brownstone he killed the engine and they sat in silence, mottled in sepia by the street lamp. A pause before the beginning of the world. She kissed him good night, a social kiss, east of the mouth, but he moved toward her and captured her lips with his and kissed her softly, tentatively, the shy date, and now fiercely, hungry, she answered him, tasted him, he drowning in her mouth, she expiring, each in the other, and then he drew her hard against him and they groaned. Laughing, she said, We're like teeny boppers in cars. He said, You can't go now. Can I come up? It was delicious, the Republican banker as horny sophomore. "It's late, I have to go to work tomorrow." "So do I." In the vestibule he crushed her against him. I want to come up, please, but she sent him gently away.

Her nerve ends hissed and whirred like Roman candles. She headed straight for the refrigerator and got her mouth around some Schrafft's cherry vanilla ice cream. Fifteen minutes later the phone rang.

"Since you won't let me stay with you, come stay with me. I'll pick you up in the car."

"Gracious, we've only just met."

"We've known each other forever. I'll be right over."

"It's past midnight."

"You know neither of us will get any sleep."

"Try eating ice cream. That's what I'm doing."

"How can ice cream help?"

"It does, it just does."

"Would you have dinner with me tomorrow?"

"Can't. Next Tuesday maybe."

"That's five whole days! All right, Tuesday it is."

Tuesday afternoon he phoned her at the office from an airplane. An *airplane*? "Sorry, tonight's impossible, things have gotten crazy. I'm far more disappointed than you. What about tomorrow?"

Wednesday he phoned from a limo to say he'd been delayed in Dallas and would call Thursday from Idlewild, but Thursday came and went, then Friday, too.

Six P.M. found her in Gina's old family car, pointed north on Route 95. She had no plan. Just to get lost in the cold cauterizing North, as far into New England as she could get before exhaustion overtook her. Dialing around on the radio, she found a station that played her favorites — the Everly Brothers, the Beach Boys doing "Surfin' U.S.A.," the Crystals singing "Then He Kissed Me." Dangerously romantic. Dial on, turn up the volume, drown thought. The snow started lightly at first, then went to feathery white flakes, faster, thicker. The car danced on the road; Gina's family didn't believe in snow tires. The front wipers kept icing over and sticking. She was driving blind.

By Holyoke everything on the road crawled, the swirling snow in her beams veiling the car directly ahead. Braking lightly she went into a ninety-degree skid, avoiding a crackup by a hair. She decided to stay alive. Pulled up at an inn, the Yankee Pedlar. A Ye Olde number, roaring fires, needlepoint samplers, copper and brick, they'd really laid it on. The check-in clerk's eyes lingered on her. She must look wild. Or maybe the world always looked askance at an unattached woman.

She'd never been able to dine solo without feeling like Quasimodo, and the tab would be steep, so she went into the bar. To the right, a fire leapt and crackled in a blackened hearth. The mantel lined with pewter plates. Suddenly she was walloped by loneliness, the effect on her of Olde American. She'd eaten no lunch and the Dewar's lit through her.

Then she saw the bulky figure filling the doorway — impossible. No. He wore a navy parka and terrible leather Stetson mashed down on his pate. She blinked and shook her head. Elation rose in her; she bit off its neck. Impossible. She turned away and leaned her elbows on the bar and focused ahead into the mirror. How had he found her? She hadn't run this far and almost died just to be found.

In the mirror she saw Straight take off his parka and hang it on a bentwood stand. He wore his country threads, an oatmeal Shetland that belled over his gut, and too-tight corduroys. His balding dome dwarfed his body. This is not a pretty sight, she thought. Relieved. She focused on the bar's impressive array of painkillers. He sat on the stool next to her. The mountain cold came off him, and the smell of snow and wet leather. What was she drinking, he asked. Better switch on the defogger. "I'll have a Coke, please," she told the bartender, ignoring Straight.

"Tell me what's going on, what're you doing? I've been calling all night. Why have you run away from me?"

"Run from you? Freud called that grandiosity. Neither the world nor I, strange as that may sound, revolve around you. I came up here to ski Mount Tom."

"Alone?"

"The lift line gets pretty sociable. Look, how the hell did you find me?"

"Oh, I have my ways," he said mysteriously.

Gina? she wondered. He might have seen them together at the Rauschenberg opening . . .

The bartender had discreetly moved away and was polishing glasses. The guests were all busy with their prime ribs; they had the place to themselves.

Straight leaned toward her. "Listen, what happened between us the other night was one of the most extraordinary things that's ever happened to me. I felt so incredibly comfortable, as if we'd known each other forever."

It was like coming home. And she, since that night, she hadn't stopped telling him the story of her life.

"Uh, have you checked in? Could we go —?" He looked in the direction of the stairs.

She jiggled her stool away. "Now it suits you? Now you can fit me in?"

"I'm sorry, my time is impossible. I never know when I'll be called away on business. I ought to have warned you."

"For your schedule you need a five-minute whore. Put a nickel in the Automat slot, and out she comes, bologna on white."

"I'm sorry, I was wrong. I hope you'll give me another chance."

"You can't just come hustling after me with this incredible grabbiness. Grab, grab, grab. Whatever you want, whenever you want it."

"There was a crisis, with millions of dollars at stake."

"And that gives you the — that exempts you from civility?"

"No, you're right —"

"And *you're* married, goddammit!"

The bartender glanced up at them. Relief smoothed Straight's brow. "Oh, so that's it. That is a bit complicated," he added. "But these things can be worked out, you know."

"Maybe I don't want your — 'a bit complicated.' "

"I didn't mean to be presumptuous. I thought you felt the way I did."

"I got ground up once by complications," she said shortly.

"But your past history — you can't ask me to pay for that."

"I would ask, though — not that I'm asking. You're looking at damaged goods, couple of cracks, a little chipped. I wouldn't go real well with the Rauschenbergs." She drained the Dewar's — his; ice cubes clacked against her front teeth. Straight signaled the waiter. He jumped to. She pictured Straight moving through the world signaling, things falling off shelves into his lap. The image didn't altogether displease her.

"I'll tell you a bedtime story," she said. "Once upon a time there was this little prince who met a beautiful gold fox with long ears. The prince wanted to make friends with the fox. But the fox said, 'If we're to be friends you must tame me. You must sit and watch me every day, out of the corner of your eye. And every day you can move a little closer. And there's something else: You're responsible forever for what you have tamed.' "

A moment. "But we've barely gone out on a date!"

Silence.

"Can't we just go along and have fun?" He put the heel of his hand to his forehead. "This is berserk. Everything I see is right. I — I really don't believe in analyzing things." Wincing, he said, "Okay. Perdita was the first woman I slept with. She was pregnant when we got married. Then she had a miscarriage. It was just as well, she's not interested in children, I can tell you. All she cares about is getting mentioned in Hedda Hopper. We didn't have a marriage, she was married to the job. We haven't loved each other for a long time." He looked exhausted from introspection.

"And you're asking me to trust you."

"I am, yes. Is that so terrible?"

"Why should I?"

"Because you can't live that way. Why should *I* trust the sun to come up every morning? I take enormous risks every day."

"That's just money."

He leaned toward her. "Take a chance on me, Daisy. Risk it. Christ, I'd get down on my knees in front of this bar stool if I wouldn't look like a horse's ass."

She had to smile. "Guarantees, I want guarantees."

Something relaxed around his eyes. "Like the warranties for a toaster, or a Hoover vacuum?"

Those parts could be replaced. "Tell me, why do you like me?"

"Because you're good. We deserve each other. And you remind me of Francie O'Brien — the girl I was in love with in first grade. All scrubbed and shiny, with freckles and the world's pluckiest smile. And I want to rescue you from your avocados. And you make me crazy with lust . . ."

So here it was. She'd been ambushed, by snow, Straight, and her own desires, not a prayer of escaping. How did you escape when all you wanted was to get your mouths on every part of each other? Would you rather be happy or right? Delphine's shrink always said. She had all the rest of her life to be right.

"Let's not analyze everything to death," he was saying. "I've always felt that things that are meant to be just kind of work out."

"Like in those forties movies with happy endings? Running toward each other across wheat fields — Darling, we've found each other at last?"

"Like that, yes."

Why fight this? She couldn't remember the reasons.

He peeked at his watch. Warily he said, "You're not going to like this."

Already?

"I have a breakfast meeting tomorrow morning at seven. To make it I'll have to drive back to New York tonight."

Knowing that, he'd driven all this way? She laughed and laughed, shoulders shaking, as Straight watched uncertainly. "You deserve a great big kiss for being so intrepid. Or insane." Their lips were rough and dry. They brushed them together, like feverish children.

"You must be hungry," Straight said. "Shall we go have dinner?"

But when the waiter arrived with their bloody prime ribs, they both looked at each other, and Straight explained to the scandalized waiter in his throttled voice that they wouldn't be dining after all.

The forgiving tea-colored light in her room was not forgiving to Straight. He was bulky and white, and she noticed a lozenge-shaped charcoal birthmark stamped on his shoulder like the mark of Cain, but her desire cut deeper, like an underground flume, and then came the silky slide of skin on skin, his chest against her breasts, his hardness, her slickness, and they had everything they desired and more, and the world closed in a perfect circle.

The crazy thing was Gina swore she had never spoken to Straight. He never would tell her how he had found her.

All the world dislikes a besotted couple. Delphine fumed at the way Daisy said "we" all the time; Gina made cracks about her soppy smile. Like astral travelers linking up in the night, she and Straight sometimes dreamt the same dream. Once they suffered through a modern dance concert in the Village, an exercise in self-indulgence, with an interminable score by Mahler. I feel trapped in a German Expressionist nightmare, thought Daisy. A second later Straight whispered the identical sentence into her ear.

"We scare me," said Daisy whenever this happened (often).

"Not me. Why do you always worry?"

"It's in the genes. We Jews from Minsk worry a lot. We take it as a personal assignment to do the world's worrying for it. So people like you can be carefree and innocent."

Laughing, Straight kissed the inside of her wrist. "A waste of time, worrying," he said, glancing at his watch. "Everything I see is right."

She could barely wait for him to come huffing up the four flights to her apartment to report his latest coup. One night it was an article in *Business Week*. The next, Xerox was sniffing around his teaching machine company. Midsentence he lost his thought, showered her with kisses. This man who made his adversaries quake looked at her, dark lashes fluttering, almost with fear. His triumphs made her feel important, as though she herself mattered and were making an impact. *Here Lies the Heart* had retreated again to the back burner. So had her designs on Time Inc.

One Wednesday Straight phoned her from London and asked her to meet him at the Hyde Park Hotel for a long weekend.

That same afternoon her boss at Aspen invited her to lunch at the Cookery.

"How'd you like an assignment that could be a real steppingstone," Nan McIver said out the side of her mouth. "I'd like you to pick up Gracchi — yes, *your* author" — she winked — "at Idlewild this Saturday. You'll settle him in his hotel and take him around to the press and TV interviews we've set up."

Daisy set down her Virgin Mary. Beneath her the floor seemed to be shifting levels. "I can't do it, I'm really sorry. I've already made plans."

"Well, for God's sake, change them. Daisy, maybe you don't understand. If you handle this assignment okay, you'd be the logical choice for promotion assistant. Now listen carefully: the promotion director, my spies tell me, wants to move to Editorial. That means you, my dear, are in the right place when *his* job comes open."

"But I'm going to London for the weekend!"

"You're *what?*"

"To meet my boyfriend," Daisy added lamely.

A moment. Nan's stare turned respectful. "Oh, I see. Uh-huh. Well, in that case . . ." She looked miserable. Pushed aside her plate of blintzes as if they'd turned rancid. "He's giving you a whole weekend? And I can hardly weasel two lousy hours outta Greg on a Saturday night?"

God, what have I done? Daisy wondered, thirty thousand feet over the Atlantic. I could have gotten a raise, a title, a real foothold. Then again, she'd been wondering lately what it was she had wanted so badly from publishing. Her happiest hours at Aspen were spent in the can reading. Now where could you get paid for loving books? Why, the academic world. As she poked at her *poulet chasseur,* she saw herself, Dr. Frank, leaning over the podium, proffering brilliant insights on her beloved Stendhal. She'd have prestige — how many women became profs? Not much money, of course. But her job would yield a second income, fill in the gaps. Of course Straight was the best reason of all for joining academe. You could work and be a wife and mother, too. She had not forgotten Straight's sourness over Perdita's "marriage" to her job.

·   ·   ·

Of course, once in London, she hardly saw Straight at all, between phone calls and meetings. She lolled about in the hotel terry cloth robe, lingered over the bidet, anointed her body with lotions from Fortnum and Mason. They managed a stroll through the flea market in the cold spring drizzle, Straight looking dopey in his tweed newsboy's hat, and he bought her an antique amethyst brooch, and they took a hump-backed cab to see *A Taste of Honey* — dozing through the whole first act — and never went, as they had planned, to the Cotswolds. He told her he loved her madly.

Love in the fast lane. This was love without foreplay — he was sometimes so pressed, he never took off his socks. ("We only want the best for you," said Franca from Cambridge. "But Peter thinks if the dear fellow doesn't take off his socks — Well, is he serious?")

Straight was married to the phone. After a marathon session, around midnight, he innocently inquired, "D'you think you might want dinner?" Nor did Daisy disclose that at his calmest Straight was a no-frills lover. He had two settings, like her broken Osterizer: fast and super-fast. She was wound up so tight from socks-on love, by the fourth fuck he had only to graze her skin and she was gone, wheeling through the stratosphere. Heady stuff. She was fucking a captain of industry and robber baron — Ira Frank's bogeyman — an American buccaneer, the Spirit of St. Louis and for spacious skies and amber grain, J. P. Morgan and raw energy unencumbered by angst, she was fucking everything that made American great. Straight had healed her. She loved and was loved in return.

Chapter 15

1963

FROM THE CLASSES:
FEBRUARY 1963

Class of '58 (Correspondent:
Sally *November* Wunderlick)

"Frank Jr. (4), Sarah (3), charity bake sales, and two sheep dogs are keeping me hopping," writes Diana *Dew* Hilliard. "President Kennedy has just named Our Leader director of the National Endowment for the Humanities. Our new address in Chevy Chase.

Delphine *Mortimer* Mikulski writes that she has just been named associate editor at Hollinsworth. Congratulations, Delphine!

We read in the *Times* that Grace *Omura* is one of a group of artists pioneering a new art form called "Happenings."

Mia *Sils-Levy* writes, "I left the road company of *Oliver!* to marry Nicholas Damiano, editor of *Erot-*

174

ica. As all the world knows, Nick is now being
brought up on obscenity charges. Any classmates
wishing to do so may contribute to his defense fund at
the New York Civil Liberties Union."

Gina *Gold* is a columnist for *Mademoiselle.* March
19 she's hosting a mini SLC reunion in her apartment.
Anyone passing thru Manhattan welcome!

"IS THIS LITTLE MAN *precious?* D'ya jus' wanna eat him up?"
Sally Wunderlick pinched Axel Tabori's little sausage arm. She wore
her pregnancy before her like Napoleon's army advancing on Moscow. Axel waggled his head, flashed a gummy smile, and upchucked
a few beige curds of milk onto Gina's couch.

"Oh, I'm so sorry," said Franca.

Gina dashed for a sponge — she'd just paid Bloomingdale's two
hundred seventy-nine dollars to recover the couch in white Haitian
cotton. Franca reached into a plastic carryall decorated with mice
holding balloons and patted Axel down with a cleanish diaper. Her
ankles were waterlogged and pink, her eyes sunken in her mottled
cheeks. She was pregnant again, and Axel barely seven months.

Daisy crouched before him on the flokati rug. A delicate scent of
Johnson's powder rose from his doe-colored thatch of hair. She ran her
index finger over his dimpled apricot knee, marveling at the silk of his
skin. He reached for her braid and pulled it toward him, eyes goggling
at the burnished copper. Daisy laughed, surprised by the strength in his
little fingers, rubbed her cheek against his. She was drowning in hormones. Bellies, babies, upchuck: they were the hot center of life. A
child at your knee, another tucked under your heart, a daddy who
came home at night — what safety! Death would never find you. To
have Straight's baby — *their* child — seemed the apex of joy on earth.
He'd be the dearest guy, gray-eyed with black lashes, plump like Papa,
who looked like Winston Churchill anyway.

"Oh, Axel jus' loves you, Daisy," chirped Diana Hilliard, bouncing
squirmy Sarah on her lap. "Somehow I never thought of you as the
maternal type."

Daisy looked at Diana, a sleek young matron in the same honey
pageboy as at college. She was walleyed from watching the kids sprint

in opposite directions; spent her days choosing fabrics for the new rumpus room; had just enough education so she wouldn't embarrass Our Leader — WHAT THEY DIDN'T WANT, BETTER DEAD! But Diana was right. The squares, the wifeys in the Kelvinator ads, they were right, too. Because what was the alternative? How else did you move your life forward?

"Didn't Freud say we have no choice?" Daisy answered sharply. She stood too suddenly and the floor billowed. *Stay here forever,* Straight had murmured last night in his pad in the Belnord. Did that count as a proposal? It had a wonderfully cosmic ring, but it wasn't awfully specific.

Delphine lit into a slice of pound cake, spraying crumbs on Gina's rug. She was worried about her plumbing. She hadn't worn her diaphragm in maybe a year. Hadn't told Jake, but in typical male fashion, he hadn't noticed. Something out of whack down there. Was she the barren woman? Christ almighty, after all those abortions? Because of them? After the last trip to Dr. Spencer, she'd bled for weeks. She shouldn't have had sex so soon after.

"Freud be damned, I for one am not cut out for motherhood," Delphine said. To Franca: "With all these hands and mouths tugging and wanting at you, what's left for *you?*"

Me, thought Franca? Who is that? She couldn't locate herself, nor did she especially want to. She only knew that lately she couldn't wait to put the babies down so she could uncork the sherry.

"Since you mention it," said Franca sweetly, ignoring Delphine's bellicose tone, "the truth is number four wasn't exactly planned. It's too embarrassing how it happened" — she looked around the room — "but you all I can tell. You see, I was still nursing Axel and, well — you know how they say you can't get pregnant when you're nursing?"

Delphine registered the arrival of that low backache that signaled — Oh *shit*!

"Well, it ain't true!" said Franca.

Laughter all round.

"The truth is, after Axel I was so exhausted, I don't remember how it happened."

Laughter.

"I don't even remember *doing* anything with Peter."

.   .   .

If only she *didn't* remember, could delete the memory . . . That little secret she would never expose to the old crowd, or even Daisy, unshockable, able to absorb anything.

After Axel, she'd wanted only to sleep; the tiredness was like inching on her belly across a vast savanna she couldn't reach the end of. He'd presented wrong, and after eighteen hours of labor Dr. Widdoes had done a C section, and then she developed a stubborn fever. Between the nurses, her mother, and the fever, she scarcely noticed that Peter wasn't around much at night — he was buried in the new production of Beckett one-acters. In a way she was grateful for his absence; she hadn't the strength to pretend, as Peter required, that she was hunky-dory. Whenever she was sick, he tried to be sympathetic — the dear fellow really did try — but irritation overtook him, and then his guilt kicked in, draining off energy that belonged to his work, and he wound up furious. At her. She was hobbling his creativity! You could be dying, and Peter would work it so he got the sympathy. She'd give it, too. Dead, she'd watch over him with a terrible caring.

Her first afternoon out of the house, the weather was blowy and moist and mild. Spring at last! Lawns were yellow with daffodils; her eye caught on a salmon-colored flowering quince. All of Cambridge was blowing and light-struck, ready to lift skyward. Her life felt full to overflowing. She sauntered down Brattle Street toward Harvard Square, smiling at strangers, humbled by her good fortune, wishing she could spread it around. Then she spotted Peter turning the corner from Church Street. With a woman. Beth Kavafian, star of the Ionesco play he'd directed.

An inner contraction, like a fist clenching: her uterus shrinking back down to size. Okay, big deal, they'd had a working lunch. She stopped to admire the bunches of yellow and purple freesias set out on the sidewalk in front of Henley Flowers. Suddenly she remembered Peter had mentioned that Beth was on the Coast, working at the Mark Taper. Franca walked on, leaving the thought behind her. No sense poking around in the mess. They said anxiety dried up your milk. The babies, the life she'd built with Peter, had the permanence of Mount Rushmore. Nothing could be altered but by a killer asteroid hurtling toward earth. So why poke around in the mess?

She crossed Brattle Street to Touraine's. Lingered in front of a lingerie display, studying her own reflection glancing off the window.

Her new layered feather cut exposed the ash in her ash blond hair — she pictured Beth Kavafian's lustrous black mane — and her molars ached. Below the neck a disaster area: cotton nursing bra, stretch marks, pouchy belly scored with a vertical raw pink zipper. It didn't seem fair: while she was spreading and loosening, Peter grew more boyish and taut. When she dropped her bra's panel to nurse, he no longer hovered around with a beatific smile, as he had with Andy. He looked as if he'd throw up. She'd taken to nursing Axel on a daybed in the third-story spare room, where Peter wouldn't see her. Her tears dripped down onto her breast and mingled with her milk, and then, when Axel caught cold, with his snot. "We're a pretty gross pair, you and me," she whispered at Axel.

She often found herself weeping like this, without knowing why. She'd had the babies so fast. She couldn't tell if she was depressed or just hormonally deranged.

Her eyes focused past her own image in Touraine's window. The mannequin wore a long blue nylon nightgown with spaghetti straps. The sort you'd wear with feather mules and ostrich boa, a real knock-out, Rita Hayworth in *Gilda*. Transparent. It brought a memory of Peter. Deepest night, and she woke to him stabbing into her from behind, she so drowsy yet right there, juicy and ready. No, absurd, out of the question. The milk stains would wreck such a nightgown. The thing would be hideously expensive. But maybe not. And worth it? Maybe? Should she? Just go in and ask?

When Peter got home that night, sometime after ten, she smelled the afternoon on him the moment he stepped into the kitchen. So he no longer bothered to cover his traces! A "nooner," wasn't that the word? An extended nooner. She had a precise image of him, lean and hard, plowing into dark voluptuous Beth, and she was amazed to feel a flash of desire. She'd reached the far side of degradation.

"Do anything, Peter," she heard herself say, "but don't lie to me anymore, it's all I ask."

He looked up from the kitchen table, where he was thumbing through *Show* magazine. She saw his reflection in the double windows giving on the garden, his fair hair and blue work shirt, and a bottle of Chardonnay on the table. The image recalled the serenity of a Flemish interior.

"Okay," Peter said simply. He dragged on his Camel. "Franca, I love you very much, you're my dearest friend and my wife and the mother of our children. But no matter how hard I try — and I have tried! — I can't fight my own nature anymore. At the thought of sleeping only with you for the rest of our lives — and I don't mean you per se, don't take this personally, I mean *only one woman* — dammit, it feels perverted. I feel trapped. Like a gelding. Can I help the way I'm made?"

She tried to remember something she'd read in Martin Buber's *I and Thou* about ethical responsibility, but she'd grown so muddled . . .

"It's not just me, it's the male animal. We're not biologically constituted to be monogamous. The fact is we're programmed to pump semen as often as possible into as many women as we can. I'm talking science here, not personal predilection."

An idea surfaced from her freshman course, *The Grand Plan of Evolution.* "Swans are monogamous," she said. "And loons, eagles, cranes, albatrosses — beavers, foxes, dik-diks —"

"Franca, give it up. Look, here's what I've been thinking. Why not work *with* who I am, instead of fighting it all the time. I can't — I won't — hide Beth from you any longer." He waved his cigarette. "You're right to ask me not to, I have to respect that. The logistics of sneaking around are unworthy of all of us. Now just hear me out on this, I'm trying to be constructive, I'm looking for solutions. From now on it's gotta all be out in the open. I want to be able to . . . to confide in you about everything and everyone."

Everyone . . . Elke, the Danish au pair; Beth — how many others?

"I want to share the love between Beth and me *with* you, so it won't drive you and me apart."

"It wasn't — it isn't — just sex?"

"It started that way, and then it — well, it grew."

Like a tumor. Franca seized an orange from a wire basket hanging to one side of the sink. She looked at the orange, felt its texture and heft in her hand. When had they started? She'd been so busy nursing Axel, a colicky baby, and then came Chrissie's earaches, and Andy so hyperactive. She hadn't paid much attention. A thought startled her: She had enough money to leave. No man would ever want her, with her pouch and pink zipper and stretch marks, but she and Mother would raise the babies, and she could devote herself to good works at the New England Home for Little Wanderers.

"What're you doing with the bloody orange, can't you pay attention? You've gotten so scattered. Now honey, listen. There's a group of revolutionary thinkers around Cambridge who are trying to push back our demeaning bourgeois boundaries. Publishing papers about their work in the alternative journals — I'll show you some clips. See, they've discovered that 'possessiveness' and 'jealousy' don't exist. They're just *words,* signifying nothing. So why should we ruin our lives for a fiction? We can have everything we need without bludgeoning each other. As I see it, you and I and Beth would spend time together without drawing arbitrary limits, and we would share everything."

"You mean orgies?"

"Now, what kind of dumb question is that?" He stood and lit another cigarette. "We could have a triad, if that's what we decide, but why must you put it in such an ugly way? Why be so reductionist? Why not be open to life?"

"And Beth likes this idea?"

"She can't see any other way."

Franca started to cry. Silent tears of rage coursed down her cheeks.

Peter groaned. Ran his fingers through his hair. "This always happens. Whenever I try dealing with you on a serious adult level, you start acting like a lunatic. Or some hick from East Jesus. The Europeans have been doing these things for years." He poured himself some wine from the bottle of Chardonnay on the table. "Franca, maybe you don't understand. This is not a one-way street. The deal is *you* would have your freedom too."

Franca looked down at the orange in her hand and she looked at Peter's blue and yellow reflection, doubled in the storm window, and then she started peeling the orange.

The next day she bought the nightgown in Touraine's.

Chapter 16

YOU KNOW YOU can handle it, you've been here before. Gina stood squarely in her empty living room in her white piqué model's coat with the strawberries, fists clenched, facing down the panic. Saturday morning, with the weekend before her, she always woke feeling weightless, skating on air, like John Glenn in his lonely capsule — till Monday morning caught her in its safety net, and just in the nick of time, too. "Bye-bye, love / Hello loneliness" she sang off-key. Love? Been a while. Like five years. *Five?*

STOPTHAT. No negative thoughts. The glass is half full, and you are in control. If you acted happy and smiley, she'd discovered, sort of by accident, you *became* happy-smiley. Bought your own act. The truth was *The Little Engine That Could* said more to her than all that gloomy Sartre and Camus in college. And the grime-smeared sign she'd once seen in a garage: THE DIFFICULT WE DO RIGHT AWAY, THE IM-POSSIBLE TAKES A LITTLE LONGER. Of course, she'd die before she'd reveal any of this to the old crowd. Bad enough that Delphine made cracks about her "Panglossian optimism" — not that she could re-member who Pangloss was. Amazing how Delphine could still make her feel like a clod.

Gina sank into her black beanbag chair; it sent up an empathic whoosh. Should she get a cat? What was she thinking? She loathed cats. And they stamped you an official spinster. She admired her spiffy new living room; it'd barely survived last night's assault by her classmates' babies. White sofa, black director's chairs, red accents, thanks to two raises at *Mademoiselle. Enjoy.* She'd throw a cocktail party. Serve onion dip with sour cream from Lipton's soup mix, low-rent liverwurst paté; if she was feeling flush, steak tartare. She drew up a guest list. It always improved her mood to make a list. She'd invite the French model downstairs, though she'd prefer just the model's beau.

To work, no more procrastinating! Sanka in hand — she avoided artificial stimulants — she sat at the Danish modern dining table she'd bought from Sally Wunderlick before her wedding. Flipped through her reporter's pad to the interview with Perdita Jekyll, a comer on the *CBS Morning Show,* and one of the few prominent women in television. An interview she'd wangled by never letting up; *a no is only the long way around to yes.* She was a crackerjack interviewer, she noted, reading Perdita's answers. Her trick was to fess up a little herself, to get her subject to spill. And had Perdita ever spilled, lubricated by three martinis through lunch. "This is off the record, just between you 'n' me, babe — but you can't work this job and lead a normal life. The hours — in bed by nine, up at four — the traveling, the pressure. Find me a man who'll put up with it. This job would wreck any marriage."

Having nothing to wreck, Gina idly wondered how *she* might do in Perdita's job. Her own face blossomed on the tube. Why not? She'd had zero qualifications when she started at *Mademoiselle;* you learn by doing. As Renato loved to say, "It's all done with mirrors." Yeah, but TV belonged to the blond and gorgeous, Miss American Pie, not a face as broad as the steppes that no makeover could transform.

She tried out a few lame leads. Finding the right lead was a unique form of torture; in fact, she hated to write. *Why do this to yourself? It's only for now; only till I meet the One.* (Nice, she now had dialogues with herself — as long as she didn't do it in the street.) At eight pop a Swanson TV dinner in the oven, then wash stockings and girdle, relax with Dick Van Dyke on the tube. That should sail her through the treacherous Straits of . . . wherever — SLC wasn't strong on geography — till she reached the far shores of Sunday, when everyone in New York wandered around in a subclinical depression.

I owe it to my public to muddle through. "Spinster's Survival Kit," in the March issue, had brought an avalanche of mail from readers buoyed by the humor-tinged advice.

> The fridge should be empty, except for orchids and Dom Perignon (get a false bottom to stow food). In the medicine cabinet, keep men's after-shave lotion, and hide embarrassing medication — no need to tell him on the first date about your colitis. Leave a matchbook from Lutèce on the coffee table.
> If desperate for the warmth of a human voice, you can always call the weather, the switchboard at the Botanical Gardens, or Poison Control Center . . .

That article had also brought a revelation: any misery could be converted into an asset, just about, if you wrote about it. If you're dealt a rotten hand, why not use it? Waste not, want not. A mild breeze blew up her white dotted swiss curtains, teasing, cruelly inviting — way too early for spring. She smelled pizza dough cut with exhaust fumes and pollution. A hunger inside her kicked into high gear, and she knew she wasn't going to win this one. There had to be someone free for a last-minute burger and flick.

She phoned Renato, who'd become one of her best "girlfriends." On Saturday night they often took in a movie together, because he was involved with a married man (!), a psychiatrist's husband who was too guilt-ridden to desert his kids. Gina sometimes joked that she and Renato were both losers in love.

(One night they'd drunk too much Chianti and, the hour being late, somehow fell together into Gina's chaste and narrow bed. And then nature, or something, maybe just the proximity of two warm bodies, took over, and they discovered themselves on the lip of making love, but Renato finally couldn't. Just short of it he shut down. "I want you to know that if I could love a woman, that woman would be you," he said in the darkness. "The crazy thing is I do love you. I adore you. What a rotten unfair trick." He rose to dress, but Gina said, No, stay. And they fell asleep together, cozy as puppies, thought it never happened again.)

"Sorry, kiddo, can't tonight," Renato said. "The missus took the wee ones to Miami for the weekend to visit family. So I'm *mucho ocupado*. Be happy for me."

"Can't make it tonight, we're driving up to Newport to visit Merry," said Delphine in a martyred voice. *We,* thought Gina. What she wouldn't give to say *we.* Flipping through the new *Life,* she paused in envy at the photos of Annie Glenn, anxiously waiting for John to come home from orbiting the earth.

"We'd love to, but Straight may be in his meeting till midnight," sighed Daisy. "Listen, if you can hold on till then, let's the three of us grab a bite together." Gina practically wept with gratitude; alone among her women friends, Daisy always looked for ways to include her, even when it was awkward. She was, after all, writing a profile of Straight's estranged wife. She skimmed her battered green address book. All the maiden names inked out, everyone married. She might as well be a leper! Only Daisy was not officially hitched. Daisy had her waiflike charm, but Perdita had cheek bones, fame, and a stepfather who was an earl — whatever that was — a tough act to follow. Gina wondered if Daisy would get what she wanted. And hoped she wouldn't. So she would not be all alone Out There.

STOP THAT! She went to the kitchen and filled a glass with spice Metrecal. What was happening to her? How could she think this way? Remaining single made you twisted and evil. Lately she dreaded visits to her family in Shaker Heights. Her aunts scoured the congregation of Fairmount temple for someone they hadn't yet fixed her up with; her father escaped to the den and guzzled Panther Piss; her mother's eyes blazed a silent accusal: to think you let Arnie Mishkin go. Though she'd tried, God knows, even endured a weekend with Arnie at Montauk Manor, and listened attentively to his lectures on the life cycle of fiddler crabs, and feigned ecstasy at the dread moment of truth — until she realized *it wasn't happening;* God wouldn't let a Nice Jush Boy do it out of wedlock.

Around midnight, Gina heard footfalls in the stairwell. The French model on the floor below — gorgeous, with a soul the size of a peppercorn — was returning from El Morocco or someplace with her date. Gina pictured this Barney Livingston. She'd bumped into him once in the hall, her arms full of groceries, and, amazed, recognized him from the photo spread in *Look.* The Singer Sewing Machine heir, an architect with utopian schemes for urban malls, skyways, whole new cities — and bachelor of the moment. Great. First there'd be fifteen minutes of moans, up through the floor of her bedroom. Then little squeaks, like mice. Was that the noise you made? Or was it just French women?

As she rummaged in the night table for her earplugs, she heard a metallic scraping. From the back fire escape? A thud. *A cat burglar!* She tiptoed to the window. Little mews came up through the floorboards — already? Lifting the curtain, Gina peered out: a shadow blackened the fire escape below, then vanished. Her heart hammered; should she dial 911? Everyone was talking about Emily Hoffert and Janice Wylie from *Newsweek,* brutally stabbed to death in their apartment on East Eighty-eighth Street — "Five blocks from where you live, Ginny," her mother repeated at least once a day.

She returned to the living room, alert to every creak. Then she saw it in the sink, *humongous!* A water bug like a miniature tank. Her flesh crawled, she seized a can opener off the counter, but the thing scuttled behind the faucets and slowly descended the wall behind the sink, over the yellow daisies she'd pasted on the rusted pipes. Something with a long handle. She ran for a mop. Tiptoed back and bent down: there it was, sonuvabitch, *watching* her from beneath the sink. With a shriek she swung the mop like a bat — a shadow moved behind the drainboard. She brought the mop down, smashing a glass, then brought it down again, and again, and again, smashing cups, smashing glass, smashing china — screaming. From a distance she heard her own voice screaming.

She slumped to the linoleum floor, sobbing. She wept because she was frigid and a freak, and had thunder thighs and a body no man could love, and was prey to all the killers stalking bachelor girls, and she wept for a future of spending holiday evenings alone at the White Turkey Inn. She should stick her head in the oven. But what did you set it at? Bake? Broil? She couldn't even kill herself properly. She bawled louder. Not that her oven worked; even her appliances were defective.

Eventually she recognized that the banging was not inside her head. It was coming from the door. Someone knocking. Oh God, the lovers. And they'd heard her — what? — nervous breakdown?

"Coming!" she called in a jus' business voice. She tamped her eyes with a dish towel. Funny, she'd never felt so sane as now. It was too scary. One taste of crazy, and she knew she would never let it happen again.

•   •   •

"Thank you, but I'm really all right. I've always been phobic about bugs." Leftover sob. Say anything, just wing it. "This one was a real mutant. And it popped out of the woodwork — practically the moment my date walked out the door. And then I heard a cat burglar on the fire escape." She fluttered her lashes and produced her best ingenue look.

"Guess you scared 'em both away, and a good thing too." Barney Livingston smiled at her. His eyes were heavy-lidded and sleepy, like a prince of Araby's. His dark hair was mussed. He smelled of something dusky — sex? She took in the dark hairs curling round his watchband and pictured the furze under his blue Oxford shirt and below, and she went all weak inside.

"Since a long time I want to tell you I love your articles in *Vogue,*" said the model from the director's chair.

"Thanks. *Mademoiselle,* actually."

"Zey give me much — Bar-nay, *comment dit-on . . . ?*" She lifted her little pointed chin toward Barney.

He seemed hardly to hear. He sat beside Gina on the couch, staring at her from some underwater place — and she in this *shmatte,* her face ruined, no eyeliner! She was crazy of course. To imagine this. Imagine he was coming on.

"She finds your articles inspirational," Barney translated, a shade late. Still underwater. "I'm a fan, too. I've read you in Monique's bathroom. You're one helluva writer, you know? You're going to be big. But you're wasted at a women's magazine. Why aren't you writing for *Life,* or *Esquire?* Tell me what else you've got in the works."

"I'm researching a piece on whether women feel their college education has made them better wives and mothers. Trouble is, my editor wants me to answer yes, of course a B.A. makes life as an MRS more fulfilling. But what I'm getting from the women is discontent. Confusion. Frustration. They're sitting at the sandbox saying, For this I went to college?"

"So your readers get the sanitized version."

"Afraid so."

Monique caught Gina's eye: *my turf.* She stood, pulling her peignoir tight around bosoms that could surely pass the "penny test." "Barnay, eeze getting late," she said with a kittenish pout. "I need now to sleep."

Reluctantly, Bar-nay stood. Gina hadn't realized how greatly she would like that he was short. "Now listen" — wagging his finger — "any more mutations or burglars come around, don't you take 'em on alone. You know where to find me — uh, us."

Tucked into bed, Gina pictured her byline in *Life* or *Esquire*. She had fans all over the place, she was going to be big. Might as well, while you were waiting for your real life to begin. And this work stuff seemed to intrigue men.

She listened for squeaks from below. Silence. By two A.M., still no squeaks. She fell asleep smiling.

The next day Gina was fired.

Big shake-up from the top down, the new editor wanted to put in her own people, et cetera.

Even Miss Alcott had "resigned."

It was worse than after Tom. At least when Tom Puccio cut out, she had a consolation prize: a job. Now she had nothing. No one.

Except yourself.

And Renato, as it happened; he'd been laid off, too, both from his layout job and his newest love affair, and often dropped by to commiserate over spaghetti marinara.

Keep moving, keep the momentum. Make lists. Get the résumé out of mothballs.

She worked her way through her Rolodex and chased down leads. Spring had arrived in earnest, a real heartbreaker, silver-green and pale yellow and rose. Rockefeller Center was banked in waxy white lilies, throats open like Gabriel's trumpet, lacing the air with fragrance. She crisscrossed midtown, feet swelling in her new Cuban heels, desperate to land a berth before the onset of New York's summer inferno. She impressed the dickens out of interviewers, who promised to get back to her if something opened up, but she shouldn't count on it — And why not get married instead, a pretty girl like you, joked the editor of *Redbook*. A recession had knocked the wind out of magazines; everywhere the same story: hunkering down, lean and mean, no hiring. Soon her severance pay would end, and then how would she pay the rent? Already she owed her shrink for two weeks' worth of sessions.

The worst was she knew that normal women didn't have such problems. A normal woman would've made it happen with Arnie Mishkin. Moaned in ecstasy while focusing on his earning potential. Fight despair. Stay positive. *The impossible takes a little longer.*

One afternoon as she stood on line at the sweltering Unemployment office — the city didn't believe in coddling losers with air conditioning — she thought, *Perdita Jekyll.* How dumb. Why hadn't she thought of Perdita sooner. Get yourself mired in a failure scenario, and you sink your own ship.

She surrendered her place to a hollow-eyed actor — his one piece of luck for the day — and phoned Renato. "But what the hell do I know about TV? Nothing."

"Not true, you shadowed Perdita Jekyll."

"But —"

"No 'buts,' just get your butt over to Perdita's. It's a whole new game. And remember —"

"Yeah, right. It's all done with mirrors."

"Waaalll, funny you should ask," said Perdita in her exhausted, overwrought way. Long exhale. "I could use an assistant, actually. Girl I just hired turned out to be a ditz. But you're a name, you're overqualified, the job might bore you."

Keeping the receiver from touching her ear — "Oh, you never know," said Gina in the voice of someone weighing a cornucopia of offers. "Tell me about it."

"You'd work for my daily segment on CBS's new *Morning Show.* We're like pygmies here of course, up against NBC's *Today,* but that's part of the fun. You'd be a, you know, booker, a guest-getter for the show. Round 'em up, get 'em on the phone, deal with publicists — *animals,* those people. Do pre-interviews — you know, be there to do all that shit that needs doing. You really are overqualified, it's grunt work, kind of a glorified gofer's job, I'm afraid. But maybe you'd find it more tempting if — Oh, hold on — *Yeah, be right there!*" she hollered. A gabble of voices. "Hi, Gina? Sorry, gotta run. I was saying, suppose we gave you the title, hmmm, let's see . . . Could you live with Talent Coordinator?"

The Saturday before she was to start at CBS, Gina went to Caruso's for a haircut. The inspiration blossomed while she was getting shampooed: why not a new Gina to go with her new job? Three hours later — the time it took for a single process plus highlights — Gina emerged from Caruso's a Spring Honey blonde.

It should have felt strange. It never did. From day one at the *CBS Morning Show,* it was like coming home. Gina loved the electric world of the TV studio, the banks of monitors, the deadlines, the frenzied pace; by comparison, magazines seemed a world becalmed. As booker, she was wanted by everyone; in her bare office both phones rang off the hook at once. PR people, flacks for this movie, that show, this wannabe, took her to lunch, dinner, flooded her with invites for openings, screenings, book parties. She was at the nerve center of the world. And to think they also *paid* her!

Even asleep, work owned her. Her best ideas arrived full-blown just before dawn. An idea for a fashion piece — Perdita loved fashion pieces. Why not get Pauline Trigère to cut an original design on camera? Gina switched on her bedside lamp, scrawled a phrase on a little pad. She was high on busyness, a magic elixir that beat off negative thinking. Because you could never get it all done; there was always some guest's *previous* book to read. So she could dream up questions for Perdita that no one else asked, to trigger some revealing story that would *make* the interview. (If you could be any character in history, who would you be? How do you feel about your mother?) She barely had time to feel lonely. Or remember she was a freak, or notice if anyone else noticed.

As a kind of bonus — a joy after the all-gals club of *Mademoiselle* — she was surrounded by men. She loved them all: Chubb Seidman, the *Morning Show*'s producer, with his bad color and little folded panda ears, scarfing Tums; the gruff cameramen who were pussycats underneath; the lighting crew; the field producers. She loved hanging out — one of the guys — in someone's ratty cubicle; loved the gossip, black humor, smart-ass repartee — she could now work the word *fuck* into a sentence without blinking. One lunch hour she sat scheming with some producers about how to ace out NBC's *Today* for Priscilla Presley, and she thought, You guys feel more like family than the naysayers in Shaker Heights. Going all moist-eyed.

Of course most of "you guys" were someone's husband. Yet didn't she have more of them than their wives? Maybe the best of them? She'd heard them trying to get "the little woman" off the phone; heard the jokes, Take my wife — No, *you* take her. If she considered the glass half full, she had a dozen weekday husbands!

Weekends, though, she couldn't dodge the sorry truth. Oh, she got squired around; the men she met through work found her ultrapresentable. But none even made a pass. She must be the original ice queen who could neither inspire nor feel desire. With envy and awe she watched Malcolm Straight hovering over Daisy in a kind of agony. Straight seemed unable to survive in Daisy's vicinity without keeping his hand on some part of her body.

One Tuesday before dawn, Gina's golden head lifted from the pillow. Why not a story on a makeover at Revlon's glamorous new salon on Fifth Avenue. Perdita could spend a day getting pampered, from split ends to toenails. To show how the other half lived to America's frumpy housewives, who were getting their grumpy husbands and bratty kids off for the day.

Perdita loved the idea. "But I can't do it myself. I wouldn't dare inflict my face on the world without makeup."

Gina could see her point. Perdita was barely thirty, yet booze was turning her into a gorgeous ruin, puffing, subtly disarranging her features. Lately she quaffed vodka straight from the Smirnoff bottle in her right second drawer, and didn't care who noticed. Mornings before makeup she lay on her desk with ice cubes wrapped in a hankie over her eyelids. Gina couldn't comprehend the romance of self-destruction. She herself had such meager gifts, yet she worked the bejesus out of them.

"Why don't *I* do it," Gina offered on a sudden impulse. "If I make a fool of myself it doesn't matter."

"My dear, it *always* matters if you make a fool of yourself." Perdita's bleary eyes assessed her. "But why am I confident you won't."

For several hours a camera crew trailed Gina through Revlon, shooting her face covered with herbal clay, head wrapped in a terry cloth turban, body swathed in a sheet, feet dangling in a little pond for a pedicure. She played it to the hilt, hammed it up; she was shameless.

The Powers joked about Gina's flat, heartland voice and matching face, but what the hell, the segment was amusing and Gina came cheap. And the girl was a natural. On camera she was absolutely at ease, with the poise of a veteran. There was no distance between Gina and the viewer.

Gina had never had such fun. She thought, Is that all? Anyone can do this stuff. The toughest part was writing the segment, but even that was a snap compared to print.

She could develop, she suspected, a taste for an on-camera job. It made her forget the life she lacked off camera. And something happened to her the moment she saw the little red light, meaning she was on air. During those minutes you owned the world. No one could take from you or do you harm. Exposed and at risk of royally screwing up turned out to be the one safe place. And afterward everyone sucked up and admired; even her pizzeria owner had seen her. Maybe the old team captains from Shaker Heights High had seen her! No one would dare mess with the Morning Girl, or cut up your heart, not Tom Puccio, not anyone, they wouldn't even think of trying.

One morning Perdita tossed a press kit on her desk. "See if you can get this character on the show. I hear he's invented — finally! — a diet that actually works. All my friends swear by him and his, uh, 'vitamin' shots."

Wondering if Perdita, too, was on his "vitamins," Gina didn't immediately catch the name on the pages before her. Then the name whacked her between the eyes. Her heart went into overdrive. The author of *The Litchfield Diet* was a Dr. Tom Puccio, a "prominent physician practicing in —" The print blurred. From the glossy promo the face leapt out at her, the clean good features, all smiling candor. Looking the same as when she'd last seen him, summer of '57. When, through a giant memory lapse, he'd forgotten all about their "pre-engagement."

Gina reached for her L and M's. She could discover in herself no strong impetus to give him a boost. But suppose he was the Next Hot Thing. And NBC got him. She'd recently lost Steve McQueen and Neil Sedaka to the competition, and needed an ace.

Gina swallowed with difficulty. She handed the sheet back to Perdita. "I've heard bad things about this guy. Let's not do him."

"What? What could you have heard? What could be bad? It's just a diet with a new angle. And he's been getting national attention. So he's a hustler. Most doctors are more interested in their accountants and brokers than medicine —"

"I've heard he's a Dr. Feelgood who hooks his patients on amphetamines," Gina improvised. "It's unethical, medically imprudent, and surely illegal, and could get *us* into trouble. The man's a sleaze-ball." Her heart was thudding and her saliva had vanished.

"I've heard no such rumors." Perdita eyed her shrewdly. Then she smiled. "Okay. You call this one. Since you seem to have your sources. Oh, and Gina?" A wink. "I'm glad to see you're human. I was beginning to wonder."

After Perdita left, Gina sat on at her desk, feeling chilly and glutted, like something reptilian that has struck after a long patient wait. She hoped — she'd make certain — that Tom found out who had struck. Heck, maybe he actually was shooting those matrons full of speed. The man had gotten off easy, the man didn't know how lucky he was. She was happy. Cold and tidy and happy.

When she got home that night, she went into the bedroom and cried for a long time.

She became known at the *Morning Show* as the girl who always delivered. People joked that Gina Gold could get any guest; if asked, she'd get you James Dean. After barely three months on the job, she was promoted to writer and offered a steep raise. She immediately went out and bought a used mink coat. What would Tom think now? she thought, admiring her furred glory in the mirror of the Ritz Thrift Shop. Goddamn you, Tom.

The Powers were less certain how they liked Perdita. It was getting hard to do business with her after three, when she'd teeter back from her liquid lunch. There were pills, too. Gina often caught her vacuuming the palm of her hand — pills to come down, pills to sleep, pills to get back up. She was a walking pharmacopoeia.

One morning Perdita arrived looking like a candidate for the sleep cure, freckles visible in her dead white face. She flung her briefcase on her desk. "He's hidden microphones in the gargoyles. But I found them."

"What're you talking about?" said Gina. Thinking, uh-oh, not the gargoyles again. She noticed the pupils of Perdita's eyes, tiny as pencil points.

"My estranged husband, Mister Malcolm Straight, has put *microphones* in the gargoyles," she repeated, irritated with Gina's obtuseness. "The gargoyles on the facade of my building." She stuck out her tongue and pulled at her ears in imitation. "To fucking spy on me."

The next day, angered by the dent Chubb Seidman had made in the show's budget, Perdita lay down on the floor of her office. "The back's out again," she explained from her prone position when anyone stopped by her office.

Her contract was coming up for renewal. The odd thing was, even in her rare sane moments, Perdita didn't seem to give a damn.

The little red light came on, and Perdita started the intro to the interview with Lesley Gore that Gina had written earlier that morning. Gina stood watching from behind the camera. As always, she was elegantly dressed, today in a tight plum silk knit jersey with notched collar, black dirndl skirt, black suede Bally pumps that somehow slimmed down her ankles. Then Perdita turned to interview Lesley Gore. Gina silently mouthed the questions she had written. On the monitor she noted that Perdita's ice cubes hadn't worked; under the makeup she looked masklike and bloated, a far cry from the fresh 'n' perky faces America woke up to. And she didn't listen. Don't cut 'er off midsentence! Why the long spiel about yourself? (How much better *she* could do this!) Perdita produced a loud whinnying laugh that went on and on. No one but Perdita got the joke.

She must have outdone herself at lunch. Walking into Perdita's office, Gina found her staring straight ahead like that *Absinthe Drinker* painting, her head jutted forward over her neck. Perdita brought Gina into focus. She jabbed with her second finger. "Honey, don't think I didn't see you."

Oh, brother, now what?

"Mouthing my words, like a voodoo queen. You trying to steal my soul? Or is it just my job you're after." Hand up, like a traffic cop: "Slow down, honey, not so fast. Plenty of life in the old girl —"

"I'm awfully sorry, I had no idea I was distracting you. You see, I rewrote the questions before the show and — guess it was just reflexive."

Perdita came out from behind her desk and approached Gina unsteadily. Navy mascara flecked her undereyes. "Oh, you don't want my job much, do you. No, not much. Wait, I get it! We're playing *All About Eve*. And yours truly gets to play whatsername, the frowsy old actress — Margo Channing," she said, raising a triumphant finger. "But guess what, you do not have to play Eve my dear. Because I" — her finger tapped Gina's shoulder — "have fucking had it. I've had the fame and the fawning, and I certainly don't need the moolah. I was so bloody clever I even blew up my marriage. Now what I wouldn't give —" She remembered Gina's presence: "Tell me, d'you ever do it to yourself?" Mimicking Gina: "Oh, mercy, a nice girl like me? Now listen, honey, you jus' slow down, okay? You jus' fucking got here."

Gina drew herself in like a purse string and mustered all her calm. "Perdita, I know I'm a beginner, I'm just trying to learn the business."

"Oh, don't make me throw up. You'll do it, too, you've got the chutzpah. But you're such a little brown-noser and goody-goody, it's truly nauseating. And your voice —" She made a clothespin of her fingers on her nostrils. "The sound of Cincinnati — sorry, Cleveland, same difference. Here, why don't you go to my voice coach?" She hiccoughed, tore a page off her pad, scribbled a number. Waved it at Gina.

"No thanks, really, this is premature."

"No, you take it, I insist!"

The paper crackled before Gina's eyes. "I don't want it, Perdita." She snapped the paper in Gina's face: "Take it."

Gina averted her face. "No thanks, I —" Perdita went on waving the paper. Suddenly Gina pushed her away, to stop the paper snapping, just a gentle push against the shoulders. Perdita opened her eyes wide. She came closer and pressed the paper into Gina's collarbone. "Take it."

"I don't want it. I don't want your paper. And I don't want your wretched job," she blurted. "I'm only here because I don't know where else to be!"

"Bullshit! You *take it!* I'll ram it down your throat —"

"What, so I can have a miserable life like you? So I can end up alone and miserable and bitter like you?"

Perdita lunged. In terror, Gina pushed her back, hard, and Perdita went crashing against a chair, overturning it, then struck the file cabinet. Rebounding, she came at Gina, flat of the hand raised. Then she wavered for a long moment, mouth forming a little black *o*. A hand went to her forehead, and with a sigh she pitched forward into Gina's arms.

Gina stood with Perdita sagged against her, holding up dead weight, smelling Perdita's hair spray, uncertain what manner of victory she'd won.

Lying on her white couch, still in office clothes, a cold compress on her forehead, Gina was too tired even to answer the phone. After eleven, so it couldn't be her mother. Renato away in Bermuda. So, her pervert checking in? Or maybe Tom, who'd found out she'd killed his segment. Calling to say You bitch, how unprofessional. Suppose he was calling to say I've never gotten over you, you were the love of my life, please give me another chance. She picked up the receiver.

"This is Pest Control Central. I'm calling to check on your water bug problem."

She hung up. Sat with her hands twitching in her lap. Usually her pervert went with "suck my dick." Wait, that voice — not the perv's. Whose? Oh my God, Barney. Barney Livingston. She'd blown it! She seized the phone book. There it was: B. Livingston, Jr., a phone number but no address. Very tony.

The phone rang.

"I'm sorry, I don't blame you. Stupid joke. I act like a wiseacre when I'm nervous. I wanted to call you sooner, but I was, uh, winding up something. Will you have dinner with me this Thursday?"

She didn't even mind that he assumed she'd known who he was.

Chapter 17

ON AUGUST 28, 1963, a crowd estimated at two hundred thousand marched on Washington to demonstrate in support of black demands for equal rights. Doubtless the crowd included few members from the classes of '58. They were busy tending children, or organizing bake sales, or potting, or riding the pampas, or were too pregnant to risk the crush — not that they'd ever been joiners. They were rehearsing, early in the game, to be the generation that missed out on the great events of the decade. For the class of '58, "The Sixties" never happened.

That same week a soggy section of ceiling came sluicing down like an avalanche not five feet from where Daisy slept. Even her lashes were dusted in ashy plaster. As a sop, Penson, her landlord, offered her the one-bedroom below — at two hundred dollars a month, unaffordable. Daisy wandered the upper reaches of Broadway in search of a solution. New York was stewing in a late-summer inversion, temps pushing ninety-eight in the shade. At the corner of Broadway and 107th, the Olympia movie house rose shimmering in the air like a mirage mosque.

The simple solution was to marry Straight. Their past several months together had passed in a kind of halcyon glaze, without incident or story; happiness needs no plot. They never quarreled. They were burled into each other, like the grain of tiger maple wood, the envy of their friends. Straight was not a deeply sensual man — but maybe the life of the senses became less important in marriage? Anyway, she'd had the whole smorgasbord, the caviar and the truffles, and could settle quite happily for just meat and potatoes.

It was for domesticity she lusted. She wanted to shop for dinner at Daitch, and press the fontanels of cantaloupe with her thumb, and hang blue and white teacups from hooks in the cupboard, and match up swatches of fabric with rugs. She wanted — coherence.

Straight, though, having married so young — Did he feel he'd missed out? Once he'd joked about his rotten timing: here he was, "spoken for," and the whole sexual revolution thing coming along. And he'd added something curious: "I've never done anything just for myself." Then in the next breath he was back talking about selling the teaching machine company to Xerox, and starting a new agriculture business somewhere in the Southwest — What was to keep either of them in cancer-gulch New York? She could write anywhere; once settled, she would, of course, get back to the writing she'd let slip.

What complicated the solution was Straight's grotesque schedule. How to nudge him toward divorce? Calm days he resembled a speeded-up tornado. And chunks of his time got gobbled by poor flaked-out Perdita. (Daisy was careful not to get pissed; she could afford to be generous!) Since getting sacked by the *CBS Morning Show*, Perdita was in a downslide, caught in a revolving door at Payne Whitney. "I was married to her for seven years, after all, and she has no one," said Straight, pleading for Daisy's understanding, his sense of responsibility making her love him the more.

Blinded by sweat, she walked into a gnome hidden behind a curtain of dark hair. Heavens, Grace Omura, her old classmate and red room regular. Wearing a black turtleneck, pants, and elf boots — in this heat!

They ducked into the Olympia Diner for iced coffee. She'd just split from her husband, Grace reported in her little singsong. She'd gotten booted from their loft on Chamber Street and needed a place to live, did Daisy know of an apartment?

Here was a temporary solution. And with Grace a fixture in the downtown avant-garde, it would be such fun.

The rest of America in early '63 grooved on Elvis Presley and the Shirelles, *Gidget* and *The Flying Nun*. But a counterworld flourished in cold-water lofts in lower Manhattan, oblivious to Elvis and mainstream America, grungy yet exclusive: the avant-garde art scene. Art was whatever you chose to call art — a notion borrowed from the European surrealists, but who cared? In his concerts composer La-Monte Young, in black velvet cape, hair in a greasy ponytail, played the same three notes over and over on a cello. People would climb five hundred steps to his loft, hear what was going on, and stomp back down — ah, the cutting edge! John Cage plunked at a "prepared piano"; Charlotte Moorman bowed her cello, boobs in the breeze; Allan Kaprow invented Happenings. There was bare tit and pubic hair by the bushel, and an occasional raid by the D.A.'s morals squad, and always, always, long saharas of silence. No one dared to be bored.

At Sarah Lawrence, Grace had been the nice token Oriental, scribbling inscrutable haiku in the Westlands apple tree. Now she was like some Art witch struggling to win wider recognition for her seminal work. When Grace moved her all-black wardrobe to Eightieth Street, she was composing an atonal opera that dispensed with singing as well as melody. And she had just completed "Penis Piece," a plotless movie composed of stills of artists' dicks.

"You'd be amazed at how different they all are," Grace piped. "This film is big departure for me," she added.

True. Most of Grace's oeuvre involved food. In "Garbage Piece," Daisy joined the other viewers in pelting a black canvas with leftovers. And in "Nut Piece," Grace tossed pistachios at the audience while whipping her long black hair around her head as musical accompaniment.

"Penis Piece" was respectfully reviewed in the *Village Voice,* and in the *Times* by one of Grace's former lovers, and Daisy acquired a sort of secondary celebrity — "Wow, you're Grace Omura's roommate?" Grace even had, in set designer Mee Young Park, a kind of Korean Boswell who trailed after her, quoting and interpreting in pidgin English. "Grace innovator of 'Concept Art,' " Mee Young informed Daisy. "I want to get in her pants."

Join the crowd. Squat and droopy, fore and aft, Grace gave the squarest tax lawyer visions of Japanese toe-blowing and sex secrets of the Orient. Her lovers came and went with dizzying speed, sometimes colliding, as in a Feydeau farce, in the little hall outside the bedroom. As Daisy turned her key in the third dead bolt, Grace sidled out of the bedroom in her little geisha two-step wrapped only in a sheet. Behind her skulked Warren Finnerty, his skin the blue-white of skim milk. He was a junkie in Jack Gelber's off-Broadway hit, *The Connection,* and barely needed to act. Within the week he was displaced by a fierce Teuton with black wire-rim glasses, editor of the avant-garde rag *Fluxus.*

In her spare moments Grace was fending off the attentions of the great sculptor Isamu Noguchi. He bombarded the apartment with white freesias and telegrams. "I *despise you,*" she wired back, spiking his ardor to fever pitch. Grace liked them Aryan and young, Mee Young Park lamented to Daisy one night when Grace had stood him up. "*Fluxus* guy, he like Grace's servant. He help her career. Grace tell me she like younger man. Good fucker! She say younger man better!"

Penson was beside himself. "Too much hair!" he growled, waylaying Daisy in the stairs. "The Chi-nee going to clog my drains."

"Uh, she's Japanese." Poor Grace, having to put up with that kind of crap.

"I want Chi-nee out."

Daisy promised to police the drains. She enjoyed Grace's deadpan humor, was fascinated by her vaunting ambition, of a scope to rival Delphine's. When not disporting with her suitors, Grace was surprisingly domestic. She rustled up Oriental-style dishes that beat Daisy's usual Swanson TV dinners of cardboard turkey, gravy, cornbread dressing, and whipped potatoes. One evening as they tucked into a splendid orange chicken with bean sprouts, Grace said, "I tell you my love secrets. I don't eat scallions or blue cheese for forty-eight hours before a date. *And*" — the corners of her lips turned up in a just-ate-a-mouse smile — "I have secret muscle." As Daisy pictured some python thigh grip, Grace added, "Way up inside. Way high up. It move and squeeze, men tell me. When we fuck. It drives men wild."

Overcome with admiration, Daisy essayed an inner clench or two. "How'd you learn that?"

Modest shrug: "Oh, muscle just squeeze all by itself."

Since Straight, Daisy had dropped out of the promiscuity game, but she enjoyed Grace's antics from the sidelines; what a thumb in the eye of middle-class respectability. So long as she kept her mitts off Straight! No cause for worry. Grace had no use for number-crunching businessmen, especially if balding and paunchy. She was ambitious in love, too, warming up for some Titan of art, someone way beyond the orbit of ordinary mortals.

By October, life with Grace had become more the problem than the solution. Daisy wondered if she hadn't taken a black widow into the apartment. It was the mess. Black clothes, mounds of gamy sheets, collages, props, edible dildos — they flowed like sludge from Grace's bedroom into Daisy's space in the living room.

"Grace do same thing on Greene Street," cackled Mee Young Park. "She make big mess, then move to new loft, ho-ho. Without paying rent."

It was the sexual circus. Grace's lovers and collaborators — usually indistinguishable — crashed on Eightieth Street at every hour. The fun and games, including something called Round the World, sometimes went on until dawn. Eightieth Street was the West Side's orgy central. Studying her blear-eyed reflection in the train window on the way to work, Daisy decided that women make pretty much the same sounds when they come. One night Froyda Maidman, from red room days, descended from nowhere, double-parked her Mercedes, and piled onto the *partouze* in Grace's room. Afterward she and Grace got in a fight over something and stood ripping up twenty-dollar bills in the hall.

One afternoon, clobbered by Hong Kong flu, Daisy crawled home from work early. Among the junk mail she noted an interesting envelope from a Peter Curry of the William Morris Agency. She stumbled into the apartment, tossing the letter in a moldering pile, wanting only bed. Hers was *ocupado*. Grace and her latest, a video artist, going at it in *her* goddamn bed! The artist so grimy he needed to be taken down with Phisohex and steel wool.

While she combed the apartment in vain for clean sheets, Grace got on the blower with her ex. Shit, wasn't Jun in Katmandu? And this the third or so call to Katmandu that week? *The phone bill,* she thought, wracked with chills. Waking sometime after midnight, Daisy smelled smoke. She tottered into the bedroom. Grace sat cross-legged on the floor, ringed by an atoll of laundry. At her feet lay a pyre of black matches. Trancelike, Grace struck a match and watched it burn. When Daisy asked what she was doing, Grace replied, in the patient singsong reserved for Philistines, "This is 'Lighting Piece.' I start working on this piece in my room in Titsworth."

After the curtains caught fire, Penson was jubilant. He had his reason for eviction! "I give you and Chi-nee one month to get out!"

Grace could not focus on something so banal. She co-opted the apartment as a rehearsal hall for her opera, which was scheduled to premiere at Carnegie Recital Hall at the end of October. All night she keened and moaned and shrieked into a microphone, an Asian banshee. Charlotte Moorman arrived with her cello. The libretto also called for a spectator in the audience to come onstage with scissors and snip off Grace's clothes, to the sound of a miked toilet getting flushed offstage, but this they would improvise the night of performance. Taking refuge in the bathtub, Daisy flashed back to Grace in the Kober House red room, sitting cross-legged on the harpsichord bench in her yellow kimono. Her dream, the avant-garde opera! She heard pounding on the hall door, Penson hollering, "I call *policía*!"

The next day Straight wired long-stem yellow roses from Milan. The card read, "I miss you, I love you, where are you?"

She was a climber losing her holds, the rock face turning to clay. She skimmed sleep, was continually nauseated; food stuck, literally, in her craw. The doctor asked, "Is there something in your life you can't swallow?" and prescribed psychoanalysis. Columbia offered it free for the right craziness. Hers wasn't. She repeated, like a mantra, the date Straight was due back home.

During a fit of housekeeping, she found the envelope from Peter Curry.

Dear Daisy Frank,

Delphine Mikulski took the liberty of sending me a Xerox of the excerpt in *Prairie Schooner* from you book-in-progress, *Here Lies the Heart*. I was enormously impressed. You have captured the people, the place, the moment, with humor and wit. You write like an angel. Where have you been hiding?

I see the germ of a really exciting book. There's a great deal of interest just now in the Beats, and you have an insider's perspective. What I need from you to move ahead with this project are three more chapters, plus a detailed outline. I believe that we'll then be in a position to get you a book contract with a substantial advance.

Why don't you call me at your earliest convenience, and we'll set up a lunch date . . .

A baroque blue and gold afternoon, such as New York grants in October. After lunch in the members' dining room, Daisy and Delphine were sitting outside in their coats in the garden of the Museum of Modern Art.

"I have to say, it's an embarrassment to me, personally, that you haven't gotten Curry the chapters you promised him. I was putting my own reputation on the line, pushing you. I mean, d'you understand what's at stake here? You could get a book contract, like the grownups. Why're you blowing it? You worry me."

Delphine's tone grated; the knowledge that she was right grated more. "Eightieth Street is not exactly conducive to work —"

"Writers have always had to buck adversity. Instead of a cold water garret and TB, you got Grace Omura." Delphine frowned at Gaston Lachaise's zaftig nude standing across from them, thrusting her boobs and belly at the world. "I get so afraid lately, afraid for all of us. They have something, these men, that we can't seem to give ourselves. It's their ambition — No, *I* have plenty of that. It's that they never get sidetracked. They are *ruthless*. And they're not even aware they're ruthless, they're as aware as a Sherman tank. I mean, look at Straight. His true passion is that job. For these guys work is sex — He probably has six orgasms in the boardroom before he gets to you."

She was knocking Straight because of Jake, thought Daisy. Sometime in May, Jake had gotten bounced from Johnson and Burgee and spent his evenings playing backgammon at the Harvard Club — and, she suspected, slapping around his wife.

"These men are building something no one can take from them," Delphine went on, staring at the Lachaise. "Investing in themselves, putting themselves out of harm's way. In twenty years they'll be calling all the shots. And where does that leave *us* in twenty years? You know, when we're not gorgeous anymore, and the heads don't snap around, and we're getting crepey and saggy and soft. Or pruney and dried up — God, remember Hannah Zimmer? Kurt treated her like garbage. Christ, are we setting ourselves up to become garbage?"

To Daisy's surprise, the letter from Franca was postmarked Haiti.

October 28, 1963

Dearest Daisy,

Here I am at the Olaffson, alone, sitting by the most glorious pool. It has *water lilies* and things floating in it! I'm trying to sort things out, and regroup, and regain my balance. (Mother is covering on the home front.)

Where to start? I always knew Peter was sleeping with other women, from the beginning, I suppose. Actually I knew *before* the beginning, when he tried to seduce my best friend! I'm still ashamed of that episode, so ashamed. How you ever forgave me I'll never know. Anyway, there was always someone, often with overlap: the actresses of course; then Elke, the au pair. His shrink's nurse — I think even his shrink! It got pretty ingenious.

I won't bore you with my quasi-fascination with the whole thing, as if I'd been hypnotized and were watching my own execution. Last year Peter started hanging out with some Zen-type psychologists in Cambridge, who were publishing papers about sexual possessiveness and jealousy. How it's unnatural and destructive — immoral even. We're just *taught* to feel jealous and possessive, they're not real emotions. These people live together around Cambridge in what they call "group marriages," where three of them, or two couples, or whatever, screw each other, and it's all out in the open.

So: Peter was having an affair with this Beth Kavafian creature (Remember her? the whole class of '57 at Harvard was in love with her), and tried to persuade me to have a three-way relationship. It would enrich our marriage, he said. We would be a triad, in the lingo. He would talk to me openly about her, include me in the circle of their "love." We would *share everything*. Daisy, am I actually writing this? I agreed! I was still nursing Axel and felt so repulsive and rejected. In some demented way I played along because I hoped to win him back. And was terrified he'd leave me if I didn't agree. Or maybe I just wanted to be part of his life. Peter's so brilliant and logical, he could always convince me of anything.

Now for the worst part. You must *swear* to tell no one (only Mother suspects). In the middle of everything, I got pregnant. It happened when [here the ink was washed away] It could just as easily have been *her*. Daisy, I couldn't. I couldn't go ahead with it. It felt monstrous. A baby conceived in such circumstances would be born under the sign of the devil.

I pretended to be ill and found a doctor who'd do a "D & C." There were complications, but it turned out to be a blessing, because in the hospital I had time to think. It took me till now, but I finally walked into Peter's den and told him I wanted a divorce. I never believed it would [again the ink had been washed away] Because of the children I didn't *allow* it to come to this. Peter said, Have you lost your mind? I said, I think I've just regained it. He said I was over-reacting. Then this torrent of rage poured out. I told him he was a selfish, controlling bastard, operating under the guise of pseudo-scientific bullshit. I said, You're right, I *am* boring. I'm an uptight, possessive square. And rich bitch! (I never told you, Peter used to say the thought of my money made him impotent.)

Naturally he thought I was bluffing. To make sure I wasn't, I brought the children to Mother's and arranged to spend a week here at the Olaffson. Now of course he's weeping into the phone and sending telegrams. He wants to go to a marriage counselor together, so we can "negotiate" a way back. I kidded him: "a *group* marriage counselor"? He wasn't amused.

Daisy, I keep remembering the last time. I'm a slow learner, but I learn! The moment Peter gets me back, we have a couple of fine months, a heavenly time — and then he reverts. To the other Peter, which I've come to feel is the real one. God help me, it's taking all my willpower to stay on course.

I've already met with Ben. Of course he's Peter's old poker buddy, but he's agreed to be my lawyer in the divorce. I'm coming to New York next week to meet with Ben again and get things rolling. Can we have lunch? I am absolutely determined to go through with this. I want to salvage something of my life before it's too late. I've got all sorts of plans. I've already offered to volunteer three days a week at the New England Home for Little Wanderers.

Am I doing the right thing? Of course Mother thinks so (she's always disliked Peter), but it's you I need to hear from.

Incidentally, I've the feeling that Ben agreed to help me as a way to be closer to you. Dear kind Ben. What a pity you could never see your way to loving him. Speaking of which, how is your Mr. Straight?

Daisy immediately wired the Olaffson: BRAVO STOP YOU ARE DOING THE RIGHT THING STOP PERSEVERE STOP MUCH LOVE.

Chapter 18

HE COULD HAVE BEEN on the phone with Nikita Khrushchev, but Miss Hickey, to whom Straight's instructions were Scripture, always put her through.

"Hello, darling, how are you? I got in early this morning, but I have to be on a seven o'clock tomorrow for Baton Rouge, of all places."

"I need to see you."

"I'm dying to see *you*." (She smiled; in the office, Straight usually displayed the passion of an actuary.) "But dammit, I'm afraid we're going to have to wait till the weekend."

"Oh?" *Don't push,* let it go.

"Perdita again, I'm afraid . . ."

Let it go.

"Really did it this time . . . barbiturates . . . accidental overdose . . . rushed to Downtown Beekman . . . stomach pumped . . . miserable business . . ."

Say I'm sorry, say how difficult for you, blah-blah-blah.

"I need to see you tonight," she said.

A phone pealed. "Can it wait till the weekend?"

"I don't think so."

"I see." She heard Miss Hickey's voice, pulling at him. "Whoops, hold on, sorry. Can I put you on hold?" She admired her Raymond

Weil watch, eighteen carat gold, a present from Straight. "Daisy, you there? Okay, tonight it is. My place at eight? I've gotta take another call."

Over lunch hour, George Michaels ironed her hair into a shimmering fall of copper. She was Moira Shearer in *The Red Shoes,* minus the tiara. After work she went to Boyd Chemists, where a makeup artist developed her face, like a Polaroid. Out on Madison Avenue necks snapped around — whatta looker. She pulled on her kelly green princess dress with the flippy hem. Musk oil to the wrists and behind the knees. Voilà. Girded to do battle. She'd lay it on the line, seize the controls. It was no good, her moving with him to Albuquerque as he'd proposed, not so long as he was still technically married. She had discovered in herself a potent need for propriety; scratch a fifties wild girl and you find a good bourgeoise. She would explain to him what he needed to do; his sins were of omission, not commission. Franca had inspired her. Little Franca, so muddled and cowed by Peter, had shown her the way.

Quarter after eight, a perfect arrival time, casual yet responsible. Her favorite guard was on duty in the Belnord's brass, glass-enclosed booth. He had burnished cordovan-colored skin and looked like the driver of a moon cab docked on earth.

"Mr. Straight isn't home," the guard told Daisy in his musical Jamaican English. She frowned at her watch: sixteen after. "Are you sure?" She felt hollowed out through the middle.

"I be sure."

Don't panic — *Everything I see is right*. There has to be a reason, a reasonable delay. The laws of the universe would not permit otherwise. She walked somewhere. Her gut had migrated up to her throat; she'd never been one to listen to her own logic.

When she next checked back: "Maybe Mr. Straight be delayed at work," the guard said with extreme delicacy.

She walked east on Eighty-sixth toward Columbus Avenue. Everyone looked ordinary. She must, too. Here she was, heading in for a crash like a rogue meteorite, and no one on Eighty-sixth Street was the wiser. In the luncheonette her coffee cup clattered against the saucer, and the coffee slopped over onto the saucer, and she gave up trying to drink the coffee, and then she noticed that the clock over the counter read nine. At Eighty-sixth and Amsterdam she crossed against the light to a chorus of horns. From the corner phone booth she dialed his number. She could see his fourth-floor apartment from the booth. As the phone rang, she heard it tinkling behind the dark windows on the third floor, in the kitchen, in the bedroom where . . . *There has to be a reason.*

She dialed his office. Not expecting an answer. Not after nine.

Someone picked up — the cleaning lady? Miss Hickey, she was on her way out, what can I do for you? "Mr. Straight? Oh, he left this evening for Frankfurt. I thought — I thought . . ."

The dim vestibule was lit by a fluorescent ceiling coil and smelled of cabbage. Daisy pressed 3A. No answer. She leaned her forehead against the cool metal mailboxes. Back out on Twenty-third Street people were pouring out of the Chelsea Cinema. They'd just seen *Psycho.* They looked as if they'd burned their retinas. They were all wearing, thought Daisy, her face. "Hey lady, you can't stand there," an usher in a monkey suit kept repeating — at her, she finally realized. *What if Ben had a date?* Of course he would have a date, what was she thinking. After five years of her rebuffs, he would have a date.

She wandered back down Twenty-third, and then she saw him. Recognized the herky-jerky gait and bow tie, the Burberry that she'd badgered him to buy, the tan attaché case. He was deep in a monologue, jabbing the air with his crooked thumb.

"Daisy, what a surprise!" Ben grasped her hand, several emotions competing for his face. "Your hair, you're so elegant!" His smile faded. "*Wait* a second. What's happened? Something's happened. C'mon, you 'n' me are going upstairs." She went along, head down, like an obedient child. His take-charge tone made her believe there might be life after the next minute.

"Upstairs" could have doubled as a motel room on an interstate: brown sofa bed with wedge pillows, a kitchenette with yellow Formica counters. Ben had never found the time to move. On the cinder-block bookshelf under the window she noticed a book: *The Leopard,* by Giuseppe di Lampedusa. Propped against it, forlorn and skinny, a record of a Bach cantata. Both presents from her. In their isolation, enshrined.

They sat on the sofa bed, flanks touching, like an old couple on the veranda. From across Twenty-third a pink neon sign winked on and off.

"So. You gonna tell me what happened?"

No sound would come, her mouth flapped open unable to organize words. Ben knew she'd been seeing Straight — *had* she? Had she dreamt Straight? Now here she sat with her burned retinas. No explanation needed. She had come to the absolute wrong person. Made her way here blindly through the night, like something crushed that comes crawling back to its hole.

"Tell me," Ben prompted.

She told him a story. "Come and play with me, the little prince said to the fox. I can't play with you, said the fox. I'm not tamed. What does that mean — tame? asked the prince. It means to establish ties, said the fox. What must I do to tame you? asked the prince. First, said the Fox, you will sit down at a little distance from me — like that — in the grass. I shall look at you out of the corner of my eye, and you will say nothing. But you will sit a little closer to me every day. So the little prince tamed the fox and —" She paused.

"What do you see in those shits?" Ben said.

She sagged against him and he gathered her in, and he kissed her forehead and then her nose and cheeks, soft moody kisses. She smelled the city trapped in his hair. His arms around her slackened; she sensed him vanishing under her hands, snatched up in some private trouble. She hugged him convulsively. Ben drew away and looked into her eyes for a long moment with a queer bitter smile. Then they were grabbing at each other. Clumsily, through clothes, too hungry, all these clothes; they scrabbled around to open the bed, he tripping, legs skinny in his goofy shorts, she kneeling, open it, fast.

He was earnest and diligent, like a good schoolboy. This aroused her more than she could have imagined, and his thinness. His face planing above her, radiant, bled into Straight's, who looked like a murderer during love. No, this was Ben. Her mind reeled and dove like a stunt plane, and she started to shudder violently, not trying for it, just shuddering away, and they both came so hard they were knocked into a different dimension. A slow drift earthward like fading fireworks. They clung to each other, laughing and happy.

.   .   .

Even before she woke, the anesthesia dropped off. She jerked upright with a gasp, pulling the sheet to her chest. Sunlight spooled on the floor by the window. Her cheeks and chin had been rubbed raw by Ben's beard.

He sat beside her on the sofa bed. He had showered and shaved and dressed for work in a seersucker suit and red bow tie. "Here, I got this for you downstairs."

She gulped the orange juice, gripping the Styrofoam cup with both hands. He watched her drain the cup, his eyes brooding and Talmudic behind the tortoiseshell glasses. She couldn't look at him quite. Last night had changed everything. She felt shame, as though Ben were kin, and a little kick of desire. She leaned her forehead against his cheek.

"Will you always look like a kid playing dress-up?"

He put his arms around her. "Why don't you stick around and see. Stay here with me."

"No, Ben, no," she said into his cheek. "It's too soon. I'm in shock. I can't make such a quick turnaround. Don't ask me to, I can't. I need time, please. This is so new and strange."

He drew back. "I understand," he said in a neutral voice.

His quickness to understand unnerved her.

"I'll let this be your call," Ben said.

She touched her index finger to his seersucker sleeve. "We're like old friends who've been through the wars, aren't we."

"*Friends?*" he said, indignant.

After that she got sick. Trying to resurrect the sequence, she would lose it. First a little man with a cigar came strolling through the offices of Aspen Press and fired her, along with two thirds of Aspen — including Nan McIver, who'd found a senior partner in love at Sullivan and Cromwell. Sometime after that — or maybe before? — her period refused to stop, the turn-off switch broken. She started hemorrhaging and landed in Metropolitan Hospital. They scraped her clean and stuffed her like a turkey with cotton batting. While high with Lucy in the sky on Demerol, she was visited by an inspiration. She'd go back to an earlier scheme and take refuge in academe. It beckoned like a tranquil sanctuary. Tenure kept away the efficiency experts. Better yet, secreted in a little carrel deep in the library stacks, you could sharply reduce the margin for human error.

Then she was back in play and pretending to be A-OK. Something in her had altered chemically. She was fogged in and stoppered, unable to *hear* the world, like a traveler permanently off a flight from Sydney. The memory was shot, too — maybe just as well. She suspected she'd had a nervous breakdown. She prudently kept it to herself.

Delphine kept to herself an item she'd read in Elsa Maxwell's column in the *Post: Perdita Jekyll and Malcolm Straight have decided to patch things up. Last night they were seen dining at El Morocco . . . The stunning Perdita Jekyll expecting a visit from the stork in May.*

Good girl, you kept your promise!

An Irish tenor penetrated the fog, a male version of Delphine's lockjaw. Daisy surfaced slowly from her *Beowulf* and brought into focus the young Tyrone Power. Beaming at her from across a table at Columbia's Butler Library. Glaringly out of place among the mossy scholars. He was eyeing her naked left hand.

She rewound to a little stone church in Newport, a preppy smelling the roses. "Oh, hello. You were the usher at Delphine Mortimer's wedding." The stoned usher.

He came round and pumped her hand. "Fletcher McHenry."

A mossy scholar went "Sshh!"

"You promised to wait for me, and so you did, bless you! I'd rather have run into you in Paris at the Flore or the Deux Magots! This joint" — Fletcher sniffed the air — "smells of glue and tired socks. Why don't we celebrate our reunion with lunch at the Plaza?"

They headed down Broadway. The afternoon had turned iron gray and raw. He was in grad school studying art history, Fletcher told her. "I'm minoring in draft evasion. They've started calling up the twenty-two-year-olds for this folly in Vietnam." He turned toward her, a butt hanging rakishly off his lip, Bogey-style. "Fortunately, married men are still exempt. D'you know how I recognized you? By the waiflike way your clothes *hang* off you. Where'd you learn to do a thing like that?"

More lunches followed. Then dinners, all lubricated by champagne, white Burgundy, Mirabelle. They lived in a parallel universe, on sabbatical from real life. Daisy thought of Fletcher as her playboy playmate. Beyond that she didn't think.

One afternoon in late November, as they headed down Broadway, they noticed people pouring out of buildings. Twelve-thirty, but far too many people at large for lunch hour. What was going on? Some cataclysm had rocked the city. Were they on nuclear alert? Was it Armageddon at last? Clamorous little knots formed in the street, people streaked toward the subway at 110th Street, disappeared into the Four Roses Bar. A woman in bangs wandered by, horror and disbelief etched on her face.

"They killed him! Someone killed the president!"

It could not be. Daisy and Fletcher rushed to his pad on Ninety-eighth Street and turned on the television. *It could not be* . . . They needed to huddle together, she and Fletcher and his roommates and their girl-friends, they all needed to draw in close. They watched the images play and replay on the screen, not trusting, needing to see them again and again.

In the days that followed the images kept repeating, yet no one could stop watching. Jackie crawling onto the back of the car; Jackie in widow's weeds walking like a tragic queen between Bobby and Teddy, eyes swollen behind the black veil; Bobby's stricken face; the funeral drumrolls, the horse with the saddle reversed. John-John in his little wool coat and bare legs and lace-up shoes, solemnly saluting . . .

Someone switched channels — and brought up Gina Gold reporting live from the Capitol's East Rotunda. She interviewed Stephen Smith, Sargent Shriver. She was adroit, emotional, but not too; not falling apart, striking the perfect tone. From deep within her fog, Daisy watched Gina Gold. Chalk one up for the old crowd. Here was a dream come true for the only one of them who had never dreamed, which felt exactly right in this theater of the absurd.

Compounding the madness, Jack Ruby broke through the police guard and shot Lee Harvey Oswald. Killed him, right on television. Right before their eyes.

One December night, the city was hit by a blizzard, marooning people in hotels, fostering conjunctions that might not have happened but for the travel advisories. Propped on his elbow, Fletcher McHenry smiled down at Daisy Frank, the snow light etching his features fine.

"Come away with me over Christmas," Fletcher said. "I know this marvelous little place in Saint Martin."

Come away? Saint Martin? Hold on there. Sex had returned her to her senses. And flushed out the mental cobwebs. Other business claimed her. She looked past Fletcher's smile to a far vista, a motel room on Twenty-third Street. A night that had stayed suspended in her mind like a bubble in a carpenter's level. *I'll let this be your call.*

A sudden pounding sounded on the outside door. Daisy raised herself on both elbows. Penson? But Grace Omura had split; Grace was in London, seducing a press lord. *Bang, bang, bang.*

"What a madhouse," said Fletcher. "Don't answer. I have a better idea."

The pounding continued, muffled, two doors away. She untangled herself from Fletcher. Sat on the edge of the bed. *Bang, bang.* Who? *Bang, bang.* Each blow drove her further and further into the clear.

And then she knew.

The pounding had stopped. She wrapped herself in the blanket and padded to the door. She heard footfalls growing fainter in the stairwell. She opened the door; a wintry blast from the foyer below nipped at her ankles. On the threshold, like an odd cairn, lay a record sleeve of Bach and *The Leopard* by Giuseppe di Lampedusa. Dried snow had left ghostly white prints on the floor. Knowing Ben, the dope would be walking around the city without galoshes or boots.

Jesus, who had alerted him?

Suddenly it was imperative that he not misunderstand.

Fletcher had come up behind her. "What have we here, the leavings of a spurned suitor?" he asked and drew her back against his warm bulk and kissed her neck, and she pitied them all.

She was due to meet Franca at one at the Cosmopolitan Club, but she needed first to get her arms around it, the momentous thing she was trying to grasp. She left the apartment well before one and headed toward Riverside Park, a lumbering yeti in her fake fur — glistening like no animal's pelt — and mangy red fox hat. She cut into the park at Seventy-third Street, boots crunching on the glinting hard-packed snow. At "dog hill" she paused to watch two Dalmatians playing. Round and round they went, leaping and nipping and yelping in delight. They were white and black against the snow; their owners wore red caps. Lovely! The white and black, the military red, the dogs frisking and chasing and arching, muscled joy.

It came clear then with a crack like ice floes snapping. The world flooded in, its wild music. She loved that man! She hugged her own furry bulk, smiling squint-eyed in the blinding light. Maybe she had always loved Ben, but needed first to dance down rainbow detours. Come to him the long way around. The faces from the past fell away, macabre masks chased by dawn. She felt new and fresh and ready to begin. Ben was like coming home. To think that they could make love again, that so vast a pleasure could be theirs. His slight body and goodness and love for her made her weak with desire. She started walking fast, boots squeaking, slip-sliding a bit on the packed snow, and then she started to run, amazingly fleet. It is never soon enough for happiness.

Franca had her old beauty back. She was the Arthur Rackham princess again, framed by the casement window in Westlands, aureoled in sunlight. Instead of the usual T-shirt stained with upchuck, she wore a blue and white Marimekko, the latest trend around Cambridge, and her hair fell from a center part in ash blond waves. She babbled on about her trip to Saks; *Billy Liar,* the new movie with Julie Christie; Andy's hyperactivity, which they'd traced to excessive sugar; Axel's hammertoes, a precocious Chrissie — why, she had a genius on her hands.

Dearest Franca. After Straight's magic disappearing act, Franca had done yeoman duty, hopping the shuttle for New York, offering phone therapy and a bed on Brattle Street. She loved Franca, and all their history. Yet now, brimming over with her news, Daisy could barely listen. To think that she'd found what she'd been searching for right under her nose.

"You could have a wonderful life together, you know," Franca said, spearing a shrimp.

Daisy looked at her, startled. Had Franca turned clairvoyant? But maybe she didn't mean Ben?

"With whom?" Daisy asked.

Franca's blue eyes shone with surprise. "Why, Fletcher McHenry. Delphine told me you two get on famously."

Laughing: "Oh, he's a nice kid. Twenty-two and planning to sail solo across the Atlantic. No job. Though when" — she grimaced — "have I ever been practical."

For some reason Franca not meeting her eyes.

"He'll *get* a job," Franca said. "He's awfully well connected. Mother knows his family."

Daisy shrugged, wondering at her sudden edginess. Now? Should she tell Franca now? "How's the divorce coming?" she said.

"Oh, as well as can be expected. Peter's insisting on keeping some Stickley pieces that've been in my family for years. Ben says, Let him *have* the wretched things." She poked at a shrimp with tiny tines. Her eyes softened. "Dear Ben. What I love about Ben is he's not a taker, not a despoiler."

Nice they got on so well.

"But sometimes," said Franca, brow puckering, "I'm afraid Ben only wants what he can't have."

"Oh? Aren't we all a bit perverse? The human condition and all." Daisy set down her spoon. The New England clam chowder had lost its flavor, which had not been much to start with. Keeping her voice neutral: "Why do you care?"

Franca's natural flush deepened by a shade. She tucked a fist under her armpit and for the first time all afternoon she looked at Daisy, looked full at her.

"Because I care. I care a great deal about Ben."

Daisy heard her own heart, its hammering filled her.

"I guess we've — Well — The fact is, we've fallen in love. Ben and I. Isn't that something?"

We?

"It happened very fast."

"When?" — Last week? Last night? While she was in the hospital? *Before the night on Twenty-third Street?*

Franca produced a strained smile. "Well, we would meet at Ben's office for the divorce stuff, and then one night we happened to go for dinner, and then — it was like an explosion. Oh, Daisy, be happy for us!"

Daisy snatched her napkin to her mouth and stared at her.

Franca's smile vanished. "Don't do this. I won't let you do this."

"*You?*" said Daisy. "My friend? Not a cat lady, not a killer — my dear friend. I trusted you. My goddamn *friend*."

"Wait! Wait a *minute*. I have done nothing wrong!"

"You're such a phony, with your saint act. You've always fed off men, their energy and talent, because you have nothing of your own, you *are* nothing without —"

"You never wanted him!"

Silence. Several lunchers watched curiously.

Franca again tucked a fist under her armpit. "You're right," she said shortly. "I am nothing — except a mother. And a woman who wants to be good to a man."

Suddenly Daisy heard the pounding on her front door — God, that very morning, now a lifetime away. She set both hands on the table-cloth and leaned forward: "It was *you* who told Ben about Fletcher —"

"But Ben and I talk about you all the time. Daisy, we both love you."

Was he doing this to get back at her? As revenge for the years she'd dismissed him? She put her fingers to her forehead. A little laugh. "Remember back in college, after Peter? How we said our friendship was stronger than anything."

"Oh, Daisy, we were dreamers, idealistic girls, baring our souls in the dorm. What did we know? Nothing's turned out the way we thought. Putting the man we love first is our real life. Be honest. You would do the same thing."

Daisy watched her light a Virginia Slim.

"My children are being beastly about Ben, by the way," Franca went on. "God, I wish things could have been different. But it's too late, don't you see? It just . . . fell out this way. And I'd like to think that we *can* all still be friends. We will. You'll see. Maybe not quite yet, but eventually. I sometimes think it's all of us, our little group that Ben's in love with."

Daisy reached for her Marlboros. Managed to light one. Couple of deep inhales. The nicotine calmed her. She sighted a golden opportunity: she had just been nominated to be a Wonderful Human Being. She would rise to the occasion, she would show a little class, she would be a good sport. She would be the best goddamn sport the world had ever known.

"You're right, you didn't do anything wrong," Daisy said. "Fair is fair."

Franca smiled at her uncertainly.

"Have a nice life," Daisy said.

•   •   •

"Yes, let's meet for a drink, by all means," Ben said in his usual voice. "I have to be at the Bar Association at seven. How's the bar of the Algonquin?"

Men. How like them to pencil in an appointment with destiny around their jobs.

"It happened very fast," Ben said.

The voice was smarmy, smug, flecked with vengeance. It was also incredibly dark in the Algonquin, like some mole hole. She focused on the ocher sconce above their table, adorned with the Algonquin coat of arms. It seemed made of scorched flesh.

"Uh, one awkward question."

"Please, ask anything," Ben said. Magnanimous.

"When I came to your place that night, why —"

"Oh yes, that night. I guess — Well, we were sitting there, and you seemed so shattered and in need and —"

"Pathetic?"

"You know you'll never be that for me." He reflected a moment. "I realize now I should have shown more self-restraint. It was wrong of me. It's just that it wasn't clear to us yet. We were both so amazed."

Us. We. He was talking about himself and Franca, she realized. "Could you speak for yourself and not the corporation?"

He laughed; good, she still amused him. "And I was selfish. I've wanted you since that night in the Fogg, six, going on seven years. I've wanted you since forever."

She liked that tense.

"You were everything I wanted."

But not this one.

"You were right, by the way. You knew me better than I know myself. You always said I needed someone motherly and gentle."

"Well," she said, stretching her neck and rotating her shoulders as though she had a crick. "Isn't this just the coziest thing. An amazing coincidence, actually." She smiled. "Because as it happens," she heard herself say, "I'm getting married too."

Ben inclined his head with polite interest. Even in the murky light she could see his skin go pale.

"Think of it," she went on, "we could have a double wedding!"

Were they really doing this? She had a sense of a horse cantering out from under her.

Ben's head remained frozen at its polite angle. He swallowed. "Actually, we haven't, uh, taken it quite that far."

He inspected the crystal of his glass. Then he met her eyes. "I suppose I should say congratulations. So." He raised the glass. "Congratulations."

She raised her glass. "And to you."

They drank.

The Algonquin lounge seemed to turn even darker, a sea of chiaroscuro, like the background in a Rembrandt, she thought she would remember forever how dark it had looked in the lounge of the Algonquin.

Chapter 19

1969

FROM THE CLASSES:

DECEMBER 1969

Class of '58 (Correspondent: Sally *November* Wunderlick)

Mia *Sils-Levy* Damiano writes that "after Nico's release from Lewisburg Penitentiary, we got divorced. I spent a summer photographing erotic Indian temple sculpture in Khajarraho, where I met the Nawab of Jaipur. We're to be married in September! All classmates invited to the wedding."

Daisy *Frank* McHenry is teaching English literature in the adult extension school of New York University. Three-year-old son Corey is keeping her busy, and she's expecting another baby in August.

Froyda Maidman has been helping hammer out "The Redstocking Manifesto," and is writing an article for "Liberation, Inc." titled "The Vaginal Orgasm: Biology or Myth?"

"My three boys love their new baby sister, Angelica, born October 4," writes Franca *Broadwater* Marshak. "My husband, Ben, has been elected to Congress from New York's 19th district."

In September Grace *Omura* staged a "Peace-In" at the Georges Cinq in Paris with her husband, press lord Jock de la Falaise.

Gina Gold must be far too busy to write, but yours truly was lucky enough to catch her on the tube interviewing the Shah of Iran at the palace of Persepolis.

And now for my own news. With both kids in school, I'm finally getting my catering business off the ground — before baby #3 makes five. The first dinner I catered for the Paoli B'nai B'rith was such a success, I have orders for several more "affairs." I'm not sure in which course I got it, but at SLC I must have absorbed the entrepreneurial spirit!

DECEMBER

"Do you have a lunch date today?" said George Byrne. "Cancel it," he added before she could check her calendar, "and meet me at the Four Seasons. At one. The usual table."

Delphine hung up, intrigued by his urgency. She and George Byrne had become tight as ticks, ever since the twin success of Aunt Hildreth on public television and *Rich and Dead* by Lucy Beamish, a cash cow for the company. The Hollinsworth publicity machine was currently cranking up to put a first novel Delphine had discovered on the coffee table of every literate American.

"I've been talking to Roger Lawson," Byrne said the moment the waiter took their drink orders. "Lawson as in Lawson Towers, Lawson City. He wants to launch a new publishing house and he's asked me to be the publisher." Her own excitement leapt to meet his. "There's just a heap of stuff I haven't been able to do at Hollinsworth. And there's so many changes coming at us from every direction. A woman's sensibility is going to be important editorially. Delphine, I'd like you to come with me as editor in chief of Lawson House. We'd be small at first, maybe thirty books a year. The money's not good, but you'd be editor in chief of a hot new house, with the freedom to create your own list."

"Thank you," she said rather formally, "thank you for your confidence. I'd like to think it over."

Of course she'd decided before he even stopped talking.

She left work early, at five, so she could put the goose in the oven. She and Jake were giving a little Christmas dinner. He'd promised to get home by six to kibitz and sharpen knives; otherwise he was hopeless around a kitchen; if she didn't cook, he'd happily subsist on Ritz crackers and peanut butter. She crossed at Fifth and hurried west on Fiftieth, past the bells and lights and Salvation Army Santa with his mangy beard. The cold stung her eyes. The reddish black sky, of a hue never seen in nature, hinted at snow. She snaked through the clots of tourists at the Rockefeller Center rink, impatient for the evening ahead.

There was much to celebrate. Her Big Deal Career Move, as Jake called it with only a hint of sourness, of course. (Well, it was a big deal: how many women — or men? — got to be editor in chief of a publishing house at thirty-two?) And their heavenly new prewar apartment, two front rooms overlooking the Hudson River, and — such luxury — *a separate dining room*. Made possible by a bequest from Auntie, poor Miss Havisham, whose will had taken everyone by surprise, since she hadn't spoken in eight years.

And Jake's career was at last on the upswing. They were the Golden Couple again, after some rough sledding. They'd fired Jake from Burgee on a Friday and told him to clear his desk by Monday; how brutal could you get. That was four years ago. Since then he'd traded down to jobs at "factories" that churned out faceless monoliths for the corporate world. Hit bottom working for Emory Roth, king of schlock. Jake drank too much cognac and took it out on her, needing to smash everything in his path. She got through the day on caffeine and prayers. Thank God all that lay behind them. Jake just wasn't cut out for the corporate scene, or piddling jobs; he felt wasted making bathrooms and kitchens, balked at limitations; he always envisioned a total space.

Now at last he'd found the right fit. At August and Nye, where he was designing a theater for Marymount College. She'd seen the sketches: a gorgeous soaring space that would revolutionize theater design. The only glitch was some minor problem about "egress requirements" from the theater. They'd gone and changed the codes on Jake, but it was way too expensive to change a whole set of working drawings, and Jake was convinced he could slide the mistake through. He had the expediter in his pocket; he'd have met with him this afternoon. Too bad Russell Nye, a real screamer, had a crush on Jake — not that she blamed him. "Whaddya think, honey, should I humor him and let him kiss my neck?" As she remembered Tim Estabrook, her laughter rang hollow. And though it was strictly professional between her and George Byrne, if she were scrupulously honest, she had to admit to an attraction. Hell, it happened all the time. It's what you did about it — or didn't do — that mattered.

The moment she entered the apartment she swung into action. She mixed up a batch of chestnut and apricot stuffing and put the goose in the oven. Then she set the cranberries boiling and washed the arugula for the salad. Rewashed it — one speck of grit and Jake turned apoplectic. She spiked some Wishbone Italian dressing with Tabasco sauce and threw in fresh parsley and dill. Glanced at the kitchen clock over the door: six-forty — Where was he? She could do with a little kibitzing. Armed with Lemon Pledge, she swung through the apartment, polishing all surfaces to erase any odor that might offend her finicky prince. She made fast, jerky motions, like Charlie Chaplin on the assembly line. Time for a hit of Dewar's to quiet the nerves. She poured herself a double, the ice cubes rattling in the glass. What was she so nerved about?

The guests were mainly old friends, family, just about. Daisy and Fletcher McHenry. An unlikely union, yet Daisy appeared content. She was disgustingly mumsy and called Fletcher Snuggy; and he called her — had she really heard this? — Mama Bear. Daisy was pregnant again, and tinkering with a Ph.D. thesis on Stendhal. Three-year-old Corey was a darling boy, round-eyed and uncannily wise; Delphine did love that child. Gina was coming with Renaldo, her fey art director — or was it Renato? Gina's date with bachelor-of-the-year Barney Livingston had been a huge success, but she hadn't seen him since. Maybe because Barney was busy working his way through every model and off-Broadway actress in New York. Delphine had also invited Sally, eight months pregnant, and Shelley

Wunderlick. After all these years, she finally had the answer to Why Sally? Sally had replaced Franca as cheering section and foil for their high-flying ambitions. The old crowd rarely saw Franca. She and Ben lived in a welter of children and dogs in Bethesda, Maryland, where they'd moved after Ben's election to Congress. And while Franca had done no wrong precisely, she'd violated some primitive female law governing turf.

Delphine watched a ship, its mast studded with colored Christmas lights, glide by on the river. Was she nervous that Jake would resent this celebration? She rehearsed a toast to him, then worried that he'd find it condescending. Jake was a sneaky one. He never actually admitted to resentment, he'd just go on a sex strike, and what was worth that?

The aroma of roast goose pulled Delphine back to the kitchen. She froze in horror. Several generations of roaches, grandads, moms, babies, skittered up the walls and scurried across the ceiling and dove into crannies between the wooden cabinets. The oven's heat or the spattering goose fat must have flushed them out of the woodwork and masonry. The kitchen roach farm, Jake had dubbed it. For some reason, the exterminator couldn't make a dent in it. Jake blamed Delphine's "slobbola" housekeeping.

The roaches sent him into paroxysms of rage. Delphine pointed out that all old West Side buildings had roaches, the trade-off for high ceilings and moldings, but Jake would launch into his tirade about old money and pathological filth, citing Hildreth's house in Marion reeking of "cat-scat." He was just venting his frustration over work setbacks. After understanding this "displacement" in her sessions with Dr. Beetlebaum, she'd learned to let Jake's tantrums rocket around her like some distant storm. But if Jake saw this — thank God he *was* late. Hell if the guests saw, even if they were old friends . . . Delphine struck back with a can of Raid. The fumes became nauseating, poisoning the platters of food set out on the counter. She retreated to the bedroom; splashed herself with Love's Lemon Cologne; she now smelled identical to her living room furniture. She stepped into a wine velvet hostess gown and pinned up her hair with the tortoiseshell combs Jake had bought her for their tenth anniversary in an antique shop on Second Avenue. She never wore makeup.

The clock on the night table read seven-thirty; guests would arrive any minute. Anger rose in her like a mushroom cloud, then dissipated to worry. What could have happened to him? She ran to the kitchen to baste the goose. Happily, the roach migration had thinned to a few stragglers. She returned to the sideboard to freshen her drink. At the doorbell, the glass jumped in her hand. Could Jake have forgotten his key?

Merry Christmas! The whole gang had arrived at once.

The only thing for it was to keep moving. She fixed drinks, passed the deviled eggs, adjusted ornaments on the tree, ran to baste the roast, lit a cigarette, forgot where she'd left it, till Gina smelled something burning, and everyone had to hunt for the cigarette. Eight-thirty, and Jake running two hours late. An *accident?* Not likely — it was she who read manuscripts as she walked and crossed against the light. She felt stood up like a college girl abandoned under the clock at the Biltmore Hotel.

"Where's the man of the house?" asked Renato.

"Oh, he'll be along — deviled egg anyone?" Delphine pushed the platter under his nose, nearly flipping the eggs onto his lap.

Daisy caught her mood and followed her to the kitchen. She laid her hand on Delphine's arm, which was trembling. "Okay, where is he?"

Delphine locked her arms over her chest. "I dunno, balling his secretary under the drafting table? I think the goose is cooked — maybe *my* goose is cooked." She laughed, and looked as if she might cry. "D'you think we should sit down without him?"

"Damn! Damn him! This should be *your* evening. Well, Fletcher can carve the roast. You know, sometimes you and Jake remind me of this joke about the piano movers —"

"Wonderful, I'm really in the mood for jokes." Delphine bent to check the goose, turning her face aside from the blast of heat from the oven.

"There's this big powerful *shtarker* of a guy, and a little weeny guy, and they're moving a piano," Daisy plowed on. "The big guy lifts the piano bench, while the little guy huffs and puffs and strains to lift the piano. That's the way I see you and Jake: he takes the bench, and you do all the heavy lifting."

"You call that a joke? Where's the punch line? And anyway, I lift the piano *and* the bench. Look, Jake's been under a lot of pressure lately, his whole career is on the line with this theater." She cut into the leg joint of the goose. "Come tell me if my goose is cooked."

At nine Delphine announced that dinner was served. "Mr. Mikulski must be subbing for Bloomingdale's Santa," she drawled, anesthetized by Dewar's number three. At that moment the lock clicked over in the cylinder. Voices faded. The door opened. Jake appeared in the foyer in his tan alpaca coat, cheeks pink and eyes starry, like a love-struck cartoon character. "And to all a good night, ho-ho-ho."

"So you *were* playing Santa," caroled Delphine. "Perfect timing, dear, we were just about to sit down." She went to the foyer and kissed his cheek, smelling cognac. "*Where the hell were you?*"

"I'm here now, aren't I?"

She wanted to damage his face. She wanted him to take her immediately to bed. "How'd it go with the contractor? Or was he at The Christmas Revels?"

"Have I told you how I hate your sarcasm?" He slipped past her. "What's everyone drinking around here?" he asked the room at large. "I could sure use a schnapps."

"But the goose will get overdone," Delphine sputtered from the foyer.

"Nah, it'll just get crisper, like a good goose should."

Renato glanced uneasily at Gina for clues on where the evening was heading. Jake filled a snifter to the brim with amber Courvoisier. He stood with his elbow propped against the mantel. His shirt echoed the cornflower blue of his eyes.

"I just saw the world's *most* pretentious movie. *Last Year at Marienbad.* Alain Resnais." Rolling the R. "Do you realize how many phonies thought that movie was profound, a work of high art? When it's just a load of shit? Mediocrity always rises, I say."

Delphine's jaw came unhinged. She hadn't budged from the foyer.

The goose was plenty crisp, especially the flesh. Jaws worked. Jake sipped his cognac, oblivious to his duties as host. Fletcher glanced accusingly at Daisy: *your* friends. He rose to pour the wine.

"I'd like to propose a toast," said Daisy, attempting gaiety.

"Hear! Hear!" said Jake.

"One night in Delphine's famous red room in college, she announced that she planned to be editor in chief of a publishing house by the time she was thirty. Of course, I was madly impressed — and didn't for a minute take it seriously. We were always high on dreams and yakking all night about the Meaning of Life, et cetera. Well, here it is twelve years later, and Delphine is about to become editor in chief of Lawson House. She's actually done it! And almost exactly on schedule. Here's to ever wilder dreams!"

Hear! Hear! Candlelight glinted off raised glasses.

"As long as she didn't sleep her way up," put in Jake.

Shelley Wunderlick chuckled; when no one else did, he brought his napkin to his mouth.

"Gotta keep an eye on that boss of hers," said Jake. "All her bosses have the hots for her."

"You can hardly blame them, Delphine is one dishy woman," said Renato gallantly.

"Gosh, I just realized," said Gina. "The red in this dining room is the same color as your old room in Kober House, Del. Remember how you used to say 'Let's unhook our bras and talk about Wittgenstein'? Just seeing this color makes me nostalgic for all of it . . . our lost innocence."

Jake raised his glass. "A toast to the good old days, before Delphine lost her innocence."

"Oh shut up, Jake," said Gina good-naturedly.

"My classmates are truly amazing," said Sally, stifling a burp. "Delphine and her job, Gina a TV star. Daisy getting a Ph.D. I just want to say how proud I am of all of you, how proud I am to know you. Now with women's lib, everyone's getting on the bandwagon. But you guys always had this . . . vision, before ambition became trendy. You were always going on about 'women like us.' And now, you know? I feel somehow . . . left behind. I'm justahousewife in the burbs, like everyone else in the class of fifty-eight." Her eyes watered. "D'you realize the last thing I read was *American Baby* magazine?"

Shelley threw an arm around her shoulders. "C'mon honey, you're the star of your Lamaze class! She *is*," he assured the group. "You should hear her pant during 'transition.' Me, I draw the line at taking home movies in the delivery room. Thank you, Dr. Lamaze, but no. I time contractions and give back rubs —"

"He nearly fainted during the childbirth film," said Sally, tamping her eyes. "They say there's one in every class."

Jake stopped guzzling cognac. "You know, Sally, I don't find you the least bit dull. What could be more important than continuing the species? After all, where would humankind be if women all went around aborting fetuses. Besides, I love pregnant women. So big breasted and luscious. Mmmm."

He still hates me for murdering our baby, thought Delphine. Jake had never forgiven her for that "D and C" right after the wedding. And now, though she'd tossed the diaphragm, no dice. Delphine drained her wine glass and looked to her left at Daisy for help — just *help* — but Daisy was looking up at the ceiling; her eyes met Delphine's and flickered a warning. Delphine glanced up and swallowed hard. A grandaddy roach was feeling its way in leisurely fashion across the ceiling, directly over the table. "Pass the gravy, please," Delphine murmured to Renato. She prayed the roach would reach its destination unnoticed.

"Yikes!" Sally pointed at the ceiling. "Will you look at that! Where's the Raid? I'm terrified of insects!" She shrank against Shelley.

Jake looked up and stopped swirling his cognac. "I must apologize to you all for my wife's rather . . . lackadaisical style of housekeeping." Speaking with the clipped diction of the BBC. "In fact," he went on, eyes on the roach, as at an air show, "I hereby formally apologize for the condition of this apartment. The mess, the filth, the chaos around here, is enough to drive any sane person round the bend."

"Well, that's the trade-off when you marry a career gal," joked Shelley. Renato glanced uneasily at Gina.

"Oh, you architects, with your craving for order and neatness — you're all so anal," said Daisy; trying to catch Jake's eye, trying to jolly him out of it. "Have you ever noticed how men your age are compulsive about cleanliness? I read somewhere it has something to do with the rigid toilet training of the 1930s."

"I tell you, the filth is gonna drive me right out of this apartment."

"I know this is not my house, Jake, but I insist we change the subject," said Gina in her most imperial style.

"Dust balls under everything, grease everywhere you turn, layer upon layer of grease. I turn on the light in the kitchen and voilà, a roach Walpurgisnacht. We could charge admission."

"So why don't *you* do a little cleaning for a change?" said Delphine, slurring her words.

"Oh, don't give me that lib shit."

Shelley's face lit up. "Golly, this dinner reminds me of a play I once saw."

Jake inspected his cloth napkin with a frown and threw it down on the table. "I can't get into my own closet. Or the bathroom. Underpants strewn about, garter belts, stockings draped over every surface. Kotex. She's driven me out of my own bathroom. I have to go pee out the window onto Riverside Drive. One of these days the window's going to slice off my dick."

Shelley stood. "I need to call my partner, please, where's the phone, please?"

"And the smells — ever smell old milk that hasn't been cleaned up in months? And you should smell her after her period —"

"For God's sake, man!" said Fletcher, pushing back his chair.

Delphine rose and swooshed the contents of her wine glass across the table at Jake's face, but the wine caught Shelley in the chest. He seized a napkin and pressed it to the maroon stain. "C'mon, Sally, we're getting our coats."

Delphine walked stiffly toward the kitchen. Jake pushed back his chair with a scraping noise. "Brandy and cigars in the living room," he said with a bow.

Delphine had no plan, nor was she conscious of her actions. She seized the carving knife and tried to carve more goose. The knife was blunt and barely cut through the leathery flesh. She sawed away, then set upon the goose, hacking, chopping, stabbing.

Jake came into the kitchen. "What're you, crazy? What're you doing?" He caught her hand, the hand with the knife in it, and without thinking, Delphine lunged at him with the knife, but he stepped out of its path in an elegant curve, like a matador. She came at him again, and this time he grasped her arm and twisted it till she sank down, the knife clattering to the floor. Bent from the waist he continued to hold her wrist in a strange pas de deux.

Delphine stared up at him from a swirl of maroon velvet, but she didn't see him, or Daisy, who stood, hand covering her mouth at the kitchen door. For Delphine understood now, understood so clearly, all anger sluiced away, she was blinded by understanding. "Oh darling, poor, poor darling, those shits, how could they, the bastards, how could they fire you before Christmas?"

.   .   .

JULY 1970, MARTHA'S VINEYARD

Delphine had always loved late afternoon by the sea. She sat in a deck chair at the Edgartown Yacht Club, wearing a long white cotton dress with a fall of lacy pleats, like a Mexican bride's, a wide-brimmed straw hat, chunky turquoise jewelry that played up her tan. The sky a whisper of peach, the water almost oily in its stillness, molten silver. Black cormorants, the shape of slender vases, dove for dinner. Toy-size in the distance, the ferry from Wood's Hole angled out to sea. Maritime sounds washed over her, familiar soothing music: a faint *putt-putt* of the yachts coming in under power, the irregular chiming of the buoy bells off the point. Then the odd queasiness came over her again; the mere sight of moving water brought it on.

She needed a gin fix; that first icy hit was the best. She sometimes believed God had invented summer so people could break out the Gilbey's. She and Jake were planning an early dinner in Edgartown, just the two of them, with cocktails first on the deck of the *Whaler*. They were in love again, the way it was in the beginning, only now they were so grateful, careful as convalescents, chastened by averted tragedy. After that horrendous, that unspeakable Christmas dinner, Jake had moved out. By day ten he was back. They couldn't live with, they couldn't live without, et cetera. He showered her with roses and contrition. They went together to Dr. Beetlebaum, despite his loathing of "psychobabble," and emerged with two ideas: more housekeeping, less sauce — it was all fixable! And Jake was working hard at not setting *her* up as the enemy. And being an awfully good sport about his own "busy work": renovating a pool house in Newport and a kitchen, jobs he'd picked up through the Mortimers. The bottom line was they loved each other, they had a mystical sense of connection, of bonds not breakable. Thus it had been from day one and thus it would remain.

To escape *les folles de Newport,* as Jake called Merry and Aunt Hildreth, he'd overcome his dislike of sailing and spent the day tacking around Vineyard Sound on a ketch belonging to an old classmate from Columbia Architecture. Barney Livingston was a failed architect who'd published a book of hare-brained schemes for utopian cities. Now, funded by family money, he'd gotten down to business and was making millions in real estate. Flamboyant, bit of a snake-oil man, thought Delphine. Amazing that he was flying an Edgartown Yacht Club burgee from his mast. Today everything was up for sale.

She'd have loved to go sailing herself, but that morning she felt sick again, an odd nonspecific malaise, and a peculiar taste in her mouth that no amount of chlorophyl gum would kill. Before taking the week at Martha's Vineyard she'd all but collapsed in the office. Was it overwork and nerves, compounded by the heat wave? Illness was a novelty; she had no idea how to deal with it. She was blessed with an iron constitution, like Aunt Letitia, who'd gone toppling over like a redwood at the Boston Symphony at age ninety-eight.

Jake was rushing toward her. How had she missed Barney's ketch coming in, *and* the dinghy? Jake was scaled pink where his curls were receding, and he walked with a sideways roll — a real gate-crasher in this old money preserve. She had to laugh. She flung herself into his arms. "Barney can't join us, he's taking the boat around to Oak Bluffs," he said into her ear. "I didn't discourage him. I want you all to myself. Tell me, do you people actually *like* to sail, or is it some perverse tribal ritual, man testing himself against the elements. The worst is the bathroom — 'Scuse me, the head. C'mon, let's go. I need a tall gin and tonic in my hand before I tell you the news."

He cocked his head back in a way he had, eyes shining with excitement. "Barney's offered me a job."

"Oh, Jake, how marvelous! Tell me more."

"Barney has decided to start his own in-house design studio to develop the designs for his projects. He's always liked my work and — Del, he wants me to be the senior designer."

"What fantastic news! Why we drinking gin and tonic? This calls for Dom Perignon. Oh, waiter." She signaled wildly.

"Barney would give me control of the design process for all his projects. I'd start with a big middle-income planned community. Del, I've been wanting this for years. Think of those eyesore Levittown tract houses. I'd design housing that complements the native surroundings. And working for Barney would be perfect for me. You and I both know I'm not cut out for the corporate scene. The deal is I'd take equity, a financial interest in the company in lieu of a fee. In the long run I'd have a shot at real money. You know how architecture fees

suck. Hell, I'd be lucky to pull down thirty-five by the time I'm forty."
He explained, a bit condescendingly, the financial benefits of being
both owner and designer.

"So you'd have no salary?" she said, a moment late.

"Not in the beginning. The money would come at the back end. As
I've explained, we'd get a percentage of a project. When the building
is rented out." Defensively: "Of course, Barney expects me to kick in
something at the beginning." He added, eyes challenging, "You could
stake me for a while . . ."

The waiter had arrived with their champagne.

"Well, sure. Fine. We can manage that. I'll stake you. Or rather,
dear old Auntie will, with the money she left me." She raised her glass.
"Thank you, bless you, Auntie! Oh, Jake, I'm so terribly excited about
this."

"I'll build us the house I've been designing for years. You go over a
stream, and there it is in the woods: layered trays that seem to float
upon each other. In every room the light changing with the time of
day." He knocked back his champagne and watched a gull standing on
a piling. "Look at that poor devil. Got a game leg." She followed his
eyes to a gull balanced on one leg. Its other was shriveled and too
short.

He sighed. "Of course, life being what it is, Barney's offer has its
drawbacks.

"Yeesss . . ." Once they drew on capital they'd eat up their cushion.
But she was earning good money, and Jake *had* to have a shot at this;
he couldn't make a life of renovating kitchens.

"I — We — The company would be based in Houston. Texas, the
Sunbelt, that's where it's happening now."

She stared at him. Shook her head no. No-no-no-no. "What do you
mean, 'based in'?" The deck was rocking, though it wasn't over water.

"Why you being dense? Barney Livingston Development is located
in Houston. We'd have to move to Houston, okay? I mean, I can't very
well work for him from New York."

"Texas? Houston?"

"Do you understand, this man has just made me the offer of my
life?"

She looked at the gimpy gull, its shriveled black leg.

"Shit, what was I supposed to say to Barney?" In a whiny voice:

"No, Barney, I can't go to Houston. I can't go because of my wife's job."

Something boiled up inside her. "Well, yes, you could've said that. You could've at least said you needed to think it over."

She realized he'd already accepted.

"I have no time for games, I'm way behind schedule. Shit, I haven't gotten a break like this in years, it's one in a thousand."

"No, you can't go back to the schlock."

They stared at each other, frightened.

They finished the champagne and returned to gin and tonic, and examined the situation from every angle. They would find a way, they would compromise, negotiate, work out a scheme, everything was fixable and they were golden. They could each work their jobs, and rendezvous midpoint on weekends. "But I could hardly bear it that you were gone five hours on the boat," Delphine lamented. "And I wouldn't trust you to be alone," she added. "Del, please, could we be rational about this?" She could be editor at large for Lawson from Houston. But George Byrne wouldn't buy it, he'd be too pissed. One idea above all tortured her. Andrea Cassidy, an editorial assistant, kid just out of Radcliffe, would be thrilled to see her leave, see it as a chance to move up. Andrea was talented and hungry and could barely conceal her impatience; she reminded Delphine of her old self. "The little bitch would just *love* to see me leave. I couldn't bear to give her the satisfaction." "Oh c'mon, that's trivial, that's bullshit." "The thing that kills me is you just accepted, without discussing it first with me. I can't get beyond that, Jake."

"Awright, maybe I *should* have discussed it with you first, but it's done, a fait accompli. Besides, I would've ended up accepting —"

"Then what the fuck kind of discussion is this? Shit, I have a fait accompli too. It's called a commitment. To George Byrne and Lawson."

Of course the weekend was poisoned. Merry and Hildreth outdrank each other and never noticed.

Back in the sweltering city they each changed their minds every second day, and then changed their minds back again. They had given themselves a week to decide.

Delphine phoned Daisy, who was spending the month on Block Island. Daisy sounded somnolent and swollen; even her speech was slowed. She was eight months pregnant, and either chasing three-year-old Corey over the dunes or napping. "I can't do it," Delphine agonized. "I can't give up Jake. I'm being asked to make an impossible choice. I don't know what I'm going to do."

"I do. You married him, against your better judgment, and now you're going to go to Houston with him, against your better judgment, and I don't see how you can fight it, Del, it's the way you are. Hell, it's the way we all are deep down. You can't ask a wolf not to eat meat. We're hopeless, we'll all always put love first."

"Sometimes there *is* no right decision," offered Gina. "All you can do is choose, and then bite the bullet and live with it."

Wednesday night after everyone had left the office, Delphine noticed Andrea was still bent over a manuscript in her cubicle. The girl had the bandy lope of a jockey, never wore a bra, and sported dark fur on her legs. She seemed to Delphine a new sex. "Andrea," she said, "I'd like to ask you a hypothetical question. If you were forced to choose between your husband and the world's greatest job, which would you pick?" Andrea offered a superior little smile. "Well, actually, Mrs. Mikulski, I don't, like, have much use for men. But if I were forced to make such a choice, of course I'd choose the job. That's where my future lies. With a husband, well" — she gave a Valley Girl eye-roll — "who knows?" Delphine looked at her, fascinated. Here it was, Brave New Woman. Her sister. Except Andrea didn't feel like any sister. This was a new species, making her kind obsolete.

Delphine went home and lay on the living room floor. She rolled on the good Bokhara rug from Rosecliff, like a horse scratching its back. She couldn't escape the family taint, everything she touched turned to horror. Raoul in his wheelchair. Dudley plumed with fire beneath her window at Kober House. Presiding over it all, her father, walking into the gatehouse, and into the shower to fry. The Furies hadn't forgotten, they'd just taken time out.

Friday night Delphine told Jake she couldn't. She wanted to, she loved him, would love him forever, but she could not go with him to Houston, physically she couldn't. She sat limply in the blue chair, looking up at him, piteous, bone weary. She'd never known such tiredness. She was genuinely sick, her body had turned against her. Good, let disease distract her from losing Jake.

"Then I'll stay here," Jake said suddenly. He knelt beside her chair.

"I can't do that job without you, I don't want any of it without you. Please. I need us to stay together. I'm not going. I'll call Barney in the morning." He buried his face in her chest. "When we were apart I used to wake in panic, my life had no compass. That's the moment of truth, when you wake in the morning, and you *know* in your gut what you've brought on yourself. During our separation I tried once with another woman. It was no good. That's never happened to me, ever, it was scary as hell. I never understood anything till now. I used to think, maybe I was just along for the ride, or settling an old score. But now I know, Del, I can't go forward without you."

Here it was. What she had always wanted to hear. Why had it come too late?"

"You'll end up hating me, Jake, I can't ask you to ruin your life —"

Suddenly she had to get to the bathroom.

She leaned over the sink while the room swayed, and she blossomed into a cold sweat, and tasted something not herself, her own spit had an alien taste, and then she stared at herself in the mirror as the news broke over her, doing calculations, counting backward over the weeks — *months?* — the idea breaking over her like a wave — maybe *two* months? — oh my God. She was beaming now, beaming at herself in the mirror, ecstatic, it was a miracle, all those abortions, she thought she'd fucked up the works, but she was getting a second chance, a boulder had been lifted off her chest, because now she could, she could go, was free to go, *had* to go, the thing had been decided for her. How had she not known sooner, that taste had been giving her the news all along, and she said, Thank God, thank God, there is such a thing as Providence.

AUGUST 1970, BLOCK ISLAND

The McHenry family beach house sat high on Mohegan Bluffs, the towering ocher cliffs that formed the southwest corner of Block Island, brunt of big blows and all the "weather." Behind it loomed the abandoned gray hulk of the Vail Hotel, the only other structure in sight. The Vail's tennis court was still visible, the asphalt cracked and overrun by grass and bayberry bushes. On the parched front lawn a shredded American flag fluttered in the wind. A spooky Gothic scene, the ruined hotel at night, its loosened windows flashing lozenges of moonlight — not to every vacationer's taste. But Daisy and Fletcher loved the Vail, as the area was known, the wildness and isolation, keening wind and wheeling gulls, even the Daphne du Maurier atmospherics.

This afternoon Daisy sat collapsed, hugely pregnant, on an Adirondack chair on the front deck. Through a glaze of contentment she looked out at the sullen sea, whitecaps boiling over the khaki waves. Storm kicking up out there, she lucky to be on solid ground. Pulling the cracked yellow sou'wester around her shoulders, she listened for sounds of Corey, who was napping in his Portacrib in the upstairs bedroom, rosy and sweaty and sweet. An elbow jabbed from within. She rested her fingertips on her taut belly. A daughter. She could sense a girl's delicate precise temperament.

She was happier than she would have imagined. Marriage and motherhood agreed with her, she reflected, eyes half shut like a slumberous toad. She loved pregnancy, the whole trip: Fletcher repeating, when she'd phoned him with the news about Corey, You don't say, well-well-well; awed, stunned, in one moment elevated to adulthood. She liked pregnant sex, the swollen juiciness of the second trimester (it had to do with "venous congestion" she'd read somewhere). Even the queasiness she enjoyed, the exhaustion; the long naps under crocheted wool throws in unheated colonial bedrooms (that winter they'd often visited Fletcher's relatives outside Boston); the mindless magazines delivered by the diaper service, with articles on baby's first solids and salves for sore nipples. She loved the abdication of responsibility. Pregnant, all you need do was exist. Amazing these younger women made a fetish of working till the first contraction. On the phone from Houston, Delphine had told her about a young designer in Jake's new office, too big bellied to reach the drafting table, who left the office directly for the delivery room, spreading her legs and panting in the cab, to the terror of the driver.

She felt blessed. A dues-paying member of the tribe of mommies, shuttling from market to park with her loaded-down stroller, mashing bananas into the Gerber's, reading aloud about Babar and the Old Lady and Zephyr the monkey. This was the hot center of life — to think she'd very nearly missed it! These days of course, with women's lib in full flower, it was all the rage to trash housewifery and your male oppressor husband. And here she was, loving everything you were supposed to hate, ever out of step. But no dum-dum and doing it her own way: wasn't she working toward her Ph.D? Making babies had raised up the ghost of her mother, a girlish figure she could only remember from photos. Sometimes she talked aloud to her mother, since she could no longer talk to Franca. Look at him, your gorgeous grandson, I had this baby for you. See his perfect fingers and dimpled knees and close-set green eyes, like yours. As though for years her mother had shadowed her, a fretful specter worrying, worrying. See, Mom, it's going to be all right.

The wind whipped wildly around, shifting direction. On the field stretching to the East Light, it tortured a gnarled scrub oak silhouetted against the sky. She smelled rain on the wind, felt unequal to the task of moving from horizontal to vertical and heading indoors. She'd give a lot to have Fletcher here. At the hint of a storm he swung into action, securing doors and shutters, setting out the hurricane candles, battening down the hatch, like the old-salt New Englander he was. Fletcher was off in the Bermuda Cup races. Stockbrokering he did half-heartedly (a boy-husband playing grown-up to please her, she sometimes thought). His true vocation was sailing. And the Bermuda Cup was the big event in the Northeast. Could she blame him for leaving? Even though she was almost into her ninth month? And couldn't exactly squat in the marshes, since she'd probably need a second C-section.

A fierce gust scraped a canvas chair along the deck and flung it upended onto the grass. The sky darkened by several shades, as if the planet were losing its light. She lazily wondered if she'd married Fletcher through the influence of Gerrit, as if Gerrit ruled her fate like some black star — a thought she rarely allowed to surface. What did Fletcher think? They seemed at times two strangers thrown into the same berth on a speeding train. Then the baby came, such delight, the joy of it astonished her, and pure nature took over.

There were worse reasons for two people to band together than to raise kids. How could you start out young and full of hope, if somewhat off-balance, and not be happy? Her boundless gratitude for their child bled into gratitude to Fletcher, coauthor of their miracle. He'd cast his lot with her; for that, too, she could only feel grateful. She flashed her favorite snapshots: Fletcher lying on his back in the grass, dandling Corey, high in the air, in his white piqué bonnet; holding him in the crook of his sailor's arm, muscled from working the "coffee-grinder" winch; hiking down the Vail beach with Corey's head bobbing in the back Gerry carrier. This was real-life happiness. Animal comfort and childish jokes about farts warming the bed, and nurturing your cubs together. The solace of rituals.

There was a lot to be said for spending the evening just sitting on the sofa next to your husband, watching TV. It was less likely than a Grand Passion to bring madness and death. And Fletcher? What did Fletcher think? After they'd eloped to City Hall, he never spoke to her again. Did he confide in his sailing pals from Groton and Dartmouth? Pregnant with their second child, she herself was not inclined toward introspection. Given the circumstances, you don't start taking your emotional temperature. Just *don't rock the boat*. Jesus, hadn't Hannah Zimmer said that? Years ago, in front of Kurt's office in Bates —

The phone rang and in the same moment rain pelted her sou'wester.

"— been worrying about you." That was Gina, she realized, over a terrible connection. "It's sunny here in New York, but Mr. Weatherby has been warning about a storm approaching New England. Most likely it'll blow out to sea, but isn't at sea where you guys are? Especially Fletcher, braving the Bermuda Triangle."

For Gina nature was a source of peril and threat. She moved in a world of climatized interiors, and hated "stander-uppers" because they forced her outdoors.

"Oh, it's a bit blowy at the Vail, but you know Block, on the other side of the island the sun could be shining. And Fletcher's an ace navigator. Gina, thanks for thinking of us. Actually it's quite marvelous here."

"Listen, be sure and give a holler if you need help. Not that I can do much from here. I wish Fletcher were — Well, never mind, it's none of my business."

The moment Daisy hung up, it felt less marvelous. The wind was slapping around the door of the back shed. She really ought to secure the latch, but the rain was coming down in sheets, and she was too fat to close her sou'wester. Upstairs, Corey was fussing. She found him cranky — from teething? — and a touch warm, maybe feverish. She carried him downstairs. A sudden cramp wrung her, and she remembered too late that the doctor had warned against lifting.

She settled them on the couch and started reading *Babar and Celeste*. When Babar, dreaming, fights off the demons of DESPAIR, ENVY, GREED, it revved up her own courage. But Corey turned whiny when she couldn't take him onto her nonexistent lap. He was spooked by the battering winds. He went to the window, fascinated by the rain spraying wildly off the barn roof. "Where Dada," he repeated. Where indeed? Had the storm hit Bermuda? She hated to think of Fletcher braving those mountainous "following seas" rising behind the stern, which he and his fellow sailor nuts found so bracing. She didn't worry *enough* about Fletcher, she thought guiltily, didn't love him properly — though she did try! — not the way Corey loved him.

They'd stumbled into marriage, he on adolescent impulse, she rebounding from too many losses. The boy-groom takes the punch-drunk bride. He like her second son, really. Maybe the business with Ben had jinxed them. The name was never spoken. Yet Fletcher knew. It wasn't fair; he'd come to her clean, and she'd come with a dowry of crossed signals. She sometimes wondered, Why had Ben come hammering on her door that snowy Sunday? Hadn't he connected with Franca by then?

She switched on the TV in search of a weather report. The McHenrys had recently imported the old Philco, and it seemed out of place in this bleached room fronting the sea. "Storm moving in a west-southwest direction, with gusts of up to seventy-five miles per hour," reported a weatherman. "Twenty-five-foot-high waves reported off Gloucester . . ." The reception was rotten, soon all she got was "snow."

She dialed around. God, maybe they were evacuating Block. Should she try to get them to the mainland? But it was often stormy and foggy here; within minutes it could all blow off. Channel 2 produced a clear image. A huge crowd moved sluggishly down Fifth Avenue in the sunshine. The women's lib march, she'd forgotten all about it! Betty Friedan had called a women's strike for August 26.

"Parade," said Corey, placing his index finger on the set. "Ladies, Mama, look at the ladies."

Thousands of ladies, flowing past Saint Patrick's Cathedral and Saks in the sunlight (Gina had said the weather was fine in New York). Chic ones in Pucci dresses, secretaries, braless girls in bell bottoms, dykey

types, women carrying babies, blacks, Puerto Ricans, suburban matrons, a few men looking sheepish and pleased. There was Betty
Friedan in the vanguard, feisty and plump and nicely coiffed. Helen
Gurley Brown. Glamorous Gloria carrying a poster of battle carnage
with the legend "The Masculine Mystique." Right on! More posters
and banners: "Pray to God / She Will Help." "Don't Iron While the
Strike Is Hot."

Gina came on with a spot about their old classmate, radical
feminist and Redstocking Froyda Maidman. Notorious for declaring
that a wife is nothing more than a prostitute. "I've come to feel that
the prostitute is the only honest woman left in America," she told
Gina. "Because she charges for her services, rather than submitting
to a marriage contract that forces her to work for life without pay."

Daisy stared dumbly at the posters moving past: "You Get Paid for
Your Brains or Your Legs?" "Up Against the Wall Male Chauvinist Pig
Doctors." "Don't Cook. Starve a Rat Today." At this moment those
posters seemed some strange intellectual game. So who *would* cook if
she went on strike? Couldn't very well starve the rat who brought home
the bacon. If Daddy was an oppressor and she was a goddamn prostitute, who gave a shit? She didn't have the luxury of giving a shit. And
hadn't she always brought in her own money anyway? Wow, was she
out of the Zeitgeist, she and her other dinosaur sisters. It was rich, she
really had to laugh. Considering how *in* the vanguard they used to be.
Sometime during the sixties, during the protests and marches and
strikes, she and her sisters, in their Lamaze classes and kitchens, had
dropped unaware out of history. They'd been born at the wrong
moment for this . . . revolution, she supposed it was. The Next Great
Moment, the *Voice* had called it. She pictured droves of tiny figures
with baby carriages falling off a precipice into an abyss.

Saw herself, suddenly, with perfect clarity. Stranded in New York
with her children. Fletcher, her boy-groom, sailing into the sunset with
a tanned hard-body in bikini. Terror grabbed her by the throat. How
could she survive in New York on no job, no money? A mild cramp
traveled from her lower back to squeeze her gut, a slow wave hinting
at power. No, impossible. Too soon, by several weeks.

She went to the kitchen. Cook dinner, do anything, keep calm, don't
let Corey see the fear. She managed to heat a can of Campbell's alphabet soup and called him to the table.

Fletcher would know about the storm. Why hadn't he called? Wasn't he worried about them?

She blew on each spoonful of alphabet soup for Corey. Hide the panic; he'd always been a remarkably empathic child. Waitaminute, was she nuts? Out of her mind? We're not talking *boyfriends* here, this is a husband, your kid's father. Dads don't just . . . desert. She had abandonment scenarios branded on her soul. Fletcher could be in big trouble, out in those twenty-five-foot waves; she looked at the ceiling: *that* height? How selfish not to worry more about *him*. Probably he hadn't called because they were trying to get to the harbor, though knowing him he'd be more concerned about winning than surviving! And the ship-to-shore phone was always on the fritz.

The lights browned and the TV dimmed. The power was going! She hurried to the phone and dialed Gina's office number, then remembered Gina was out covering the strike. "Tell her to call Daisy, it's urgent." She left her number with the secretary. She switched channels in search of weather news. "Hurricane Grace battered Bermuda early this morning." *Oh my God* — "A piece of her energy spun off and was absorbed by another storm percolating over the Atlantic . . . A strong low-pressure system over the ocean coming up against a strong high-pressure system over Canada" — Who gives a shit! — "A monster hundreds of miles wide bludgeoned coastal areas of the Northeast . . . Tides four feet above normal . . . Seas as high as a two-story house."

The set dimmed and the lights died. Corey started to bawl. Wanting to bawl herself, she cried, "Sweetie, let's get our candles! Won't it be fun to light candles?" She made a game for him of setting them around in the clamshells they'd painted on rainy days.

A second cramp squeezed her. This one meant business. The last cramp — she checked her watch — had come ten minutes earlier.

She went on red alert, focused, efficient. She knew only that she must get them to the mainland. She dialed the Coast Guard. The line was busy. The fifth try it rang through, thank God! A strange whistling pierced her ear. She yelled into the phone, but couldn't make herself heard.

A cough and the line went dead.

Merde! She stared at the receiver in her hand. Pretend it's all right, don't frighten Corey.

Get moving, get it organized. We've got to get to the mainland. She bundled Corey into his red slicker and rain hat. He was cooperative, fascinated, understanding, somehow; he'd always been a wise child. She poured the remaining soup into a canteen and threw it into an L. L. Bean bag with a carton of milk, cognac, Corey's blankie. She told Corey she was sorry she couldn't carry him. She opened the kitchen door to a blast of rain and wind. Heads down, they struggled toward the Volks station wagon. The path streamed with mud, but some mussel shells they'd laid down kept them from slipping. When she turned the ignition, it yielded a pathetic wheeze. Please God, let it start. Battery dead? No, the car lights worked. Several tries, and she knew she'd flooded the engine. She made a game of counting with Corey to twenty. Pumped the gas, as she'd seen Fletcher do. This time the engine caught.

She crawled along the road leading to town, but sheets of rain defeated the wipers. She was driving blind. Blasts of wind rocked the car, light as a Fisher-Price toy. She inched forward, belly against the wheel, staring into nothing: fog and premature night. The road was flooded. She sensed water halfway over the tires, and feared the car would stall.

"Look Mama, boxes!" cried Corey, forehead to the windshield.

Sure enough, several strange crates floated in the road. Lobster pots, with live lobsters — you could see green claws. Power lines sparked above them, spraying eerie blue lights through the rain. They came to a house whipped into scattered piles of lumber, its furniture half buried in sand. She recognized that house, though! She took hope, they were getting closer to town. Keep focused, just get to town. Keep driving . . . the Coast Guard . . . the mainland . . . the doctors.

Here was the worst part, section where the road dipped low, skirting the coastline. She heard the surf roar above the wind. The engine died under her. They were flooded out! They were lost! She spun the wheel and the car slipped sideways into a swampy bed and stopped dead. A glacial coldness circled her heart. She reached for Corey and gathered him into her arms, with his soggy blankie, saying, It'll be all right, they'll be out looking for us, we'll be rescued, just like in *Babar,* and she hugged him close, and thought of the many kindnesses Ben had shown her, and prayed to any God that could hear.

PART THREE

Chapter 20

OF COURSE the place looked smaller. Even with the naked new dorms spilling unevenly down the hill from Westlands, like a dinosaur's spine, and the new wing of classrooms and studios piggybacked onto Kober House, and the soaring glass and stone library by Richard Meier — freestanding, a Statement; no more apology tucked into a dorm. It looked suburban and somehow diminished, the old college. A flaky heiress's estate. Patched together, still groping for its identity, as they might have said in Zimmer's course, The Search for Authenticity. Makeshift and pieced together — reflecting their catch-up lives?

The alumnae strolled up the path from Bates in their light summer dresses, skin already sticky from the heat. A grassy perfume rose off the lawns. Mingled with the powerful scent of wisteria — oh, remember? — choking the arbor. They looked a bit vague and tentative, the alums, as if returning here they'd reverted to girls, but with blurred silhouettes and dimmer eyes and skin like finely cracked Meissen china. They would not have missed it for anything, this chance to see what the real world had done to everyone (and wonder what it had done to themselves). They poked around the deserted dorms, looking for ghosts. Disappointed to find only deserted dorms. They twittered in pastel knots near the Westlands apple tree, perched awkwardly on the rock outcropping near Bates, their old picnic spot. Spiral notebooks in hand, they trooped off to seminars on "Homosexuality and the Brain" or "The Language of Seduction" to try out their minds. Several alumnae stood slightly apart, nursing vague artistic impulses, as yet unfulfilled; measuring the distance between girlish aspirations and how it turned out, vowing to get it down on paper — oh, did they have a story to tell, they'd get it down for sure, one of these days . . .

The fact that Gina (*Ginny Goldberg*) Gold, class of '58, was keynote speaker had attracted a larger than usual crowd. Gina Gold was talismanic. Strangers wrote her letters, plucked at her sleeve, sighed their tales into her ear, paid five thou a pop to hear her speak. They wanted her, *it,* the fairy dust. She had tangoed with death and stared it down and come back with her pockets full of gold.

Few of Gina Gold's classmates were in evidence. Not surprising. The class of '58 had barely gathered for their big one, the twenty-fifth. You could never accuse '58 of sentimentality. In the *Alumnae Bulletin* the space for '58 sometimes came up alarmingly blank. As though they were a class of Lost Members, the whole lot of them swallowed in time.

Only Reisinger — its white cinder-block walls and proscenium stage — looked exactly the same. For a second Gina saw a flash of copper and pink on the stage behind the mike: Daisy in that dance — "Wings" was it? — Daisy in her glory days, owning the audience; the whole college always turned out to watch her. Well, look who's the star now. She admired the ivory silk sleeve of her Armani, the David Webb gold cuff. For shame! Just setting foot here she regressed to the old loser.

A trio of male students slouched in sporting "buzz cuts," earrings, and — heavens! — nose rings. A far cry from the old Joe Colleges. She nodded hello at women in pastel shirtdresses, strangers who recognized her. She savored it more than usual. Say hi to the former Ginny Goldberg, Delphine Mortimer's sidekick and Nowhere Girl.

Her eyes trolled up the steeply raked rows. A flutter kick in her chest. Would he come? She'd asked him not to. *I want to soak in nostalgia, too silly, I know*. She sighed. At forty-seven, her age for the past several years, you mainly wondered if love, or whatever you chose to call that big blip on the radar screen, was worth the commotion. She'd interviewed him in January for a Special. Kurt Zimmer, her old prof — and Delphine's old flame — had been reborn as a publishing phenomenon. His book on myth and masculinity had struck the proverbial nerve, flown off the charts; he'd become a rallying point for men in search of their *cojones* after the pounding by feminism.

During the taping something had clicked between them — no, ignited! She always had preferred the tried and untrue to the new. Even paunchy and silvered. They reconvened the next evening, she and Kurt, at Bouley, a bistro in TriBeCa transplanted from Paris. They closed the place, recounting all their stories. At forty-seven you were rich in stories. They closed the next restaurant too. She said, "I'm suspicious. This is happening too fast." He joked. "At my age, it better happen fast. Besides, I've known you since you were a girl." "Kurt, I sometimes wonder. Were you — are you — infatuated with our little group?" He smiled. "Well, it's fair to say that collectively you used to pack quite a wallop. But now" — he brought her hand to his lips — "*you* are the fairest of them all."

Quickly, they'd also reached the familiar impasse. Kurt was due to leave in two weeks for Edinburgh for a post as distinguished lecturer.

He paced her cream and gold living room overlooking Central Park South. "Hell, find me a couple who *isn't* juggling two careers now. We can't be defeated by schedules. Let's just sit down and plot this out, week by week, and jigsaw our lives together. Did I ever tell you what Hemingway said?" "No, Kurt." "He said, work and obligations we always have, but you have to engineer your pleasures, *make* them happen. Of course, Papa put it better." Feebly she protested, "I don't know if you understand quite. I have to be on call, I have to follow the story, I have zero control over my time."

Too much like the last time. Did she have to remember? Lord, was it worth the effort? Under the New Age rhetoric, Kurt was a bred-in-the-bone fifties man. He spoke the correct language and struck the poses, but at bottom he was a benign despot expecting to be catered to. She'd even done a show on men like him; she could write the whole script. And she need never be alone: a squadron of Jerry Zipkins stood at the ready to squire her to the latest event. Maybe her real reason for holding back, absurd to say, was Renato. Dear Renato — the last time he'd been devastated. Could she really do this to him again? And she would so miss their gossip marathons and fashion confabs and blissful stolen weekends at Caneel Bay. Renato offered unconditional support, the loyalty of an attack dog, zero demands — maybe *he* should marry Kurt!

Someone arrived to fiddle with the microphone. Gina consulted her notes for her talk, "Starting Over." She'd give 'em the truth, as much as they could tolerate. She was a master truth teller, she'd gotten rich on candor, like emirs on oil. Who else could be funny — cute, even — about the unspeakable? Not that she was heroic. She simply went with her journalist's instinct: the truth made the best story. The downside was she'd put her whole self out there. She occasionally wondered if she still had a private self. The old crowd (returning here reminded her) had written her off — such a fifties idea — as superficial. Of course, they would need to. To justify their own choices.

Start with the morning I got fired from *Mademoiselle*. Joke number one. Started over in TV. Joke number two. Then, when the boss gets bounced, starting over yet again. And she'd give them what they came for: starting over when the fight is rigged. The shit-to-gold stuff. Oh, she would amuse, she would inspire; she could do this with her left hand. And omit that every morning she woke to stark terror, lay rigid in bed, fists clenched. Till it hit her: she'd been granted a stay of execution, this day was hers, and she climbed into it, fists swinging.

Froyda Maidman sauntered down the far aisle in engineer's overalls and spiky punk hair, a butch Woody Woodpecker. Gina waved. There was Sally Wunderlick. Designer bob, sinewy and gaunt, in fighting trim for some corporate battle. She looked like a wolf, the former class floozy — this *would* be amusing. Diana Hilliard followed in sleeveless shocking pink, a page from Talbot's. Tanned arms, chin line going. Still married to that Washington lawyer? And there was Franca, dear Franca, hair wild and graying, mismatched linen, doing a sixties flower child. How did she get away with it? She must be awfully sure of her husband.

And Daisy? Gina craned her neck. Why wasn't Daisy here? She'd taken over as the old crowd's chief instigator, it was she who'd been agitating for a minireunion after the speech. *We'll mosey over to Kober, open some rotgut Chianti, and talk about boys and hair.* Without Daisy the reunion might unravel. Gina was surprised at her own eagerness for a bull session with the old crowd. As if it might yield . . . answers. Only what was the question? Of course she really couldn't afford the time. And it wasn't as if she needed friends. In fact, she wasn't accepting new friends, just as her radiologist had closed his practice to new patients. Sourly she remembered what had become of her good buddies when catastrophe struck. So different from college. All those heart-to-hearts in Delphine's red room, or the overheated dorms with the radiators hissing and the smell of wet wool. The fierce loyalties. Passionate affinities. To think they'd once had an SOS Club!

The club had saved at least one soul, she reflected. She had snatched Daisy from the jaws of a hurricane, summer of . . . Was it '70? She'd raised hell to get the Coast Guard to comb Block Island for a woman alone with her child. They lacked the "resources," had their hands full with swamped boats, et cetera. She made noises about exposing them on CBS. Resources materialized. They located Daisy, well advanced in labor, Corey asleep in her arms, in a flooded-out car on the road to town. Flew them to Westerley, Rhode Island, just in time to get Miranda born. How, without clout, did anyone survive?

Lately, even with all their history, she saw little of Daisy. They simply moved in different worlds. Her own included heads of state, financiers, the crème of Washington and Hollywood, a community of the powerful and superrich busy running things for everyone else. Daisy was also writing that wretched novel. Went around like a crazed Pac-woman, snout in the breeze, ingesting chunks of people's lives. Open your mouth in her presence and you'd find yourself immortalized. She wanted to copyright her life to keep Daisy's mitts off. She didn't believe in fiction. Tolstoy and Dickens wrote fiction. Nowadays people just looted their friends' lives and made things generally unpleasant. And why bother with fiction? Her own life to date made melodrama look restrained.

At the thought of melodrama, she craned her neck in search of La Delphine. Delphine, since her return to New York, had become uninvitable. Perhaps she had never wholly recovered from the "tragic event" of twenty years back, as people referred to it. Gina hadn't seen her since that appalling dinner party the past spring, when the pork roast skidded off the platter onto the floor and Delphine set to carving it right where it fell, juice running into the floorboards. As though it were perfectly normal. My dear, it's no longer *deep* to self-destruct.

And the morbidity. Delphine's current obsession was the Lockerbie plane crash. Ancient history now, yet Delphine couldn't stop talking about the "starfish couple." At the time of the crash the evening news carried an image of a couple lying on the floor of Kennedy Airport. The footage kept repeating, at six, six-thirty, and again at eleven. The couple had a son on board Pan Am Flight 103. The camera panned to them just after they'd gotten the news. The wife folded to the floor, and the husband fell onto her and sprawled crossways over her body, his hands pinioning her open palms.

The starfish couple. She knew all about that. Must she remember? She focused on her French manicure. Shuffled and reshuffled her neatly inscribed three-by-fives. Feeling teary and oddly unhinged, most unlike her. She shouldn't have come back here, not even for an hour. Damn place got you crazy. Raised up the old girlish dreams, romantic garbage, all of it. And the old heartache. So much heartache. *Must I remember?*

Perhaps it had started, the story she kept sealed in some sunken inner vault, in the fall of '71. She was heading to work along Fifty-seventh Street in New York's predawn stillness, when only the street cleaners were about. She was playing Good News/Bad News, a game that organized life like her new Techline closet organized her wardrobe. The good news: she was a crackerjack writer, great on camera, the show's best interviewer, worked harder than anyone — wasn't she always on the set afterward for a debriefing? And she clearly outclassed the current Morning Girl. For almost two years she'd been lobbying Chubb Seidman to make her the Girl. Courting the executives above Chubb. Flattering Chubb shamelessly, giving him credit at meetings for story ideas that came from *her*. She knew she could do the job. *And* save Chubb's ass. He was racking up a long list of losers.

The bad news: she couldn't budge the head of Sales, who was worried she lacked the household recognition — the "Q" factor — to move the merchandise. So every time the newest girl bombed, Chubb replaced her with a fresh semicelebrity — and disaster. The latest was a dimwit actress. Daisy's son, Corey, understood more about broad-

casting. The past week LaDonna had broken the nincompoop record
when she announced — everyone in the office was still snickering —
"The Pope beautified a caramelized nun."

The good news: suddenly the rest of the world had caught up to her,
and she was an old maid no longer. In 1971 they called it an action
heroine! She was a role model for younger women. Fortunately, her
fans didn't know that at thirty-five, after exactly one encounter of the
close kind, she'd relapsed to the virgin state. Now men felt intimi-
dated. Or dated her to brag, Jeez, I go out with the gal on *CBS Morning.* She'd signed off romance altogether since the stockbroker from
Bear, Stearns. Republican, three-piece suit, ultracorrect. After dinner
he invites her back to his Park Avenue apartment for a cognac. Puts on
a flick he bills as "cleancut hedonism." It turns out to be *Behind the
Green Door,* and next thing the guy's ripping her clothes and unzip-
ping, exposing his — *thing* — purple like gizzards . . . She raced by
the snooty doorman in her black Emba mink, lipstick schmeared,
holding her skirt closed . . . *Can I get you a cab, madam?* Wall Street
was slow to get the message about MCPs.

She swung into her cubicle and lit the first of her three daily L & M's.
She tipped back in her swivel chair, her thoughts settling deliciously
around Barney L., her phantom lover. A single enchanted evening that
she turned over and over like a relic. They'd cruised the night city,
talking, talking. She'd preserved the details of each station: the hearty
welcome accorded Barney, a regular, at Lutèce; their taxi hung, un-
believably, with valentines from Jesus; the warm smoky womb of
Chumley's on Bedford Street. He told her terrible stories, as though
he'd been waiting all these years just to tell her. A wife had hanged
herself in the shower. A mentally impaired daughter was secreted in an
institution. Only the discipline and distractions of business had kept
him from coming unglued. He had never, he confessed, spoken to
anyone of this. An unorthodox seduction, yet seduced she was. She
absorbed his confidences like a chalice receiving holy water. Eight
years later she could still hear his precise language when, after waiting
ten days, she phoned him. He could get "too serious." Right now it
wasn't "where he was at." He had just "come off" an affair.

She developed a phobia about sentences ending in prepositions. For
years she read about his models and off-Broadway actresses in Suzy
and Earl Wilson.

Daisy said, "Just get it on with anyone reasonable, just to prime the pump."

"Maybe some of us only love once. What do you think of that?"

"Well, sure. Women back in the twelfth century, when they didn't live past thirty."

As Gina stubbed out her L and M, her phone rang. Chubb Seidman wanted to speak to her.

"Gina Gold from Shaker Heights is not exactly a household word," he started before she could sit down, his sallow face set in a scowl. "You got a Q factor of minus zero."

So here was the answer, after all her campaigning. She could taste the disappointment. What a pack of old biddies, terrified to take a chance.

"And you've also made one helluva pest of yourself," he said, rubbing his little folded ear, more panda than human. "Gotten all your pals upstairs on my case."

Her eyes smarted. She'd overplayed her hand . . .

"Sooo, to get you off my back, I decided, Awright, let the nervy broad do it. We want to give you a trial run as coanchor."

The lurch of joy pitched her forward. "Thank you, Chubb. You're not going to regret this."

"Of course, I got plenty of resistance from Sales, I don't need to tell you. How's Gina Gold from Cleveland, Ohio, gonna sell the Alpo? But after a nice lunch, coupla cigars —"

"When do I start?" said Gina hastily.

"How's about next month? We'll sneak you in a little at a time, over a fourteen-week period. To see how it plays."

So if she fell on her face, no big deal, no one would notice.

Back in her cubicle she smoked the second, then her third and last L and M. It was only nine-fifteen A.M., but what the hell. The alternative was to holler from the rooftop, *I've just gotten the best goddamn job in television! Her?* The best job? She'd bamboozled Chubb, but now she'd have to deliver. What if she flubbed the first four words, or her jaw locked? Who was she, to have such a job?

STOPTHAT. She ground out her L and M and spun her Rolodex. She'd make certain her arrival at *CBS Morning* did get noticed. That way she'd be tougher to get rid of. She dialed the number of her pal Bob Thomas, TV columnist for the *Post*. Better leak the news now, before her next attack of nerves.

In the hall she heard LaDonna chattering, laughing, still high from the show. She was heading for her big office, the one Gina often mentally redecorated in the French provincial style, with pink velvet pillows, pink velvet chairs, and a pink-sprayed typewriter.

"Hi there!" called out LaDonna, dipping by. "Don't *you* look dishy this morning, you have a hot date last night?"

The number ringing in her ear, Gina stared into space. Gosh, they played rough around here. No one had bothered to tell LaDonna yet.

The moment she hung up with Thomas, she remembered the bad news: Daisy stuck with her babies, Delphine in Houston, Renato off somewhere with his latest paramour. Here she was, about to conquer America, and she had no one to celebrate with.

Less is more, Delphine used to say in college, its mystical ring impressing the hell out of everyone. Except Delphine was wrong: *more is more.* Her job was a nonstop high, it was like being in love. Didn't she, under the lights, feel warm and adored? She loved the midnight blue limo CBS sent to collect her before dawn at her new atelier-style duplex on Central Park South. And her corner office with its pink velvet pillows and chairs. Loved the constant attentions to her body: manicures while dictating correspondence; fittings by Casper or Donald Brooks, a different ensemble for every day of the week. She loved traveling first class with the retinue of producers and her hairdresser, and gaining access to all the people who counted, and feeling connected to every event in the world. She loved her hundred thou a year and worries about tax shelters (which Daisy, perennially broke, called an "uptown problem").

And yet: wouldn't she trade it all in to marry Barney Livingston? She could dance on the high wire because a part of her didn't give a damn. It was heady up here, *in the interim* — until Barney saw his massive error and returned from Houston to marry her. (So she was nuts; so long as no one else knew.) It was grand up here until her real life began. And now she finally deserved him. With her star luster how could he not want her. Single, meanwhile, had its advantages. When everyone else hurried home at night to the family, she could work away at her typewriter. What else did she have to do?

Chubb usually tapped her to do the celebrity interviews. One day he tossed her a plum: Mamie Eisenhower. "For God's sake though, stay away from the dipsomania stuff." But wasn't that precisely what ev-

eryone wanted to know? She interviewed Mamie at home in Gettys-
burg, and then they walked arm in arm in the woods, two chatty ladies,
and she circled and feinted, and then just kind of dropped it in toward
the end, as they were shuffling through the leaves: the question. And
Mamie eagerly explained she was no lush, she suffered from a balance
problem, having to do with a carotid artery, et cetera.

Chubb busted a gut. And tossed her plummier plums. She noodged,
she intruded, she pried — and got away with it, the Mother Confessor
of the morning. Pretending to open herself, she pulled secrets from her
subjects. The exercise gave her all she needed in the way of intimacy;
who had time for more? She decided to make herself the female equivalent of Edward R. Murrow on *Person to Person*. Like Murrow, she'd
become as celebrated as her subjects. But she needed more exposure in
the press, and a showcase outside the format of *Morning*. She hired a
PR firm at eighteen hundred bucks a month. On May 22, 1975, *Look*
ran a story titled "Early Rising Star of the Morning," with full-page
photo of Gina Gold in Monaco's palace gardens, lemon silk hair curving over her molded cheekbones, herself an American Royal, schmooz-
ing among the bougainvillea with Princess Grace.

Gina privately regarded the story as a teaser sent to Barney Livingston. Surely they read *Look* in Houston. According to her sources, he
had never remarried.

And then one day she heard he was coming back East, like a Christmas present in July.

One indisputable fact: Barney was handing over the business to his
deputy manager. The rest was just stories. Barney was sick to death of
Houston. He'd grown bored building shopping malls the size of Luxembourg. He'd become allergic to his own ability to make money
every time he turned around. Or allergic to Houston's climate; he'd
once collapsed on the tennis court, there were rumors he'd had a health
scare, and decided it was now or never, the moment to make good on
forgotten dreams.

As a generous donor, Barney sat on the boards of Houston's major
art, design, and development nonprofits. At one museum fund-raiser
he got to chatting with a board member of New York's prestigious
Gotham Art Society. Sensing that Barney was looking to come back
East, the gentleman mentioned that the director of the Gotham Art

Society had just resigned. And perhaps Barney, with his background in design and preservation issues, might consider coming on board as president?

The GAS fought developers to keep the city quasi-livable, and was involved in every major land-use decision in New York. As president, Barney would wield influence at the crossroads of architecture, politics, and business. He saw a vindication of his thwarted artistic dreams, the admiration of his peers, power harnessed to Goodness and Beauty — wasn't it time to give something back? A potent cocktail. Barney barely needed to think it over. The lack of salary, of course, was not an issue.

Gina schemed how to engineer a chance encounter. She wanted Barney because they'd connected "back when," she a mess and freaking out from burglars and loneliness, and she wanted him because he was familiar from her fantasies (unlike everyone else, she found the familiar arousing, novelty merely alarming), and she wanted him because she wanted him.

"Hey, are you crazy, it's been over ten years," said Daisy. "You, the model of rationality. Why when it comes to love are you like Madame Butterfly?"

"It's all that Verdi Tom Puccio used to drag me to."

"Uh, Puccini."

"Just don't tell Gloria on me. Or Froyda. Or Ti-Grace."

Her sources disclosed that Barney was planning to be in Southampton the weekend of July 24 for an auction of weathervanes to raise money for the Parrish Museum. He was expected afterward at a party for the trustees, hosted by her old colleague Perdita Jekyll and her husband, Malcolm Straight.

The rare weekends she wasn't working, Gina went to her eighteenth-century farmhouse in the toniest section of northwestern Connecticut. (She liked Connecticut; it was nature at its most genteel, and too buggy to go out of doors.) The weekend of the twenty-fourth she arranged to borrow Chubb Seidman's Italian-style villa in East Hampton.

Toward five P.M. she discovered a ravening need to look at weathervanes. She dressed carefully, choosing a white Mollie Parnis jumpsuit artfully scooped to serve up bosom. Cursed the sea air poodling her fair hair into ringlets, then decided she liked the effect. She looked prettier, she knew, off camera. The camera couldn't capture the matte silk of her skin, its glow of a dusky pearl.

She swung through the Parrish wearing the pleading smile of celebs: be a good soul and leave me in peace. She was in luck. The old guard in Southampton considered fame to be in bad taste, and she was outclassed by Lauren Bacall. She joined a group clustered around something psychedelic by Peter Max. The harder she stared at the thing, the less she saw, as though her vision could dissolve matter. Her heart thudded in her ears; she had worse stage fright than when she'd interviewed Che. She who remained, under the gush, as warm as steel. Her noodle legs barely got her down the steps into the grass courtyard. Above the trees a brightness lingered, silver and mauve, holding out against the gathering dark. She mingled with *le tout* Southampton, a blur of red pants and Dick Tracy jaws and debutante stoop, weaving before anyone could attach, nauseated by lurches of perfume.

A sleek dark head appeared in the crush at the top of the stairs. Her heart staggered in her chest. The same hooded eyes and lush mouth. Her Arabian prince. Bit of a gut, hair going south. His jacket a phosphorescent white. She could make out blue points of beard above his lip. Then a crane tied up in organdy bows appeared at his side. Bent to whisper in his ear.

She'd been stabbed clean through. You could not feel this pain and live. She heard a crack, looked at her hand: she'd broken her plastic glass. Her hand was sticky with champagne. Oh, goddamn, oh, you fool. Of course. What had she been thinking. His role model was Hugh Hefner. She pictured Chubb's pale yellow BMW, parked in the lot behind the Parrish. Getting to it seemed a daunting task.

He saw her, his eyes came alive, and he bowled down the steps. "Gina Gold, what a surprise. I'm so happy to see you."

"Yes, this is a surprise," she squeaked. She lowered her register. "But I'm afraid I'm on my way out."

"Why? Why must you leave? I've just found you. I'm so happy, you've no idea." This kept her in place. His eyes licked over her. "You've captured the sun." He noticed the wrecked glass, her wet hand. "Goodness, what happened? Let's get you another."

He steered her toward the bar, expertly dodging people they knew. A line from Stephen Sondheim popped into her head — *He assumes I lose my reason, and I do.* They strolled along the edge of the crowd beneath a feathery cover of evergreens and caught each other up on ten years. He had followed her career. Could it be? Was he as nuts as she? There was no mention of the crane.

"And tell me, how is your daughter?" she asked, dizzy from two sips of champagne.

He stopped and looked past her, a tiny muscle twitching under his eyes. "She's been diagnosed a paranoid schizophrenic. It's now official. She'll never live in the world, not ever." He brought her back into focus. "You know, I've never told anyone about Nadja but you. It's been — what, ten years? And you remembered."

She looked full at him, her identical height, her lips, throat, pelvis, every inch of her offered. "Yes, I remember." In her best deep-throat delivery: "I remember everything."

"So do I. Fondly."

Fondly. Hope died. Though he was no word person.

She materialized from hell, a walking boneyard, taller than Barney by a head. Hovered at his elbow, poised to be introduced.

"Serena Fosburgh," Barney said, opening his shoulder and admitting her, "I'd like you to meet an old friend."

Oh, Barney. Too corny, too predictable. First models, now socialites. Upwardly mobile fucking.

"Shall we bid on the Rosenquist?" Serena was saying to Barney.

"Oh, don't tell me," chirped Gina. "Do you also collect art?" She checked her watch. "I'd better be off. I'm house-sitting for Chubb Seidman."

Barney's eyes smarted. "Don't go yet. Why don't you come with us to the auction, and then on to Malcolm Straight's. I'm sure he'd be honored —"

"But perhaps not Madame Straight."

At least, she thought, pushing off, he'd become a cliché. With all that turnover how did he tell them apart? It was hateful, it was disgusting, he was beneath consideration. She fumbled with the car key. And no other man would do.

Around eleven, Gina lay in a circular bathtub in Amalfi-on-the-Atlantic, chin high in bubbles, woozy from Chubb's finest Pouilly-Fuissé. She pictured Barney's almond eyes and childishly loose mouth, and felt a tortuous tingling in her crotch. Her rosy nipples peeped through the foam. She wanted him to touch her all over, invade her, she wanted to take him in her mouth. She sat up, amazed by her own depravity. That was the acid test, whether you wanted to get right down and root and sniff and lick — it was no different than dogs. Through half-shut eyes she studied the diamond zodiac in an indigo sky that Chubb had hired the local Michelangelo to paint on the ceiling. As she searched for the Big Dipper, the phone rang. What a bother, let it ring. Had to be for Chubb, no one knew she was here. She noticed a phone nestled among some cactus plants next to the tub. Right at eye level. Could she muster the energy? She'd have to explain that Chubb was in . . . Rapallo? Or was it Positano. She watched the little white Princess phone jangle with self-importance. Oh, shut up. She reached out a sudsy arm, and lifted off the receiver, and reluctantly murmured Hello, and so it began.

Chapter 21

THEY MET at La Ferme Saint Siméon in Normandy. After she finished the interview in Paris with Yves Montand, the world's sexiest man, lost on her. It had been Barney's idea to meet at La Ferme, an inn in the harbor town of Honfleur (and a weekend retreat, Barney joked, for Parisian husbands and their mistresses). The main building was a fairy-tale farmhouse, low-slung and rambling, timbered in the Norman style. Spires of blue delphinium hugged its walls. They were shown into a low-ceilinged dining room with carved wood mantels, terra-cotta tiled floors, copper gleaming in candlelight, tables notched into cozy corners. A kind of charged silence prevailed; the three-star cuisine was not the main attraction. Their entrance excited a ripple of curiosity. They were like allegorical figures for North and South, she all vanilla and gold, with broad glowing *pommettes,* he drenched in dusk, his eyelids and mouth the color of plums, both dressed in ceremonial white and the same height. On second look they might be some royal half-brother and sister, their retinue of servants tucked away in the Ferme's *grenier.*

"The French really know how to do this stuff," joked Gina. Suddenly miserable. She hated the elegant couples around them, discreetly murmuring, pressing each other's hands across the crystal and the white linen, oozing savoir faire. In her initial euphoria, then the rush of preparing for Montand, she hadn't thought this through. She was here under false auspices. Somehow she'd imagined that she and Barney could sail into the sunset, like the end of a fifties movie. Leapfrog over the part following the slow fade into happily-ever-after. She barely listened as Barney detailed his morning alone on Omaha Beach, the very air still haunted by all those casualties. She saw only the casualty of her own body. Thunder thighs, Mediterranean hips (in the euphemism of a charitable beau). And Barney accustomed to Bo Dereks and perfect tens.

"Why now?" she interrupted (an old interview trick: catch the subject off balance). He looked puzzled. "Why, after all those cupcakes, do you suddenly want me now? After all these years."

"Well, for one thing, *you're* a cupcake, especially as a blonde. And I've always wanted you." At her skeptical frown: "I was an average adolescent when we met. Playing macho games and notching my belt. You have to picture it. All us horny boys back in the fifties, jerking off to *The Amboy Dukes* and trying to score in the back seats of jalopies. Then the sixties comes along, and suddenly they're giving it away, it's a sexual free-for-all, pig heaven. Before that I was married, and when my wife got sick, I just cut myself off from anything resembling pleasure." He shook his head. "Gina, when I met you I was a total jerk. An asshole. I wasn't ready to be happy. I thought — I thought I had all the time in the world to be happy."

I thought I had all the time. The sentence echoed peculiarly as they walked arm in arm through the flowery dark to their room in a modern annex. The ruffled heads of the dahlias looked black along the path. She smelled crushed apples and thyme. "I know you won't believe this, but you were always in my mind in some way," Barney said in his rich baritone. "I always imagined you as the woman I'd come home to."

What she'd always wanted to hear. And now all she could feel was nausea, as though going on camera without a script or TelePrompTer, or even a topic. She couldn't deliver the goods. She was a fraud. An impostor of love. Calvados and nerves had upset her stomach. She'd have to spend the night in the W.C. — very romantic, and it was located in its own room, so she couldn't pretend to be having a long bath.

Upstairs in their beautiful blue and white bedroom it was mortifyingly awkward. They couldn't navigate the room without colliding. How could you relax, do your business, do anything around this stranger? If only he were Renato. She and Renato would guzzle eclairs, and massage each other's backs, and lie around in their *gottkes,* watching *The Thin Man* in French. She pictured all the suave Parisiennes down the hall. Lingered in the W.C. in a cramp of misery.

He lay in bed under the sheet, propped on his elbow, eyes aglow. Chest just the right hairiness. She sucked in her breath. Sat beside him on the bed, in the ivory satin and lace gown she'd bought in Paris at Dior. Manicured fingers on the bedspread, not touching him.

"Okay, I might as well level with you. I'm afraid I misled you. I can't do this. I'm thirty-eight years old and I never have. So there you have it." A moment; the muscle twitched under his eye. "Okay," he said pleasantly, as though it made perfect sense. He relaxed back on the pillows, hands clasped behind his head, and smiled at her. "You saved yourself for me. The worldly gorgeous woman on everyone's screen. How delightfully old-fashioned." She cut a nervous glance below. In a faint voice, she said, "I don't mean technically. In college there was a, uh, nasty skirmish, and I, well, signed off love after that. I'm not —" "Yes?" "I'm not all right. In any way." He nodded. "I see."

She twisted her hands together. "I don't believe I'm saying this" — she glanced around — "here, in this beautiful place. What a waste, huh?" "Oh, who gives a damn about this place. Europe's a dead museum, as far as I'm concerned." He sat, drawing up his knees and wrapping his arms around them. "Listen, we can just do whatever we want. Nothing. Everything." He shrugged. "Something in between. Who's to know? It's just between us."

She searched his face, the misery ebbing a little. He smiled a luxurious smile. "Just think: we have the whole rest of our lives to do whatever we want." Oh, she breathed out. Oh. "Listen, I'm a bit of a fraud myself. All the cupcakes, as you put it — I even love it when you knock me! — I used to run through women because I was, well, sick in the heart. I couldn't feel anything but self-disgust. Guilt at how little I could offer them. So I kept it light, I kept it 'fun,' I kept moving. Before anyone got hurt or hated me too much. Before I could seriously hate myself." Outside a bird warbled and trilled. A scent of jasmine wafted in through the open casement window. "And now, since you've been so candid with me — frankly, my dear, I'm pretty lagged out.

Could we — Would it be okay if we just went to sleep? Would that be all right? Come sleep in my arms."

She was shocked by his strong musk. Was this a man's smell? Tom Puccio had smelled of Phisohex. The moonlight petaled the bedspread through the lace curtains. Sleepily, he moved against her and she felt him prodding her thigh, hard, like something mineral, girded up for a night tourney. She smiled in the darkness: he found her desirable. Even jet-lagged he wanted her. Her own body was numb, dumb; only her mind buzzed. His breathing evened. In a panic almost, she noticed the sword had softened and shrunk. With a little moan she pressed herself into him. His breathing altered and slowly *it* swelled. She exulted in her power.

When it began she couldn't have said, maybe she dozed off too, but suddenly he was kissing her, soft, sleepy kisses like puppies, scented with Calvados, dry, then wetter, drawing her in, and she felt him butting high into her pubic bone, though he raised himself off her, maybe not to scare her — but she wanted him back, precisely *back there,* lower somehow, she needed him lower, so she slid slightly upward till he was nudging her right *there,* where she wanted, and suddenly her body got away, moving all on its own, ruthless, wanting his hardness . . . and then he drew back — she gasped in disappointment — but he found her, stroked her there, and traveled down, fingers playing and probing her wetness, she praying he'd return to the lovely place, and he did, then his fingers dipped back down, and slowly, he groaning in his throat, back up to the beautiful place . . . as he came into her, and she moved with him, got it, she got the idea, so this is it, this is, this is — her mind blanked, she was purely this wave, about to crest each time, higher — higher — she was *there,* wave upon wave, exploding through, the gorgeous amazing thing, she bucked and heaved and flopped about, crying out in a strange hoarse voice as he met her, both of them shouting.

The next day they strolled around the Old Harbor at Honfleur. They admired the blue and white boats, and one with a red sail, and the narrow houses with terra-cotta roofs, casting their reflections, tall and wavering, into the blue-green water. For lunch they ate crevettes with a fine Meursault in a bistro overlooking the harbor. Like ordinary tourists, they asked a French papa to take a snapshot of them. Honfleur rhymes with *bonheur,* said Barney, smiling into the camera.

After lunch they went back to bed. At teatime, hungry, they feasted off each other. Gina slept a great deal. Rapture exhausted her. She woke weeping. To think I might have missed this, missed you, what was I doing before this. Let's drop out together, he said deep in the night. She sighed into his armpit. My public wouldn't hear of it. Screw your public, he murmured, I don't want to share you. You won't, she promised, it's just a dumb job . . . Rising over her: Let's do nothing again. I like doing nothing with you. You're so lovely. Perfect. Everywhere. Everywhere. Let's put the light on. Let me see you. She fought him. She wanted to die with embarrassment.

Later he said, Promise me that whatever happens, we'll never not make love. She sat up like a shot. What do you mean, *whatever happens,* don't say that, what do you mean, her mouth kept repeating it under his kisses, but he made her promise.

It was like a montage, that year and a half: apple green and gold through a gauzy scrim, always a perfect season, Chopin on the sound track. Happiness. *Le bonheur,* the French said, the article like a consecration. The only sadness was Renato, playing the spurned lover, sulking, bad-mouthing Barney. She'd never dreamt the extent of Renato's possessiveness, never intended to exclude him. He accepted a job at the French *Vogue* and moved to Paris.

La Ferme Saint Siméon in Honfleur became their place, whenever their schedules allowed. And the Connaught in London. La Samanna in St. Martin. They owned New York: Gina Gold, the rising star of TV's popular morning show; Barney Livingston, the handsome, mercurial president of the Gotham Art Society. *Women's Wear Daily* captured them at "21," their heads touching, eyes comic-book starry, but wary, protecting their luck. Between them they met everyone; they had global reach; the best part of success was never having to suffer boring people. Barney preferred spending the rare weekends she wasn't on location at Dunesmere, the sprawling heat-guzzling mansion in East Hampton he'd rented. They walked along the winter ocean ("I'm teaching you the out-of-doors," he joked), and Barney set pine-scented fires in the fireplace while Gina shivered — it was always too cold for her — and they filled the country kitchen with faience from Normandy, and dined on the bouillabaisse she'd learned to cook from La Ferme's own recipe.

They slept curled into each other in the big upstairs bedroom, windows open wide to the stars and the booming sea.

Reasons. You can turn them every which way, count them all you like, but they only add up, reasons, explaining nothing.

The change was in him, secret and silent and dangerous, like shoals shifting under the sea. She went faster. He went slower, his every motion, even the way he sipped his morning decaf. He delegated more work to his deputy director and activist board, and discovered navel-gazing, gurus and brown rice and self-actualization. A California heart doc who taught type A blokes like him to live forever. He needed the sun — *for five lousy days, Gina, not even a week!* — and she needed to cancel. Over and over — first it was the Ford-Carter presidential debates, then Queen Elizabeth's Silver Jubilee. Then came the blowout with Chubb Seidman. She spent all her off-air time — after finishing the afternoon tapings — hunkered down in her apartment on Central Park South with her agent, negotiating a move to NBC to cohost *Sunday Seven*. She was asking for a million — *How can we go to La Ferme right now? Next week, after the contracts arrive, I promise.* He: *Okay, I understand.* But just before the signing, she hopped the shuttle to Washington to interview Kissinger. That, too, he understood. A charitable hostess mentioned she'd seen Barney escorting Serena Fosburgh to a Fresh Air Fund dinner-dance at Tavern on the Green. Now *she* understood. Forget it. Don't create an issue. The woman was the female equivalent of a walker. And she needed for Barney to be occupied.

Were they casualties of trendiness — his? In 1976 people nurtured and watered their Needs and "grew in different directions" and "got behind their potential" — she sometimes wondered if the psycho-babble didn't produce the behavior, instead of the other way around.

Sometimes the only reason is that someone wants out.

He sprung it on her fully hatched, before she could mount her artillery. A sneak attack, a Pearl Harbor of the heart.

That Saturday he showed up as planned to take her to dinner, with a bag of bagels from Zabar's for Sunday breakfast, and announced that he loved her and would never love anyone else. He didn't take off his coat, he just stood in her rose marble foyer, clutching the plastic bag of bagels, his brown gabardine coat buttoned to the neck like a good schoolboy, saying he loved her very much. So she knew.

"But I can't have you. I got to you too late. You're already married — to your job. I resent and hate it. But that job *is* you, and partly why I love you. I'm so proud of you, so in awe of you, really."

Her heart was running away from her. Her mouth opened and closed. No awe, she thought. *Don't give me awe.*

"Would you come in and sit down?" she said finally.

He unbuttoned his top button and followed her into the living room, but remained standing.

"Look, we can work this out, it's all doable. You're right to be impatient. Give me one more week and I promise we'll go to Cancún." Why was he pulling this now, with her still trapped in marathon sessions to hammer out the new contract? Any moment she expected her agent to call about one last sticking point.

"Uh, Cozumel, Gina. It was Cozumel."

"So sue me, it was Cancún — Cozumel!"

"It's no good. Your job owns you. You're superb, Gina, you're a star, you're the best. But I hate the bullshit life, the glitz, the — the tempo. In bed by nine. Sex every third week, not even. It's not what everyone's gonna say, you know, that I resent playing Mr. Gina Gold, that's not the point. I want a life. Time together, kids — I wanted *you.*"

"You knew, Barney, you knew —"

"People grow in different directions."

Gina covered her eyes with both hands. Please God, not psychobabble.

"And I've had time to think. Lots and lots of time. I feel abandoned, with you away twenty-four days out of the month. It's too lonely loving you. Funny, I can really understand all those women who bitch about their workaholic husbands —"

"But they hang in. They manage."

"Yeah, they manage to get laid in the afternoon."

Poisonous silence.

"Besides," Barney continued, "most of them have no choice. The women with guts walk. You just did a story on one —"

"All right. We'll have children. We can, you know. I'm only thirty-nine."

He noticed the plastic bag in his right hand, distractedly handed it over. "Here. Bagels. Poppyseed and whole wheat. Dammit" — he shook his head no — "I — I don't see you as a mother. You're barely a wife." They both looked startled by the term. "I want a normal, corny family life. I wanna get out of cancer gulch, spend long weekends in the country — I've set it up so my deputy and board can spell me. I want to play softball with my kid and go ice-skating on the mill pond —"

"What mill pond? You sound like a Hallmark greeting card."

He said nothing.

"You don't even ice-skate. Since when do you ice-skate? You know you have weak ankles." She hugged her satin dressing gown to her. "Okay, I'll retire, that's what I'll do. For a few years, while we raise a family." The words tasted funny. "You know, Hugh Downs just retired —"

"Gina, you're about to start at NBC, for a million bucks —"

"DID YOU HEAR ME? I'LL RETIRE."

"Hugh Downs can take time out. He's a man. For you it would be professional suicide. I — I wouldn't let you. Besides, I don't believe you. I don't believe you'd do it."

Thrusting her chin: "Try me." For a millisecond she was distracted. Why hadn't her agent called by now? Would they use her trivial little demand as a deal breaker?

He was staring at her. "You wouldn't do it. Would you."

She needn't decide this instant, she need only keep him from leaving her apartment.

"Would you."

"I will do anything to preserve — us."

"Baby, you're kidding yourself."

She looked out the window at the swath of Central Park stretching north, an ugly barren gray. Suppose she quit, and then he discovered she was a boring hausfrau. Or she couldn't produce a male heir.

"You're some kind of monster, you know?" said Barney. "I love you very much, but you're a monster."

Flash bulbs popped behind her eyes. "Okay, who is it."

"Who, what, what are you talking about?"

"Who is she. I want to know."

"Oh Gina, don't."

"The mommy on the mill pond."

"Don't. I don't want to remember this."

She rushed at him. "Who is she. You tell me goddammit, who is she. You tell me."

He grasped her shoulders. "You know, we don't have to lose each other."

The panic receded. She must keep her head, not say things she'd regret. Maybe he'd just been testing her.

"Do you remember our promise in Honfleur?" he asked.

She stared at him, not getting it. Then she got it. She swung the plastic bag of bagels like a cudgel, brought it down hard on the side of his head; again and again and again she socked him with the bagels. *You tell me who, tell me.* He shrank from the blows but he stayed, he held his ground, not protecting his head, only flinching a little from the blows, looking bewildered, still in the overcoat, and she kept on swinging, and now he was bleeding, near his eye, the outer corner, and still he didn't move. And then he turned and walked out the door.

When she saw him next she was dying.

Certain events alter the terms so radically, you spend the rest of your life in a race to catch up to yourself. Nine days after she'd closed the deal with NBC, becoming the first woman in television to receive a salary of a million dollars, she felt the lump. That morning, as she was showering, she felt it in her groin, slippery and discrete under the soapy washcloth — the Big Find, the big dread. She stood unmoving under the water a long time, the news raining down on her.

Her job ferried her like a life raft through the nightmare that followed: the tests, the trips to ingenious regions of pain contrived by modern medicine, the waiting to hear the verdict and her sentence. Her fame made these medics snap to, she was getting the best; imagine how much worse it must be for everyone else. Somehow she always managed to work. Even through the fear, the worst part. No, the worst was the plunge, after stupid blind hope. No, the worst was no Barney. It would even be possible to die if there were Barney.

Finally the doctor said, You're a reporter, I can give it to you straight, and said she had high-grade invasive lymphoma. *I'm a reporter . . . What am I feeling?* He told her that, untreated, she could live several months. With aggressive therapy she might live as long as

eight years, the course of the illness was unpredictable and as yet —
I'm a reporter. She never heard the rest. *Carpet beige,* she noted before
blacking out.

She was determined to keep it from the press. The big C was surrounded by medieval superstition; it might destroy her, but she must
not let it wreck her career, she cracked to herself. Not yet. Play for
time. Someone leaked the news. The press was delirious. They'd been
ragging her for weeks — all those clams for an entertainer, not a serious journalist, who'd reduced TV news to a game show. And now,
ta-da, tragedy — almost as good as the Kennedys'. The nervy broad
torpedoed on the eve of her greatest triumph. The big C punishing
hubris. Tabloid heaven.

Her mother's hysteria and need to blame — "It's Barney's fault" —
made things worse, if possible. Gina sent her mother back to Shaker
Heights. People made gestures, wrote notes, sent flowers — and grad-
ually disappeared. Renato, her dearest friend, flew in from Paris — but
business snatched him back. Only Daisy, bless her, never disappeared.
Daisy juggled jobs, babies, sitters, boyfriends, to sit out the hours in
waiting rooms, walk her through Admitting, fetch her home in cabs,
even though the mere sight of a hospital terrified Daisy. Swimming
back up to the world after they took out her spleen, Gina opened her
eyes to Daisy's peaked little face floating over her. Later that night:
"Why you still here? Go home to the kids." "Honey, I'm here. What
are friends for? What can I get you?" "My dancing shoes, let's go
dancing." An hour passed, or a day. "I thought what you can get me,"
she said through dry, cracked lips. "Get me Honfleur."

Six months later Gina was a hundred pounds, hairless, something
not fully human. At least Barney couldn't see her. Always look on the
bright side. She turned her head to the wall. A magic lantern brought
her the lovely days in Honfleur. She saw it through a faint haze, the
lovely late summer in Honfleur, the dark crisscrossed timbers of the
Ferme, the ruffled heads of the dahlias, the road to town scented with
jasmine and thyme. Houses shimmering pink and gray in the blue-
green water of the harbor. Honfleur rhymes with *bonheur.*

A low voice was repeating, You have a visitor. After a long, long
while, she turned her head.

"I'll never leave you again. I was a fool. Forgive me." Gina shut her eyes. She opened her eyes. The vision was still there. Her lips too cracked to smile. "Don't speak. I'm here," the vision said. Later: "It was no good, you see. I'm divorcing Serena. I can't live without you." "You may have to now," she managed. He smiled. "Now that's more like it, now that's what I like to see. The old wise-ass." "You mean" — raising one eyebrow — "you don't like the new me?" "C'mon, we're gonna beat this, you're a fighter." *We,* she thought, waking during some strange hour in hospital limbo. Lit by a cone of light from her bedside lamp, he kept watch. Happiness could find you in the damnedest places.

He fired her doctors and assembled a new team from the National Cancer Institute who were working the cutting edge of cancer research. "Manhattan's enough to make anyone sick. We're getting out of cancer gulch." Defying all the doctors, he drove her out to Dunesmere in East Hampton. He carried her from the car to the house. The February garden was blanched and dry, an assortment of brittle sticks. Like me, thought Gina. A mild lurch of air against her cheek hinted at spring. *Give me the spring, one spring with Barney.*

From the "command center" in the lower guest room, Barney was in touch with cancer researchers the world over. New discoveries were breaking all the time. He came bounding, vibrant with animal health, into the sunroom, where Gina lay on a chaise. He waved a telex at her. "MX4935, that's our ticket. It's a promising experimental drug being evaluated by the N.I.H. Available only to the investigators — and you 'n' me, babe." She smiled at him sadly. He thought he could buy her life.

One evening she couldn't swallow. Barney got onto the bed in Southampton Hospital and lay beside her. Suddenly he raised himself on one elbow.

"Gina, will you marry me?" She could barely talk. "Don't you have to stand up to get married?" she managed. "Where is it written?" he said. "And haven't we always written our own rules anyway? I'll carry you to the altar. I'll hold you in my arms." "But why?" she said. "We're as close now as we can be." "I want the whole world to know. The ritual means something. Guess I'm just an old-fashioned guy who wants to make you an honest woman." "Yes," she croaked, "I'll marry you, Barney. If it's the last thing I do."

They decided to marry in Dunesmere. Barney telegraphed invitations to friends and relatives: Daisy McHenry, Franca Marshak (and to hell with old feuds), Sally and Shelley Wunderlick, Gertrude Alcott from *Mademoiselle* days. Delphine and Jake Mikulski flew in from Houston, Renato Russell from Paris.

A chamber music group played Mozart and Purcell and Cole Porter. Barney carried the bride down the stairs to a little raised landing that overlooked the living room. Her long rose silk dress hung off her in odd folds. The new medication bugged out her eyes; thin strands of hair lay plastered to her skull. A local rabbi performed the ceremony.

Barney looked out at the small gathering, Gina in his arms. "I want to make a toast. To this woman, who has brought such happiness into my life, and filled this house with joy." His voice broke. "I am the most fortunate man."

The guests raised their glasses and smiled uncertainly. "L'chayim," said Shelley Wunderlick. "To life," echoed Delphine. *To life.*

It was spring in earnest. Sun flooded the upstairs solarium. One day Gina felt well enough to sit on the chaise longue wrapped in her red mohair afghan. The following week she was able to walk on Barney's arm up and down the hall. I'm hungry, she said in amazement. The doctors declared the new cocktail was working. Over their protests, Barney bundled Gina up and half carried her a few feet along the beach. Even with the wind, the air was always somehow warmer by the ocean. She grew stronger; her color improved. He spoon-fed her powerful broths in the big country kitchen he'd piled round with Norman faience, as if with these emblems of joy he might tether her to life. She gained weight; her hair grew back, slate-gray but abundant. He forced her to "train" with him, swimming laps together in the pool. Tanned from the sun, each day they lengthened their hike along the surf by an eighth of a mile. By Labor Day they made it twelve miles to Amagansett and back.

Sometime in mid-September Gina's doctors pronounced her cancer-free. They refined their cocktails and wrote articles in *Lancet* that were picked up by the *Times*. Gina's friends privately observed that the doctors had neglected to mention the key ingredient in the cure.

Barney returned to the Gotham Art Society and launched a brilliant campaign to quash a mega—office tower positioned to shroud Central Park in shadow. Infused with energy and nowhere to put it, Gina started caroming off the walls. "Why don't you call your agent and rattle his cage?" said Barney. Her old job at *Sunday Seven* was not available, her agent reported. Gina's replacement had done better than anyone could have hoped for, and the ratings were up. Nor could her agent get much enthusiasm from the other networks. She thought, Disappear from the biz for a year and the waters close over your head. It's totally irrational of course, her agent was saying, but there's still a stigma attached to cancer, the fear it'll spook the viewers. She hung up on him.

She signed up for a local gardening course, then one on Thai cooking. In the middle of the first lesson on wok maintenance, she thought, What am I doing here? She'd never been interested in cooking, even when women were compelled to be. Then she did what she used to in her magazine days when she was hurt or mad. She wrote an open letter to the world. About the medieval attitudes and taboos circulating that blamed people for their disease. The letter expanded and put out leaves — and ended up an article in *Redbook* that drew mountains of mail.

Gina's phone came alive. A literary agent saw a book. No, no book, thought Gina; it would somehow jinx her to relive her ordeal in writing; she felt superstitious about disturbing her equilibrium with Barney, as though it were a gossamer web. But when a producer from PBS phoned about a six-parter on the Art of Healing, and his need for the personal dimension — experts and medics he had up the kazoo — Gina saw a way to use what had happened to her. She took viewers through a story about beating illness. Told them they never had to give up, new therapies, promising new protocols were coming available every day.

But mainly she talked about love and miracles and Barney. And hope. Hope as a moral obligation. Corny as all get-out, but she *felt* corny. Now it was her moment to turn the tables and use cancer. The way she'd learned long ago to use the other rotten blows life had delivered. Gina the alchemist, turning shit to gold.

Chubb Seidman, Gina's old boss at CBS, was starting a newsmagazine at ABC, and looking for a woman anchor. He had watched Gina Gold's performance with growing excitement. Of course he and Gina had had that nasty spat — but old grudges had a way of evaporating when a common interest was served. Their agents made the *shiddach*.

"Gina old pal, how are you? What wonderful timing, really seren-dipitous," Chubb purred into the phone. " 'Cause right now I could shir use a seasoned old bird like you."

Gina sat on a blue-and-white-striped lounge chair under a matching umbrella alongside the pool at Dunesmere. On her lap lay a pile of clips for the interview with Anwar el-Sadat. The new show had taken off, even positioned against 20/20. She was too happy to read. She wanted, for the moment, just to *be*. Through heavy lids, she watched Barney swimming laps. It was hypnotic as a mantra. He would reach the far end of the pool, push off with his feet, then arms and shoulders flashing silver, heels fluttering, he would start the steady crawl back. When he reached the near side of the pool, he'd execute a fancy un-derwater flip and shoot back the other way. All tanned and stream-lined and muscled. The sound of him snorting out water like a sea lion made her smile. Brimming with contentment, she focused her eyes on her notes and read a couple of bios. She melted in and out of sleep, lulled by Barney's water noise.

She woke shivering, chilled. A cloud must have passed over the sun. Something else had changed. She no longer *heard* him. She looked up. Barney floated facedown at the far end of the pool. *Don't, don't scare me like that.* He was still floating facedown. He would flip over soon. Any second now. Shoot skyward, slam into the butterfly stroke. Any second —

BARNEY! She stood, notes slapping the wood deck, moving for-ward, pleading, No, Barney, don't, don't scare me, don't do this.

The official cause of death was listed as coronary arteriosclerosis.

Over the months, bit by bit, she sketched it in. There had been a history of Type 2 familial hypercholesterolemia, Barney's doctor told her. There had been a warning episode in Houston: chest pain, the collapse on a tennis court. She remembered that now, remembered everything. He had gotten the verdict of the angiogram: the condition was inop-erable. He had refused to lead a "limited life," refused the medication, refused the side effects. Inderal, the doctor explained to Gina, fre-quently affects potency. Barney had preferred to take his chances. She understood now. The abbreviated time frame had taught him what was important. He had left Houston and come back for her. They walked to their room that first night in Honfleur, past the black heads of the dahlias, the air scented with apples. *I thought I had all the time in the world to be happy,* Barney said. Now she understood.

Kurt Zimmer paced her cream and gold living room, waving a Phillips calendar. "It's all manageable. You'll fly to London on the fifth. Or I'll come to you in Washington."

She was distracted, she couldn't focus on this. She kept seeing the starfish couple splayed out on the bottom of a pool. Why start over? It was like taking a homicidal maniac into your house. She'd made her deal. She understood the terms: no gain, no pain. She preferred it like this, living "over" life, like an opera singer she once interviewed, who said she sometimes sang over her own voice. Control, the main thing was to keep control. She was keeping control. Except for the silent screaming in her head, she was perfectly in control.

The new president was introducing her. A pleasant, plucky woman, the new prez, but without the panache of their own dear Harold Taylor.

Smiling into the applause, Gina spotted a figure slipping into the back row. So Daisy had come! Suddenly Gina longed to get down with the old crowd and unhook the bras and break out the Chianti and escape into the warm bath of the past, when they'd gotten it so wrong. She wanted to laugh and cry and get drunk on the worst Chianti in the land, yes, most of all she wanted to get very, very drunk.

Chapter 22

I AM GRATEFUL to cancer, it has made me hoard every minute.
From her perch in the last row in Reisinger, Daisy heard a collective gasp of admiration, like wind soughing through a wheat field. She too was perpetually amazed by Gina. Gina's take on cancer was a wondrous feat, the mental equivalent of erecting the Great Pyramid at Giza.

Half listening, Daisy looked around her at Reisinger, the white cinder-block walls, the apron of the arena stage, outthrust like a giant tongue — scene of her old triumphs. She hadn't been back here since 1958. *We had our whole lives before us then.* The idea cut her breath. She saw herself pooled in a white spot, downstage right, left arm outstretched, palm flat. Flashed to the four-year-old in a black short-sleeved leotard, leaping across the New Dance Group studio, eating space. To think of all the little girls who wanted to be Pavlova!

She scrawled on the back of the stapled blue booklet titled *The Perfect 30th Reunion:* "What became of all those dreams? Were we derailed by lack of staying power? Anemia of the will? Simple vagueness? Or because none of us believed we were in it for the long term." She quoted from memory a recent study in the *Times:* "Even women who were college students in the late sixties did not expect to spend much of their adult lives on the job . . ." Hey, who knew? So today we lead catch-up, pick-up lives, cobbled together like this campus.

Setting down her pen, Daisy continued talking her book in her head, telling some invisible choir of readers how it was with the class of '58 . . . Joe College followed a different blueprint, of course. By sophomore year he'd drafted a Life Plan. Today he's a CEO, or editor in chief, or partner in a white-shoe law firm, or enjoying the views from a golden parachute. He's acquired a second home and second wife (investment banker, Yale '78); with just a few bumps marking the transition, he's acquired a second life.

And what of the brides of '58? The last generation who expected to make wife and homemaker their life work, dinosaurs, really — how are *they* making out? A few remain cozily married. Or maybe they're just hanging on by their fingernails, riding it out, counting on real estate, male aversion to change, and clogged arteries to keep their husbands in place. Guilt and gelt. *Don't rock the boat,* Hannah Zimmer said in the corridor of Bates some thirty-five years ago. Would someone tell me, please? In thirty-five years, what exactly has changed?

As for the divorcées of '58, a few are doing splendidly. Hats off to Gina Gold! And Sally Wunderlick, who woulda thunk it! After all the bumbling and false starts, Sally corners the market as Ms. American Homemaker, and winters in Aspen. I suspect many more are slogging away at odd, catch-up jobs, fodder for studies on "the feminization of poverty." Not many CEOs from the class of '58, I can tell you. No Mistress of the Universe, no Elaine Garzarelli in our crowd; old Elaine might as well hail from Krypton.

So I worry about the class of '58. The Lost Members. The ones who bolted from the doll house and fell on their faces. The ones fired from marriage, the Displaced Homemakers. The ones on their knees in the dark, still feeling around for their second lives. Where are they now? How are they making out? It's hard to know; the lines are down, we're all so cut off. Flashing little distress signals across the land, winking out of sight in the darkness. What became of that warm bath of sisterhood? Today it has the flavor of a brief intoxication, like sex with a married man. When the musket smoke cleared and the rhetoric faded, did it all shake down to the old couple thing?

Gina drew another gasp from the audience, jolting Daisy back to

Reisinger Theater. Returning to SLC had been an inspired move. She had only to touch down here and her chemistry altered, as in the old days, when they ran up the flagpole on no sleep and grandiose dreams and those green heart-shaped Dexies. Perhaps a ramble through the old haunts was just what she needed to jump-start her stalled book. Drafts for her prose epic on the class of '58 slopped onto the floor beside her desk, collecting dust. She'd gotten hopelessly lost in a jungle of her own devising.

"Just forget about that tome. Why don't you write something commercial, like Nancy Friday or John Bradshaw? People want the inspirational, the upbeat."

The Luftmensch speaks! Her current beau meant well, but didn't do a hell of a lot for morale. When the Luftmensch talked like that, she just smiled inscrutably and returned to her computer. Sat there by the hour, yanking at her hair like a lunatic. She needed to write this book. The voices left her little choice. They echoed eerily down the corridors of time, the voices, buzzed her ear at four A.M. like gnats. Delphine going on in her honk about "women like us." *To our brilliant futures! We're going to play it different.* And Zimmer: *You all go for cruel flashy men.* And Diana Dew: *Lord knows how y'all will end up . . . I'm going to have a wonderful life . . . wonderful life, wonderful . . .* This book was her bridge back, to a self she'd been forced to abandon twenty years ago. Twenty years ago she had sat out the night in the 16th Police Precinct and made the permanent acquaintance of panic. Knocked off course, she'd been forced into a winding detour. Now she'd returned. Blown back into town like a mean hombre in a Western, full of piss and vinegar, bent on settling an old score. A score with herself. If she didn't get this book born, she wasn't sure in what form she would survive.

Thank God someone else, besides her children, that is, thought she had a story worth hearing. Last month at a book party, she'd run into Andra Cassidy — formerly Andrea — Delphine's old slavey at Hollinsworth. After that, the editor of *Woman Today.* Now one of a handful of superagents, just profiled in *Vanity Fair.* Oiled by her second Chablis, Daisy pinholed Andra and told her about her pages. Andra — board-chested, bandy-legged, of no discernible gender — listened in a kind of agony of impatience. Here she was, *trapped* by Nobody, when Tina was here. And Si Newhouse. And her two hundred dearest friends. Suddenly she focused in on Daisy. Daisy saw something crystallize in the lupine eyes: dollar signs.

"I like it," said Andra, "I like it. A big serious look over thirty years at the women who came of age in the fifties? The timing is just right for a book like that. Hell, I'd take it on for the premise alone. The story of the baby boomers we know. The women taking hold in government, business, the media — Hillary and friends. *My* generation. We set out to have it all. Old story. But *your* group was positioned to miss it all. I mean, there they are, and suddenly all the rules collapse from under them, the marriages go bust. They're out on their ass. And they'd never thought to take care of themselves. Never even framed the concept. What happened to that generation? How did they reclaim their lives? I love it! I see an M.O.T." (A *what*? thought Daisy, not daring to interrupt.) "I mean, tell me, I'm curious for myself. How in hell did you people survive?"

The only sound for days was the palsied Philco air conditioner changing cycles. *I can't, I can't, I can't,* racketing through her head, waking and dozing. She lay jackknifed in the king-size bed in the upstairs bedroom, sheet pulled over her eyes, hands between her knees. How many days up here? What was the date? — 1970, sometime in late September. All she knew. A golden muscled figure appeared on the prow of a ghost ship. Stood admiring his golden bicep, flashed a devilish grin, cigarette butt dangling off his lip, then tacked off into the wild blue yonder. That was Fletcher McHenry, father of her children. Converting the *Playboy* philosophy into action. During the hurricane he'd bailed out of his eight-meter racing boat, and in the same breath bailed out of his marriage. Resurfaced in Bermuda as captain of a tourist schooner. Suffering from amnesia about his previous life. The worst was how easily her heart let go. Like a bad tooth giving up the ghost. They'd never been connected except — big "except!" — by the babies.

Downstairs, Leopoldine, the human tourniquet, was binding up her hemorrhaging life. She'd surfaced from the underground of illegal Haitians with little English who were willing to work cheap. She was blind in one eye and devoted to soap operas and had trouble negotiating the third floor walk-up.

I can't, I can't. A different voice said, Waita sec, what about *them*? If you can't, who can? If you don't, who will?

This conundrum absorbed her through several cycles of the air conditioner.

Maybe you can try? came the new voice. You could at least try. Just take it one step at a time.

Slowly she sat and swung her feet to the floor. Now: set one foot in front of the other. Keep in forward motion. That's right, to the bathroom, turn left. She splashed cold water on her face. She brushed her teeth. She pulled on an old maternity smock. Suddenly she remembered Zimmer saying that the one unacceptable trait in a character is self-pity. She made a vow: *the world will not know.* The world would see a winner. She looked at herself in the closet mirror: limp, greasy hair, puffy eyes, dress stained with breast milk. The image needed work. With the slowness of a moonwalker, she descended the stairs to the living room.

Leopoldine sat on the couch in front of the TV, mouth ajar, snoring. Phil Donahue was talking about multiple orgasms. Corey watched beside her, eyes round, serious and whey-faced as a dust bowl kid, a dark crust under his nose. He wore his navy wool stevedore cap pulled to his eyebrows. Miranda lay snoozing on the coffee table in the cardboard carton from the hospital, tiny fist gripping a silver rattle. Her amazing copper hair fanned around her head. Such abundant hair for a baby — Miranda. That was her daughter. Her throat constricted and an ache shot from her palms up through her arms. The children were part of her, pieces of her soul; how monstrous to hole up in the attic. Swell, but how would they manage? *His* baby too, dammit. Where the fuck was Fletcher. This wasn't the deal, I'm not ready. *This was not the deal!*

True. But do you have a choice?

"Hi gang," she said, supported by the newel post, "I'm back."

She hurried down Seventy-fourth Street, her face stung by the mean wind ripping off the Hudson. Corey insisted on "helping" push the carriage, a huge battered Rolls from Salvation Army. She was in a rush to get home and perform the switch from harried mom wearing an epaulet of upchuck to cool candidate for tenure track. A rare job — and a plum — had opened up at Columbia: teaching a Great Books course in General Studies, the adult extension school. Kurt Zimmer, her old SLC prof, had fired off a recommendation. At three o'clock she was planning to impress the hell out of the chairman of the Comp Lit Department. A big deal specialist in semiotics, Professor Otto Schiff had been in the French Resistance during the war and lost an ear, no one knew how. He seemed to enjoy disliking anyone who came within range, though he was less venomous around pretty women. As she and Corey negotiated a slippery patch, she saluted her own progress.

They'd made it to the new year. January 1971. Gina Gold had just positioned herself to become a household name, while all *she* had done was survive, but hey, you adjust your sights a bit. An autumn of chasing down leads had finally yielded the tutoring job at the Balfour School for rich nut cases. She got strafed by paper airplanes, and Eliot the doctor's son preferred spitting into his collar to learning irregular French verbs, but never mind! She could buy Pampers and strained apricots. Pay the pediatrician on the installment plan. And when Fletcher sent the odd check she would buy a new parka for Corey at Morris Brothers. They were at the mercy of Fletcher's largess. Matrimonial lawyers shuddered at the word *enforcement*.

Sometimes their trio even felt like a family. Wobbly as a three-legged chair, but it stayed upright. Fletcher owned the brownstone, so they lived rent-free. No one maintained the building, though; the place was a genteel slum. A slow leak in her living room ceiling had produced a wonderland of white stalactites. Wind seeped through chinks in the facade. Periodically something would back up and explode in the building's innards, and the tenants would place frantic calls to Bermuda. I'm gonna kill McHenry, the parlor-floor tenant advised Daisy as she tried to butt past him in the hall with Miranda's battered Rolls. A clogged chimney had filled his toddler's bedroom with black smoke.

One night after the kids were down, Daisy sat at her desk to pay bills. Dribbled out the amounts owed in checks for twenties. Her math had never been good. But tonight it was good enough to see that she'd run out of cash. The bimonthly paychecks from Balfour barely covered cigarettes and carfare. Balfour was one of those "little jobs" wives worked, an inoculation against the dread phrase "I'm justa housewife." And she'd run through the eighteen hundred dollars Fletcher had sent three months back. She broke a sweat; lately she sweated like one of the damned in any climate, as though she'd hurdled twenty years into menopause.

She went to the phone and dialed Fletcher's number in Bermuda. She got only a coughing on the line, then a buzz. The ship-to-shore was always out of order. She had no backup. No slush fund, like Delphine; no husband *and* slush fund, like Franca. No big-bucks job, like Gina — what you needed in this town with two kids to make it above the poverty line. Who were they kidding? So get a serious job! To get launched, you needed a serious sitter. No way out. She was being dragged toward Welfare. Except how did you "go on Welfare," what was the protocol? Somehow they'd neglected to teach that at SLC, between Marriage and the Family and The Search for Authenticity. She was cornered, like a rat. Exhilaration seized her. It was her, just her, against IT. A mighty steamroller she'd stumbled in the path of. She shut her eyes and clenched her fists, mouth stretched, teeth bared. She needed all her cunning. Like a rat.

The following week she heard about the opening at Columbia.

Pulling the carriage backward up the slick stoop, she felt the creepy tingling in the vertical pink scar partitioning her belly; she sometimes thought the scar might rip open, her innards spilling out like glistening pomegranate seeds. With icy fingers she fumbled in the bag for the keys. Dug deeper. No keys. She started sweating. Oh not again, she'd locked herself out, second time this week! She could picture the keys so clearly, hanging from the painted wood key ring Corey had made at West Side Montessori. She'd blown it for the interview . . . only opening around . . . her one ticket out . . . how could she? . . . this was not working . . . she wasn't hacking it.

The temperature had dropped ten degrees. She'd get pneumonia from this wash of sweat. Corey was poking at icicles hanging off the stoop with the corn tongs he carried everywhere, his "woofa-snoofa." "Ma-Ma-Ma-Ma, I have to pee," he chanted. She hit all the buzzers. At least get them into the hall, get out of this cold. No one answered. Hold it — June, the Barnard baby-sitter should be here by now, June had keys! Where the hell was she? Daisy scanned the block. No sign of June. They were the worst, the Barnard girls, too busy pondering *Das Kapital* to change a diaper. To think this job would've allowed her to hire a decent sitter! The tears welled. *Stop it,* don't let Corey see you cry again, don't fuck up your child. Saskia Levin, the shrink's wife in the brownstone across the street — could she leave the kids with her?

Forget it, by two Saskia was always stoned. Last time Saskia made it clear she wanted no part of their mess. The whole block viewed them as a crisis waiting to happen.

Corey was watching her with his weird, sly smile, navy wool cap pulled nearly over his eyes, nose streaming. He'd acquired that smile after Daddy split.

"Oh, Mama, you're not going to cry again."

In a sudden inspiration she scooped Miranda and her nest of blankets from the carriage. Miranda flailed her tiny fists and gave a great squawk of protest. "Honey," she told Corey, "we're going to hop a cab and visit a big school for grown-ups where they have bathrooms. And then, as a special treat, we'll go have sugar doughnuts and hot chocolate at Chock Full o' Nuts."

"Do we have to take the silly girl?"

The origin of all his troubles, Corey had decided. "Oh, we wouldn't want to leave her behind. We're a team, we three, right?"

Halfway up the block she turned and saw the giant black carriage, poised on the stoop, hearselike, shuddering in the wind.

"Excuse me if I don't sit, but I need to make this brief." Her chest was clammy with sweat where she cradled Miranda, and her shanks were shaking from the cold. Schiff wore a white Irish-knit sweater under a thick tweed jacket. If he found anything amiss, he didn't let on.

"I know this is irregular. We've, uh, got a problem on the home front, purely logistical, you understand, nothing that can't be solved. But I'd better be brief." A corner of her attention strayed to Corey, plying the hall outside with his woofa-snoofa. *Damn,* he always drifted off.

"I think I could do a superb job teaching this course. I know those books better than I know myself and —"

A thud from the hall. Schiff raised an eyebrow. "Uh, would you excuse me a moment?" She sped out the doorway. Down the corridor Corey lay sprawled beside a crate, rubbing his leg. She hissed, *Get back here this instant* — the voice of the food-stamp mothers in Daitch; they all had the same Ugly Mother voice. Miranda jerked awake and started fussing. Daisy jiggled her against her chest.

She returned to Schiff. Corey had gone very still. Then she felt it, burning into her haunch where Corey rested the back of his head: the question taking form in his mind, the question he was preparing to ask about — Schiff's ear. It'd been sheared right off; where the ear had been, there was only smooth skin. She tightened her grip on Corey's shoulder, tapping in a prayer.

"I know my appearing here like this" — she indicated the babies — "is unprofessional. In fact it's out of the question — believe me, I know. But I'm asking you to take a chance on me anyway and give me this job. I promise you won't regret it."

Schiff had adopted a *faux* earnest expression. He picked up a turquoise egg-shaped paperweight from his desk and studied it in his palm. "Mrs. McHenry, I appreciate your situation. But I need to interview several other applicants. They are highly qualified, you understand."

"With all due respect, *I* am highly qualified. Dr. Schiff, there's something crazy going on out there" — she gestured with her chin toward the window — "something's coming apart, it's like an epidemic, and I got caught in it. And I wasn't ready. You're looking at a middle-class disaster." She fought back tears. "But I am fighting very hard to stay afloat here."

"Yes, and I applaud you," said Schiff testily. "But how can I just sidestep the usual procedures, and hand you this job?"

Sudden flash to a girl in a kelly green dress pitching herself to the boss of Aspen Press — just a game back then. "Because I'm good enough," Daisy said. "And I need it the most."

"I see." He cocked his head at her, amused. "I tell you what. Why don't you give me a ring next week, sometime around . . ." He picked up his calendar.

"I can't wait till next week, Dr. Schiff. *I need this job. And I need to know now.*"

He set down the calendar. Adjusted his shoulders under his jacket. Oh God, she'd overstepped. She watched him riffle through papers on his desk. He went on riffling. Looking for what. Had he forgotten all about her?

Schiff thrust a sheet at her. "Here's the syllabus for the course. We'll give you a Monday, Wednesday, can you manage with that?"

Her hand holding the syllabus shook from elation and the cold. "Mama," Corey started. "Mama, why does the man —"

"Honey, why don't *we* go to Chock Full o' Nuts and have a nice sugar doughnut," said Daisy with the timing of an aerialist.

In 1972, you could just about smell it in the air: couples itching to split and leave the stagnating marriage and actualize their potential. "Divorce Fever" they called it on the cover of *New York* magazine. A book caught Daisy's eye as she wheeled Miranda's stroller past the Brentano's on Broadway: *Creative Divorce;* the following week she spotted *I've Had It, You've Had It.* Maybe Fletcher had caught the divorce virus. Daisy felt vaguely comforted to have been overwhelmed by something enormous, a plague, or a major tectonic shift, not just her own fuckups.

Sally Wunderlick phoned late one night from suburban Paoli, Pennsylvania, talking in slogans almost. About Wanting More. Wanting Space. Actualizing her Potential. Being her Own Boss. "Shelley is stunting my growth, yet he's also very closed off and only comfortable with a low-level intimacy. Of course he won't hear of couples therapy. Daisy, I can't help wondering — Is this all there is? I mean, is this, like, *it?*"

"But isn't it nice having a daddy around the house?" Daisy offered sleepily.

"You gotta be kidding. Shelley works so late he's never home. And when he is, he's like that faceless husband reading his paper over breakfast. Life imitating cartoons. At night he's asleep before I'm done flossing. I have to choose between healthy gums or getting laid. My gums are in glorious shape." Daisy heard her light a cigarette. "*Entre nous,* Shelley's got these hangnails he never trims. It does nothing for our sex life. But whenever I try to talk about it he gets pissed. The other day at the car pool, I realized something horrifying: it's only his good graces that stand between me and poverty! And now" — dramatic pause — "there's someone else. A lawyer from New York who's been working with Shel on some dreary 'matter.' We snuck off during an office outing. He told me I look like a voluptuous Audrey Hepburn. I think Shelley last gave me a compliment circa 1964."

Blear-eyed, Daisy checked the clock radio: one A.M. "Uh, Sally, can we continue this tomorrow? I was up all last night with Corey's ear infection and Miranda's teething." Today she'd raced from Balfour to

Columbia, a sort of traveling pedagogue paid for piecework, like turn-of-the-century immigrants on the Lower East Side.

Intimacy was confined to discussing Gretel, the class guinea pig, over Spaghetti-O's with Corey. And planning the McHenry Expedition, their joint assault on the north face of the Matterhorn — *Heidi* and Dr. Seuss had made Corey an armchair mountaineer. Next they would take on the Eiger, and after that the Jungfrau or Mount McKinley.

Corey was a spookily wise child. He hung around the kitchen, trying to decipher her least shift of expression. "Have hope, Mama."

Was he also clairvoyant? She had just been considering that it might be the package — not just her — that scared off serious suitors. One session with Miranda shrieking and Corey yanking at her hem, and they were gone, tripping over a squeegee or catapulted to the stairwell by some launch pad Corey had built with his Erector set. There was Byron, the go-go bond trader, who dipped by on the odd Tuesday, offering Colombian gold, the wisdom of Esalen, and stoned sex. Dennis the anal art dealer, who turned psychotic when Corey returned a book to the wrong place on the bookshelf of his restored farmhouse. Bernie the engineer, berating Daisy for diluting the blood of the Chosen People with a goy.

And now, finally, Howard the urologist. He courted her with Tales of the Divorce. "I paid for Arlene's nose job, even after she told me she wanted out, and now she's in love for the first time in her life, she says. With a *dyke*. So what was I, chopped liver?" But unlike the others, Howard didn't seem to mind the Lego that stabbed the bare soles in deepest night, or the empty roll of White Cloud bobbing in the toilet. They played doctor; it was important to determine whether her diaphragm was behind the right bone. "Whooo!" he said, sitting up in bed. "You're much more responsive than Arlene. Phew!"

Flashing his pale mortuary smile, Howard liked to joke about spaying the cats in heat who patrolled the brownstone gardens below. He stood perpetually ready to relieve living creatures of their parts. His fellow man he regarded as a walking prostate spoiling for trouble. And he got depressed when he had no patients in the hospital — but never mind. Howard felt *familial*. He prescribed Amoxicillin for Corey's earache, Bacitracin for Miranda's diaper rash, a "D and C" for Rosalba, the new sitter, after she broke down one evening in tears. Poppers for him and Daisy to blast off into the stratosphere. Then one Wednesday Howard looked up from the loin lamb chops she'd splurged on at Oppenheimer's and announced, in the mealy voice for conveying the biopsy report, "I want my own children."

"Daiz, is that you under there? I recognized those spectacular legs. What on earth are you doing under the table?"

Daisy eyed the metal undergirding of the table. What *was* she doing down here? She must be clobbered. She'd crawled under here to chase an earring . . . She inchwormed out. There sat Froyda Maidman-Dichter, cross-legged, cigarillo in hand, nostrils dilated. Nureyev in velveteen knickers. From another room pulsed the disco beat of the Bee Gees — *Stayin' alive . . . dah-dah . . . stayin' alive.*

"Men," said Daisy, rubbing her head. "Have you ever noticed how they're always involved with two women so they can keep *both* of them off balance?"

"Yeah, given their druthers, men want two things: Mommy — that is, their wife — and a new woman to fuck every day. So what. You know your trouble? You're man-addicted." Froyda blew smoke out the side of her mouth. "What do you need a man for?"

"Uh, sex?"

Froyda looked at her pityingly. "My dear, you are living in the Dark Ages. The only way to complete autonomy — and self-respect — is to depend on men for nothing. Zilch. M'dear, you don't need anyone but yourself for sex."

Daisy pointed out that she, Froyda Maidman-Dichter, had both a husband and a girlfriend, so who was she to talk.

"I take full responsibility for my own sexual fulfillment," Froyda said righteously. "Listen, I have just the place for you. Why don't you sign up for Betty Dodson's workshop in self-love."

"You mean, masturbation?"

"Well, that's part of the work, but really it's about having a love affair with yourself. No, go there fresh, without preconceptions. Here, lemme write down the address. Just bring a towel and your lousy self-image."

"Froyda, I've never been a joiner."

Unfortunately there was a doorman. When she mumbled "Betty Dodson," avoiding his eyes and shifting on her feet like Corey needing to pee, he said "Fie E" and flashed a gold-plated smile. She stood before

Fie E, index finger poised over the bell. *You don't have to do this.* You can just rewind the evening like a backward movie and be safe on Seventy-fourth Street with the kids and *Babar,* and Zephyr's green monster aunt in her grotto. Oh, *do* it. It'll be better for your complexion than the Clan MacGregor.

The door opened on a bald Buddhist monk. Actually, it was a small naked woman with a shaved head. She wore a radiant smile and large hoop earrings that dragged down her earlobes.

"Hi there, I'm Betty. You must be Daisy McHenry."

Oops. She'd also shaved her pubic hair. Daisy followed her down a hall hung with watercolors and charcoal drawings, unmistakably of labias. Georgia O'Keeffe sans poetry.

"Why don't you get undressed and join us," Betty said like a matron from B'nai B'rith. She waved at a row of pegs. "You can leave your stuff here."

It felt perverted to be naked with women. Oh c'mon, it's just like the dressing rooms in dance studios. She'd make mental notes. As protection.

She walked into a low-lit room that smelled of incense, hunched forward like Eve fleeing Eden, wishing her towel could be her fig leaf, but maybe that was poor form? No furniture, just wall-to-wall carpeting. In a circle on the carpet sat eight or so naked ladies of all shapes and ages. At the far end Dodson presided, legs crossed Indian-style. She introduced Beverly, a woman with a scrubbed, rosy face who could be a cheerleader from Winnetka, except she too had a bald pubis. Daisy's smile froze: she'd just recognized — oh migod, a neighbor from Seventy-fourth Street, a fat woman with salt-and-pepper hair and thick glasses whom she sometimes saw in Daitch. How could she face her over the broccoli bin!

"Let's chant again," said Dodson, closing her eyes. "Everyone join hands and say *om.*"

"Ahh*mmmmm.*"

"We were saying that self-knowledge leads to self-love," Dodson took up in her chipper voice. "Most women don't even know how they look. We have never really looked at our own most precious part. We've been conditioned to think pussies are ugly and evil smelling and yucky, and that's exactly how the male patriarchal establishment wants it. 'Cause that keeps us in our place. Self-love is power. So our first exercise is to explore ourselves visually, revel in our own vaginal flowers. We're each beautiful in a different way. Anybody want a mirror?"

Thank God she'd taken a shower before coming, thought Daisy. Her neighbor from Seventy-four Street sat pretzeled over herself, scowling, her view obstructed by rolls of belly.

"I see an orchid!" exclaimed a platinum blonde with black pubic hair. "I never realized!"

Daisy heard Mr. Rogers singing, "Boys are fancy on the outside, girls are fancy on the inside."

"And now, dears, a little voyage of inner discovery," said Dodson. "This is a speculum." She brandished what looked like a stainless steel garlic press and a tube of jelly. "Who wants to look inside?"

Blondie volunteered.

"Eeeek! Cold!"

"At the end of the speculum you should see a lovely pink place," Dodson prompted.

Blondie fiddled with her mirror. "I see pink!" she cried, like Columbus sighting land.

"It's called the os."

"I see it! I see the os!"

Next came a lecture on hygiene and something called smegma.

"Ha-ha. Sounds like a Czech composer."

"That's Smetana." More laughter.

"Okay everyone, *Ommmmmm*."

Daisy's neighbor from Seventy-fourth Street had finally managed a look-see with a mirror. "I don't think I'm beautiful. It's goddamn ugly, all this stuff hanging. And I have saggy boobs and black hair on my nipples," she said angrily.

"Honey, real bodies don't look like the high-tech bodies that we all try to live up to," said Dodson.

"To me," said Beverly, "you look Rubenesque."

"Like the Venus of Mittendorf," Daisy put in.

"*Who?*"

"Or Willendorf. Something. She symbolized fertility and the eternal feminine," Daisy improvised.

"You can talk, you look like plain Venus."

A woman across the room with a butch haircut winked at Daisy.

"And now on to masturbation, the ongoing love affair that each of us has with herself. You should set aside one evening a week for self-love. Make a date with yourself. Put on erotic music. Massage yourself with oils. Try a dollop of K-Y jelly —" She demonstrated. "Or use Jergens, whatever does it for ya. A lot of us get hooked on men because we think we can't live without sex. And we're right! But expecting to get all your orgasms from a guy keeps you stuck in sexual insecurities and romantic illusions. Husbands and lovers come and go. But the right person we've been seeking to bring us true love is ourselves. Beverly here will demonstrate!"

"I'm my own best partner," Bev boasted, flashing her cheerleader's smile. "I almost never come with a man."

"Me neither."

"Not me. 'Specially with a slam-bam-thank-you type."

"Is there another type?"

Laughter all around.

"They think they're giving us so much pleasure with all that in-out, in-out."

"So," said Dodson to Bev. "With a vibrator tonight, or without?"

"With, I come in less than a minute."

The room was silent but for an electronic hum. In no time, as promised, her eyes rolled back and she thrashed and moaned.

"Oh, I get it," said a pale underdeveloped woman. "Sex is physical. You were moving."

"Okay, your turn!" said Dodson to the class. She jumped up and put on a record with the throbbing beat of a porn movie sound track. "Bev here's gonna take five."

"The hell I am! I was just warming up!"

"At ten we break for refreshments," said Dodson.

"Can we smoke a cigarette afterwards?" someone cracked.

"Wait a sec," said Blondie, "there's something I wanna share with the group. For the first time in my life I feel self-sufficient. I can do for myself. I don't have to beg, I don't have to need, I don't have to demean myself taking shit from Tony. Thank you, Betty. I'm so happy, so very, very happy to be free at last."

Then she burst into tears.

"I mean, *do you believe that scene?*"

Daisy heard a clink of ice cubes. "Just barely," said Delphine, her voice slurred.

Lately, every time she phoned Houston, Delphine's voice was slurred. She and Gina had been badgering her to join AA, but it was tough to keep after her from New York.

"In Houston people think the libbers are all Commie lesbians," Delphine said. "The only good thing here is no one's ever heard of Nora Ephron."

"Would you believe I'm going back?"

"You're not."

"It's good for my complexion, and it does take the edge off desperation. I kind of view it as a stopgap, like the steno we took after college. Something to fall back on. I know this sounds corny, but there's more good feeling in that room, more real support for women —"

"Why don't you write about it?"

"Oh I couldn't."

"Call the piece 'The Eleventh Commandment: Love Thyself.' "

"I couldn't. I mean, how could I?"

Why not, though. Why the hell not.

She was posted at the sandbox in Riverside Park, on a bench sticky with melted orange popsicles. It was late May. The trees in Riverside Park bowed under a froth of mauve blossoms. The funky air — pollution and exhaust cut with dog shit — gave her a rush. Beside her Sonny Liebowitz jiggled a carriage and regaled her neighbors with The Labor Story. "I was nine centimeters dilated — *nine,* you understand — when this cute intern marches in and . . ." Such a cozy sorority, the mommies, only she was not in it. Mateless like Lowly Worm, Corey's favorite critter from Richard Scarry, she was an impostor here. She watched Corey cede his turf in the sandbox to a commando wearing a yarmulke fastened to his hair with bobby pins. Corey was a dreamy, empathic child, uncannily attuned to any unfortunate in the vicinity. He was always giving pennies and oddments to a street hustler on Broadway he called "my favorite bum." Daisy's heart ached for him.

Shifting her sticky haunches, she took a sounding. She'd come a way from the wreck of last September, hiding under the sheets in the attic. Okay, you survived. Congratulations. What next?

"I'd have finished my degree in sociology, but David wouldn't hear of it," Sonny Liebowitz was telling her circle.

Ah, the excuses and cop-outs. They never lacked for excuses, she and the mommies. *We got too many mixed messages. I'd have gone to Law School, but . . . I'd have kept on painting if . . . If not for Sam, I'd be singing at La Scala.* Oh, Delphine, what will your excuse be? They were nothing in the arc of a life, the intentions and ifs and regrets counted for nothing. Her old dreams tugged at her. Women everywhere were churning out articles and books. It seemed every mad housewife and ex–prom queen in the land was locked into a room of her own, pounding a typewriter. Writing stuff that no one in the past had considered fit to print, words that were new and exciting and steaming with rage! And it paid. Gina had just done a story on a housewife who wrote a mystery about a randy suburban psychiatrist, and then sold the thing for a fortune to the movies. Clay Felker, the editor of *New York* magazine, was making his girl reporters into stars. It figured in a way, women all scribbling; you didn't have to go to Columbia Law or Wharton or the B School or anyplace but the hard-knocks school of life to start writing. Magazines had O.D.'d on consciousness-raising groups. But no one had covered Betty Dodson. What a bizarre mix of raunch and kindness. Delphine was right, Dodson would make a marvelous story. And no one had written it — not yet. Why not catch the cresting wave? *Why not me?* She glanced at the *Village Voice* crumpled beside her on the bench. She'd just read the cover story, "The Next Great Moment Is Theirs."

Who was "theirs"? Her gang had missed it, the next great moment. Vivian Gornick, the author of the article, had gone on about the paralysis afflicting them all. Yet Gornick had gotten off her ass to write about paralysis.

Seated at the kitchen table, she typed draft after draft, over a week of afternoons and the weekend, going through a half carton of Carltons. Sunday midnight, smelling like a chimney and hugely pleased with herself, she mailed six perfectly typed pages to a name she'd gotten off the masthead of *New York* magazine. She sent a carbon to the *Voice,* too. This violated article submission etiquette, Gina had warned her. But she'd never sold that piece on career girls back in the sixties, and she didn't seriously believe she would sell this one, so screw etiquette.

An image from the piece woke her up laughing in the middle of the night. Thank you, Dr. Howard. Without you I might never have gotten to Dodson.

Tuesday morning when the phone rang, Daisy hauled out her list of questions on projectile vomiting, bracing herself for the aggravated voice of the pediatrician.

A man on the other end introduced himself as Ron Carroll, executive editor of *New York* magazine, and asked her where the hell she'd been hiding. "I love your piece. It's witty, hilarious, fresh. This is great stuff. We're going to banner it on the cover. What else can you do for us? Can we have lunch?"

Lunch! Banners! Great stuff!

Corey wandered into the kitchen with *Babar* and a question on Zephyr's aunt. When he saw Daisy's face, he didn't need to ponder the message.

Chapter 23

AND SO, DEAR CLASS of '58, I got my fifteen minutes of fame, wrote Daisy in an early draft of her book. I became a chronicler of feminism and its fallout — well, one of a herd of chroniclers. Suddenly in the early seventies, all the voices belonged to women. And everyone listened. We wrote about vaginal politics and hookers' rights; body hair and witches' covens; Jayne Mansfield and SCUM — Society for Cutting Up Men — and suctioning-off periods; Miss America, the mindless-boob-girlie symbol, and marriage as legal whoredom, and the sex life of spiders (he fucks her; she bites off his head). My articles struck, as they say, a nerve. I appeared on talk shows: Donahue in Chicago, Joyce Brothers in L.A., Charlie Rose in D.C.

In D.C. I saw Diana *Dew* Hilliard, busy with baby Nicky, number 3, while husband Frank helms the National Endowment for the Humanities; Di is indeed having a wonderful life, as threatened. In Houston I looked in on Delphine *Mortimer* Mikulski, who raises money for the homeless and is unrecognizable, but I'll let *her* tell you all about it! And in L.A. at the Beverly Hills Hotel, whom should I meet poolside but Mia *Sils-Levy* Damiano, now Princess Mia of course, after her marriage to the Nawab of Jaipur, which I'm sure you know unless, *my dears,* you've been living under a rock. And *then* whom should I see taking a stroll in the pool but Gina Gold, who's making waves as the Morning Girl on CBS.

It was all going so well, if we leave love out of it. Can we do that? Please? Or consider it this way: losing in love became fodder for winning copy. Ms. Heartbreak became — don't laugh — an expert on "the sexes," spokesperson for singleworld! In any case, in 1973, a card-carrying feminist was supposed to leave love out of it. Love was so . . . *diminishing*. The big romance was women, all doing such exciting things. The big romance was work. I was hot for the writing game, journalism, dancing two steps ahead of the trends — no, *creating* the trends. Magazines gave us entrée, exposure, a stairway to celebrity. The fun would never end! The articles also devoured our time and talent and paid shit. It was my academic piecework that paid the bills.

But we were thirtyish and everything was possible! I was riding the cresting wave! Sniffing out tomorrow's news, prospecting for the big story that would splash my name over the cover. A story that would dig behind the party line to capture what was really happening to women in '73, the real lives beneath the rhetoric. Finding the story would take some fancy footwork. Luck, timing, the right friends. Oh, I came close. I came so close I could smell it. Almost get my arms around it. The story that made it happen, almost, turned out to be Sally. Sally *November* Wunderlick.

I found her one glowing fall afternoon on her knees on the sidewalk in front of her building on Seventy-seventh and Riverside Drive. Crawling on the pavement, butt in the breeze, attracting dismayed glances. Jus' pass 'er on by folks.

"I'm looking for my earrings. No, keys. I'm looking for the keys." Her voice strangely hoarse. As if she'd been garroted.

Then Daisy saw her hands. "Jesus, Sally, what happened?"

Sally held up her bandaged mitts. "I just got discharged from Bellevue, actually." And, it turned out, evicted from the apartment belonging to the lost keys.

"C'mon," said Daisy, "you're coming home with me."

She settled Sally on the couch. Corey and Miranda, the trauma team, tootled in with a tray of Sleepytime tea and a box of Fig Newtons. Before coming to New York Sally had the lubricious bloom of a

Playboy centerfold. Couple of seasons in the Apple had drained her color, and cords stood out in her long neck.

Some of the history Daisy already knew. Sally had left Shelley in Paoli, Pennsylvania, two years back to come to New York with the three kids. It was early seventies and Sally was part of a mass migration; across the land, wives were walking, marching off into the wild blue yonder to the cadence of Self-fulfillment and Autonomy. Hadn't Sally's best friend Lottie just left her CPA husband to hit the road with a Dominican bandleader? Sally arrived in New York spouting the jargon. *I need space . . . need to grow . . . actualize my potential . . . I want to be someone.*

More specifically, she would expand the catering she'd done for suburban garden parties to corporate clients. She would launch a newsletter, *The Compleat Homemaker,* with recipes, entertainment ideas, gardening tips. She would write an article, "Living the Dream: Notes of a Recycled Homemaker." "I had to leave," she told Daisy on the phone from her new apartment. "I've never been anything but a daughter, wife, or mother. Where do *I* figure in? Isn't it *my* turn?"

Several months in, she still hadn't found the fun. She plodded through charcoal slush to job interviews; rode the West Side IRT, nauseated by the smell of wet wool and gamy breath and the cheap soap used by the poor, not that she wasn't one of them now — well, it was *la misère* or self-loathing in Paoli, Pennsylvania! She failed a test for a slot as copyeditor at *Gourmet. Food and Wine* said we'll call *you. Are we having fun yet?* She thought her phone must be out of order until her periodontist's nurse rang to say the mouth guard to prevent teeth grinding was ready. Eventually she landed the job as administrative assistant to the comish of the New York Parks Department. It was an opportunity to hone the writing skills she would need for *The Compleat Homemaker,* even if she was only writing about inadequate park lighting in the Bronx.

"Then I fell in love with Ike Handman, the lawyer I met at Shelley's office party." (And stopped calling her "girlfriends," Daisy noted.) "We were soul mates, Daisy. He told me I was the one that got away. The sex was — God help me, I'd forgotten how it could be. Shelley couldn't find a clitoris with a road map. And his hangnails . . . Then Ike cut out. Just like that. Said things like, 'Nothing lasts forever.' And he never wanted children, much less three not his own. He wanted space, blah, blah, blah. It was like, 'Thanks for the beer, honey, sayonara.' I went bonkers. Wrote him *scorching* little letters. On Valentine's Day I sent him a dozen red heart-shaped balloons. I called at all hours. He had his number changed. I showed up at his apartment wearing only a baby doll under my Burberry — Oh God, leaving the kids alone. The doorman wouldn't let me up.

"I got fired, of course. I mean, without Ike in my life, I couldn't find any meaning in writing about lighting in the Bronx. Then the rent check bounced. I was overdrawn — all those nighties I'd been buying at Bendel's to feed Ike's fantasies. One rainy day I interviewed for a gal Friday. They gave me the usual we'll call *you*. I went and sat on a bench in Central Park, depressed as hell, and I thought, What is this? Here I'm miserable about a dreary gofer job I don't even *want*? Even the car pool was better than this, and the bridge games, and the silly country club scandals, and those parties we 'surprised' our husbands with. This career thing, what a crock. We've been sold some bill of goods. Yet could I really go back to Siberia and Shelley? I used to stab myself with a paring knife just to make sure I existed. So I lay around the apartment with the kids, watching the Watergate stuff on the tube, waiting for the luck to change. Then Shelley showed up in the Country Squire in his new body shirt and bell bottoms. Waving a court order to take custody of the kids.

"One afternoon I'm standing on the checkout line at Zabar's with my stash of Nova Scotia and white chocolate, and I start chatting with this cute guy behind me. Pink cheeks, blond hair, like Dink Stover at Yale. We kind of fell in love, right there on the checkout line, you know, one of those mad things, like in college. He invited me back to his place for lunch. He had his Lincoln Town Car and driver waiting outside.

I went home with him and never left. He's this Wall Street wunderkind from Texas who made a pile in hedge funds and semiretired at thirty-five, and sits on the board of Lincoln Center and Legal Aid — you've read about him in *Town and Country*. He lived in a five-story mansion downtown — a renovated bank, actually — with a marble staircase, and wood-paneled library, and Parisian cage elevator. It got pretty wild — 'ludes, poppers, threesomes . . . Meanwhile, Dink is getting weirder and weirder. I used to lie awake at night petrified, thinking of those 'snuff' porn movies, where the big *O* is death. Then one night I'm up in the library working on entertainment ideas for *The Compleat Homemaker* — I had *fabu*lous ideas. A giant chocolate swag for July Fourth. An outdoor omelet party. A *soirée dansante* with desserts for forty. Poached pears with crystallized violets! Rhubarb Crumble! Kiwi tartlets! Gooseberry Fool —"

"Yes, so what happened then?" Daisy interrupted.

"That night Dink comes into the library dressed in a gorilla suit and says, 'I'm gonna fuck your brains out.' I don't think he talked like that at his board meetings. Then he wanted to — Oh, it was too awful. He had these catalogues from the Pleasure Chest with leather masks and rubber aprons. Daisy, I can't" — she started to shudder like she was sitting atop a 7.7 on the Richter scale. She put her white mitts over her eyes. "I'm sorry, I can't say it —"

"It's all right, don't, it's all right."

"Later that same night I knew I had to split," she continued in her scratchy voice. "I decided to slip out the back on the elevator. I got in and suddenly the elevator rattles to a stop and it went dark. Totally black. He cut the power! I banged on the cage, banged and banged." She looked at her white mitts. "I screamed till something popped in my throat. Snapped. I still can't talk. How much time passed I don't know. I peed in the elevator. Like a vagrant. Like a dog . . ."

The next evening Daisy placed a discreet call to Paoli, Pennsylvania.

Within the week Shelley Wunderlick dismissed his live-in secretary. He had decided to try again with Sally. For the children's sake.

"He's the proverbial loyal husband," said Sally, sucking an Elavil off a bandaged hand. "And he's agreed to go into couples therapy. I believe it's possible to grow and self-actualize *within* the marriage, don't you? You know, I've been thinking" — she cocked her head at Daisy — "Why don't *you* write 'Living the Dream.' Tell my story, minus, well, the gorilla suit." Nervous laugh. "It shouldn't be a total loss."

"Oh, I couldn't," Daisy protested. Smelling a great story, maybe the one she'd been looking for. Sally leaps to liberation — and lands in a bed of nettles. Why? There was the story. And how many other wives who walked were now adrift in America, blowing around the land like so much tumbleweed? (In retrospect, dear class of '58, how pathetic we were. What would Hillary and Marian, and the new women senators and V.P.'s, make of our clumsy efforts?)

Daisy sighed. "I'd feel like a ghoul, Sally, using your life."

"Oh, but you *are* a ghoul, everyone knows that! Nothing anyone says or does is safe from you! Now listen, I want you to write this story. I'm asking you to, for me. Here. Get me my bag. I'm gonna give you all my tapes."

"Living the Dream" made the cover of the September 4, 1973, issue of *New York* magazine. Shortly afterward, Daisy was invited to contribute to a rotating women's column in the Thursday *New York Times*. She might have moved to a different planet. Pre-fame, she was one more broke single mother with the clout of an illegal alien. Now she displaced space. Went to A-list dinners. Basked in compliments. An editor at Doubleday paid her ten grand to finish her memoir on Paris in the sixties. She flew around America to promote *Here Lies the Heart* on radio and television, high on semifame and vodka gimlets. Sally, too, found happiness; Shelley trimmed his hangnails and helped her incorporate *The Compleat Homemaker*. It seemed, in those days, the only direction you could go was up.

It was a good time, too, with the children. One morning when Félicité, the current sitter, came down with acute vapors, Daisy hustled the kids into a cab to the WPIX-TV studio where she was being interviewed for a show called "A Second Look at Women's Lib." From her perch facing the generic A.M. blonde, Daisy could make them out in the live audience: Corey's pale bowl haircut and round eyes; beside him, a head lower, Miranda's flame hair and foxy little face. Given the cue, her kids applauded vigorously with the others, clap-clapping away, important and proud at being members of the wedding. Proud of their old mom, the mess in the attic. *I dug out, I did it.* For them. My team. What's it all for, if not the children. They played for keeps, the children.

Like the nuclear families, they had their rituals. Maybe it was Corey who got them started on the hiking, with his penchant for sauntering down Riverside Drive and never looking back. (How he frightened her with his disappearing acts. Several times she'd nearly called the police. Since the Etan Patz horror, which continued to fill the tabloids, mothers throughout the city measured delays in seconds.) They hiked Central Park, wandering by accident into the Rambles, the homosexual cruising section. They tooled upstate in their leprous '64 Dodge Dart, its chassis gnawed by rust. Trail maps in hand, the McHenry Expedition conquered the Catskills, the Shawangunks, the Berkshires. Even doll-size Miranda was of the party, the "sweeper" trotting along in the rear on her small legs with her Snoopy backpack (often finishing the climb on the shoulders of the reigning "uncle"). Corey was in training to become the next Edmund Hillary. He led the expedition, first to spot the blue trail markers painted on tree trunks, rationing out the Hershey bars. He scooted up ahead, stopping to lean on an improvised alpenstock and call back with manly condescension, "Pick up the pace, goils."

That was on the Longmeadow approach to Mount Greylock in the Berkshires. In the late spring, the sun warming their backs. Along the spongy streambed they discovered yellow dogtooth violets and the rose-flecked throats of jack-in-the-pulpits. Time for a breather, called out Corey, pronouncing it "breath-er." They ate their heroes on a log fretted with silver lichen. A velvet carpet of moss, psychedelic green, stretched down to the stream. Daisy jotted an article idea for her *Times* column on the pad she always kept at the ready — because of the column, nothing went to waste; everything became material. A piece on female sex drive, she scrawled, picturing herself with a Satyr asprawl on the velvety moss. Call it "Randy Jane." How to package such a subject for the prudish Gray Lady . . .

A riot of birdsong stole her attention. You couldn't see any birds in the pine tree, yet there had to be a major convocation tucked in under the boughs; the entire tree was piping with song. *Remember this . . .*

"When are we going to climb the Alps?" asked Corey.

Another ritual, their plans for a Swiss holiday. A single mother doubled as father, purveyor of big-ticket dreams.

"Oh, I'll need to sell a few more articles first," said Daisy with a sigh. More than a few. She was richer in praise than money. A new boiler for the brownstone had swallowed her advance for *Here Lies the Heart.* Switzerland seemed as attainable as Jupiter.

"And after you sell the articles, *then* we'll climb the Matterhorn?" Corey persisted.

"Yep. And maybe the Jungfrau."

"Me too," piped Miranda, her refrain.

"Tell us about the Matterhorn again," said Corey, wiping mustard off his mouth with the back of his hand.

"Well, let's see. First you take a little red cog railway that goes clackety-clack, up to the village of Zermatt. And there it is, the Matterhorn, like a cockeyed pyramid with snow on top."

"Like the hat in *The Cat in the Hat*."

"Right. And sometimes it wears a little ruffle of pink cloud around the summit, maybe because it's bashful."

"And what's it like at the summit, Mom?"

"Oh, it's like looking 'out the windows of Heaven,' one climber put it. And in the meadows below you hear the sound of cow bells —"

"And see mountain goats."

"Yep. And we'll go bounding up the slopes, just like the goats."

"Me too," said Miranda.

"But the silly old girl is too slow," said Corey.

"I am not, I'm coming too!"

"Of course you are. We're a team, we three." A team in need of a leader . . .

She rarely thought about Ben Marshak outright; he rustled through her nights like ghost music. Sometimes she read about him, with proprietary pride, in the papers. The resolution Ben had introduced, while still in the City Council, to impeach Nixon for the bombing of Hanoi. His triumphant run for Congress from the 19th Congressional District. The economic conversion bill he was sponsoring that would take people from a war preparedness economy and retrain them for peacetime. Ben Marshak had rapidly become known in liberal circles as the conscience of the House (making up in principle what he lacked in effectiveness). In her personal mythology Ben embodied the goodness that she failed to discover in the men it was her lot to fall for; that Ben was good enabled her to survive the scumbags. He was her phantom fallback. Whenever she was bone weary from fencing with editors, creditors, and her newest date, and ready to forfeit all claim to being a grown-up, she would screen a grand reunion with Ben. Usually it was set near the Great Barrier Reef in Australia, *Tristan and Isolde* on the sound track. He was well married, they said, but where was the harm? The idea of Ben made the world safer, like Snoopy and Jenny Kanga and the other button-eyed fuzzy-wuzzies posted around Miranda's bed at night.

Corey was studying her face. "Don't be sad, Mama."

She shivered. Downright spooky, the way he read her.

"Why're you sad?" Miranda asked.

"Actually, I'm the world's happiest mother. I've never been so happy as I am with you," she said truthfully. "It's just that sometimes I get lonely."

"But you have us."

"Sometimes grown-ups need other grown-ups."

"You know," Corey said to his sister. "For smooching."

"But you can smooch with us."

"Not that kind, silly old girl," said Corey. "Like in *Playboy*."

"Hey, guys, you're the best. I love you madly. C'mon, three-way kiss."

Corey leaned in and gave her a noisy wet smackeroo on the nose. He smelled of clover and Italian salami.

"Me too." Miranda pressed in between them in her quick, febrile way.

Remember this. She closed her eyes, inhaling her children.

Was it hormonal, some female deficiency that kept her from converting success into serious money? Even the fancy *Times* paid a lousy three hundred dollars a column, and it was only a ten-shot deal. Hardly a sum to buy them a safe apartment with heat. Fletcher's second wife was pregnant; requests for donations to family number one only fattened the phone bill. Fortunately, a children's guardian angel kept watch. Preventing the local cat burglars from breaking into the apartment from the fire escape. Staying the hand of the junkie who drilled cylindrical holes from the stairway landing into their hall. Holding up the sagging ceiling in the living room. Her most pressing need was for a reliable sitter. The going wage was two hundred bucks a week, plus separate room with TV and bath. Fat chance! Félicité had a habit of collapsing on the couch, hand trailing, à la *Dame aux Camélias*. Corey and Miranda often took care of *her,* curing her migraines with their all-purpose remedy, mint tea and Fig Newtons. They'd become bizarrely parental, assuming that uncoupled female adults required coddling. (A great subject for the *Times* column, Daisy scribbled on her pad, rocketing homeward on the IRT.) Félicité's brother Albert, melancholy and elegant as a Parisian dandy, usually picked up Félicité in the evening. "She is not happy, *ma soeur*," he confided to Daisy. "Her son and husband they stay back home." My God, her *son*? thought Daisy. She herself couldn't get into the morning without a session of bone-crushing hugs with the children. Hers were white middle-class problems, even if she was hanging on by a thread.

"Who woulda thunk it," said Daisy to Gina one evening over the phone. "I used to think life would be about Love and Art, in caps. Now I lust for Benefits. A dental plan. More steam heat. If I'd known, I'd have gone to law or business school. Like the class of seventy-three. They won't ever get caught like us."

"No, probably not. But why do I think you're still dreaming about Love, capital *L*?"

New York is of a size to swallow all crimes of the heart. Everything is permitted because most everything disappears; what goes around seldom comes around. Nor does the city offer chance encounters, like those that occur in gentler milieus around the village green, a shot at repairing breaches opened in a fever of distemper. In New York when people quit the frame of each other's lives, they're gone for good. Daisy was unprepared, then, that February afternoon she was heading down Fifty-ninth Street toward Bloomingdale's, visions of white sales dancing in her head, to collide with her past.

She recognized the man who was talking to himself. Jabbing the air with his thumb. Her heart banged around like a trapped bird. She lowered her head. Just butt on by, for vanity's sake; this morning she'd forgotten the Maybelline.

He grasped her upper arm and swung her to a halt. "Daisy Frank, you're not going to just walk by me without saying hello." Crooked smile. "Daisy, uh, McHenry, is it?"

Since the Algonquin she'd seen him only in the paper. His dark hair spilled onto his collar, trendily shaggy, and his eyes were watery behind the black eyeglass frames. Same mashed nose. His small ruddy face now scored with lines. He looked like an aging boy.

"So, you're in New York," she said idiotically.

"I'm in town over the weekend to open another district office. My fifth," he added proudly.

They stood disrupting the flow of walkers, both grinning, and she saw them standing just so, ten years back, on a different street.

"Listen, I'm late for a meeting, but are you — Would you by any chance be free tomorrow evening?" He rushed recklessly through the words. "I have tickets to *The Cherry Orchard* at the Vivian Beaumont. Could you come with me? I hear Irene Worth is marvelous." His eyes anticipating refusal, but *come, won't you come?*

He pronounced Irene "Ee-ray-nee," like people in the know. Her old rough diamond. And what of the missus? Tending the hearth in D.C.? Daisy scented danger. There was every reason to pass.

"Yes," she heard herself say. "Yes, I could."

All the critics had given the production raves. Raul Julia played the nouveau riche Lopakhin with just the right swagger; an electric new actress named Meryl Streep was a scene stealer as Varya; and of course the sublime Ee-ray-nee as Madame Ranevskaya wrung every heart in the packed house. Every heart but one, that is. Daisy, who loved Chekhov with a passion, would have to take the critics at their word. She was busy imagining how very lovely it would be if Ben were to reach over and tuck a hand under her knee, in that delicious silky hollow where it joins the thigh.

Afterward they went for a drink to a new French bistro several blocks north of Lincoln Center. The place was done with chrome and black and white tile, to reassemble an art deco bathroom. It rang with braying laughter, the sound of the Me Generation at play. There were no vacant tables, so they stood at the bar, propping their elbows on the cold zinc, facing each other and nipping at Glenlivet single malt. She watched his thin childish mouth, charmed by the odd catches in his voice, the minipauses before words.

They talked about the peerless performances that she hadn't noticed. And Ben's efforts to push through an act in Congress to protect from reprisals the "whistle blowers" who expose fraud and abuse. And they talked about her columns for the *Times*.

"I read you every chance I get," Ben said. "You're good, you know? You've really done something. I'm impressed."

She'd partly written those supervisible pieces, she realized, from an urge to *gall* Ben.

They talked about his daughter, Angelica, and difficult stepchildren, and her Corey and Miranda.

They were as correct as two English butlers. Fine. Anything else would be folly, of a sort to pirate away her concentration, a writer's crown jewels. He also belongs to your old classmate, remember? She sensed the potential here for a test of sisterhood. Better not test it. She preferred not to discover the true dimensions of her character.

Abruptly Ben said, "I dream about the colors you are."

A woman behind her shrieked with laughter. Daisy wasn't certain she'd heard right.

"I seek pink, rust, lavender. You always used to wear lavender. Like tonight."

She held very still. Don't move, don't breathe, let it blow off.

"God help me, I've never stopped thinking of you," Ben said. "You're like a piece of me that's missing."

She closed her eyes, swept back to the night on Twenty-third Street, then she joined him in the madness.

"When I had the babies, it was you I wanted there —"

"I wish I had been there."

They stared at each other, and a rent opened in time, exposing that murky afternoon in the Algonquin. What had they done that afternoon? How much had been improvised from spite?

She laid a hand along Ben's shirt front, silky cotton with a thin pink stripe. "I've always meant to ask you, When did you take to wearing bow ties?"

"I used to get food on regular ties. And shirts are easier to clean."

They laughed.

His eyes pleaded. "Daisy, I —"

"My dear, you're a married man." Abruptly she saw herself on Peter Tabori's floor in Cambridge. Little Franca had certainly evened the score.

Sighing, Ben sloshed Scotch over the ice cubes in his glass. "Do you ever think we're going to wake up old one day and it'll all be over? And we'll have missed it. Missed the best part."

Spoken as if it were a fait accompli. "What do you want?"

"All I know is I want you," Ben said, eyes flashing.

An influx from the door pushed her against him. She shifted away but he drew her to him, his lips opening hers. "What I want is to come home with you tonight and hold you."

His mouth the shape of her smile.

"Let me stay with you tonight."

"And afterwards you'd go home to your life."

"You're right, it wouldn't be fair to you."

She drew away from him and gripped the bar. He must hate her, she'd once treated him so carelessly, how could he not.

"We must see each other, there has to be a way," Ben said.

"Well, maybe we could meet once a year, like in that play, *Same Time Next Year*."

"If only you were married, too, then we could be together."

She watched the bartender expertly pouring with both hands from his spigot bottles. This was not the Ben of her imaginings. "Tell me, why do you stay married?"

Ben focused on the bartender's motions for a long moment. "I know why," he finally said, "but I can't tell you. Obligations I can't explain. Yet."

Yet. Goddamn lawyers!

"But as of tonight everything's changed," he said. "If you asked me —"

"No! Then it would fall on me to thrill you, make it worth your while, worth all the mess and suffering. Not to mention a damaged career. No, you'd have to come freely, be already free. Take the same risk as me."

A long sigh. "Would you do one thing? Come close again, just for a minute."

"Aren't you afraid of being recognized?"

"They're theater groupies here. Besides, I've committed worse crimes."

"Taken bribes, have we?" she murmured into his mouth.

"I'm more attracted to you than you are to me. Always have been."

She assured him not. Their tongues melted together.

"Could I meet your children? Could we at least do that?"

"Tomorrow I could bring them to the playground at Central Park and —"

"Where?" said Ben feebly. "Tell me which one."

"Which what?" A woman behind Ben in a raccoon coat watched her in disgust.

"Which playground. No, don't move, let's stay like this —"

"Eighty-first Street."

"East?"

"West."

"You haven't even gone yet, and already I'm longing for you."

She felt him longing, like trapped lightning, through layers of clothes.

All night she trembled uncontrollably, she might never be warm again. Sunday morning the sky promised snow. At the Eighty-first Street playground, her children, their exquisite antennas picking up her tension, were cranky and listless.

Ben appeared five minutes later, the collar of his rust tweed coat turned up; it looked like a kid's coat. Ben sat on a bench across from her and the children. Daisy poured hot chocolate from a thermos, and rationed out the Gummy Bears, and then she pulled the children to her and hugged them, all the while staring at Ben. She must memorize him.

Ben stared back, eyes pinpoints behind the black frames, ears rimmed pink with cold. Miranda glanced his way.

"Is that man a bank robber, Mama?"

Miranda's catch-all term for anyone violating standard decorum. Daisy laughed and kissed her chapped red cheek.

"Why don't you guys go swing on the Tarzan rope."

On the way Miranda tripped in the sand and started howling because she'd swallowed a Gummy Bear whole, and Daisy ran to administer first aid. Then several people recognized Ben and closed in on him, blocking him from view.

All the way home she kept seeing his face, a mask of regret.

That evening, she stood in her bay window with a double vodka. Doing the right thing could just about kill a person. The snow had started. Thick flakes swirled under the conical beams of the streetlights, bearing her back to the white nights of their youth, and the morning she'd been in bed with Fletcher, and Ben had come knocking on her door, and everything set in motion had been wrong.

It was rich: here she was at the peak of the sexual free-for-all, women all gung ho for recreational fucking. Look, Ma, no strings! We can be heartless, too, just like men. And she acting like someone in a nineteenth-century opera. Give me everything or give me nothing. Could she be more out of step?

Wasn't there something in between?

"You are right," she wrote Ben in her mind, "there has to be a way."

Instantly she felt better. Like a wretch at the foot of a guillotine suddenly granted clemency.

She rummaged on her desk for a presentable sheet of stationery. She sat with her pen poised to write the sentences crowding her head.

The phone rang.

"I'm calling to thank you," Ben said, his voice muffled across a bad connection. "Thank you for sending me away and being mature for both of us. We did the right thing, Daisy, didn't we? It would've been dangerous, so dangerous, my darling, do you realize?"

Daisy agreed with Ben that they had indeed done the right thing. Then they talked for a minute about nothing at all, unsure how to cut off, and Daisy hung up a shade too abruptly.

She wanted to bellow, throw things — burn the letter. But there was no letter to burn.

Of course, Ben had merely respected her wishes. How could he have guessed her change of heart? Were they fated always to cross wires? Her only recourse was to get wildly successful. She would flay him with her fame. Obviously, teaching was not the ticket. She would become a hotshot journalist, with a front-row seat on the world — as written about as the stories she covered. Like that Oriana Fallaci. No one remembered what Fallaci wrote about. Her single best subject was always Fallaci.

"What you need is a forum," said Gina over lunch at La Réserve on her expense account. "That means getting a staff job. No more freelance. Shouldn't be too hard to find. You're a name, you've got your finger on the pulse. Any publication would be lucky to get you."

Daisy hunkered down on the living room couch with a yellow legal pad and a pack of Viceroys to plot her campaign. After the splash made by "Living the Dream," she'd been a lunch away from making it to the coveted ranks of contributing editor at *New York* magazine; but a sudden takeover at the top had neutered Ron Carroll, her one-time boyfriend and sponsor. On her pad she listed every other publication she could think of. Scanning her list, she underlined *Newsday:* a hot book, but not sufficiently "in" to be off bounds. Its Part 2 magazine insert would be a perfect showcase for her Lifestyle pieces.

Forget it, a veteran staffer told Daisy after the Part 2 editor had jerked her around for a month. They want young, they want male, they want a background in hard news.

Keep moving, put the word out, schlepp to all the parties — So-who-do-I-have-to-fuck-around-here? It *was* all about connections.

Then she picked up word of a new magazine targeted to upscale urban women. *Woman Today, Savvy, Smart* — they hadn't settled on a title. The editor was the formidable Andra Cassidy, who'd just put out a special women's edition of *Esquire*. She had started out in book publishing; in fact — and how long ago it seemed! — she had once been Delphine's assistant, snapping at her heels at Hollinsworth; Andrea with an *e* back then, instead of androgynous Andra. After a four-year struggle to get backing for her new magazine, she'd finally put together the money.

Daisy tossed her hat into the ring. She fired off letters, followed it with clips, telephoned everyone she knew, called in favors. She brainstormed with Gina over lunch, and Delphine on the phone. Then she sat down at her typewriter and knocked out the best list of article ideas of her career.

Andra Cassidy, she was told by a snotty underling, had an impossible schedule and was not making appointments for several months.

Next day Andra phoned. Brimming with apologies about the avalanche of clips. Wondering if Daisy could make lunch on Thursday the twenty-fifth.

Here we go, thought Daisy, soaring through the kitchen skylight: the right place, the right moment, all vectors converging.

At twelve-ten of Thursday the twenty-fifth, Félicité still hadn't arrived. Daisy paced the living room, chain-smoking, checking her watch every minute, cursing the festering bulge in the ceiling. How to synchronize all the parts? Miranda grounded with an earache. Corey needing to be picked up at his school across town on the East Side. She already late for lunch.

She pounced on the ringing phone. Surely Félicité, explaining the delay.

It was Professor Schiff. Calling long distance from Oneonta, a college in the state university, where he had recently been appointed Distinguished Professor. Some time ago she'd told him she couldn't accept "piecework" anymore, only a tenure-bearing "line."

"There's an opening here in Comparative Literature," Schiff said in his "Tcherman" accent. (Daisy anxious to get off the line, in case Félicité was calling.) "It's a full-time appointment. You'd start as lecturer and move to a tenure track once you finish your dissertation."

What perfectly wrong timing! She needed like oxygen the pace and drama of journalism. Besides — Oneonta? She pictured a snowy wasteland way the hell away in upstate New York. Near Albany? Buffalo? Somewhere north of nowhere. She'd be trapped in the boonies. Exiled in cow country. Cut off from the culture beat, the action, the clearinghouse of ideas, all her big plans.

"Thank you, Professor Schiff, but I have commitments in New York. I couldn't possibly leave now." She was warm and munificent, like someone who has received a proposal when already engaged to another.

By twelve-thirty, as she was foraging in the drawer under the phone for the grease-spattered list of sitters, she heard the downstairs buzzer. Félicité at last! Thank God! She must've forgotten her keys. Up the stairs tromped Félicité's brother. Albert explained that his sister would be a little late. Apparently the husband in Port-au-Prince had run off with her cousin. "She eez *triste,* my sister. You know, *les chagrins d'amour.*"

Daisy knew, always the same shit, no matter the culture, where did it all end. But right now SHE DIDN'T GIVE A DAMN!

Miranda started to cry; she wanted Félicité, not Albert. "Are you certain your sister will get here in time to pick up Corey?" Daisy repeated it in English, then French. Guilty about asking, Albert might construe the question as one more slight to blacks. Albert drew himself up, offended. "Madame, I already promise she come *tout à l'heure* — soon."

Daisy pulled on her raincoat. "Don't go, Mama!" Miranda screamed. Oh my God. "I have to. Do you want the goddamn ceiling to collapse on us? No, don't worry, honey, just joking. Bad joke. Why don't you show Albert your mourning dove. There's a dove building its nest on the fire escape," she called up, already in the stairwell.

She raced through a mild drizzle to the Seventy-second Street subway station, Miranda's wails echoing in her ears. What if Félicité didn't get to the Day School by two? Should she go back? Oh, Félicité would come through. She always did, didn't she?

Sardi's at lunchtime was favored by theater folk, *Times*men, and cigar-chomping deal makers out of Damon Runyon. Its walls were plastered from ceiling to floor with autographed photos and caricatures by Hirschfeld. When Daisy blew in, the noise level had built to a critical mass.

Waving away Daisy's apologies with her celery stick, Andra Cassidy introduced Ellen someone, her managing editor. Ellen wore a little string tie. Andra's chopped-off hair was defiantly gray.

"I'm really pleased to meet you, I've been a fan for a long time," Ellen said. "You're a terrific social critic," added Andra. Their "angel," she explained, was Philip Fertig, who'd made his money in cut-rate drugstore chains and now wanted a forum to extend his influence. He'd committed four million for the first two years of operations. They planned to use direct mail to launch the magazine.

Daisy was fascinated by Andra's cost-effective voice, devoid of emotion and produced with minimal jaw movement. Maybe if she worked real hard, in twenty years she could become as aerodynamic. Her eyes kept wandering to the wall clock above Andra's head.

"Excuse me a moment," she interrupted at a pause in Andra's spiel. "Emergency on the home front."

As she dialed the number, she could still see Andra and Ellen hooking eyeballs. She was willing to bet neither was a mother. A busy signal, damn! Happened whenever Corey hung up the phone wrong. But Corey wasn't home — Was anyone? Was anyone in charge? Don't panic, not now for God's sake.

When she sat down again, Andra asked what she thought she might contribute to the magazine. Daisy led with her list of ideas for "First Person," a column on women's issues. Every so often Andra nodded excitedly; Ellen jotted notes on a reporter's pad. "Fantastic . . . Oh, I like that . . . Why has no one covered that? . . . It's the last taboo." They tossed in their own ideas. The three of them were really cooking.

A piece of her mind kept hearing the phone's busy signal.

"We'd like to send you almost immediately — if everything works out — to Zaire to cover an international women's conference. Would you" — Andra hesitated a beat — "be able to leave early May?"

Africa! The world! Good-bye to the 104 bus! "I could arrange it," said Daisy evenly.

They ordered espresso. Daisy would have preferred Pepto-Bismol. She took a deep breath. Palms on the table, she said, "What kind of money are we talking about?"

Andra's face betrayed no expression. She told Daisy what kind of money.

Daisy swallowed hard. Had she heard right?

"Listen, we're not happy with it, either, but it's the policy set by Fertig. A year in, when we have a better idea of our prospects, we're hoping to pay the columnists more, uh, competitively." A moment. "As I'm sure you know," she added carefully, "it's a very crowded market out there. The odds that a new magazine will fly — well, it's a crapshoot. But we're confident the concept is unique enough to carve out a niche that's profitable." She drew on her cigarette and eyed Daisy narrowly. "Once we're launched, of course, everyone will want in. Right now you'd be in on the ground floor."

"I'd like to think it over," said Daisy, masking her elation. Of course she wanted the job, she would gladly gamble, she couldn't pass this up. A steady column, the forum she'd been looking for . . . Zaire! She was really moving. Surely by May she could find better coverage on the home front. This magazine *was* gonna fly, because Andra would not have left *Esquire* to flop on her ass. Everyone else would be hammering at the door, and she'd be on board.

At two-forty Daisy pushed back her chair. "Excuse me for running off, but I have to attend to the family crisis."

"Nothing too terrible, I hope?" said Andra without visible warmth.

"Oh, just the usual trials of the single mother," said Daisy, gathering her things. "Now *there*'s a column!"

She aced out a lame person for a cab. A sea of honking cars locked them in front of Rockefeller Center. By the time she got to Seventy-fourth Street, she calculated, Corey ought to be home. The kids would be so excited; she couldn't wait to relay the news to her cheering section. She loved their pride in her. Of course, they'd have to remain in Fletcher's slum until Fertig decided to shell out for writers. So the guardian angel could moonlight a while longer. Everything was falling into place.

She flung herself into the apartment.

Miranda stood on a chair by the living room bay window, holding Jenny Kanga by a foot and looking down at the street.

"We're looking for Corey, Mama," she said.

Ice needles pricked her heart. What the — Where —

Félicité was seated on the daybed in the back bedroom, hands folded in her lap, staring moodily into space. Noticing Daisy: "When I get to school, Madame, they tell me Corey leave —"

"But what time did you get there?"

"Corey maybe leave early."

"But what time, dammit —"

Félicité looked indignant.

Daisy ran to the phone and dialed the Day School. Corey McHenry? No, they hadn't seen him leave, the voice said.

But had he in fact left? she cried.

"Mrs. McHenry, please hold on, let me ask —"

She had a vision of Corey wandering off in that way he had, heading into a Central Park bristling with kidnappers and perverts. She put her hand over her heart. To this degree she'd been selfish, that she'd endanger her own child.

Another voice came on. "Mrs. McHenry, Corey left with his sitter."

What sitter? Daisy started to weep. "Corey's sitter is here. *Without Corey.* Okay, who saw him leave? Who was in charge? I'm coming right over."

Instead, her finger dialed 911. While she stammered out her news, she heard the slow roar of a cataract. Daisy dropped the receiver and ran to the living room. Miranda stood dusted in white, a few feet from a mountain of plaster, gaping up at a huge hole exposing wire mesh and wood beams.

Félicité appeared in the doorway wearing her coat and hat. *"C'est ici une maison maudite.* I leave forever. *Je m'en vais."*

The cops asked questions, so many questions. Has your child ever run away before? they asked. Has there been a recent fight? What was the child wearing? Did the child favor certain locations? Playgrounds?

Then they were sitting on a bench at the 16th Precinct station house. The station house was somebody's former mansion. There was a lot of yelling and smoke. Most of the yelling came from a cell where several men appeared to be chained to a pipe, and one of them was being forcibly wrapped in blankets.

A cop led her and Miranda up a marble flight of stairs. To the squad room, to be interviewed by the detective. Sloping indentations were worn in the marble of each step.

The detective had slicked-back hair, beautiful Italian eyes, and a gold bracelet. Miranda sat quietly on a chair beside her, saucer eyed, clutching Jenny Kanga.

You yourself are a suspect, the detective said. And Corey's father, he said. He wrote down Corey's father's address.

Missing Persons is contacting the area hospitals, the detective said. If the hospital search is fruitless, we'll search rooftops, alleyways, sewers . . .

Sewers . . .

Daisy rose from her chair, swayed uncertainly, then folded to the floor.

Dear God, just give me back Corey, God, and I swear I'll live my life to protect them, just make Corey all right.

Okay, stand back, came a voice. Get her off the floor.

The fluorescent light above had a piece of pink bubble gum stuck to it. Miranda's face floated over her upside down, braids dangling, mouth stretched in a sob.

Missing Persons learned that a male child roughly resembling the description of Corey McHenry had been admitted to Saint Luke's Hospital. Every sinew in Daisy's body melted. Someone transported them to Saint Luke's. To identify the boy. The boy was bandaged and plastered and attached to an IV and wasn't Corey. The third boy was Corey. She went to throw herself over his body. A nurse pulled her back.

Only weeks later did the cops piece together the story. A disturbed, well-dressed woman who hung around the private schools had presented herself as Corey's new sitter. Since he'd had so many different sitters, no one suspected she might be bogus. Eventually Corey smelled a rat and lit off through Central Park. Somewhere near the Rambles he'd run afoul of a pedophile, again escaped, and run into a cab on the park transverse. He would need months of physical therapy, the doctors told her after the first operation. Maybe years. It wasn't clear yet how well he would walk. But Corey was a sturdy fellow, he was going to make it, the doctors assured her. He was lucky.

She was also looking at years of medical bills, a staggering array of bills.

When she phoned Schiff, the job in Oneonta was still available. She was lucky. Corey was lucky. They were all tremendously lucky.

Chapter 24

DEAR CLASS of '58: My daughter Miranda is a campus activist, national coordinator of college pro-choice groups (how different from our Silent Generation, when any commerce with causes was hopelessly uncool). Son Corey is a scholar/poet and world class flaneur, off to Magdalen College in Oxford . . .

And will doubtless never climb to the summit of the Matterhorn . . . Nineteen years later the sight of his lurching gait is my guilt made palpable.

And I am back in New York, teaching English at a Jesuit college in Westchester.

She had done the right thing. Fashioned a life for herself and the kids in snowy Oneonta, with its red barns and striped barber pole and general store mimicking Norman Rockwell. Corey mended. Both children grew robust and red cheeked and boisterous like country kids. They started hiking again. Slowly at first, adapting to Corey's pace, over the shallow rises of an abandoned golf course. Then they tackled Mount Marcy in the Adirondacks. Next, Whiteface. And finally Mount Washington. Slowed by Corey's lurching gait, they needed the whole day to reach the summit, and rode down on the cog railway.

Daisy played the academic game. Her thesis on Louise Colet, a nineteenth-century poet and novelist, made a big splash in a small pond. She put in her time on committees where the chair limited the long-winded with a stopwatch. She loved her students, more than she could have predicted. She courted the powers who voted on tenure, and made associate professor. There was even a gentle interlude with a tweedy visiting prof, on leave from East Anglia College and a fraying marriage. It was an honorable life. It just didn't feel like hers. Still, she was grateful, humble. She had made her deal. She moved through those years with the dreamy distance of someone impersonating herself.

Now the children were launched. Superb human beings, even, with a sense of humor, even. ("Yes, Miss Lucky-in-Love," said Miranda whenever Daisy offered social advice.) She had come home to New York with visions of a big book, to settle up a debt to herself. She had returned, a graduate of many therapies, certifiably sane. No more moonlighting husbands or emotional bandits. She was undeterred by her own history. She felt she had one last love in her, the way Mahler must have felt before composing his Tenth Symphony. She wanted someone to recuperate from life with. To go gently with into the good evenings.

She'd forgotten about New York's hordes of unattached women, sellers in a buyer's market.

"You can't become a shut-in. You mustn't give up hope."

"The statistics —"

"Forget statistics."

"The odds —"

"You can beat the odds."

Swell. She should believe in miracles? For this she paid seventy-five dollars an hour? Forget Vienna. New York's mental health mavens must have trained at Lourdes.

Without someone to love, I will die.

God heard.

She opened the door one May evening to the friend of a friend who worked in advertising. Sandy Ehrmann was tall, rangy, with thick dark hair and close-cropped beard, sort of a *haimish* Westerner. Smoky eyes of the race, like, God help us, Arthur Frank, and never mind that he was in advertising. What was he saying? Did he like her, too? *Whoa, slow down!*

Her second idea of the evening: I'm gonna marry that man.

He took her to L'Alouette on East Forty-seventh. Pricey and dim, more waiters than diners, the smothered hysteria of a place going under. She acted impressed.

"Ending the marriage was not my idea," Sandy confessed on their banquette, gray eyes turning haunted.

Splendid; he'd never leave her — Oh, slow down, you idiot.

They agreed that couples who'd hung in together for the long haul knew something that had eluded the rest of them.

Clearly a man of substance.

Once when his baby son was down with strep and he wanted apple juice — orange, pineapple, grapefruit, wouldn't do — he braved a blizzard to comb Manhattan for a jar of Mott's.

Mott's! In a blizzard!

As they leave the restaurant, a bag lady weaves in front of them. Stumbles and drops her bundle. Apples, comics, socks, belts, fall to the pavement, a trash can smorgasbord. Sandy squats down and helps return every sorry item to the bag.

A mensch!

Back in her apartment, she collapses on the couch, overwhelmed by the evening's implications. Sandy sits at some distance in the wing chair.

"Something happened tonight," he observes with awe.

He comes to her on the couch and kisses her breasts. Though the fabric of her dress she feels the nuzzle of his beard. His hair smells of Johnson's Baby Shampoo, which has aphrodisiac properties. She rests her hand flat upon a stiffness under the Paul Stuart.

"Thank you," Sandy says. Then, "I'm sorry. Why did I say that?"

The self-deprecating charm.

I'm going to court you a little, he announces on the phone the next day, endearingly boyish.

They do everything right, like not make love right away. She congratulates herself. She has always jumped first, and pedaled in air later. She has not survived Gerrit and the bandits just to push the old self-destruct button, oh no. They wait till evening seven, an effort worthy of Hercules, a biblical span.

When it happens, not a lot happens. Shit, Sandy says, nose pointed toward the ceiling. She looks up at him, brimming with solicitude, loving even his nose hairs. She tells him everything's fine and how happy he has made her. (She has love/lust enough for both of them.)

And now the first weekend in his country house. They drove to Pound Ridge on 684. A golden late-September day, humming, full of gladness. The leaves this year were muted, rusty mauves and honey, the brights leached out by a long summer drought. They passed Sunnyfields horse farm, its meadows dotted with cylindrical bales of hay. Beneath the warmth lay coiled the evening chill, a hint of winter that for Daisy heralded the onset another solo season, which lately had the flavor of a life sentence. Sandy hooked a right onto 172, then a sharp left onto a curving road shadowed by giant oaks. They passed a white Georgian mansion — home to a Wall Street titan under indictment for embezzlement — with its groomed fields and paddocks, a flock of Bo Peep's sheep, their neat black legs looking shod in patent leather. In Pound Ridge nature was tamed and manicured; they must deodorize the manure.

"I still feel amazed at owning a house here," confided Sandy, the self-made man. "One winter we're skating on the town pond, and I felt I'd walked into a Currier and Ives. I thought, Not bad for a kid from Paterson, New Jersey."

She loved his ties to the old neighborhood, an inoculation against arrogance. She loved his stand-up comic shticks, and the rough of his beard and urban cowboy lope, and the monogrammed L. L. Bean bags in the back, and this car, a well-worn Volvo with a Diesel purr, of a piece with Sandy: family values, no hit-and-run stuff. Solid. The gray and black Cairn terrier that lay snuffling and farting in back she loved less. Jules smelled like rotting meat and was incontinent and neurotically dependent, and humped anything vertical. Sandy was much attached to the creature, the last vestige of his old family life; that, too, bespoke loyalty, good character. How had she gotten this lucky? Finally, she dared rest her weight against someone. Was that her purring or the Volvo?

He pulled up the driveway of a newly old white farmhouse built into a hill. Vast, sheltering willow out front. Red mansard roof, half-moon windows and dormers. Inside American Country rubbed shoulders with funky Yard Sale. Daisy instantly saw herself curled up on the worn colorless sofa facing the hearth, notebook and brandy in hand. Sandy steered her toward an oak hutch and proudly showed her his treasured collection of antique creamers and syrup jars.

He led her upstairs to the guest bedroom. "Here's where I thought you could write. We'll build you a little office right here. Overlooking the pond." He glanced at her, eager for her approval. High above the pond, a kingfisher hung motionless. Sighting prey, it dropped plumb to the water, zinged back up to its sky-perch, wings whirring, its dark crested head like a pterodactyl's.

They slept in the soundless country dark, Sandy's blue pajama'd bottom nestled against her crotch, her left hand clasped to his heart in a night tango. Next day they hiked the autumn woods off High Ridge Road. Panting, they talked their way up the trail; so much history to exchange, they'd need the rest of their lives to fill each other in. She had not imagined romance could be this friendly.

Sandy always closed the house at exactly five P.M. on Sunday, one of many soothing rituals. Then they drove back to New York into the dropping sun, past the phallic silver silos and ocher haystacks, shadows lengthening over the fields. Ravenous from talk, they'd make a little jog off 172 to Jackdaws, a fast-food joint with a kitschy windmill, where they gorged on fries and vanilla shakes.

One Sunday they went antiquing along Route 7. Daisy drove them home, down the Main Street of Kent, all white clapboard and olde shoppes with gold leaf lettering. The town could be a theme park by Disney. Daisy kept it to herself; for Sandy, owning property near posh Connecticut was emblematic of making it. The car was fragrant with Jules, who lay snuffling across Sandy's knees. Daisy glanced at Sandy's profile; all afternoon he'd been strangely moody.

Abruptly he said, "Now what do we do?"

Did he mean a better way to go? "Should we get off Route Seven?" Daisy asked.

"No, I mean, you and me — What do we do now?"

Somehow that didn't sound like a proposal.

"Do we go on like this?" he pursued. "Get married? Break up?"

A summit meeting. She was back in Mattapoisett with the crickets, swamped by the old terror. She veered toward Ye Olde Milke Pail — cut the wheel just in time. Jules was thrown to the floor.

"Hey, watch it! Poor baby, poor sweetheart, did Aunt Daisy scare you?"

Jules responded by humping his leg.

She wanted to whack the goddamn dog. "For goodness sake, it's only been three months," she said in her best adult voice. "Isn't a decision like that a little premature?"

Especially since, after three months, their love had yet to be consummated. A cottage in Truro on Cape Cod she'd rented over Labor Day. Through the bedroom's opened windows they could hear the cadenced *whoosh* of the surf. The moon shot out from behind scudding clouds, silvering the room, and their bodies as they grappled like gladiators, he over, she under, she above, he below. He found her, lushly wet. Moved over her, then — *nada*. He fell onto his back. "I don't understand what's wrong. Why is this happening?" His voice choked with self-hatred.

He'd confessed this was not his first encounter with the Problem. She thought if she were a man, surely her body would pull the same rotten stunt. She raised herself on an elbow. Moonlight shone on his white back sown with sparse hairs; he seemed terribly vulnerable. She told him she would never leave him, giving him permission to proceed on his own timetable, which would of course heal him. Breaking the cardinal rule, Don't Expose Your Hand First, but Sandy was too tortured to play deep games with. And she was as confident as she had ever been that she — her love — would heal him. His cock could misbehave for only so long. It didn't have a prayer. And anyhow, didn't the current manuals say the vagina was basically insensitive and penetration overrated? She was not going to be greedy. Oh no, she would not make that mistake, thank you very much, she would not be a pig!

Incredibly, they could talk about it, talk about everything. Sandy was wonderfully adept at articulating his angst, which usually took them to Jackdaws, and sometimes as far as Taco Bell. The Problem was due, they decided in concert, to Sandy's troubles at work.

"It's a nightmare at the office, ten times a day I'm on the verge of quitting," he would start. They'd been driving around South Salem in search of antique syrup jars and creamers to add to Sandy's collection. Daisy couldn't quite see the appeal of the jars, but she loved shopping together like a little bourgeois couple.

"Miserable timing. I meet you, I fall in love, and then, bango, this nightmare at work."

For two years he'd had an affair with a junior copywriter in the ad agency. He loved her, but did he love her *enough*? To up and leave his three sons, their mother, and Jules? (Daisy wondering with what calipers you measured "enough.") Then his wife ups and dumps *him*. On top of which the beloved Jules becomes incontinent. Then the creative director of the New York officer calls in Sandy's mistress and names her deputy creative director. Sandy's been there fifteen years to her seven, and now *he's* reporting to *her*. Oy oy! Every day a new indignity, a new ball breaker. Then at an office party Sandy drinks too much and lets fly at the boss, tells him, the boss, he's never had a single creative idea, he's a cannibal living off other people's brains . . . Oy oy! Should he quit before he's canned? Or relegated to Limbo, that floor where fired execs were permitted to use the phones?

Daisy counseled, commiserated, propped up Sandy's collapsed ego; she felt reincarnated as a giant ear. Sometimes the angst took them all the way to the George Washington Bridge, even in holiday traffic.

What, in the age of recovery, could not be fixed? He could take the cure at the Payne Whitney sex clinic; they could go in for couples counseling. Then one evening on a program about men's health, Sandy heard about the penile erector. A little coil buried under the skin, a hand-held radio frequency generator held next to the coil and presto! A hard-on! Like the raunchy old days in Loew's balcony. Trouble was, a burned-out component might generate a different frequency, confusing the message. Parking the car, he'd get a hard-on; in bed, the garage door might fly open. The good news/the bad news. They cracked up. Was it not wonderful? That they could laugh like this?

In December, as a sop, Sandy's agency sent him to Paris. He and Daisy decided to spend New Year's there. The Hôtel des Grands Augustins was on the Left Bank, just off the Boulevard Saint Germain. Narrow, discreet, with claret carpets, light-struck crystal, burnished copper. While Sandy checked them in, Daisy noticed a couple in the glassed-in court, sitting over their *cafés filtres,* foreheads grazing. They sat in that peaceful, clean silence that follows a rousing session in bed. Daisy inhaled the lobby's venerable musk of damp and Eros. Who needed Payne Whitney? Over dinner in a little bistro in the Rue Napoléon, Sandy watched her uneasily through the guttering candlelight, a goldfish eyed by a cat. She'd never met a person so mobilized against his own pleasure, except in a Woody Allen movie. But tonight in the city of love was *the* night. She was afire, inspired, a profane saint bent on converting Sandy to carnal bliss.

She emerged from the bathroom. From the bed came a low snore. Oh, no. No-no-*no*. He'd never get away with that! She pulls out all the stops; he must feel attacked by a dervish, a hydra, caught in a maelstrom, the war of the worlds. Success! Sort of! It happened! Something! Yes! She swallowed.

"Feh!" he said, shaking his hand in sympathy, gesturing her toward the bathroom. Afterward they lay entwined in the Parisian darkness, triumphant comrades in arms.

"Shit!" came his voice in her ear.

Ooooh, so *quick* — Not again. It felt like grit in your eye all through your body.

Still, things were looking up. It was springtime in Upper Westchester, late afternoon, and she'd finished putting in the phlox seedlings, and they'd fallen onto the bed for a nap before going to dinner with Leo Salkind, a bond trader who piped New Age Muzak through his Japanese garden. "We won't fuck, we'll save that for Sunday morning," Sandy murmured. (Or Tuesday after squash; or Thursday after his stress reduction workshop — Sandy *scheduled* sex.) Then ole instinct outwits him. . . .

"Shit!"

The "squeeze" technique wasn't working. Her body was jangling, ringing off the hook. Could a steady diet of almost-coming give you cancer? ("He needs a cost-effective yuppie who comes in seven seconds," Delphine had cracked long distance from Houston.) Lately she felt more like a service than a person. Sandy's cock was coming between them like some bratty kid: Does it want? Not want? Now? Later maybe?

Jules set his forepaws on the bed and started humping it. She'd sneak rat poison into the Super-Lite Natural Dog Food that night. She, a dog lover. She was really losing it.

Sandy sat up against the pillow, dark hair mussed, eyes glinting with danger. He rubbed his beard.

"Dammit, I'm tired of making women unhappy."

Daisy leapt out of bed and stood clasping her body. What kind of mind-fuck? No, sign-off, a mind-fucking sign-off. The panic siren bleated. Hold it, don't pile on the past shit. Sandy's your friend. He's in a snit because *he hates to fail*. Why did the sum of her psychological wisdom sound like some article in *Cosmo*?

"Sandy, that's really not fair, throwing a tantrum whenever we run into a problem. Turning it into a game breaker. You know that most of the time we make each other very happy."

He looked doubtful. Then he got out of bed and put his arms around her. "Hello there," he said to one breast, and kissed it. "Hello to you, too." He kissed the other, his tickly beard setting her ajangle. "Guess we better go back to plan A for a while," he said.

A spell of abstinence, they'd agreed, took the pressure off. Hell, if it would help, she'd take the veil.

She kicked off the damp sheet: three-alarm flash alert! Careful not to wake Sandy — he hated her insomnia — she peered at the digital clock on his side: five-ten. Lately she rarely slept past five, for hormones and anxiety. At fifty — Gina's "forty-seven" — either you put it together or slogged toward the finish line alone, joining an army of women in "the colourless years," as E. M. Forster had charmingly put it. A population about as welcome as Haitians in Miami — let them all go gently into some black hole! Hey, except for a few superstars, they're invisible already.

Don't get crazy. The glass is half full. She had a life, after all; she had her children, her work. The thought of her book triggered a fresh oven blast. Her agent had messengered her baby to three likely publishers. And struck out. Suddenly the agent's not returning her calls. Then, before she can fire her agent, the agent fires her. And whose team was Sandy on? "Oh, Daisy's been working on the tome for years," he told the city squires at a dinner party in Pound Ridge. In the tone she thought of as Banter Lite. "I'm always telling her, Why not write something inspirational, like Rabbi Harold Kushner? Make people feel good about themselves. In hard times Americans want happiness. They're not going to pay for gloom and doom."

Sandy never struck her, she thought abruptly — in fact, he was a physical coward — but wasn't Banter Lite just a milder version of battering? She thought of the retarded girl abused by the high school jocks; the papers were full of the trial. The girl let one jock put a broomstick and another a bat in her vagina. Even though her "bottom" hurt afterward. She let them do it because she wanted to be wanted.

Daisy unstuck her hair from the clammy pillow and lay staring into the gray dawn, hands clasped behind her head. Listening to the even snoring beside her. The last chance café.

She felt curious to learn exactly how far she might go.

A soggy tropical weekend in late July. She'd brought up from New York the heavy artillery: a filmy black teddy from Victoria's Secret and almond-scented massage oil. So far so good. Eight o'clock on a Sunday morning, and it looked as if Sandy might not get to his doubles game. He'd make her pay — but later, later. She tasted almonds and essence of Sandy. Easy! *It* was skittish as a unicorn, mustn't alarm it. Cleverly, by degrees, she maneuvers them into "scissors," a great honey cup of bliss. There. Oh yes, so deep . . . And it's lasting . . .

"We're fucking," Sandy crows, "we're fucking."

Don't *think,* she silently prays. The joy of it . . . pure heaven . . . a record . . . on and on . . .

"Now what?" Sandy said.

Her eyes fluttered open.

Now what? Oh my God. She slipped backward, but only for a second, then crushed him to her with demonic force.

They drove home through a heat wave, green boughs along the road swaying in the feeble hot wind like swags of velvet. The smile never left her face. She felt like William the Conqueror; she'd vanquished Sandy's craziness. Yes, face it. There was something seriously *nuts* about saying "now what" in the middle of everything. Did he want dancing girls? A juggling act? The Flying Wallendas? At some point they had assigned her the job of justifying their union to him. Well, she could rest her case. Coast. The stupefying heat canceled conversation. They couldn't close the windows and put on the air conditioning because the beloved Jules stank up the car. Such a luxury not to *have* to talk. She need no longer audition. She felt like one of those enviable couples eating in silence in highway McDonald's, trusting each other not to go to the rest room and hightail it into the night. They passed the Mobil station just before the turn-off to Jackdaws.

"Can we talk about us?" Sandy asked.

"Hmmm." She stretched luxuriously.

"It's just not all there for me," he said.

She was still back at the Mobil station.

"You're wonderful, I love you, but is it enough? Do I love you enough?"

He turned into the parking lot for Jackdaws. Killed the ignition. She stared out the window at the red windmill. It was part of a pocket amusement park in a hollow to the right. The park crawled with hideous munchkins in play togs.

"Talk to me. Oh shit. Listen, I'm starving, what about you? Shall I get you the usual?"

Hearing the car door slam, Jules wakened from his beauty sleep and tried to migrate to the front seat. "No. *Sit*. Dammit, *sit!*" Jules whimpered and farted and circled. From the car Daisy could see Sandy in Jackdaws's plate glass window, giving the waiter his order. It seemed to be a jumbo order. His back was to the car. Jules kept trying to clamber over the gear shift to the front seat. Now that they were motionless the stench was stronger. Daisy rolled up the Entertainment section of the Sunday *Times*. The moment she swatted the dog she realized how long she'd been waiting to do it.

"Are you surviving having a relationship with me?"

She stared into the phone mouthpiece. Was this the way he did love? He had once confessed that "tumult" gave him a rush. Her it gave spastic colon. After they hung up, she switched on her answering machine. Over the next forty-eight hours, Sandy's messages went from cajoling to pissed. "We *must* talk. You better call me. Where the hell are you? Are you listening to this?"

She decided to burrow into a movie. Something jolly, like Robert De Niro slicing up women in *Cape Fear*. She headed down Broadway, giving little snorts of rage, attracting stares, even with all the local competition. So what percent *is* "there" for you? Seventy-five? Eighty? In the calculus of self-indulgence, do you round off the numbers? In Sandy, consciousness was a disease. He was seriously, well, impaired — she still needed to protect him, even in her thoughts — yet he'd worked it so *she* didn't measure up? She was lover, cheerleader, sex therapist, social worker, human rotorooter, a white-glove, full-service woman, and she also loved the schmuck — and it wasn't goddamn enough? A block away she spotted the movie marquee. It suddenly seemed part of some continuum: De Niro playing meat cleaver. The jocks shoving in the baseball bat. Prince Sandy taking his emotional temperature. As she walked, she revved up the engines. She would ride her fury like a rocket clear out of Sandy's orbit.

She stopped at the Cineplex Odeon, eyeing the long queue stretching around the corner. The gang flashed her the New York welcome: why honey, just step into this line anyplace you please. By now she was basted in sweat from the heat, lost hormones, greasy moisturizer to combat lost hormones. She noticed a space cadette making her way down the other side of the line. Mumbling at her own image in a compact mirror — maybe coked up. She wore a filmy Indian shmatte that reminded Daisy of the bohemians in college. Heavens, that was Mia. Mia Sils-Levy Damiano, now ex-Princess of Jaipur.

"Is that really you?" they said simultaneously.

They decided to skip De Niro and went to a white stucco joint next door, Mykonos-sur-Broadway. Mia ordered with elaborate graciousness, as though conveying instructions to the palace hands. It didn't go over big with the waitress.

"I know, don't even say it, don't even try to deny it, I look like shit," said Mia in her weird accent.

Daisy had been trying to conceal her shock. At college Mia had been a major campus beauty, with her heart-shaped face and tragic eyes and chestnut hair in a chignon; Lillian Gish updated with Susan Strasberg. It was all still there, but with the youth sucked out, she resembled a fossilized girl. "Just changed is all."

"Gina Gold actually looks *better* than in college, don't you think? Isn't science marvelous? Cigarette? I'm afraid I still smoke."

Daisy still couldn't fathom the accent, that of an English nanny in India, talking to her charges.

"It's losing the teeth that's done me in," Mia continued. "Plus a few other holes," she added mysteriously. She flashed a demo smile, displaying two black vacancies, upper left. "The new ones are still in the shop." Surveying Daisy: "But don't *you* have marvelous genes. Gina — I saw her at the Temple of Dendur — in New York, not Egypt — Gina said you've met this *charming* man. Wish I could say the same. You probably heard that after Nick, I married the Nawab of Jaipur. Didn't I warn everyone back in college that I'd marry royalty?"

The passing waitress paused and rolled her eyes.

"I met Prem when Nick sent me on assignment for *Erotica* to photograph dirty Indian sculptures at Khajarraho. We lived happily ever after for ten years, until I discovered Prem was screwing everything in sight: male, female, castrati, quadrupeds, feathered friends." She made a little sucking noise through the vacant spaces in her mouth. "When I announced I was leaving, he screamed bloody hell. As if he hadn't *forced* me to leave. The passive-aggressive style cuts across cultures, it's alive and well in Rajasthan. D'you suppose we've had passive-aggressive men since the dawn of civilization in Mesopotamia? Oh, waitress! Two more, deah. Please, yes, the Chardonnay, that would be *lovely.*

"But we're survivors, our little group. I returned to New York dead broke, and I said to myself, Let's just see what we can put together here. I remembered a contract I'd written back at SLC for a psych course. And I thought, Why not plug into one of these est-type therapies proliferating around the country. I found a place called the Forum, which teaches people how to get out of their own way — and voilà, I'm a facilitator at the Forum!" She fished in her bag and handed Daisy a card. "Why don't you come for one of our weekend marathons. And do bring your friend, uh —"

"Sandy Ehrmann." She decided to launch a test balloon. "Actually, Mia, I just broke up with him."

Mia's eyes opened wide. "Oh deah, what a dreadful mistake!"

"He's turned out to be a Luftmensch. After a brilliant first act, another man of air."

"Gina said he was so dear."

"To everyone but me."

"Oh, *that* type. I prefer the out-and-out shits, don't you? That way you know what you're dealing with. It's positively toxic when the vileness is marbled with niceness." A pause. "But don't you know what it's like out there? I recently went out with an endocrinologist who said to me, 'Menopause is nature's way of telling women that, in the evolutionary scheme of things, you're through. No longer needed.' He told me that, my date." She lit up again. "Of course if you're an heiress or takeover artist, like that Linda Wackner, whoever — you know who I mean, they just did a profile in the *Times* — there's some wiggle room. But there's only *one* of Linda. That leaves the rest of us. We kind of fell between the cracks, didn't we? We didn't gear up for big careers, but we don't have the protection our mothers had, either."

She exhaled. "Y'know, Mother nagged Father and bitched and moaned, but she had a nice apartment, the country club in Pelham. A social context. And companionship — more durable than happiness, this bluebird we've messed up our lives chasing. Hell, at least Mother never had to go to a Yale Club mixer, where you stand on an auction block with women twenty years younger, and you say to some guy, 'Hi, my name is Mia,' and then he walks right away. I sometimes think that if I don't pick up the phone, no one will ever call me again. I've already started to worry about a date for New Year's of 2000, only eight years off . . . But hell, I'm not ready for the rocker yet. Even if biology thinks otherwise. I don't need those dratted hormones either, I'm plenty juicy. So I nosed around in the Personals. Kind of enjoying the surreal aspect of it. Imagine, a one-time princess answering the Personals! I went to benefits, pay to play and all that. There's no shortage of married men cruising parties like sharks. You know the ugliest word in the English language? 'Fun.' It means 'fuck and run.' Finally, in a bar in Soho I met — are you ready to hear this?"

Did she have a choice?

"This performance artist who worked at the Public Theatre. Really sweet, divine in bed — he was only thirty-four. But I worried about the drugs, or whatever he was up to in the john. He had an odd scar on his arm. I never quite knew. Then one night he showed up wasted, something, turned into a raving Mr. Hyde and started socking me around. I crawled to the phone to call the police and he pulled out a gun and shot me. Left me for dead."

Daisy shook her head no. No-no-no.

"When I was in hospital, I sometimes wondered if he thought of the evening as, well, performance art. He's completely disappeared." Mia studied her wine glass. "Then the other night in a bar in TriBeCa I ran into a guy who claims to have been his lover."

No. Hand over her mouth, Daisy kept shaking her head. No-no-no.

Mia eyed her piteously. "I'm too petrified to get tested."

Tears had started up in Daisy's eyes.

Mia wagged her finger. "Uh-uh, now none of that. The crazy part is — you've got to believe me — I'm happy. Honestly. Hell, I'm alive. I feel terrific. I can't *wait* to get up in the morning and run a workshop. I'm studying Buddhist Vipannassan meditation and learning to live in the Now. Happiness, they teach, comes from letting go wanting what you don't have. Like a mate. Good health. All the things we used to assume you needed as a bare minimum!"

"Where the hell have you been?"

Sandy slammed his door shut and retired pettishly to the couch. "Jesus, you had me worried. I was worried — well, to tell you the truth" — he hung his head like Peck's bad boy and stuck out his lower lip — "I was afraid I can't manage without you."

Later, kissing her breast — "Hello, you." Kissing the other — "Hello to you, too."

She suddenly wondered how many times he had said that.

Chapter 25

DELPHINE

DELPHINE SAT on a slatted bench of bleached wood, Smith and Hawkens's finest, staring into the Kober House orchard. The apple trees had passed their flowering and formed a dense tapestry of green. Beside her towered a giant stand of rhododendron, the pale pink blossoms fleshlike and vulnerable, throats gaping. The old college still had the lushness of a hothouse, like the one that had forced the girls of her class into exotic blooms, suited for practically anything but the world outside.

From behind her in the circular cobbled drive she heard a rustling. Hoarse cries. Her skin prickled. No need to turn her head: she knew that Dudley Hunnewell stood on the cobblestones beneath her old window, his back plumed with fire. Dudley dissolved into a different scene of mayhem. The one after which she had only imagined you could go on.

Not her finest idea, coming back to the old school. She'd come mainly to humor Daisy, put in an appearance at the private reunion. But first she'd have to listen to Gina Gold's deep thoughts. Afterward maybe they'd unveil an equestrian statue of Gina on the front lawn;

329

she wouldn't put it past them. And class reunions required a clean presentation of self. Who she was these days had become a shifting proposition. She commuted with the speed of light from the heights to a dark undertow. One minute she's airborne on big dreams. The next she's barreling out to Long Island, planning to drill Jake full of holes like some tin cutout. She tried to picture Race Ranch, the baby banker's spread in Bridgehampton. A ranch at the *beach*? She slid her hand beneath her bag and cupped the reassuring heft of the .22 automatic . . . To hell with class reunions. She would phone for a taxi to the station and hop the first train back to New York. Right away, before she lost her momentum.

The plan had alighted on her yesterday like a giant black crow. She'd been standing in the darkened packed ballroom of the New York Hilton. The Emily's List fund-raiser for women running for the Senate had drawn a huge crowd. Applause and whoops greeted Carol Moseley Braun, striding onstage in a turquoise suit, smiling the big smile. Right on, Carol! Way to go! Delphine cheered with the rest, lofted high on the energy of a thousand women. Jeered, fist in air, at the name Arlen Specter. Barbara Boxer came on next, in fireman red. The Senate may soon need to rearrange its plumbing, Boxer warned, to cheers and laughter. It was all wide open for women now, at least the ones poised to take power, younger than she by maybe only ten years. Yet those ten years were like the distance between the Mesozoic era and today. Who among them would have signed over her life to a husband?

Now, through a bizarre chain of events that always amazed her, she'd almost caught up to them. Traveled 360 degrees to end up where she'd started out. As an advocate for the homeless, she was riding an updraft. She'd just testified at a hearing to prevent the city from lodging the homeless in city offices. She got quoted every third day in the Metro section of the *Times* . . . For her, too, it was wide open. She could use her job as a springboard to something bigger. Maybe Housing Commissioner. Or head of a new umbrella agency for homeless services the mayor was proposing. She was an ace administrator, loved to *hondel* and press the flesh. Or maybe she would run for City Council. She wrote the campaign flyer in her head: "Someone once said that people get the government they deserve. But *nobody* deserves the government New Yorkers are getting . . ." She could extract money from her old Newport friends. And a few remained. Nowadays suicide by gin was out; the rich had decided it was more amusing to live forever.

Hell, if Patty Murray, the mom in sneakers, could get to Congress, if the other PTA types and fund-raisers could do it; if the community activists and teachers and county recorders of deeds, barely younger than she, could do it, why couldn't she?

Then she saw Jake. The wired hair and narrow shoulders. Several heads forward. An ice pick lodged in her breast, she couldn't find her way to the next breath. With expiring eyes she watched Jake drape an arm over the banker and murmur in her ear. She knew all about this banker, who looked like Rebecca de Mornay and probably had her intellect. There's always a kind friend on hand to tell you how the person you've loved more than life itself is currently amusing himself.

It was the first time she'd seen him since Houston. He'd lost more hair and gotten his eczema back. Fuck, what was he doing here? The gall coming here and poisoning this women's moment! Then she remembered that Rebecca gave handsomely to Emily's List.

She butted her way out of the ballroom, ignoring indignant glances. Past a guy wearing a sandwich board studded with buttons that read "A Woman's Place Is in the House and Senate." Arrived at the lobby, she fell into a bar. *Don't.* Don't do it. You've come this far. You owe your future. Your constituents need you. Order a Sprite, Diet Coke, designer water.

"Double Stoli on the rocks," she told the bartender.

She'd stuck by Jake, given up her own dream, staked him with her family's money. There was something seriously out of balance here. And she was powerless to right it. The Stoli took down her rage a notch. Maybe not as powerless as all that. A sojourn in the rootin' tootin' West gave a gal ideas about how to right the balance. Jean Harris had leveled the old diet doc and done her part to right the balance. She would drive out this weekend to the banker's spread and force Jake to ante up. The precise choreography she couldn't envision, but she would come forearmed, then just let 'er rip, the final bloody scene in her melodrama. After all, a deal's a deal. As no one but the Mafia seemed to recall anymore.

She suddenly remembered the interview with Tipper Gore in this morning's *Times*. "Why," the reporter asked Tipper, "did you give up your dream to become a psychologist?" "It made sense to me at the time," sez Tipper. And would go on making sense, so long as Al honored the deal.

To her, too, it made sense at the time. Even if it hadn't, wouldn't she have followed Jake to the ends of the earth? It *was* the end of the earth, let them call Houston the New York of Texas all they liked. In New York you could walk in the streets. In Houston you'd get steamed to death. The natural medium was a canned deep freeze. In summer everything was overgrown and overripe; the air smelled of rotting berries. The heat melted attention spans to the size of a watermelon seed. The incessant racket of cicadas brought on her migraine. And no foreign outpost could feel this alien. The natives here ate rattlesnake. They ate chicken-fried steak: pounded cube steak rolled in bread crumbs, then *fried,* the whole mess washed down with iced tea — the thought made her gorge rise. Lindalyn Woodruff invited her to join the Ladies' Auxiliary of the Houston Salvation Army. After one meeting Delphine begged off, pleading pregnancy ills. (In truth, the nausea never let up and she'd had early episodes of spotting.) The husbands, mostly in oil, of course, had something porcine and compressed around the snout. They were clones of Nelson Bunker Hunt or W. C. Fields. She preferred the rednecks gassing up their pickup trucks in a lone dust-blown Mobil station out by Almeda Genoa, beyond the city proper, the wilderness known as Outside the Loop.

The Texas big rich whom she and Jake met through his partner, Barney Livingston, made her old Newport crowd seem austere as Shakers. "You would not believe this scene," Delphine wrote Daisy.

All the new mansions in River Oaks are built to look old: French chateaux, Tara-style plantation houses, etc. One local legend is a lady billionaire named Ima Hogg — not kidding! She used to dress all in pink and ride a tricycle around her digs, summonsing the servants with tweets on her whistle. People go on safari and then mount his-'n'-hers critters on the walls. You sit there in someone's "trophy room," *surrounded* by the beady eyes of a Bengal tiger, water buffalo, rhino, warthog, you name it. The wives throw theme parties to raise money, for which cause no one much cares. Over two weekends we went to a "Soiree on the Sewanee" benefit, complete with Aunt Jemimas (only Jake and I were offended by the racist overtones). And a gala with the theme Renaissance England, with fire-eaters and jousting knights, and the beer-bellied host playing Henry VIII. Modesta and somebody Twinkle have a mansion flanked by two stone lions that talk to you thru a microphone hidden behind their fangs. Bronze pixies lounge about the lawn. And the Twinkles are considered tastemakers . . . Where am I? And oh, Daisy, where are you? I have no one to talk to here, no friend of the heart. I even miss Sally November . . .

At night, in her dreams, she smelled the briny coast of New England, heard the mournful clang of "groaners" at the harbor's mouth, calling, calling her home.

She took herself in hand. Too much had not been asked. She had not understood till now the depth of her wedding vows. She must make of Houston a broadening experience, treat it like one of those tours of the Continent taken by turn-of-the-century gentlemen. She found things to love: the glorious fields of bluebonnets she and Jake discovered out toward Brenham. The live oak trees with crocodile bark, touching their heads together on Main Street, like beneficent oaks in fairy tales. The stark octagonal chapel where the Rothkos vibrated in the dim, beacons from the beyond.

She even got a chuckle out of their sublet ranch-style house. A low sprawl of white brick, it sat on a lawn the size of Prospect Park. Out back was a gazebo and lily pond, lost in the great expanse of carpet grass. The sunken family room sported an oak cabinet displaying guns that were illuminated by little lights, and a TV the size of a tank. Mounted on racks at each side of the fireplace were deer heads. Their big brown glass eyes observed her as she moved about or read. How could anyone be seriously discontented in such a dippy place?

And there was Franelle Lacy. The widow of an oil baron and major Houston hostess, Franelle had adopted her and Jake and Barney as her East Coast project. She had a chipmunky charm and went in for deep decolletage, more to display a fortune in emeralds than cleavage, which was also impressive. Her speech was, to put it politely, nonlinear; without the bankroll, she'd be packed off to a course in remedial thinking. But Franelle, as Jake had pointed out more than once, was on the board of the Houston Museum and chairman of its Building Committee.

It was Franelle who got them invited to that party for the movie celebrating the war in Vietnam. Was that the evening it began? The evening that set in motion all the rest? The party was, incredibly, a Combat Chic affair. The hostess had converted her Georgian mansion into an Asian jungle. "M.P.'s" parked the cars. Potted banyan trees towered in the living room. "Army nurses" passed hors d'oeuvres. Delphine blinked at the lights popping on the dance floor. Jesus, was that supposed to be napalm? She wanted instantly to leave. She felt huge and ugly in her muumuu, especially around all the copper-tone bazooms. But Jake was busy chatting up Franelle, who wore a strapless jumpsuit with a jungle camouflage pattern. Cleverly Jake steered the conversation to his concept for a new museum to house southwestern and primitive art.

"What's needed is a building that doesn't shout. Sensitive both to the climate and the light, yet also at ease with modernism . . ."

Delphine cast a look of longing toward her usual salvation, now off limits: a tile basin full of champagne. Over it presided a Neptune who seemed to have a hard-on.

"And I'd want no bookstore near the entrance, no signs of commerce." Jake pressed Franelle's forearm. Delphine studied his fingers splayed on Franelle's caramel arm, between the elbow and the wrist cuffed in gold. Mr. Finicky, Jake was, never one to play touchy-feely.

"What I see is a cluster of small buildings," he went on, "with a bookstore and museum shops housed in a separate space and —"

Franelle leaned toward him, all teeth and cleavage. Delphine didn't catch the rest of Jake's sentence, for he turned abruptly and shut her out of their circle. She stared into the ivory weave of his jacket. Banished.

Tears stung her eyes. She took the true measure of her position, the thing she'd not allowed herself quite to see. She was exiled in East Jesus with nothing to do and utterly dependent on Jake. And she'd brought it on herself! She left hurriedly and had an M.P. bring the car around. How Jake got home was no concern of hers.

Delphine was waiting up for him when he rolled in, eyes rimmed pink.

"We need to talk —"

"Not me, I'm bushed," Jake said.

"That party was disgraceful, a show of support for genocide —"

"Could this wait till tomorrow?"

"I will not be ignored, publicly humiliated."

"Hey, who was left stranded? You expect me to hitch home?"

"How *did* you get home?" When he didn't answer: "That woman can't get out a coherent sentence. She talks in circles."

He flung his tie toward a chair, missing. "Who cares about circles. That woman, as you call her —"

"Has a circular cunt?"

"Christ, I'm not in the mood for this. Look, she happens to chair the Building Committee. Which is going to commission the architect for the new museum. Oh, to hell with it, I just can't make you happy. You used to put me down for *not* sucking up."

"You're using my advice from the heart to bludgeon me."

He sat on the immense bed and unlaced a shoe.

She came and sat beside him, hands resting on her watermelon. "Jake," she pleaded in a low voice, "I'm so scared, so alone here. I feel uprooted. Literally like I'm dangling in air."

"Well, if you'd just get cracking, get your freelance editing going, instead of sitting on your butt all day —"

"Jake, I gave up my life to come here with you." *What she'd promised herself never to say.* She started to cry, knowing it enraged him, crying harder at the injustice of it. He grabbed her shoulders. She recoiled, shutting her eyes, on the edge of screaming. She felt his hand on her cheek — stroking, tenderly stroking her cheek. She opened her eyes and saw his fear.

"I know what you gave up. Believe me, I know. But I'm going to make this work for us, you'll see. Help me, Del. We've got to pull together here. We've got to be each other's team."

Numbly she looked at him.

He drew her against him. "Poor darling. That *was* a vile event. On the dance floor — D'you see the napalm?"

She was very pregnant. Inspired, they discovered an ingenious position. Later Jake groaned, "How we going to survive an entire month?"

She raised herself on one elbow. "Promise you won't make love to Franelle Lacy."

He sat up, blue eyes blazing. "I'll not promise anything so absurd." He nosed her girth. "Truthfully, I don't know if I could with anyone else."

"Swear to me you won't make love to Franelle. Swear on the life of our child."

His head snapped up. "I will not. What's wrong with you? What's gotten into you?"

"Swear to me, Jake. On the life of our child."

He was about to get royally pissed. He rolled his eyes. He groaned. And then he swore.

The next day Delphine started staining.

The doctor ordered her to bed for the final five weeks. She sprawled on the salmon velour comforter, watching *One Life to Live* and the game shows. Willing herself into a vegetable torpor that would forestall labor. After she was born — she was certain they had a girl — it would all be wonderful. They would be a family. She would do this thing better than Merry. She remembered Merry always dashing off in her terrible mink "piece," its two heads with their beady eyes dangling near her waist. Looking for a place to set down her old-fashioned . . . And after she got her strength back, she would start her freelance editing in earnest.

Little Hildreth was beautiful and perfect, with hair a brighter auburn than Delphine's. Delphine held and watched her by the hour. She was astonished: after all she'd inflicted on her own body, God had allowed her this perfect being. Wearing a white hospital gown, Jake cradled Hilly in his arms. He told her in a husky voice, "We've been waiting for you for a long time."

Delphine rejoiced. That they were now three bound Jake closer.

After that, Jake pretty much disappeared. Vanished into work, as though he had enlisted in a distant war. She was alone in the ranchero with Hilly and Elberta, the sitter.

How could she begrudge Jake, he was drunk on opportunity. In Houston it was boom time for developers. For B. J. Livingston there was gold in them thar hills. Jake was designing corporate headquarters, shopping malls, residential hives outside the Loop. To think that two years earlier he'd been renovating dens in Scarsdale! Unique among American cities, Houston had no zoning; the place just kept oozing outward, like a giant oil stain. Barney would lay claim to a cow pasture along a new highway, and lo, a planned community took shape on Jake's drawing board. He wanted to take the kitsch out of mass housing, Jake explained to her late one night, pacing their bedroom. "I'm designing houses that relate to the austere landscape of Texas and do minimal violence to the natural surroundings, not an atrocity by Lefrak."

She tried to ride the current of Jake's excitement, like the hawks riding the thermals out by Dripping Rock. His success was hers, too. Theirs. *We're a team, Del, we've got to pull together.* This was real. The rest — her college dreams, the years in publishing — seemed a feverish detour. Love changes the terms.

Daisy phoned, elated by the writing assignments coming her way. She had just finished a piece for the *Village Voice* on the first hookers' convention. "And I've proposed a piece to *New York* magazine on Sally November Wunderlick. I see her as a fumbling Everywoman. She bought the promises of women's lib, then fell flat on her face and went crawling back to Shelley. I need to understand what went wrong."

As Daisy yakked, Delphine heard an odd noise. She glanced at Hilly in her portachair on the kitchen floor, gurgling and waving a yellow squeegee. Abruptly she realized the noise came from her, grinding teeth. While the world surged forward, she'd fallen out of history. She was trapped in Togetherness without the togetherness. The life she'd most dreaded! For a wild second, she saw herself joining the army of deserting wives, fleeing with Hilly to New York.

No. She would stay right here. She had her reasons. She'd burrow deep into the ordinary, hidden from the Furies assigned to the Mortimers, stalking them for generations, avenging sins real and imagined — after all, what self-respecting Fury could tolerate the climate here? Sheltered here, she would elude the curse that turned her brother's brain to rutabagas. Fried her father. Guided her mother's bullet to Raoul's spine. For the first time in months she thought of Raoul Peña, their feverish nights, sentenced for life to his wheelchair by Merry's bullet. The guilt that used to gnaw at her was just a faint neuralgia.

By some mysterious alchemy, the harder Jake worked, the less Delphine felt impelled to edit freelance.

Jake nagged her to get started. "Honey, how many editors can pull a book together like you?"

Jake did so want this to work for them.

But the alchemy had mysteriously transferred all her energy to him. At the thought of blanketing her old publishing contacts with letters, she'd yawn and retreat to the black leatherette couch in the family room for a sex fantasy. Even at his most abject, she had found Jake arousing. Now with his new success he seemed lit from within, aloft, *electric,* always talking and in forward motion. She would watch him at parties, surrounded by admiring women; his Tartar eyes and sultry mouth and adder-thin body — and she'd cramp up with fear. Was she expendable? Spooning out Hilly's strained apricots in the kitchen, she became swollen with lust. She would ravish him under his drafting table. Where else could she have at him? Usually he got home after midnight, dropped instantly into sleep, and was out of the house by seven. Never in the years of their marriage had she felt so tantalized.

One night he sat on the bed, absently watching basketball on the tank-size TV. She wriggled across his knees in a naughty spanking position.

"Hey, cut that out. I'm trying to watch the game."

He didn't know Walt Frazier from Joe Montana. She gave his thigh a puppy bite. "Since when do you watch basketball?"

"Del, for Chrissake, it's the NBA playoffs." He shifted her head out of his line of vision.

Since when did he care about the NBA? She went downstairs to the family room and picked up *The Beautiful and the Damned* without reading it. Just *back off.* The surest way to short-circuit a blowout. The deers' brown glass eyes seemed to agree. Besides, she was clearly un-desirable. Can't argue with that. Stretch marks on her breasts; a peculiar brown seam bisecting her middle, which wouldn't quite deflate. Maybe Dr. Huggins had forgotten the "husband stitch"?

So what was Jake doing for sex?

A wife always knows, she and Daisy had decided back in Kober House days. What she does with the knowledge is another matter. Delphine's antenna shot up. One evening she walked into the kitchen to hear him signing off on the phone. "Thanks a million," he said sweetly. *Thanks a million.* The phrase sounded bogus. Un-Jake-like. A switch flipped for her benefit?

She began to study Jake and Franelle Lacy with gimlet eye. At a Safari Party for the Houston Symphony, they were cordial, yet several degrees cooler than formerly. Come to think of it, they were downright niggardly with the warmth. Delphine smelled a rat. Oh, she knew Jake like herself, how pitifully transparent his maneuvers. Watching him at a buffet dinner where Franelle was present, she thought, I, too, would take care to keep my eyes *off* the object of desire. She stood by Jake's side, registering in her own body the effort this must cost him.

She ate. Binged in private — no one ever saw her — with the absorption of a lover or killer. She returned to the muumuus of her pregnancy, now her uniform. She adored Hilly, but erratically, in bursts. She had no patience and grew quickly bored; often she called Elberta to take over. For Franca and Daisy, the babies became the nerve center of life, a consolation for everything denied. She herself would look at Hilly, her eyes the color of bluebonnets, like her father's, and think how deprived she was of Jake. She decided that she lacked the maternal instinct, like some killer with a broken gene. She judged herself monstrous.

She started drinking in the late afternoon, an hour she defined as three. Soon she stopped defining it. Before an evening out, she'd lay down a base of Jack Daniel's, and boost it with blue parrots and margaritas through the rest of the evening. Her parched sleep was haunted by nightmares. She dreamed she found Hilly floating in the bathtub, rubberoid and bloated, eyes swollen slits. The cops came, the doctors. They couldn't take Hilly from her.

For weeks afterward, she never let Hilly and Elberta out of her sight.

If Jake noticed the drinking, he didn't let on. He broadcast a silent prayer: Let me keep in forward drive and don't give me grief.

One afternoon she walked Hilly in the stroller, stopping to point out the mesquite trees with their odd bean pods and deeply furrowed bark. When they returned, she noticed a woman watching her from a car parked across the street from their house. She had the hollow gaze of a zombie. White hair in a chignon, like Norman Bates's mother in *Psycho*. Powder blue bell-bottoms. An eerie figure, somehow familiar. Delphine turned Hilly's stroller up their long poured concrete driveway, wishing it were shorter. She kept glancing backward. The woman's eyes were following them. The next day the lady from *Psycho* wasn't there, or the day after. Delphine forgot about her. Then the following week, like an ominous pain, the woman reappeared. She stood leaning against a giant live oak across the street, slightly hidden by a hank of moss, watching.

"Don't you think you're being a little paranoid?" Jake said distractedly when Delphine mentioned the woman that evening.

"I think we should call the police."

"And tell them what, honey? That Norman Bates's mother has been sighted in the Montrose area?"

"But, Jake —"

He rushed to get the phone. Problem with materials for the Glencoe office tower, he told Delphine. He didn't know what time he'd be home.

Thanks a million, he'd told the caller.

They planned, that Saturday afternoon, to drive with Hilly to the country, out toward Brenham, to see the fields of bluebonnets. At noon Jake phoned from the office. Something had come up. A glitch in the drawings for the Glencoe job, he needed to meet with the contractor. Maybe they could go to the country the next day.

"Jake, we haven't seen you in daylight in weeks. Hilly doesn't know who Da is."

"I don't think you realize. What I'm doing is for Hilly and you."

The hell. You also fucking Franelle for Hilly and me?

She filled a glass with bourbon and ice and returned to the black couch in the family room. Bringing the bottle with her, why not. For days, it seemed, she'd been stuck on page 71 of *The Beautiful and the Damned.* Some women were floating "helpless and uncontent in a colorless sea of drudgery and broken hopes." Broken hopes. Join the club. She read on, distracted by the watchful deer. Trying to tell her something? Getting blotto here. Can't remember why in college we loved Fitzgerald. She tried to focus on the lily pond out back.

Picking up the *Houston Chronicle,* she thumbed through the Lifestyles section. Her eye snagged on an item titled "Tuscany Comes to Texas." The print zoomed out at her. "After a lengthy search, Mrs. Franelle Lacy has finally selected architect Jacob Mikulski of B. J. Livingston to design an Italian country house, or rather, an Italian farm, which she describes as 'a Tuscan village, complete with several campanile' . . . plans to call it Villa Amore."

She sat unmoving for a long while with the paper on her lap. A python digesting a pig. She felt almost reassured. She loved Jake this much, knew him this well, that she'd seen right into his heart. She heard him say, But Del, I simply forgot to mention it . . . Too tied up with Glencoe . . . What's gotten into you? She could do his end of the dialogue, she knew him this well.

Elberta came into the sunroom holding Hilly by the hand. Seeing the bottle, the glass. Behind the downcast eyes thinking, *Whatta lush.* Elberta said, "I'll be leaving now, ma'am, if you don't need me." She was going to a cousin's wedding in Conroe. Hilly was flushed from her nap, and her eyes had the cranky uncertainty of a just-wakened toddler. Her royal blue playsuit set off her copper curls. "Poor Sleepy, come give Mama a hug," said Delphine, holding out her arms. Hilly blinked at her suspiciously, made a little shudder through the shoulders, then picked up a Fisher-Price mower filled with colored balls and pushed it along the carpet. The child loved Da and Elberta, thought Delphine distractedly. Not the wicked stepmother.

Delphine went inside to the kitchen and phoned Jake.

Barney answered. In a surprised voice: "Jake? I haven't seen him all afternoon." Sudden pause. Cautiously he added, "Come to think of it, he did say he had to visit a building site."

"The site of Villa Amore by any chance? Nice try, Barney. Do tell Jake I called. And tell him I said *mazel tov*."

She dialed a number she had committed to memory. Ear to the receiver, she heard the balls in Hilly's mower rattling in the sunroom. Or was it cicadas? Or the ring in her ear of Franelle's phone? Hard to know which sounds were in, which out — Fisher-Price, the cicadas, the phone.

She hung up. Cicadas outdoing themselves, a fucking concert. Thank God you couldn't hear the buggers when the door was shut. An image of the door with glass louvers — Her blood turned to ice. Oh my God — *the door to the garden. Open.* "Hilly!" She raced to the sunroom.

The mower lay on the floor. The door to the garden stood ajar. *Hilly!* She hurled herself about, checked around the gazebo, underneath, behind the crape myrtle. She ran back inside and checked the house. Hollering Hilly's name. Every room. The upstairs bedrooms. She flung open closet doors. Water, she heard water trickling. She ran to the bathroom. Just the broken washer in the tub. *Water!* She looked out the window at the back garden. In the lily pond, among the waxen yellow and rank green, she saw a patch of blue. She fell back down the stairs.

Over the sunstruck pond hung a gaggle of dragonflies, wings an iridescent blue.

She sped to the front of the house.

Then it all happened in slow motion. She saw the woman with the white chignon watching her from across the street. The woman reached into her purse and took out a gun. The woman aimed the gun low down, at her knees.

"Mama!"

There was Hilly, running toward her from the right, arms outstretched. *No, Hilly, stay there, don't come, stay where you are!* But Hilly kept coming, feet churning in the white lace-up shoes, reaching out her arms and fingers, mouth a downturned crescent.

A glance at the gun aimed low. *Get between Hilly and the gun.* She lunged. The same moment a loud bang, like firecrackers. Hilly knocked to the ground. She gathered Hilly to her. The blue eyes stared up, seeing nothing.

Across the way the woman looked at the gun, dropped it, and shambled off down the street.

There were sirens, cops, the static of radio cars. A forest of legs all about her. More sirens. A man with white sleeves, trying to take Hilly from her. She wouldn't let them, not yet.

Much later that evening someone managed to locate Jake.

The Houston tabloids were delirious. BULLET INTENDED FOR MOM KILLS TODDLER, et cetera. The story made the Rhode Island papers, too, of course, and even the New York tabloids, but not the *Times*. Mrs. Sandra Peña of Newport, Rhode Island, the papers said, had had a long history of "mental troubles." After Merry Mortimer's bullet pierced her son's spine, she'd been dispatched to Westwood Lodge outside Boston. She was diagnosed a paranoid schizophrenic, though you didn't have to be loco to imagine that after Merry shot Raoul, the Mortimers had bought off the Newport P.D. Several weeks prior to her appearance in Houston, Sandra Peña had slipped through the Westwood Security and disappeared.

For many years she had assured anyone inclined to listen that she intended to even the score. A crippled daughter for a crippled son. What goes around comes around.

Chapter 26

DELPHINE II

FOR MONTHS after the trial, Delphine held to an unswerving routine.

Mornings she sat in the Rothko Chapel, a dim octagonal space with dove gray walls and concrete-tiled floor, a vestibule out of time that pertained to nothing on earth. She sat on a brown wooden bench, hands resting palms up in her lap, fingers aching, her spirit yearning toward Rothko's brooding rectangles, as if there in the radiant penumbra behind each one she could join Hilly.

Afternoons she drove. She sought the landscapes of desolation, outside the Loop. Empty weed fields, fast-food dives, the grungy motels sometimes raided by the Houston P.D. She would park the Thunderbird in an abandoned development and sit looking at the streets all laid out, the electricity hooked up, and a few empty tract houses trailing off to nowhere.

She and Jake moved to a house in West University, near Rice. Between them not a word of blame. Jake was gentle, solicitous, somehow gallant. They had become each other's only recourse, bound close in an unholy tie. Between them was the smell of blood.

Jake prospered. He designed a shopping mall cum sculpture garden; an office tower like a silver-skinned abstract rendition of the Chrysler Building. And his long-postponed project: clay-colored notched towers for middle-income housing, which the shelter magazines likened to Italian hill towns. For him and Delphine he built their dream house, outside the swank River Oaks section, the one they'd conjured some five years back — a lifetime, it seemed — in Edgartown. You approached the house over a bridge and came upon it in the woods, a grid of unevenly stacked boxes that seemed to float upon each other. In every room the windows varied, the mullions creating dialogues with the trees outside.

The house was applauded in *Architectural Digest* for its dynamic use of light. *Town and Country* did a piece on Texas "Young Tycoons," and shot Delphine and Jake in their all-white living room. Jake wears a delphinium blue shirt and green Irish wool tie and stands behind Delphine, right hand resting, proprietary, on her shoulder. Delphine wears what looks like a pale yellow chiton, her violet eyes slightly upturned, registering Jake's hand on her shoulder, impossibly lovely. They create the only colors in the room. They are lapidary, perfect, with the insolent self-sufficiency of the well mated. A fortress.

Delphine went to AA. She got involved. Like wives of rich men everywhere, she was perpetually busy without pay. She occasionally "plumped the pillows," as she called it, of the odd manuscript sent her by Andra Cassidy, her former secretary, now an editor at Hollinsworth. Mainly she engineered the transfer of funds from Houston's deeper pockets to the coffers of worthwhile causes. Unlike the Houston do-gooders who didn't know which good their charity did, Delphine chose her projects with care: the Peaceable Kingdom, a utopian commune an hour north of Houston. Theatre on Wheels, which brought professional dramatic productions to public schools. Her greatest joy came from needling, badgering, shaming the city government, into forking over for three shelters for the homeless.

There was even talk of Delphine running for office. Though she was regarded somehow as a foreigner, like her neighbor, the Marquesa di Portanova, who was neither foreign *nor* royal. Something un-Texan, un-American about Delphine's attitude toward fun. She gave off an aura of glamorous doom, like some ill-starred queen. She never wore makeup; her only jewelry was a Cartier gold link necklace and a collection of drop earrings, left over from bohemian *Village* days. With her dark auburn hair pinned up with tortoiseshell combs, violet eyes, jutting jaw, and powerful neck, she was considered a "natural English beauty." But Lindalyn Woodruff sometimes wondered aloud why Delphine didn't check into the fat farm at Duke. Didn't she fear a new edition of Franelle Lacy in the wings?

What Lindalyn failed to understand: for Jake, the Polish immigrant's son from Greenpoint, Brooklyn, Delphine was the woman he'd grown rich with, beyond his wildest imaginings. She was talismanic, like the copper bracelets worn by Californians. Money was balm to Jake's lacerated pride and all the slights of his youth; now the revenge was complete. Jake's euphoria spilled over onto Delphine. As always, money didn't register on her; to see it at all, she needed to view it through Jake.

The coffee table of her glass-walled sitting room overflowed with magazines and books. Become what you marry! said Gloria. Daisy had touched a nerve with her *New York* piece on Sally November, and was writing a woman's column for the *New York Times*. Gina Gold bowled through like a tornado, on a tour to launch her network TV newsmagazine. Legions of women were living *her* old dream. It floated in a far-off bubble, that dream. Jake, with his thinning hair and inflamed pink eyelids and full quota of exasperating traits, had become her world, eclipsing any other. Her passion for Jake came as a continual surprise. There was in it something absolute and barbaric, like whatever had impelled those Aztec priests in Chichén Itzá to drown virgins.

It would be fair to say that for some twenty years, Delphine and Jake, within the frame of a chastening sadness, were happy.

In 1990, Livingston, Mikulski, leveraged to the eyeballs, went bust, one among many big Texas tumbles.

Delphine sat on the raised bed in their aerie high among the trees, letting the housekeeper field phone calls downstairs, bracing for whatever might come next. It was early morning, and she was still in her forest green velvet dressing gown — the one, Jake said, that made her look like Maid Marian — burnished hair rippling over her shoulders. Disaster had mobilized her Yankee fighting spirit. When the going gets tough, et cetera. They were not young, exactly, but they were healthy — she had the same energy as at twenty — Jake had a name, they could go anywhere and start over. A change might be exhilarating. Seattle, Hawaii, Maine — *anywhere*. She looked around the room at the paintings by Jasper Johns and Kenneth Noland and Jake's cherished Navaho rugs. They might need to auction off their treasures. What did it matter? Wherever she went with Jake, the world came with them.

The phone continued to ring. Damn, was no one answering? The housekeeper must have gone out. Delphine picked up the receiver.

It was Jake.

He was weeping.

Delphine's hand flew to her throat. He'd gotten sick from all the stress. "Darling, what is it?" she cried. "What's wrong?"

"I'm crying because I have left you."

Have left. It kept catching in her ear, the tense, like a needle on an old 78. *Have left, have left . . .*

She ran to his dressing room and flung open the closet door. A narrow gap produced by departed suits. A ghostly scent of Armani after-shave.

She headed him off at the office, where he'd been sleeping. *Why?* Another woman? No? No other woman. So why, why, *why?* For God's sake you owe me that, at least, it's been thirty-three years . . . Jake, *you can't just stonewall me after thirty-three years.* She crumpled to the floor, raking her nails down his legs. Jake's Judas eyes skidded away.

Finally Jake said, "It wasn't working for me anymore."

And disappeared. Skipped the state, like a car thief. Leaving her broke, semibroke, she wasn't sure, having retained her innocence about money. Certain crucial facts emerged: there was not enough money left in their joint account to cover expenses, and the bank was foreclosing the mortgage on the house.

Jake, went the common verdict, had snapped.

Delphine rode the Greyhound back to New York. A blur of depots and fluorescent lights, stale smoke and recycled coffee and crullers with runny white icing. She crashed in sublets, generally in Chelsea, where AIDS was emptying whole buildings. Wherever she landed, she would set on the coffee table a silver-framed photo of Hilly. She sat on the couch staring at the photo as afternoon faded into dusk. The street sounds of Con Edison drills and car alarms barely reached her. She wanted to climb backward twenty years toward this child she had never known. She invented a life for Hilly. Imagined her grown, slamming doors, bratty teen–style, like Daisy's Miranda. At her college commencement (she would *not* go to SLC). Hilly would be her best friend, the way Daisy said Miranda was hers. But then she got to explaining about Da, and there she grew muddled, since she herself didn't understand about Da. The light fell from the day and she sat on, crafting the speech she would uncork when Jake finally appeared on the doorstep.

Franca, mothering and gentle, was the only person she could endure. She sometimes phoned her in Georgetown.

"Loving Jake was my life work, my masterpiece. We're the end of a line, the last fools for love, like the dodo. Nevermore. No woman will ever again be stupid enough to live like us."

"You'll start over. I did, after Peter."

"You were young. I'm fifty."

"But what else can you do but start over? What other choice do we have? Listen, you've always been smarter than any of us. Remember, in Houston you raised money for those shelters for the homeless? Why not get involved with social work again." Silence. "Or go back to publishing."

Then Franca would launch into her count-your-blessings spiel, a tale of someone saying yes to life even after the cruelest blow. "Senator Cutler's wife is in remission from Hodgkins. She said to me, 'I'm lucky to have this kind of cancer, there's a ninety percent cure rate.' " The next week: "This friend of my mother's? The doctors just rebuilt her rectum. She says, 'It's all patch, patch, patch. But they'll fix the next thing, too!' "

At this point in the conversation, Delphine usually discovered some compelling reason to hang up.

When trying to start over in New York, it's imprudent, she discovered, to present yourself as anything but a winner. One whiff of need or distress, and people fade away, don't return calls. Sometimes for days her sole human contact was via answering machines. Or the post-human sound of voice mail. Only Daisy remained loyal, in the spirit, Delphine thought, of a first aid vessel plying the Gulf of Maine.

She hit the employment agencies. At the umpteenth one, someone discreetly advised her to lose the dates on her résumé. And maybe consider dyeing her hair?

Finally she got sent on an interview for assistant editor of an engineering magazine. The interviewer wore his glasses cocked forward, so they could function as bifocals. His capped front teeth were like stained Chiclets. She guessed he was roughly her age. As she explained why they should hire her, he scrutinized her strangely. Well, so she wasn't dressed for success; her clothes were scattered in different sublets or still in Houston. She glanced down: a tit hanging out maybe? At least she could be sure there was no blood on the back of her skirt.

Abruptly the man asked, "What class were you at college?"

Oh, I get it. By way of answering, she launched on a riff about her publishing triumphs, a trick she'd picked up from watching Gina on the tube.

"Ah, you worked in publishing in the sixties, then. So when did you graduate?"

Delphine eyeballed him. "When did *you* graduate?"

He cocked his glasses at her. "Uh, in the sixties."

"Well, that's exactly when *I* graduated," she shot back in a bellicose tone.

She should have said, You SOB, I can take you to court!

That evening she sat in her dim living room before the photo of Hilly, working her way through the Jack Daniel's. Why, there must be a whole invisible contingent throughout the city of women like her: aging, jobless, unattached. A kind of throwaway population, hanging on by a thread. She mentally jotted notes for a "Letter to My Generation": "In New York there's a critical mass building of women like us, sinking into isolation and poverty." She got no further. The phrase "women like us" called up the old days in her room at Kober. When those words had an altogether different resonance.

After piloting *Woman Today* to record profits, Andra Cassidy had returned to book publishing as editor in chief of Hollinsworth. Got dumped in a palace revolution. And reincarnated as a power agent, the sort who leans across the table at the Four Seasons to breathe into the ear of Tina Brown the title of The Next Hot Book.

"Publishing's been hit bad by the recession," Andra told Delphine, speaking ungrammatically like the young barbarians dominating the profession. "No one's hiring. If I hear of anything . . ."

Delphine learned that George Byrne, who'd been thrown out of the loop, was about to resurface in a new publishing venture funded by a real estate magnate. The magnate's chief mission, Delphine read in the *Times,* was to sell the hell out of their product. Publishing, since she'd last looked, had changed.

After a week of "Mr. Byrne is in a meeting," she got through.

Why, Delphine Mikulski. Long time no. Lovely to hear. Must have lunch. Give you to secretary.

On the morning of their lunch date, the secretary phoned to cancel. The following week she canceled date number two.

On the morning of date number three, Delphine dressed in slow motion, superstitiously keeping the phone out of her line of vision so it wouldn't ring. She put on her beaded black Donna Karan with plunging *V* and Cartier gold link necklace — not ideal for lunch, but her other clothes were at the cleaner's or in the previous sublet, couldn't remember which. She did up her hair, now threaded with silver, with the jade-edged combs Jake had given her for their twenty-fifth anniversary. She inspected herself in the full-length bathroom mirror. Her eyes were circled by shinerlike shadows. Even so, *pas mal.* Good bones and all that.

She'd once had a yen for George Byrne; perhaps they could team up again, in more ways than one. She reflexively checked her wrist, then remembered she'd pawned the Movado watch, another present from Jake. How he'd loved to spend money on her! The alarm clock on the night table read ten to twelve. She popped a Valium, to take the edge off, even though she'd swallowed a couple sometime before dawn. Then she remembered that it was her last day in this apartment. The owner, a friend of Gina's old buddy Renato, was due back in the evening. She would deal with where to go next after Byrne gave her a job.

The phone ripped the silence.

Delphine clutched her heart, unable to lift the receiver. "Mr. Byrne had to leave town on a sudden business trip," said his secretary.

The moment she hung up, the phone rang again. It was George Byrne, apologizing for canceling at the last minute, but a dear friend had just dropped dead on the tennis court. He was sure Delphine would understand.

"Actually I don't," said Delphine. "I mean, which is it? Did your best friend leave town? Or did you drop dead?"

Nice going. She'd just severed her lifeline.

It was stifling in the apartment, the ancient air conditioner neutered by a heat to match the Houston tropics. Suddenly she felt, why, almost festive. Like dancing, drinking Dom Perignon from a crystal flute, laughing and flirting with the men hanging all over her. Why not go someplace mah-velous, like in the old days, a place to buoy the spirits. She tried to imagine where that might be. The Oak Room at the Plaza, maybe? She was dressed for it. Or maybe the Café de la Paix in the Saint Moritz? There were so many ways in New York to be festive.

The smell of horse shit from the carriages on Central Park South mingled with exhaust fumes. At least it was a touch cooler here on the terrace of the Saint Moritz. As though Central Park, its foliage a tired sooty green, were exhaling on them. Delphine sipped her kir royale — she'd lost count which one — and watched the man at the next table lay his hand along the side of his girlfriend's breast. It always surprised her, the shared vocabulary of desire. She averted her eyes. She rarely thought directly of Jake, yet his absence, a black hole at her center, was company of sorts. She watched a family of blond Germans in shorts; some Japanese with elaborate halters of equipment. They were replaced by Iowans in pastel polyester leisure suits, and then the Iowans left as well. Delphine marked each changing of the guard with a kir royale. Afternoon melded into dusk. The horizon beyond the buildings on Fifth Avenue turned a malignant red.

She fuzzily remembered she had no place to sleep. Call Daisy. No, Daisy gone to France with Sandy the Luftmensch. She had no plan B. Panic time! She called for another kir royale, and paid with a ten. Her last. By the look of the waiter, the old sourbones didn't like you to linger. Didn't he know that lingering was the raison d'être of cafés? Well past nine, and still sweltering . . . Maybe it was cooler in the woods across the street.

She threaded her way unsteadily out of the Café de la Paix into the street. The light must have changed. Cars, honks, a flood of hysteria bore down on her. She held up her hand like a traffic cop. *Odeur de horseshit* baked by the heat. She hurried past and followed a little path into Central Park. The coolness a benediction. She sat on a splintery bench, eyes adjusting to the dark. Smelling piss now — Honestly, where could you *go* anymore in New York? It took an enormous effort to remain vertical. She noticed a body covered with newspaper stretched out on the next bench. She'd lie down, too. Just for a bit.

She awoke stiff, with a furious need to pee. She eyed the bushes behind the bench. *Ocupado*. And to judge by the fragrance, the local outhouse. She'd head over to the New York Athletic Club across the street. Dudley Hunnewell's old haunt, gracious she hadn't thought of him in years. To think he'd proposed to her in that cozy bar to the right of the lobby. Or was it at the Rathskeller in New Haven . . . She could picture, like nirvana, the ladies'.

The lobby of the N YAC was underdecorated and dim. You could practically smell the old boys' sweat socks. Delphine hooked a right toward the bar. Same oak wainscoting and low-wattage chandeliers, place hadn't changed in thirty years. It was empty but for three graying preppies at a table. She narrowed her eyes — Dudley? Could it be? Dudley Hunnewell of Saint Marks and Yale? Same fussy chin and florid cheeks — well, jowls. Hard to say, his profile was partially in shadow. The man glanced in her direction. His eyes locked into her.

A concierge detached himself from the front desk. "Madam, may I help you?"

"You may indeed. I'm looking for the ladies' room, please." Doing her Empress Josephine. Oh dear, she might not look quite regal. She tucked up a hank of hair and adjusted her dress, which exposed half her bosom. She was all but boogying in place.

"Madam, I'm afraid the rest rooms are for patrons only," he said in a low voice.

Delphine glared at him. To think poor folks put up with this shit every day. "What a despicable policy! Don't you realize you're identifying with the oppressor?"

Head lowered, the concierge reached for her elbow. "Madam, I'm sorry but —"

She shook off his hand and wheeled around toward Dudley. He was watching, taking this all in. He must rescue her, like the gentleman he was. Class is thicker than money. She remembered there were rooms upstairs. They could catch up on old times, she and Dudley. Maybe pick up where they'd left off, who knew? God, how she wanted to sleep.

"Hi there!" She took several steps toward Dudley, waving gaily.

The man exchanged a sheepish smile with his cronies. "Excuse me, have we met?" he asked without standing.

"Delphine Mortimer, don't you remember?" His brow and eyes were in shadow; suddenly she was no longer sure. "We once had a rather, uh, *momentous* encounter in this very place," she prompted. Or was it at Yale, at the Rathskeller.

He raised his chin slightly. The light shone full on his face, and a smooth, shiny scar above his left checkbone — a burn scar — and she saw the Dudley of her youth.

For a long moment they stared at each other across that dim space and thirty years, her eyes beaming a plea: for God's sake, in the name of all that's decent . . .

"Excuse me, but I believe you've got the wrong man." He leaned toward his pals and murmured something. Judging by their low laughter, it amused.

The concierge and a new cohort flanked Delphine and gripped her arms.

"Gentlemen," she said loudly, "either you let me through, or I pee on your rug, which is not of the first quality. The choice is yours."

"Filthy bastard, communist spy! Get your fucking hands off of me!"
Black Cat's voice yanked her back. She jolted upright on her cot. She must have dozed off. Even with the stop/start ranting of Black Cat, several cots down. The Musak of hell. The woman had one scarred eye pasted shut, a tongue trawling in air. Now she was throwing punches at phantoms, delivering the coup de grace with a karate kick. Delphine cowered in terror. She also longed to spirit Black Cat off to some repair shop of the body and soul. Judging by the gray light in the high windows, it must be dawn.

Couldn't remember how much time had elapsed, or the transitions. She'd gotten bounced from the NYAC after first ruining their rug. She had simply reached the point of no return, which coincided remarkably with a point beyond shame. Out on the street she found the twenty in her purse . . . bought a fifth . . . back to the park . . . Then the cops came — when? And a film crew. Impossible, yet she remembered lights and cameras. They'd been rounded up by cops, corraled, herded into this place — an armory? She glanced up the rows of black iron and plywood cots.

"My cunt! They've taken my cunt and given me syphilis! *You! The Jew!*" Black Cat was shouting at a space of air above her head, hovering near it, jolting away, hovering, jolting . . .

Delphine rested her head in her hands, grateful for the lull. *You gave me syphilis!* came the voice on top of her. Hands gripped her throat. "*You the Jew* —" Delphine flailed and choked, eyes fixed on the battered face, the lolling tongue — "*Stole my cunt.*" She pushed hard against the woman's shoulders, struggled to free her throat . . . Her whole being rebelled . . . The obscenity of *disappearing forever* . . . She couldn't cut off here . . .

Everything going black, thought dimming . . . She was blind need . . . Get to the next breath — *Give 'er the necklace!* Her fingers clawed behind her own neck at the clasp. She felt the clasp snap open, and fell backward, released to the world. She lay on the cot, ears filled with her own rales. Black Cat had scooted with her booty. Around her she heard laughter.

When she could stand, Delphine tottered into a scarred front hall. A security guard was heading toward a flight of stairs.

"I almost got choked to death in there!" she rasped.

"Honey, it ain't the Helmsley Palace," he called back.

She headed toward the door, colliding with two men carrying clipboards.

"Christ almighty, I almost got murdered in there!"

The men exchanged grim looks; the older one pushed on. The young one jotted something on his clipboard. He glanced at Delphine, then looked again, hard, as if adjusting his vision four different ways.

"There's a psychopath in there," she said hoarsely, shaking both grimy hands. "It's criminal, unconscionable to throw the mentally ill in with everyone else. This is why the homeless prefer to freeze to death in the streets. You people ought to be sued —"

"And where exactly would you have us send them, madam, to the city shelters?'' the man asked wearily. He gestured with his Styrofoam cup. ''They're even worse, just places to warehouse the sick and desperate.''

She noted the good diction, L. L. Bean shirt, tanned hound-dog face. Fortyish. Not your standard social worker . . .

''Well, if this hellhole is private, dammit, surely you can organize some system to separate the mentally ill, the folks who've been dumped on the street by institutions, from the merely homeless —''

''Which requires a staff to supervise intake,'' the man snapped. ''And we've just lost a major portion of our funding. Dear madam, have you ever dealt with foundations who choose causes like some flavor of the month? Or the city bureaucracy? The massive cynicism of bureaucrats crying 'broke' while permitting giant tax abatements for developers? Have you? The shelters are already packed. By winter there won't be any room at all, and already they're living in cardboard boxes along Ninth Avenue. We're suing the city. But what the hell do you know about any of this?''

He stared at her: sunken eyes, sooty cheeks, auburn hair snaking about her, black dress molting its beads, and he thought he had never seen anything so exquisite.

''What are you doing here anyway? What's your game?''

''What kind of elitist shit —''

''No, don't tell me. You're a journalist posing as a homeless woman to gather material. Or let's see, you got bored with lunching at Le Cirque and went back to college, and now you're researching your term paper. How'm I doing?''

''Swell. Just great. Is this what they taught you in social work school?''

''Oh, I've got it, this week you're *slumming*.''

''You're a real smart-ass, you know?''

''Or is it *la nostalgie de la boue*?''

''You sonuvabitch —''

''No, you started, you attack *me* when —''

They were hollering in each other's faces, all lips, teeth, and spit, an inch from blows. She felt his breath on her. Hers must be foul.

Suddenly she was basted in cold sweat and her stomach bucked wildly. She was about to throw up. She swayed in space, fighting for control. Stretched out her hand. ''Excuse me, I think . . . Excuse me —''

His arm clasped her about the shoulders. She folded into him, smelling his after-shave, and herself — stale piss, like the people she moved away from in the subway.

He got her to a metal folding chair. Squatted beside her. "Here, take a slug of this."

Both hands gripping the cup, she sipped his coffee through a hole cut in the Styrofoam. She sipped and sipped. The coffee was hot and had an excellent taste. The nausea receded. She felt amazingly well. In a flash she departed her body and looked down at the scene from on high. Oh, Delphine. For shame. She was a dilettante, dabbling in degradation. When she got bored with the lower depths, she could just climb back out. Regroup, reconnect, take a hot shower. She could. Unlike the real thing back in that toad hole.

It was her first clear idea since Jake left. She sat in silence with her idea, and a bad case of shakes, gripping the half-empty Styrofoam cup to still her hands.

"You're right," she said, half to herself. "I am an imposter."

The man was squatting at her knees, watching her. He shook his head no. "Listen, I was way out of line. Here, put this on." He stood and draped a jacket over her shoulders.

"A fraud."

"No, I had no right. You hit me at a bad moment. You can't imagine the frustration of dealing with those bureaucrats and policy wonks —"

"Oh, but I can," she sighed. A peaceful silence. He stood above her, so she couldn't see his face. "You asked me what I was doing. Here's what. I think I've been — throwing a monster temper tantrum."

"I've thrown a few of those myself."

She looked up at him and offered a wan smile. It hurt to smile; her lips were dry and cracked. "Friends?" She stuck out a begrimed hand. "Delphine." She hesitated, then said, "Delphine Mortimer."

"Whit Thayer. This may sound nuts —"

"No more than anything else."

"Then why don't you come have breakfast with me."

They took a cab to Whit Thayer's townhouse in Gramercy Park. He showed her to a Russian green bedroom on the second floor. The entire third floor housed a skylit studio where he painted. Delphine showered, savoring water as though she'd just discovered it. Fancy nozzles were positioned to hit in strategic places. Feeling as if she'd wandered into a fairy tale, she slipped on a papa bear's terry cloth robe. A maid served them breakfast in a sunroom hung with paintings that Delphine judged mediocre (her eye having been educated by Jake). Their table looked out on a garden with a stone fountain. Water spouted from the mouth of a dolphin. It was the sort of tranquil oasis that could be bought in New York for a vast sum. Hair up in a towel turban, Delphine gobbled scrambled eggs, ham, scones and marmalade, slices of melon and kiwi. Whit Thayer, his tanned pedigreed face attentive to her every expression, watched her eat.

Back in her Russian green room, she slid under deliciously clean sheets, marveling at this latest twist in her tale. A cautious elation spread through her. She fell asleep avid to learn what would come next.

In the days that followed, they swapped stories, she and Whit Thayer. They strolled arm in arm around Gramercy Park, deserted in August, with the local gentry out of town. They ate dinner at the half-empty Gotham Grill on Twelfth Street, or Florent, the new French bistro over on Van Dam in the meat district. She drank Chardonnay, he Pellegrino. They communicated in code — each could fill in the other's blanks — like two battered survivors of war and pestilence who discover their common origins. Whit was a painter and an advocate for the homeless. "I got involved in the Coalition for the Homeless through a friend, Vernon Mack, who's the executive director, and now I'm on the board. The morning I met you, I was down at the armory shelter with a staffer from the coalition, hoping to get a hands-on sense of the situation. We're about to approach the commissioner of housing about reducing the number of homeless we're forced by law to take into our SROs. We want the number down from sixty percent to forty, which is still way too much, of course. I despise policy wonks, and I wanted to make a tangible argument. You, my dear — your experience there — is the tangible argument."

Over dinner Whit told Delphine that his wife had shipped out three years and seven months earlier to go work for Mother Teresa in Calcutta. "She perceives herself as some sort of secular saint. After she left, I went on a marathon bender. All but killed myself. AA saved me. I show at a gallery, I sell my work, but through my new prism of sobriety, I've had to admit I'll never be anything but mediocre. I'm highly suspicious of my do-gooder stuff. I suspect I've adopted a project to rival my wife's. Or maybe it's a more constructive way of continuing the tantrum, as you call it. No matter. At some point I understood I had no right to destroy myself, not while there was so much suffering around me that I had the power, in some small way, to alleviate. My wife's legacy again?" Wry smile. "Of course I also still hate her guts.

"The morning I met you I'd just received a revoltingly righteous letter, and, I'm afraid, vented my fury on you."

While helping administer a shelter in a downtown settlement house, Whit had hatched a scheme for combining his two passions. "Art has grown elitist and lost touch with a popular audience," he told Delphine over coffee in the library (as Delphine calculated when she could sneak out for a cognac). "So I thought, Why not commission work from artists for the shelter? After all, what population is more in need of beauty than the homeless? I wanted them to live one small part of their lives like the rich. Like I do."

"What a marvelous idea!"

"Now that social activism is P.C., I had no trouble finding even name artists to create works for the shelter. We've gotten foundation grants, a write-up in *People*. Here, let me show you the piece."

Over the course of several weeks, Whit pestered Vernon Mack to put Delphine into a recently opened slot as assistant to the housing director. Vernon objected that the many staffers in line for the job would raise hell, and exactly what were Delphine's qualifications, but Whit said he'd pay Delphine's salary for a year. And that was that.

On June 6, 1991, the *New York Post* carried the headline HOUSING EXEC KNIFED IN WEST SIDE SRO. Delphine's boss. She badgered the coalition's chief financial officer to give her a crash course in the myriad maneuvers needed to convert a building into a home for street people. Then she persuaded Vernon Mack to name her housing director. Within the year, Delphine was overseeing five SROs and controlling a big budget; hiring and firing staff; jockeying with unions; lobbying the city commissioner of housing; displaying the administrative skills of Houdini. And working up an appetite for a bigger job. Like the boss's job. Vernon Mack was stale and played out and dreaming of Arizona.

She kept her thoughts away from Jake. A question of discipline. A question of survival. Jake was a killer disease from which she was in remission. Besides, by evening she was too bone tired even to miss a private life. She lived purely in the public dimension, for which she felt grateful.

She and Whit came and went in the townhouse like two compatible siblings. It had been a long breakfast, they sometimes joked. Then they kissed good night, both cheeks, and went upstairs to their separate quarters. That Whit was an attractive man she had not failed to notice. He was sexually unoccupied, so far as she could see. Not gay. Maybe still sulking over his secular saint? Or, like many New York men who poured their libido into work, just neuter? He was also fourteen years younger than she. This eliminated any sexual static. Fine by her. She had opted for early retirement from the life of the body. Since the evening she had first sighted Jake at Peter Tabori's party in Katonah, she had not thought to sleep with another man.

Then one night as she and Whit stood chatting in the stairwell, he reached his hand behind her head and pulled out, one by one, her jade-edged combs. Her hair slipped down. Whit inhaled its perfume. Delphine reached her hand back to the newel post and shut her eyes, confused, uncertain where to go with this. Surprised, but not entirely. Suddenly she saw Jake. Loitering over by the porcelain umbrella stand, clear as can be, hip out, mouth sultry, blue eyes mocking. *Go to hell, Jake, I'm done with it. You offer nothing.* She could come in from her cold, dark limbo to warmth and light. The tender damage she could barely remember. Could she? Begin to remember?

Would Whit throw her out if she refused?

"You should know that I want you to live here as long as it suits you," Whit said. As always, reading her.

She opened her eyes and looked at his handsome hound-dog face.

"I'm overweight, going gray, everything going south. I'm fourteen years older than you and I just lost a tooth and another needs root canal and —" She brought the back of her hand to her lips. "I don't think I would even know how."

Whit considered this gravely. Then, his voice low in his throat, he said, "Do you have any idea how incredibly arousing you are?"

Afterward Delphine wept loudly without troubling to cover her face. Whit Thayer understood that she wasn't weeping for joy.

Chapter 27

Daisy had already heard the gist of Gina's speech at their annual lo-fat-hi-fiber lunches. Fortunately, she'd chosen an aisle seat in the last row. Gathering her things, she glided with her airborne step out a side exit of Reisinger.

The weather was holding its breath before unleashing a serious storm. The rain-colored sky accentuated the green, invasive, an excess of green, Westchester aspiring to the jungle. Daisy checked her watch. Too soon to head over toward Kober House for the old crowd's private reunion. She was in no hurry. Over the years, the SOS Club had deteriorated badly, like most alliances based on neither tribal ties nor money. She and Franca hadn't spoken in two decades; even now, people avoided mentioning Franca's name in her presence. Gina, when she talked to her old friends at all, talked down. She seemed to consider them an adolescent phase she'd put behind her.

As for Delphine, would she even show? Since Jake had taken up with the baby banker, as Delphine called her, she was like a keg of nitroglycerine. You didn't want to jostle her. She'd surfaced for a time in Newport. Camped out in the empty Rosecliff, bedding down on a mattress in the middle of the living room in her vintage over-the-top style. She had actually visited her old beau, Raoul Peña, even after the horror in Houston — to accomplish what, Daisy had never learned. Now she lived on and off with a youngish painter and worked "in the poverty racket," as she put it. At times she was almost like the old Delphine, steaming with excitement, cooking up big plans — Gonna sue the hell out of the city . . . Get named to a commission to overhaul the homeless shelter system . . . Run for City Council . . . Then bango, she's off on a bender. When Daisy had last had dinner with her at Caramba! Delphine downed three margaritas and slid off her chair onto the floor. Daisy would make noises about AA. Delphine would dismiss AA as "religio-fascistic," and couldn't Daisy see she had the drinking under control?

Without any precise plan, Daisy cut across the grass and strolled under the arbor of wisteria toward Westlands. She inhaled the whorish perfume of yesteryear, hoping for a Proustian epiphany. All she got was a sneezing attack. Snuffling, she entered the sepia gloom of Westlands. There, to the left, the grandfather clock with its painting of a leering tipsy moon; ahead, the leaded windows of the back vestibule that opened onto the great lawn and the one apple tree. She half expected to see Grace Omura perched in its branches, composing haiku.

She climbed the oak-paneled stairs, past the windows adorned with stained glass coats of arms reading *In Cruce Salus* and *Dieu et Mon Droit*. Then she turned up a small spiral staircase. She was headed for a room with casement windows, and a rocker and paisley throws and faded Persians, a room bathed in sunlight, motes dancing on the rays. In search of that April afternoon that brought Cambridge and Gerrit and Ben — and all that followed. Life seldom offered neat time lines, yet the sense was upon her that there in that room, some thirty-four years ago, her story had begun.

She reached the landing, light-headed, heart knocking about her collarbone. The floor was strewn with student discards: empty bottles of Snapple; a spindly plant; red term-paper folders; a jockstrap — the place was coed now; and, salute to the times, surgical rubber gloves.

She walked down the corridor to Franca's old room. It was mean and dusty and dim. The mattress drooped sideways across the bed. Franca's old rocker was pocked with knife wounds. Daisy sank onto the rocker and sat staring out the casement windows into the trees. Down the hall the custodial people were banging around furniture. She had heard no footsteps, yet suddenly she sensed she wasn't alone. Gooseflesh prickled her arms. She swiveled her head. There stood Franca.

"So you're here," Franca said. "I've been wanting to talk to you for thirty years."

She came swooping over and expertly kissed the air near Daisy's cheek.

The politico's wife, thought Daisy, stiffening. Discomfited at being found here. "Has it really been that long? I've *seen* you, though, of course, in the papers."

"And I've seen you on your book jackets and the talk shows."

Generous, considering her last book had been published almost fifteen years ago.

They exchanged quick appraisals in the pitiless way of women tallying time's insults.

"You look amazingly the same!" Franca said, continuing the generous mode.

"You look well, too." In fact, she didn't. For a second Daisy saw a radiant face framed in sunlight, the crown of blond braids, the heedless magnetism of youth. Franca now had a frosted lady-do, and one eye gaped slightly, perhaps from a ministroke, and nasty tucks notched her jaw, mirroring her own. Franca, too, turning that hard corner. And protected by a doting husband. Malice crackled through Daisy like the distant thunder outside. Oh, let it go, all so long ago, what does any of it matter now.

Franca took up her old perch on the window seat. "I've missed reading you. I used to look forward so to your Thursday column in the *New York Times*. That must have been around, uh, 1976? I would also dread it."

"Dread? Why?"

Franca opened her mouth to reply, then thought better of it.

"So, you've been wanting to talk to me," said Daisy.

"I've been wanting to tell you about my life."

"Oh? But why after all this time — Why me?"

"Because you're the only person who would understand."

"I see." She had seldom wanted to hear a life story more.

"My daughter's name is Angelica. My child with Ben." ("Ben" spoken awkwardly.) "Pretty name, don't you think?"

Angelica. Mystified, Daisy nodded. "A name in your family?"

Franca only studied her inquiringly. Flexed stiff fingers. "I guess you could say I've had a storybook life with Ben. There's been plenty of excitement. Ben generates excitement around him."

Daisy kept her face expressionless. She pictured a marine parasite drilling a little hole into a mollusk and sucking out pulp.

"Ben" — still awkward about the name — "is a good man. He has been a good husband."

Has been. The tense resonated.

"If by 'good' one means loyal-in-his-fashion. He's good to me, you see, out of honor. Decency. Respect. History. Those things are not the same as love, are they."

Something within Daisy brightened, shaming her.

"Ben's real passion is his work," Franca went on in a monotone, a voice coming through a confessional grille. "He's purely about ambition. Even his daughter he loves only intermittently, with huge displays of affection. He would never leave us, though. So many bonds besides love. Love is the least of it. How naive we all were." She looked around the dimming room and tucked her hand into her armpit, in a way Daisy remembered.

"Bonds," Franca repeated, cueing herself. "Gratitude, there's a bond. Ben considers that he owes me. Mother and her pals from Saint Botolph's helped finance his campaigns — poor Mother's been an awfully good sport. First Peter, a manic-depressive from Hollywood. Then Ben, a Jew from Brookline who didn't even go to Harvard!" She sighed. "Men are more governed by inertia than we ever imagined. What they hate above all is change, upheaval. A woman's rage. So what they do is quietly make a new life without leaving the old one. Add on secret wings and turrets instead of buying a new house."

A mistress, then. Daisy wondered whether with *her,* Ben would have made his life in one place. She was flooded with sweet poison. She had always, she recognized, wanted Franca to pay. Even with that goddamn halo around her head.

"But a prominent man in Washington?" Franca was saying. "He'd have to be brain dead not to succumb to temptation." A little laugh. "Know that fellow Stephen Hawking, the physicist who's crippled from Lou Gehrig's disease and talks through batteries? I just read in *People* that he traded his wife of twenty-five years for a new one. And how did they meet? She was the nurse who fed him dinner through his feeding tube. Now does that say something about men's options or doesn't it?"

She glanced at Daisy, mouth twitching, and for a moment they both teetered on the edge of hilarity. Then Franca foraged in her bag and fetched up a Chap Stick. "Heavens, I was thinking we still smoked. This place puts you in a time warp. I was saying, Ben has — Oh dear, have I said this? — a second household. There's even a child, I'm afraid, yes," she added wearily. "When I found out, I . . . collapsed. It'd been a disaster with Peter, and now . . . *again.* I had this perfect life, in the world's eyes, but for me there was nothing inside. It was all icing, no cake. We were purely a ceremonial couple. Ben put his life as a man in a separate compartment. I didn't want to live. Needless to say, I botched that, too. Twice. The second time, in the hospital, Ben vowed he'd never leave me. We had this understanding that I was fragile and would self-destruct without him, and he was the strong, steady good husband who held me together. Except" — her voice turned rancorous — "if he'd been truly good, I wouldn't have needed the rest."

Pieces from a past puzzle clicked into place. She heard Ben that night in the Café Luxembourg. *Obligations I can't explain,* Ben had said.

"Then Ben's second household created unforeseen expenses. The child, it turned out, had a defective heart valve and required expensive surgery. Charitable soul that I am, I wasn't going to ask Mother to donate to that! The mistress became too depressed to cope. I believe at one point she attempted suicide — Ben had two crazies on his hands! The man gravitates toward unstable women. He needed money. Ben became involved in some, shall we say, questionable activities. Which I alone know about. For the moment. Another bond."

"Wait, hold it," said Daisy, presenting her palm. "You've been through some rough stuff, and I'm sorry. But why . . . Why me? What does any of this have to do with me?"

Franca leaned toward her in the falling light. "I came back here today because I wanted to ask you" — clasping her hands — "Daisy, I'm asking you to forgive me."

"For what?" said Daisy sharply.

"For stealing your life. I've always had the ghastly feeling that I stole the life that was meant to be yours. And Ben and I always felt that you regretted losing —"

No! She sprang from the rocker. She could hear them commiserating over poor Daisy, taste the smarmy sympathy. No, they wouldn't have it!

"That's your fantasy, something you and Ben got off on. You enjoyed thinking I was eaten up with regret so you could give your own wretched marriage a jolt. Well, sorry to disappoint you! Oh, there were times when I may have envied the material ease of your life. You've never had to struggle. One marriage sours, and you fall into a tub of butter: the lap of a new husband. You've never earned a living. You're part of a tiny mandarin class that doesn't live in reality. You know nothing about the world! Your words, *you* — have no weight, you have zero credibility." Sputtering, shaking: "I — I've always thought of you as a parasite, you feed off the energy of men, live off *their* excitement, what *they* create, suck it out like pulp. It was the same with Peter. Envy you? Hell, no, it's not you I envied. It's Ben. *His* life. His achievements and energy and vision. The thing we dreamed of doing ourselves. You — you're just a product of our age. When I think of you at all, it's with contempt."

Oh, that felt good! She'd blown out of her system years of backed-up rage.

Then she saw Franca's bad eye, and the tremor of her mouth, and the loose skin beneath her chin. Franca twisted around toward the window, a small matronly figure with swollen ankles and shoulders in a defeated slope.

"Oh, shit," said Daisy. "Look, I've overstated things as usual. It's being back in this place. It makes you imagine how one *could* have done things." Franca said nothing. "It's the hormones. I finally couldn't take it anymore and said yes to the damn hormone pills," she offered. "Even though Froyda Maidman — remember her? — insists they're a conspiracy against women by the pharmaceutical industry and medical establishment." Still, Franca wouldn't speak.

Daisy sat back down in the rocker, took a deep breath. "All right, look, it *was* a blow when you married Ben. Because, dammit, I lost you both. Then Delphine moved to Houston, and Gina got all chilly and brittle and . . . there went the SOS Club." She put her fingertips to her forehead. "Anyway, it's all past history now."

Franca swung around to face her. "Not for me. Scarcely a day goes by that isn't poisoned." Almost to herself: "D'you know what partly drives Ben?"

"He always was impossible," said Daisy, eager to have Franca talking. "He used to make appointments with himself to relax. Deliver closing arguments in his sleep."

"Ben was forever trying to prove himself to you. Win you. Make himself finally worthy. *Show* you, and fling it in your face. He's stuck back in 1957."

Daisy looked at her dumbly.

"He named our daughter Angelica while I was knocked out from the C-section. After some character in a book that you and he once read together."

The Leopard. She remembered now. She saw the book lying on her doorjamb that Sunday morning, white patches where snow had dried on the dust jacket.

"He admires your independence, your talent. The other women of our vintage climbed on the career bandwagon once it became the thing to do. But you, Ben used to say, you always had a dream."

"I've failed miserably," Daisy blurted.

"Who says we're talking about reality here? You were the unattainable princess of his youth. Dismissive and snotty to perfection. Oh God, did that drive him wild, that he couldn't have you! Once, after one of your books came out, he got hold of a video of you on Charlie Rose. I found it in the back of his closet. Ben, a man who never once had time to go to his daughter's school play!" Franca tucked a fist under her armpit. "D'you know how we got married? D'you want to know the way it happened? After the last time you saw Ben, and you told him that you were marrying Fletcher — that was the night Ben proposed."

Franca placed a hand over her mouth and stared at Daisy. "I do believe I hate you. I have wished you dead. Then I would think, dead you would have even more of a hold on him. Oh, then he could really have a field day, mythologizing you."

Daisy closed her eyes and bowed her head. She wanted to wrap herself around Ben's love and take it in, all that love streaming toward her, beamed out into the heedless dark without ever finding her. She felt consoled, almost, for the dry, dry years, and all the loneliness.

She became aware that Franca was standing.

"Well, guess I'd better go take my Prozac," Franca said. "Before I say something even uglier. Besides, I have to tinkle," she added in boarding school lingo. "Listen, I'm, uh, sorry about all this. How did we contract this dangerous habit of telling each other the truth? I'm sure men never do it. Maybe that's why they accomplish so much."

She slung her bag on her shoulder and headed toward the door.

"Wait," Daisy said. "Stay. Why don't you stay a little while. I mean, now that we've both scorched every bit of earth in sight . . ." She shrugged and a smile stole over her lips.

At the door Franca wavered. Then she smiled, too. "We did scorch a lot of earth, didn't we."

Daisy exhaled luxuriously. "I feel good, actually. How about you? Like we can talk again, after all these years. Sort of take up where we left off."

"Yesss," Franca breathed in a way Daisy remembered. She returned to her perch on the window seat.

"Long ago you once told me Ben only wants what he can't have," Daisy said. "How right you were."

"Mm-hmm. I saw it all at the outset. The terrible thing is we see the truth, then march right into the bear trap anyway, like sleepwalkers."

Daisy leaned toward her. In the dim light they were like two shades. "It's that we imagine we'll change them."

"We were all crazy back in sixty-four."

"Out of our minds."

"I was in a panic after leaving Peter, ready for the first tub of butter, as you put it. And Ben married me out of rage at you."

"Surely out of love, too."

"Oh, ten percent. The other ninety was to make you writhe. He thought, *Now* she wants me because Straight dumped her. And it didn't help that you were sleeping with Fletcher. That was the last blow!"

"Did we fuck it up."

"A comedy of errors, without the laughs. In that one moment of madness our lives got changed forever. Oh, think of it, Daisy, so much waste."

So much waste. Daisy felt the years exhale into the room their bounty of loss.

"No, not waste. We have our children."

"Yeesss."

"You know, I used to blame, blame, blame — you, me, Ben," said

Daisy. "But it was nobody's fault. We were all just young and driven by gonads and out of our gourds." Shyly: "D'you remember how we used to say that the men come and go, but classmates are forever?"

Franca smiled. "I do, yes." A pause. "I often think about leaving Ben, you know. We last made love" — little laugh — "sometime in the eighties. We stay together out of habit, inertia, sheer busyness. Because Ben can't pencil in the time to get separated. And because of *my* sense of obligation. I suspect he's about to get pilloried for — well, writing checks he shouldn't have. He may be forced to resign his seat. An awkward moment for me to leave. Oh, and a part of me has always enjoyed" — her eyes flicked away — "the ceremonial aspect. Then I'm sitting at some state occasion, chewing rubber chicken, and I think good God, how much time do we have left, anyhow? We're all going to be dead soon, and this is what I've chosen?"

An old longing rocked Daisy. Subsided. It was some vestigial habit, wanting Ben. The clock had long ago run out on her and Ben.

"I have to admit, I've been seeing someone," said Franca in their old just-girls manner. "Whenever I can sneak away. Wait, don't say it, I know. Another tub of butter. That's how I am, Daisy. Don't despise me for it." She smiled. "Jamie Smithys is an old family friend. When I was a child and he was teaching drama at Harvard, I remember him coming out to the house with his wife to our musicales. She died several years ago. I recently ran into him, at Mother's nursing home, of all places. We started meeting for tea, and one thing led to another and — How can I put this. I feel I've discovered my soul mate. Finally, in middle age." She sighed. "But Daisy, he's seventy-five. What folly. And there's the sheer *mess* of leaving a marriage. What's to become of us all."

They sat in silence in the dusky light like exiles from the world. Outside, beyond the casement windows, voices and laughter floated up like colored bubbles. That would be the reunion classes, pouring out of Reisinger and onto the graveled path, heading over to the president's house on Kimball Avenue for pre-dinner cocktails.

"What are you thinking?" asked Daisy.

"I'm thinking that I'm happy."

"Yes?"

"Happy enough. Maybe we weren't put on earth to be happy in the way we imagined. That delirium with men that we used to live for."

"Ecstasy is so tiring. Thirty seconds of ecstasy a year is more than enough."

Laughing: "I'm happy just pulling up radishes in Jamie's garden. I'm happy having my grandchildren come to stay. I'm happy doing my silly volunteer work to relieve some small amount of misery in the world."

They sat on in the dim peace, neither wanting to leave just yet.

"I'm happy," said Franca, "sitting here in this room with you."

Chapter 28

WHEN DAISY AND FRANCA rolled in, arms about each other's waists, jaws dropped, conversation withered.

"We love each other again," Daisy announced simply.

"I think I'm going to throw up," said Gina in her Tallulah voice.

Daisy cut Gina a knowing smile. To leave in the middle of her speech was to spit on the shroud of Turin.

The others continued staring in disbelief. Phone wires had burned — How to finesse a meeting of Daisy and Franca after all these years? Heavens, wasn't it disorienting enough to be in McCracken's new Common Room, done up like a Motel 6 with orange Naugahyde chairs and sofa and walnetto tables, a rude change from the old slip-covered gentility. Mia had arrived at Kober House first, to find their old dorm metamorphosed into an early childhood center. Luckily, she remembered the new Common Room and taped a note for the others on Kober's door.

Everyone jabbered at once — Diana, what a surprise . . . Mia, last saw you in Jaipur . . . Franca dear, where you staying . . . Daisy, that miniskirt . . . Really carry it off . . . Who does your color . . . So which is it going to be, girls, color or cancer?

"I say we're a pretty dishy bunch," said Sally. "No one gone to fat."

The sinews displayed by her black halter dress reflected long hours on the Gravitron. "We certainly look better than our mothers at this age. What do you put it down to?"

"The need to survive without a husband," said Daisy.

"Must you always take such a bleak view?" said Gina irritably. "I'd say it's because we're not defeated, like our mothers."

"I say it's the boys in Brazil and personal trainers," said Sally. She struck an Atlas pose. "Look, girls, delts, lats, muscle definition!"

Daisy flashed to her old partner-in-crime on the road to Harvard, the class nympho with the fastest diaphragm in the East. Cut to young matron. Cut to deserter wife. And now the New Entrepreneur with the fastest Filofax in the East, just profiled in *New Woman* in "A Business of Her Own." Sally encapsulated every convulsion of the age. It was exhausting even to think of it.

Daisy's eyes wandered over the others. Mia's alarming apricot hair, eyes lined in parrot blue, the flowered sari offering a generous scoop of perfect breasts. She was a gorgeous ruin with only her bosom intact, like that lone tower in Frankfurt that survived the blitzkrieg.

Diana Dew Hilliard with the same honey pageboy and barrette as in college, bronzed upper arms just going puddingy, a fading prom queen. She'd delivered on her threat to have a wonderful life.

From the middle of the couch Gina commanded the room. She was of no discernible age. Hair like some gold pelt, lips, suit, and nails the same beige — a confection tied up in cellophane. And in the flesh somehow reduced. Only TV brought her fully alive.

Sally poured Pellegrino into plastic glasses. "There's wine, too, for anyone who hasn't read the latest reports."

Damn health fascists, thought Daisy. After the soul-baring in Westlands, her mouth wanted gin. She inhaled the resinous dorm smell, hoping to conjure the fever and clamor of youth. Vivaldi's *Four Seasons* burst from an open door . . . A mist of Réplique . . . The muffled footfalls of girls in pink curlers and plaid bathrobes dashing down the hall for the phone. Then they were in the cab and boarding the train for Princeton Junction, Amory Blaine, the grab bag of happiness . . .

No, just a closed-up space in need of airing.

"Well, here we all are," said Sally rather grimly. "Except for Delphine. She *is* coming, isn't she?"

Everyone looked at Daisy, who glanced uneasily at the door. Since her return from Houston, no one could get a bead on Delphine. It was said she was big as a house, hitting the sauce again, looking *wild.* Then next thing, there she is in the Metro section of the *Times,* getting quoted on the latest plight of the homeless. There was even some cockamamy rumor about her having been a street person herself.

Daisy was kind of hoping Delphine wouldn't show. She wanted to shield her from the old crowd's fascination, which would be of the sort reserved for the crocodile boy or bearded lady. "I haven't seen Delphine. I doubt she'll show up," she said shortly.

"But Delphine *has* to come," protested Mia. "She was our ringleader, our beacon. I can still hear her going on about 'women like us,' how we were going to set the world on fire."

"Remember how she used to play the harpsichord naked? Anyone visiting Kober, it was the first thing they saw."

"Okay, girls," said Sally in a Delphine drawl, "let's all unhook our bras and talk about Schopenhauer."

"Wittgenstein," said Daisy over the laughter. "It was Wittgenstein."

The outside gloom invaded the room. McCracken shifted and groaned in its joints. With one move, they all looked toward the door.

Diana switched on a lamp. She smiled brightly. "I could really use a smoke. Would anyone mind if I smoked?"

"*I* would," said Gina in a way that closed the subject.

What's bugging *you*? thought Daisy. Gina ought to be celebrating. Over their annual lunch of mung beans and sprouts, she'd hinted at making it official with Kurt Zimmer. Maybe this exercise in nostalgia had been a lousy idea.

"Here, I'll open a window," said Franca. With a whistle, the wind blew the curtain straight into the room. A storm was gathering.

"I have an idea," said Sally in her new managerial mode. "While we're waiting for Delphine, let's go round the room and hear everyone's news. Me first." She made a birdlike preening motion with her long neck. "Seven years ago, I finally got divorced from Shelley. The divorce freed up all my energy. I expanded my catering gig from suburban garden parties to corporate clients, and business really took off. Now I'm starting a home-arts magazine on gardening, cooking, decorating — I have all the backing in place. This spring I did a trial segment on *Good Morning America* on making Easter eggs and baskets. Now my agent is negotiating with ABC for a regular slot. Remember in college how I used to grow pot in a planter and bake hash brownies?" she said giddily, the old Sally. "I guess I just made the most of my two modest talents. Who's next? Daisy?"

She'd get this over with fast. "I'm teaching English at Mercy College in New Jersey." No need to mention that she taught remedial compostion to the postliterate. Her novel lay in ruins, a slag heap of aborted inspirations. And she'd just managed the unusual feat of getting fired by her agent.

"I help run workshops at the Forum," said Mia in her weird English nanny accent. "The Forum's an offshoot of est. We teach people how to get out of their own way. I'll see if I can swing an invitation for you all for one of our weekend marathons. At the group rate."

"That would be nice," murmured Gina. She reported in a bored voice that she'd just interviewed "the Bushes" on *Frankly Speaking*.

As in George and Barbara? thought Daisy, longing for the old Delphine mischief.

"I've organized a program of volunteers to go to hospital nurseries and hug crack and AIDS babies," offered Franca.

"Just hug?" asked Gina.

"Just hug. You'd be amazed at the good it does both baby and hugger."

"Fascinating," said Gina.

"Dearie, we don't all have to be attorney general," said Franca amiably.

Diana was lighting a cigarette off the butt of the old one. "I raise General Jacqueminot roses and I have two golden retrievers and three wonderful grandchildren . . . and . . . and" — she sketched a figure eight with the cigarette, then brought her left fist to her eye — "Frank wants a divorce."

A chorus of Oh, Diana, no's.

"Last November he had to be in New York to see a client. He took me to the Rainbow Room — sort of our place, it's where he proposed — and told me he's fallen in love with a litigator in his firm. Now all our old friends avoid me as if I were infectious. Though they see Frank and — the woman." Diana ground out her cigarette. "I said to Frank, 'Why the Rainbow Room? Why did you take me to the Rainbow Room to tell me?' And he said, 'I thought we could at least have a nice evening.' The thing is, he really meant it. He couldn't see why I had to ruin the evening." She looked confused. "And then I couldn't, either."

Daisy heard a voice float up from the past: *Lord knows how y'all will end up. And I'm going to have a wonderful life.*

"She's not even a bimbo, or anything. She's a ranked squash player, and bills millions of dollars."

"Now listen, Diana, you can turn this into a positive experience," said Mia, donning her Forum hat. "Use it as an opportunity to grow. Consider that you were addicted. Why not take all that love you used to give Frank and give it to yourself."

Diana stared at her dully.

"Just imagine," Mia went on. "For the first time in your life — the first time ever—you'll be *independent*."

Diana opened her eyes wide in horror, then burst into tears. "I'd rather be married to a wife beater!" she sobbed.

At that moment the door opened and the wind sucked the curtain hard against the screen, then blew it straight into the room.

In the doorway stood Delphine.

She was wild and gray and fat, *voluminous,* with a harrowing beauty, Brunhilde come striding over the crags through storm and flood and fire. Her hair was caught above the ears with combs and streamed over her shoulders. She wore a yellow muumuu and scuffed tan sandals.

"Wife beater?" she echoed. "Good grief." She walked unsteadily into the room, clipping an end table with her right hip. A bottle of Gordon's bobbed in her Mexican wool shoulder bag, a relic from the fifties Village. "Am I in the right place? I expected something jollier — straw boaters, school songs, champagne flowing . . ."

A chorus of greetings.

"Pellegrino?" offered Gina.

"Thank you, no, I brought my own." Delphine sank heavily onto a chair catty-cornered to Franca and pulled a quart of Gordon's vodka from her bag. "Snort, anyone?" Poised to swig from the bottle, she seemed to think better of it and poured the vodka into the plastic glass Franca handed her.

"*So* sorry we don't have tonic," said Gina.

"And I'm *sooo* sorry I missed your speech," said Delphine, matching Gina's tone. She flashed her smile at the group. The bluey shadows around her eyes gave her a vampish allure. The only woman, thought Daisy, who could look both gorgeous and like Queen of the Bag Ladies.

"Well, well, a toast to old times. Let's all unhook our bras and talk about the meaning of life." Delphine knocked back her drink. She noticed Diana's tear-stained face across the room. "What's this about a wife beater?"

Franca filled her in.

"Oh, that," Delphine intoned in the familiar honk. "Join the club, dearie. Every woman thinks it's only her, but it's happening across America at the rate of a hundred per minute." She loudly chased phlegm around her throat. "Who woulda thunk it, Di. You and I started from opposite points on the spectrum. Yet we both ended up in the same place, what with the death of morality and men fucking their daughters."

Her eye caught on Mia, to her left. "My God, your hair! Where did they *find* such a color? It's so . . . *Cabaret*."

Daisy saw the muscles working in Gina's clenched jaw.

Delphine refilled her glass. "Well, Diana, surely there's a nice widower in the wings, some fusty old colonel, who'd be happy to jump into the breach."

"Such tact," said Gina between her teeth.

Delphine looked at Gina. "How do you do that — speak without moving your mouth?"

"C'mon, none of that," said Sally. "I came here to mellow out and wallow in nostalgia, dammit. Delphine, stop destroying your liver and tell us about your exciting job."

"Actually, I'm writing a book."

"You always were the most talented of any of us," said Franca.

"It's called *The Thinking Gal's Guide to Firearms*. 'Cause those scumbags should all be lined up against a wall and shot. Just" — she aimed her index finger — "shot. I mean, they've set the tone of lawlessness. We women have no choice. D'you know how *easy* it is to buy a gun? In New York you hit the pawnshops on Eighth Avenue. In Houston you could buy a gun in any hunting store. A girl wants something dainty and feminine she can tuck into her purse with the tampons. A twenty-two automatic. Maybe a twenty-five. In Houston the store owner will actually teach you how to fire it. You don't slap the trigger, you need to *crawl* the hammer back." She eyeballed them, as though to divulge a capital secret. "Princess Di took lessons in marksmanship at a police weapons training center."

No one knew where to look. Daisy kept her eyes focused on the window. A group of alumnae in light dresses fluttered by, like spirits from reunions past.

Delphine crossed her arms in the old chest lock. "Face it, girls, we're casualties of history. Farmed out to the soap factory in the middle of the party." She hiccoughed. "Our profession was wife. Then we got laid off — Au revoir, honey, thanks for the ride. At fifty-plus, we're out on our ass, with our memories. Our regrets. Our king-size beds. Our empty houses that we can't afford to keep. Our 'little jobs' that can't keep us . . ."

McCracken shifted and groaned on its foundation. Diana sat doubled over, arms wrapped around her ribs.

"Wine," said Daisy abruptly. "Did I hear something about wine?"

"Good thinking!" cried Sally. She hauled out a magnum of Chablis from under the coffee table and started filling glasses. "Oh, damn! Phew!" She fanned her face with her hand. "Another 'hot,' and I can't do hormones on account of my fibroids. How's *this* gonna look on *Good Morning America?*"

"No money is worse," said Daisy. "What is more precarious than being out there at fifty with no significant money?"

Mia said, "I read somewhere that female MBAs get fifty-four thousand bucks one year after graduation. I'm twice their age and I don't earn half that!"

Sally upended her glass. "Naah, the worst is having a hot-flash attack while you're trying to get laid. I was thrashing around in the sack with this whale with a huge potbelly, and he's trying to put on a Trojan, but he's having trouble finding his dick he's so fat, and meanwhile *I'm* worried I'll be too, you know, *dry?* but I'm also slimy with sweat, having a major flash attack, fireworks, it's fucking Pearl Harbor. Then the guy loses his erection."

"Remember when it wouldn't stay *down?*"

"Thank God I'm married," said Franca. "You don't have to deal with sex at all!"

Laughter. Even Daisy laughed. Especially Daisy.

"When I push the covers off at night, my boyfriend goes berserk," she said. "He can't even acknowledge what's happening."

"Of course not. One gray pubic hair and *they* have visions of mortality."

"Y'know how *they* talk about us? 'Old pussy,' they say."

"Thank you, Norman Mailer, such a way with words."

"My last date was this grizzled anthropologist with white hair," said Mia. "He told me he isn't aroused by women who aren't still fertile. The guy was decrepit!" She looked around in disbelief. "I feel I've woken up on a strange new planet. A village of women with all the men gone. Welcome to Gal City."

"Except they're not making war, the men," said Delphine. "They're making love with their daughters."

"The crazy part is so many women asked for it," said Sally. "Remember all that consciousness-raising in the seventies? Remember the *term*? In my CR group we used to cheer and egg each other on when someone dumped her husband. Little did we realize: the women who ditched their husbands were hurled into poverty for life. When I go back to Paoli I sometimes see this crazed woman from the group driving around in a battered Country Squire. I think, There but for the grace of God . . . Hell, that *was* me. Until my business took off. Until I got lucky."

"*I* didn't ask for it," said Diana in a small voice. "All I ever asked was to keep on loving Frank."

A little whiffle snore. Delphine sagged sideways toward Franca, mouth ajar.

"Whatever happened, I'd like to know, to sisterhood?" Daisy rushed on, partly to distract from Delphine. "For a moment there was this great surge of female solidarity. We were all going to be each other's chosen family, a community of friends always there for each other, remember?"

She looked at Gina. Gina stared stonily ahead, her spiky black lashes like barricades.

"Now, so many women are isolated and cut off — anyone who's not cozily coupled. It's exactly what we were warned against in the fifties! Okay, it's not Somalia. But it's a famine of the soul. Death by invisibility. How did we end up so alone? Yeah I know, I'm 'with' Sandy. But I'm one male midlife tantrum away from Siberia."

Mia looked around and smiled. "God*damn*, it feels good to talk the truth. Part of what's making us crazy is the conspiracy of silence. Just stay cheery and chipper and pop your Prozac and baby-sit the grand-children. Better yet, just go the fuck away." She shut her eyes. "I haven't slept with a man in three years. I feel so juicy. I sometimes think I'm going to start screaming and never be able to stop."

"Hang in there, honey," said Sally. "I ran into Helen Gurley Brown at a fund-raiser the other night, and she told me about this woman who got laid at ninety-two."

"Listen," said Mia, "if I ever met someone I could care for, you know what? I'd run as fast as I could in the opposite direction."

You people make me sick.

Heads jerked toward Gina.

Delphine shuddered awake and blinked her eyes. She reached over her belly for the Gordon's.

"You made your choice," said Gina. "Who ever stopped you from doing what you wanted? No one. Absolutely no one. So I guess you'd better just live with it. It's called being a good sport. Delphine, why don't you put down your glass and walk it off around the block. The self-destructive act is not cute anymore. Look at you. What are you doing? Why are you doing this to yourself?"

Delphine looked around clownishly, like the class cutup.

"When I think" — Gina threw up her hands — "of all you had going for you. A shot at editor in chief, a chance in a million. And you walked away from it, you walked clean away."

"Coulda been a contenduh," Delphine mumbled.

"Her husband did get transferred to Houston," said Diana timidly.

"Commuter marriages weren't exactly in style twenty years ago," added Sally.

Gina shrugged a silk shoulder. "Well. I guess you can't have it every which way, can you." She sipped her Pellegrino.

Anger rose in Daisy's throat. "Who're *you* to be so righteous?"

"You're another one," Gina shot back. "You're blowing it with Sandy and blaming it on ratios —"

"*Me* blowing it? I'm a fucking Florence Nightingale, a one-woman sex clinic. What would you know about it?"

"You're just like Delphine; you had a shot at a great job. But no, you hightailed it to the boonies."

"Daisy is a college professor, after all," said Franca, ever the little Dutch girl plugging up the dike.

Gina looked blank; if it wasn't fame and power, it didn't register.

"I had a severely injured child and I needed a secure income with medical benefits," Daisy snapped. "I couldn't afford to gamble. Shit, why should I justify myself to you?"

"You could've stayed in New York *and* had the income and benefits," said Gina smoothly. "Right after you left, I had lunch with Andra Cassidy. Andra said to me, 'I don't get it. I offered Daisy a great job — a column plus longer pieces — and a contract. It's as much security as you get in this world. But she was dead set on leaving.' You did the same thing with dancing. You were magical on stage. You threw that away, too. So don't go on about casualties of history. You had the talent. You just didn't have the guts to run with it."

"What could you possibly understand?" said Daisy, voice trembling. "The only thing you've ever cared about is your own advancement." Murder sang in her hands. Gina had exposed the nerve and blown air on it.

"Well, maybe *you*'re looking out for number one, too," Gina said to Daisy. "Why do I have the eerie feeling that you convened us all here today so you could gather material?"

Daisy stared at Gina, fingers twitching, not seeing. A fine idea percolating through her. Why not start the novel here, with the reunion, in the present? Then cut to the past and each woman's story. Zigzag back to the present and the wrong side of fifty. Maybe here was the shape she'd been looking for. She couldn't end, though, with a catalogue of botched lives . . .

Delphine cleared her throat loudly. She looked at Gina, shadowed eyes glowing dangerously. "Now, Gina, you are the class success, so no disrespect intended. But your work is dreck. That Special you did with George and Barbara? *Aaahh,* I ran screaming from the room."

Sally clapped the heels of her hands to her head. "Would you guys give it a rest? It's just like in college, you're monopolizing all the attention! And you are ruining our reunion!"

"You and the lies you propagate, you're everything that's vile about network television," Delphine went on, ignoring Sally. "You're what's toxic about this country."

Gina eyed Delphine as she might a cantankerous guest. "I may not meet your high standards. But you might want to thank me anyhow. For getting you edited out of a film on the homeless in Central Park."

Horrified murmurs.

"Nice, Gina, real classy," said Daisy.

"You just spew out the lies Cap'n Bushy wants to feed the public," Delphine barreled on, beyond humiliation. "And the smarmy way you play Mother Confessor and suck up to the power. Your 'patriotism' during the war in Iraq." She threw back her head. "AAAHH, RUN SCREAMING FROM THE ROOM! Hell, no one's seen your face in years, it's so far up the behind of Cap'n Bushy. You're not a journalist. You're an Establishment toady sellout star fucker. And I'll tell you something else."

"I think not."

"The moment you made it, you dumped your old friends."

Gina looked around the couch for her things.

"And maybe, Ginny, *you're* not a real good sport either. In fact, maybe you're the worst sport in this room. You wanna know why you're such a rotten sport?"

Gina shrugged on her jacket.

"You're doing your Ninja number on us because you're still furious that Barney dropped dead. I'll tell you something Jake once told me, after Barney left Houston."

Gina froze, her face a mask.

"Jake said that Barney knew exactly how sick he was when he returned to New York. He came back to you because he needed someone to die with. He came to you to die. Barney never wanted you when he could live."

"You broken-down bag lady —"

"Fag hag." Delphine pitched forward and spat at her.

The spit landed in a spray on the couch and also hit Gina's cheek.

Gina seized an ashtray off the coffee table and hurled it at Delphine, but Delphine shifted sideways and the ashtray sailed into the wall and fell to the floor with a clunk.

"*Stop it, both of you. I can't stand this!*" Daisy was on her feet, fists clenched. She looked from Gina to Delphine, tears streaking her face. "I just — can't — bear — it."

Gina sat canted forward, staring unseeing into space, her cheek still wet. Then her mask melted, like a spooky special effect, into the face of rapture. Everyone watched, mesmerized.

"Barney is the best thing that happened to me," said Gina in a thrilling low voice. "I would have died if Barney hadn't loved me."

No one moved or spoke. McCracken sighed mightily through its timbers.

Gina seized her glass off the coffee table and held it up. "Oh, hell, make me a spritzer someone."

The room exhaled.

"You bitches," said Sally, looking from Gina to Delphine to Daisy. "Still hogging all the attention."

"Yes, it's my turn," said Franca. "I came here today because I once loved you all, you were the best friends I've ever had. Since college my friends have been social fixtures. Mommies, other political wives. My only true friends are my children. But we do have to let our children go, don't we. The truth is, I've missed you. I came back here because I want you all in my life again."

To old ties! Everyone toasting and chattering and laughing.

What I want now is revenge, came Delphine's voice over the babel. "To revenge!" She lifted her handbag off the table and cradled it on her lap. "I want Jake drawn, quartered, and ruined — of course, he's already bankrupt."

Daisy shot her an uneasy look. She had a good notion of just how far Delphine might carry the blood and thunder.

"No, no, that sort of revenge is tacky," said Mia. "And where does it leave you? What does it get *you?* No, the best revenge is simply to become" — she leaned forward, boobs swinging — "marvelous."

"Happy," said Franca. "Happiness is the best revenge. Okay, so we've missed a lot of the fun. But we're not helpless. We've got a few resources. Lately I've been thinking, there's so little time left, only a few good years before we're really in for it. These years are a gift. They're like a free zone, almost, on the other side of life."

Delphine had turned, fascinated, to watch Franca, her face a field of warring emotions. " 'The second half of joy' " said Delphine. "That's what Emily Dickinson called it. 'The second half of joy.' "

Yes, let's make whatever time is left a celebration!

A celebration! Pour me some vodka!

"I'm starting right now," said Franca, blue eyes shining. "I just realized that I don't have to answer to anyone anymore. It's sort of a booby prize for being so insignificant."

"True, since we barely register on the charts, we can do whatever we goddamn please," said Mia. "Become eccentric old biddies, *les Folles de Bronxville*."

Disgusting . . . Outrageous . . . A lesbian — No, I already did that in college.

Franca held up her hand. "My daughter Angelica plans to devote her life to reforming the health care system. Me, I've devoted my life to reforming men. I now have to admit that by any standard I've been a failure. So, ladies" — laughing giddily — "I hereby announce my retirement."

Hear! Hear! Where's the gold watch?

"I finally found a man who doesn't need reforming. I can take him right off the rack."

Oh, Franca, do tell.

"For months I've agonized. I can't do this *again*. The disruption, the mess, the lawyers. He's also — ancient."

"Victor Hugo could get it up at eighty," offered Delphine.

"Just so," laughed Franca. "There are other advantages. As Jamie said to me, I'm too old to screw around." She raised her glass. "You people are the first to know it. Because you've inspired me. I'm leaving my husband to elope with my seventy-five-year-old soul mate!"

Daisy drained her glass. *I'll drink to that.* So Ben was free. A rush, as though she'd busted through a dark rabbit warren and stood on a peak high in the Swiss Alps, among snowy cones dancing into the distance — Oh, you fool. Wanting Ben was like an ache in an amputated limb.

"I have a confession," said Diana, looking around the room with a sheepish smile. Her lashes fluttered. "Delphine, dear, you weren't entirely off the mark. You see, there actually *is* a fusty old colonel. Well, retired admiral, to be exact! He keeps asking me . . . to *tea*."

Well, there's a beginning! To the admiral! A toast to Diana and the admiral.

"I could care less if they're old farts or young studs," said Sally. "Getting rich is the best revenge — Who needs sex? Money!" She ran her hands over her breasts. "I want to rub it into my skin and lick it and stick it in all my orifices. I'm getting richer by the minute, too. Call me the Doyenne of Domesticity! And doing a lot better than Shelley. His law firm's down the tubes, what with business off in mergers and acquisitions. Guess the times have passed him by. I hope his new bride won't walk out on him when she gets the picture. Seduced and abandoned, he'd be a terrible role model for the children."

"I'm going to buy a little house in the country," said Mia. "And garden and have animals and keep an open house, where my friends — you, all of you! — can come and hang out and recharge. It'll be a commune, the one we imagined in the glory days of feminism."

"And you'll install a handyman lover, the local Mellors," said Daisy.

"*Hell no!* I've spent my life's blood agonizing over what kind of mood some asshole was going to wake up in. C'mon, *enough!* I recently went to Jack LaLanne, and this guy was lying there, straining to lift a gigantic barbell, and he was making these noises: growls and snarls and grunts, like a wild boar taking a shit, and then . . . *barks!* He was actually barking! And I thought, Behold a man."

Gina was waving her hand in the air. Was she actually tipsy? Daisy wondered. "My turn!" she said. "Professor Zimmer has got it in his head that the world would be a better place if I married him." She turned toward Delphine. "We seem to recycle men, it's our contribution to the environment."

Nervous laughter; everyone was still terrorized by Gina and Delphine.

"Of course, it makes perfect sense to marry Kurt," Gina went on. "But oh dear, he's like the wolf in Red Riding Hood. Underneath the P.C. rap, it's the same old Kurt, an unreconstructed fifties man. He's already pestering me to take time off, do it *his* way. That old battle makes me want to curl up and go to sleep. Besides" — the eerie radiance again — "well, let's just say I have a promise to keep."

Daisy felt the skin prickle on the back of her neck.

"The truth is, since Barney," Gina went on, "I feel an overwhelming desire to *not* make sense. In fact, what I really want is to set up house with my best friend! Renato is the perfect partner. Supportive, utterly loyal, grand escort, superb cook, cheering section, masseur. He's everything a woman could want. The perfect wife. Face it, I've always been a queer bird. He's queer. We'll be two old queers together!"

Hear! Hear! To Gina and the perfect wife.

Gina turned to Delphine. "By the way, fag hag isn't quite accurate. Renato, uh, likes to *watch*. I doubt he's exchanged any fluids in twenty years. Which gives him a good shot at outliving me!"

A somber moment, as everyone digested that.

"Well, guess it's *my* turn to play," Delphine drawled. "The truth is I just swung by here as a detour. I was actually on my way to Jake's bimbo's place to right the balance. Fire a shot for womankind."

Glasses froze midair; Franca shot Daisy an alarmed look.

"But I guess I'll have to leave that sort of work to the next Jean Harris — I'm sure there'll be one. I seem to have lost the momentum. It turns out I really stopped off here to say good-bye. So" — she raised her glass — "good-bye, Jake. It's been a great show." Her hand remained in the air. "Oh, why is it all so fucking hard?" she said brokenly.

She drank and set the plastic glass down on the coffee table. "I guess I couldn't desert my little boyfriend either," she went on. "I don't think he'd enjoy the visits to Bedford Hills. Though it wasn't *my* idea to become romantically entangled," she said with the old belligerence. "Whit just sort of ambushed me one night on the stairs. And voilà, I'm responsible for someone's happiness. Even though — I can see it from here — Whit will cut out when I'm sixty and he's forty-five. But why worry about the future? There's only *now* now. And so much work to do. Ah, such epiphanies . . ." She raised the back of her hand to her forehead.

Then she eyed Gina mischievously. "Actually, Gina, you're the best deterrent. I mean, when I think of the fun you could have had with my story! Former Socialite Goes Gunning for Ex, et cetera. Or maybe not! Maybe you'd say, Not another woman gone round the bend for love. What a *bore*. The thought of you dismissing me as a cliché — it's the best deterrent a girl could want!"

Gina looked uncertain how to react.

"Oh c'mon, Gina, just joking. A joke, Ginny, a joke! Sort of."

"I wish I could turn my life around, like you all," said Daisy quickly, sensing the need to divert the current. "And come steaming into the free zone. Tell Sandy to go stuff it. Throw down my crutches and walk, ta-da! But the trouble with heroic gestures is the morning after. When the band has stopped playing, and you have to live with the consequences. And I'm not heroic. I just want to muddle through. So I'm gonna play a waiting game, even if I have to eat shit now and then, and hope that Sandy gets so used to seeing me around he'll give up his adolescent fantasies. Which he couldn't do much about anyway. He's not a bad sort, just majorly impaired. The fact is Sandy needs me, even if he can't admit it."

Hiss . . . Boo . . . Fists pounded on the coffee table. Oh c'mon, Daiz, you gotta do better than that.

She shook her head no. "I know myself. I'd turn into one of those crazies, talking to herself on the checkout line."

Phooey! Whatta cop-out! You gotta come up with something better. Even if you change your mind tomorrow morning.

Hell, she'd better give them something. She sipped at her vodka. *You brought us all here as material.* Well, yes, Gina. Maybe so. And maybe end like this: zigzag to the present and the wrong side of fifty. And then the friends reinvent themselves in the free zone.

"Well, said Daisy, laughing, holding up her hand for quiet, "since you're all such bullies. I guess I'd better go home and write the story of our lives."

Chapter 29

TWO MONTHS LATER, Daisy and Sandy were throwing a brunch at his house in Pound Ridge. The hottest Sunday of August, temps hitting ninety-eight in the shade, and everyone sunk in a vegetable torpor — even the Nova Scotia was perspiring. Though she ordinarily loved domestic routines, Daisy kept sneaking looks at her watch and privately wishing the guests Godspeed.

On Wednesday of that week she had messengered to Andra Cassidy the revised two hundred pages of her novel, along with a ten-page, single-spaced outline. Since June she'd worked without respite, going on five hours' sleep a night, fueled by caffeine and some unholy joy. She had run with the story shape she'd hit on at her . . . class Götterdämmerung. She'd also semifollowed Sandy's advice. Forked in some fancy plotting, what Hollywood called high concept. Delivered happy endings. A lotta pluck, a little luck, and the world is yours. Why clobber America's readers with unvarnished truth when pink slips were descending on them like locusts . . . With the big push over, she collapsed on any horizontal surface, as though drained of blood. Now came the waiting to hear, a ritual rivaling in exquisite suspense the wait to hear a biopsy report. Lately, so went the horror stories in publishing, unless you were a brand name, agents and editors took months to respond to a manuscript, or never responded at all; might as well pitch something into the space beyond a black hole . . . On Friday evening, she and Sandy drove as usual to Pound Ridge for the weekend. As they slowed for the Ardsley toll and Sandy switched on the radio to "All Things Considered," she was fingered by an urge to open the car door and walk over the grass divider in a straight line to nowhere.

"We're short on food because Daisy went and bought shrimp salad at Fairway. And she *knows* that the Salkinds are kosher."

She tuned in Sandy and the sound of Banter Lite, her private term for his ribbing. Sandy ribbed her a great deal. It had become his preferred mode of recognizing her presence in the environment.

"Blame it on the tome. When Daisy's writing the tome she goes into a trance. Hears voices. She actually talks to herself."

Leo Salkind chuckled. Sandy the *tummler*. He'd just made everyone roar with a story about taking Jules to the vet.

"I keep telling her, for God's sake, write something commercial for a change. Like a thriller about a serial killer with a female detective. And make the detective a lesbian. The killer, too."

Underneath the table Jules found her leg and started humping it. Daisy thought, with one well-aimed kick . . .

She couldn't trust herself. Without a word, she left the dining room and locked herself in the bathroom. She climbed into the empty bathtub. Lay back, letting the porcelain cool her arms and calves. Lifted a section of the Sunday *Times* off the hamper. No danger of wetting the paper.

A knocking on the bathroom door. "D'you know how long you've been in there?" came Sandy's voice.

"Sorry, I have heat stroke."

"Well, *we* have guests. Or had you forgotten? What are you doing in there? Have you gone mad?"

He mumbled something else, but she wasn't listening, she was riveted by a name: *Ben Marshak*. A story on page fourteen. Her eyes skated around the newsprint: "Small private plane made a crash landing this morning in an industrial complex near Teterboro Airport . . . No one killed, the authorities said . . . The six passengers sustained minor injuries . . . Among the passengers Ben Marshak, the Congressman from New York who has recently submitted his resignation after the check-kiting scandal . . . Passengers residents of Manhattan . . . The plane, a two-engine, six-seater Piper Aztec, took off at 8:30 P.M. last night from the airport in Teterboro."

Daisy lay very still with her eyes closed, the *Times* forming a tent over her chest. She was husbanding energy for what she knew she would do next.

Now she moved swiftly and with economy, like someone bailing out of the *Titanic*. She fetched her L. L. Bean bag from the closet. Emptied into it the contents of the oak bureau's top drawer, the single drawer Sandy had allotted her in his bedroom, since any more space would have signaled commitment. She threw in her toothbrush and moisturizer. Then she walked, bag in hand, into the dining room.

"What, what's this with the luggage," said Sandy. "You going on a trip?" His dark hair was plastered to his forehead in a way that always made her think bed.

"I'm leaving."

"Oh, are you? How about clearing the table first and bringing in the strudel."

"Tell me, Sandy, what makes you think you can talk to me like that?"

A hole of silence.

"Uh, could we, uh, discuss this later? Sorry, everyone." His compressed lips had turned white.

"There is no more discussion, Sandy. Finito. We talk and we talk, yet nothing ever changes. 'Cause you're a bullshit kind of guy."

"*Later*. I said *later*."

"There is no 'later.' I can't afford it anymore, getting picked apart and belittled. You're always picking, nicking, whittling away at me. I'm writing a 'tome.' I'm too old. I don't have a power job or a power serve, or rosebud lips, like the girl of your dreams. Oh, let me count the ways I fall short! Talk about abuse! You don't strike me, you batter with words. I tell you, every time you withhold love, you batter me. I'm one giant bruise. Beaten to a pulp, even if you can't see it. You've robbed my concentration, my belief in myself, my sense of worth. That revolting dog of yours gets more love. I've had it. You can just fuck off. I'm tired of waiting for you to figure out if you're willing to settle for me!"

Sweat ran into her eyes. She saw a wash of faces, mouths opened in an *o*. Suddenly she realized someone was clapping. It was one of the wives. Eve Salkind had gotten up from her chair and stood there, loudly clapping.

Happily, none of the guests' cars were blocking Sandy's Volvo. Daisy felt under the front seat, where Sandy kept the keys.

She backed out the driveway.

People burst from the farmhouse door, jerky and fast, making gestures in her direction. With a screech of tires, she turned the car down Pond View Road. Eventually she hit 172. She didn't miss him already.

They kept an apartment, she knew, on West Eighty-sixth Street. She had always known where they lived; he was the orienting pole on her compass.

Franca, she knew, had moved to the Cosmopolitan Club.

Hand trembling, she punched 411. Then she hung up and paged through the phone book. Like a teenager, she couldn't have said his name aloud.

He wouldn't be home. He would be off with his spare wife. Getting rehabbed at Rusk Institute. He would be chilly and brusque — No, not Ben. Over the years, Ben had become in her imaginings everything good. Far worse, he would be nice. Don't risk it. How much of your life can you toss in one afternoon?

"Hello," Ben said.

Her heart raced, her mouth had gone dry. They ran through the pleasantries. He sounded weak, his Boston accent more pronounced, and he didn't seem especially surprised by her call.

"I was hoping I could see you."

"I've been in an accident."

"I know."

"I'm pretty beat up. I'd be rotten company."

"I know."

A moment. "Could I ask you, then, to come here?"

She dressed carefully, as if for some gala performance. She put on a cream silk teddy and tap-dancing pants, and a black organdy dress with tiny lavender and rust flowers. She stood in front of the bathroom mirror and considered the possible scenarios. They would wander off, hand in hand, over the gorse-covered moors. (God, was it possible she'd learned nothing?) She would drive a stake through her romantic heart. They would end up with something wildly unsatisfactory in between, the way life usually worked it.

He looked smaller and pitifully fragile. One eyelid drooped at half-mast, and his smile was lopsided — nerve damage in his cheek, he explained — and his hair was sparser and grayer. Otherwise he was Ben.

They sat on the living room couch. "Can I get you something? Some wine? Yes, let me get you some wine." Ben hobbled off to the kitchen. From behind, with his pants hanging off him, he looked like a starved cat.

She was glad for his absence. It allowed her to unstick herself from the ceiling. The couch faced away from the window and the view, as though no one here had given much thought to interior design. A cup with congealed coffee stood on the coffee table beside a saucer containing crusts of toast. An odor of bachelor disarray. Daisy recognized a Stickley buffet from Franca's Peter days. On it stood silver-framed photos. She decided not to look.

Ben came limping back with a bottle of wine and two glasses. He kept his hurt shoulder hitched up in a shrug. They sat side by side on the couch and talked about children, safe subject. Her Corey and Miranda, his Angelica. No mention of his second child. The gathering storm cast the room in a pewter light that resembled no recognizable hour.

"We were lucky," he said of his accident, she registering the "we." "I'm sort of holed up here. A lot has happened. A lot of things came apart at once."

Suddenly she wondered if he knew the details of her chat with Franca.

"I'm going to be okay, though. The doctor says I'm a fighter. Says I have to be patient — easy for *him* to say. I've got all sorts of things in the pipeline. I may end up living in Geneva, of all places. I'm talking to a firm with a branch there."

She wasn't ready to hear his career plans. "Ben, you must think it strange, my calling you after so many years. But when I read about the accident I wanted — I had to know that you were all right."

He turned toward her stiffly and winced. "Thank you, that's really kind of you. So thoughtful. Thank you."

Now she winced. Okay. Information. She'd come on a fact-finding mission. Forget the Eternal Return, this was the nervous nineties.

"I gather you know about Franca and me," he said neutrally. "We parted as friends. No reason not to. She told me you two have reconciled. I was surprised. You always were a sore subject. To her you were, well, the ultimate threat."

"Was I?" she said, feigning innocence. Meaning *am* I?

Suddenly he stood. "I want to play you something." He put a CD in the stereo and limped back to the couch.

A song of love remembered filled the room with its poisoned honey. Daisy smiled. Brahms's *Liebeslieder Walzer*.

"I think that's why I proposed to you on our first date. Wow, did you snow me with all that 'kultcha,' me a yokel from the wrong part of Brookline."

"I was an arrogant little fool." She added, "Actually it was two weeks later that you proposed. On the hall phone in Titsworth."

"No, you've got that wrong."

"You sure?"

"Would a man forget such a thing?"

Something had altered. It was the wine and the silver half light of their enchanted space, and the Brahms, these songs drenched in regret that only now could they understand. He turned his head with difficulty. He looked at her with his ruined squinty gaze, thin mouth in a crooked smile. She felt the heat coming off his skin.

"You were dreadful back then —"

"Dreadful," she echoed. "We were in some kind of strange combat." Then, frowning, "But who won?"

"For a while I believed I won. Now I wonder if maybe we both lost." A moment. "Everything's turned so ugly and sour and sad."

"Do you still hate me?"

His eyes flicked away. "You know, I didn't want to see anyone. I just wanted to crawl into my cave and hide." His eyes returned to her. "Now nothing feels so right as you being here."

Outside, the first heavy raindrops hit the asphalt. They swam in that medium of desire where it seemed as though they had already touched, and would touch any moment, and were touching now.

"Think of it, Daisy, after all these years."

"All those years."

He looked at her, transfixed. She shivered. She knew that he saw a radiant, mocking girl in 1957.

"Oh, Daisy."

"I know."

The taste of him, that she remembered, and his oddly jointed thumb, and this, and this, too.

"Can we? I mean, can you?"

Smiling, he said, "We'll see what happens."

She followed him to a small guest room. Avoiding the bedroom, she noted. They stood before the window in the summer heat, hearing the rustle of rain in the street below, smelling the sooty freshness. This was the good time. They were the same height, comrades, their hands reading each other, gingerly, because of his shoulder. He buried his face in her neck and they stood like that for a long while, trembling. His pauses, that, too, she remembered. They tore at each other but were forced to slow down. Everything hurt him. Slowly they eased off his shirt. He still wore goofy red bikini underpants. She remembered the hair on his chest. His cock aloft like a child's play sword. He stood looking at her. "You're exactly as I remembered." Blind to the evidence.

He'd had a lifetime to learn love. The idea made her crazy with grief and desire. Shame fell away, they couldn't say where he began and she left off, they were exiles reaching for home. He pressed into her. Wait, she pleaded. Wanting it never to be over.

"Yes."

"Are we dreaming?"

"Uh-uh."

"Wait. Those things."

"Really?"

"We should."

"Like the old days!"

Laughter.

"Where?"

"Here, in the drawer."

"No, let's not. I could die happily now."

"We're just beginning."

"I'm too happy. I'm going to cry."

"Don't cry, my darling."

"Wait —"
"Yes —"

She sat in her teddy and tap-dancing pants at a table by the window, sipping coffee and talking too fast and filling the air with plans. Ben stood looking down at Eighty-sixth Street. Horns blared. A fight broke out between two cabbies, yelling in a mysterious language. The streets were flooded from the rain storm, unleashing the usual New York bedlam.

"Come to Zermatt at the end of August," Daisy said. "Corey and Miranda and I are planning an assault on the Matterhorn. The McHenry Expedition. We've been planning it for years. We're not climbing to the summit, of course. But there's a glorious, and manageable, hike to the Hörnlihutte. That's the jumping-off point for the real mountaineers. On the way up, we'll get some of the best views in the Alps. And the mountains are the perfect place to convalesce."

Ben ran his hand through his damp hair. Abruptly he went and sat on the rumpled bed. "Daisy, it can't be."

The cabbies were cursing each other in Yugoslavian. Or Bulgarian. Or maybe Serbo-Croatian. A siren bleated, then cut off right beneath the window.

Wait. Stay with it. This is worth fighting for. "Of course, I forgot," she said. "Your . . . your companion. And child. I know the whole story."

"Oh, Franca," Ben said irritably.

"Hell, why not invite them to Switzerland. We'll be an extended family. Kinda warmed-over sixties, but that's okay. We missed the sixties anyway."

A weary sigh. "Actually, that came apart too. Call it a clean sweep. My 'companion' and I — her name's Nydia Garcia" — Daisy recognized the name from a race for Congress — "we've gone our separate ways. She ended up hating me. Because I could never leave the marriage. When it came right down to it, I guess I was the loyal husband to the end. Nydia got involved in local politics, at my urging, through my connections. I created her," he said with a touch of anger. "And then she blossomed. She's making a run for the incumbent's seat in South Carolina. Once she found her calling, it became clear that she valued me mainly for my contacts. Fair is fair. Now that I'm political

poison, I'm out of the picture. She'll invent a new past for the résumé.
If she runs for president, which wouldn't surprise me, the dirt diggers
will be in pig heaven. We have a son. Of course, I wish her well."

He paused. She noticed that she'd forgotten to breathe.

"So you see, it's not Nydia. It's me. After everything that's happened, I despise myself. I'm starting from ground zero. It's like being
twenty-two all over again —"

"But you're not twenty-two! There's no time left, Ben! Time's moving so fast it's like the future is hurling itself at us."

"That's what's so awful. What could I offer you now?"

A moment. "Everything I could want," she said.

Lamely: "I don't even have a job."

"What does it matter? You'll find one." Hands clasped on her knees,
she leaned toward him. "Ben, don't you feel it too? This, us, last night.
We're the last thing in the world that makes sense."

He threw her a tortured look. "Too much time has passed, too many
years. We missed it, Daisy. We lost it. Why kid ourselves? It's too late."
Pettishly: "Maybe I'll never stop being angry."

"Bullshit!"

"I associate you with pain."

"No, that's not it. What —"

"I can't tell you," he said sheepishly.

She waited.

He sighed. "When I fell in love with you, I couldn't conceive of ever
wanting another woman. I was certain I would always be faithful to
you. Now I don't believe that I could make that kind of commitment
again. Not to you or any woman. The only thing that makes sense to
me now is freedom. When I was married to Franca, you see, I had that
freedom."

The words were mere sounds. The sense followed after.

"But I could never live that way with you," Ben went on. "You
mean — you've meant — far too much to me."

It shattered then, the bright thing she'd been trying to build. For
several long moments she sat in the cruel comfort of clarity.

"So, this 'freedom' — after everything — this is what you want?
This . . . narcissism and catting around, this is what you, as a man and
a human being, really and truly want? The acme of what you aspire
to?"

She stood and looked down at him.

"You know, Ben, you used to say, long ago — you used to say to me, 'Daisy, you don't know the man I am.' Well, now I know. Yes, I'm afraid I do. I now know the man you've become."

She pulled on her dress and looked around for her bag. He watched her from the bed, small and dark and squinty, like some changeling.

"Another thing," Daisy said. "Sometimes it's better not to win. Because I don't want the man you've become. I wanted the other man, the one I've dreamt about for thirty years. But maybe he never existed. Good-bye, Ben. I wish you lots of luck." As the dirty old man of two continents, she added to herself.

She walked to the door and turned to look at him. A final snapshot, the one that would last her. She shook her head. "Oh, drat, I did so want you to meet my children. Properly, this time."

"Wait, Daisy, don't just go off like this, who knows," he began, but she waved her hand in front of her eyes and walked out the door.

There were seven messages — she counted the blinks — on her answering machine.

Ben had metamorphosed while she was walking home!

"You behaved badly, but let's talk."

Oh shit, Sandy.

"We need to talk . . ." Blah, blah, blah . . . *Beep* . . .

"Daisy? Where the hell are you? Where the hell have you left the car? Blah, blah, blah . . ." *Beep.*

"Okay, *forget* the car, we must talk, we *must* . . ."

She was about to flip off the machine when a new voice spoke: "This is a message for Daisy Frank from Andra Cassidy. I have great news. Three independent producers are bidding for the the rights to your book — Lorimar, Viacom, and Hearst Entertainment. I need to hear from you immediately. Call me even if it's over the weekend."

Daisy smiled wolfishly. She replayed Andra's message. She let out a loud whoop. A movie, imagine! That meant money. She could smell the money from here. At long last she had gotten the timing right. The world seemed rich in consolations.

The train went through red-roofed Montreux, passing Lac Leman on the right. At Brig in the Rhone Valley they changed for the red cog railway to Zermatt. As the land outside turned vertical, excitement mounted in the crowded train. They rose past blue-green vineyards, and women scything in the fields, and herds of sheep. Below, the swollen river boiled between rock walls. Tourists walked about the car, pointing, exclaiming in several languages, aiming their cameras at the views. Corey consulted his guidebook. Grabbed Daisy's shoulder. Mom, Miranda, look over there! The Weisshorn! At Stalden they caught a long view of the green Bernese Alps. Corey pointed out the avalanche barriers girding the mountains high above the train. The Breithorn and Klein Matterhorn appeared at the head of the valley. And then, as the little train labored around a corner, there at last towered the Matterhorn. Daisy and Corey and Miranda stood, shoulders touching, without speaking, and looked at the lopsided pyramid thrust into the clouds.

They checked into their hotel, a luxurious chalet with a pool and views of Alpine meadows. By God, they were doing this right. Why not? They'd been planning this trip for more than fifteen years! The Movie of the Week they were making from her book had permitted them to do this right. Tonight at dinner they must remember to drink a toast to Andra Cassidy and her negotiating finesse. They strolled through town in the rosy dusk, arms about each other, unable to take their eyes off the Matterhorn. "It really *is* like the hat from *The Cat in the Hat*," said Corey. When they next looked, the summit was hiding modestly behind a pink curtain of cloud.

At dawn the next day, Miranda set off with a pack from the base of the mountain. Toward noon, Daisy and Corey took the cable car up above the timberline to Schwarzee. Ahead loomed the rocks of the Hörnli, jumping-off point for climbing the Matterhorn. Miranda met them on the porch of the Hotel Belvedere. They strolled around a melancholy mountain lake bordered by a white chapel. Then they hoisted their day packs, and Corey seized his walking stick, and they struck out along the mule path to the Hörnlihutte. Daisy was soon panting. Corey was slowed by his pitching gait. They soldiered upward. Soon they were traveling through the top of the world in a dazzle of sun and snow. Around them, to every side, lay the playground of the gods. They were drunk on light and air.

"Time for a breath-er, Mom?" asked Corey, mimicking his childhood pronunciation. "I'll meet you farther up," said Miranda, shooting on up the trail. "Silly little girl, you think you're a big shot," Corey called after her. He and Daisy rested for a while on a rocky platform. They looked without speaking at the circle of shining cones and glaciers marching into the distance. Corey poked her shoulder with his alpenstock. "I love you, Mom, you're the best." "I'm so proud that we actually got ourselves here." "Hey, Mom. *You* got us here."

Someone yodeled. They glanced up. There stood Miranda, her hair aflame in the snowlight, waving at them from an overhang above. Daisy and Corey waved back. Daisy looked down, impressed by their progress; even at their pace, they'd come a way. The trail was a steep spiral banked with scree, the gray broken only by lavender heather and orange lichen. She pointed out a white patch below to Corey: might that be edelweiss?

A group of expert mountaineers in lederhosen were making their way smartly upward. They disappeared along the switchback. Next came a lone figure laboring up the trail. Wearing blue jeans and a baseball hat. A compatriot, thought Daisy lazily. The Swiss wore the proper gear and seldom hiked alone. The figure disappeared, lingering in her mind. After a long while it emerged in the curve of the switchback. A small figure, chuffing along, ever so slowly. Limping almost. Daisy had to smile. The American team here making a sorry showing. She waited for the compatriot's next appearance round the switchback. That limp — No, ridiculous — Could it be? Did miracles exist? Was it really he? Not likely. She focused her eyes on the bend where the figure would next emerge. But if it were, how very nice that would be.